Sins and Secrets

Sins and Secrets

P. F. KOZAK

APHRODISIA

APHRODISIA
KENSINGTON BOOKS
http://www.kensingtonbooks.com

KENSINGTON BOOKS are published by

Kensington Publishing Corp.
850 Third Avenue
New York, NY 10022

ISBN: 0-7582-1418-9

First Trade Paperback Printing: October 2006

10 9 8 7 6 5 4 3 2 1

Acknowledgments

Thank you to my husband, whose constant love, infinite patience and professional editorial skills supported me through the writing of this book. From my heart and soul, thank you to IK. Peter and Pamela would not exist without you. To Hilary, my editor at Kensington, thank you for giving me plenty of head room. I needed it. A particular nod of thanks goes to a wolf in sheep's clothing, who became my pertinacious muse while writing *Sins and Secrets*. And to the Burning Love, Hot to Trot team, *alla famiglia! Ti amo!*

Prologue

THE PLEASURES OF LOVE

Pressed in the arms of him I so adored,
The keeper of my charms, my pride, my lord!
By day experiencing each sweet delight,
And meeting endless transports every night

When on our downy bed we fondly lay,
Heating each other by our am'rous play;
Till Nature, yielding to the luscious game,
Would fierce desire and quenchless lust inflame!

Oh! then we join'd in love's most warm embrace,
And pressed soft kisses on our every grace!
Around my form his pliant limbs entwined,
Love's seat of bliss to him I then resigned!

We pant, we throb, we both convulsive start!
Heavens! then what passions thro' our fibres dart!
We heave, we wriggle, bite, laugh, tremble, sigh!
We taste Elysian bliss—we fondle—die.

THE PEARL
A Journal of Facetiæ and Voluptuous Reading.
No. 1, July 1879

Chapter One

Peter glanced at his pocket watch while he waited for his coachman to bring round the brougham. He had just over two hours before meeting Pamela at the London Bridge Railway Depot. He tucked the watch back into his vest pocket just as his man Jack rounded the corner with the carriage.

"No need to get down, Jack." Peter opened the door himself. "We will be making a stop at Nellie's, then going on to the depot to meet Pamela."

"Yes, sir."

"Oh, and Jack . . ."

"Yes, sir?"

"Once we get to Nellie's, you may have one on me. But you must get me to the depot on time."

"Yes, sir!"

As the carriage rolled down Chancery Lane toward Thames Street, Peter stared out the window. Pamela's return would bring changes to his life, changes he had postponed as long as he had been able. He remembered the days before her father died. She had been a headstrong child, and only grew more so as she matured.

Once he became her guardian, he had immediately sent her to boarding school. Then she wanted to go to University, which her father never would have allowed. But, the alternative of having her live with him seemed far worse than invok-

ing the old man's ghostly wrath. Through his connections at
Cambridge, he managed to enroll her in Newnham Women's
College. For the last several years, he had only seen her at
Christmas and for short holidays.

Now, she had completed her studies. Surely, the girl should
have married by this time! But she hadn't. The old man had
locked up his will with a chastity belt. Pamela had to live
with Peter until she married, or he forfeited the rights to
manage the estate and his share of the trust. He would need a
stiff drink at Nellie's and the company of a woman before
Pamela took up residence as lady of his house.

The carriage abruptly stopped. Jack hopped down from
the driver's seat and opened the door for him. "How long do
we have, sir?"

"About an hour forty-five."

"Jolly good, sir. I'll be sure to have you to the depot on
time. I'll come and fetch you, I will."

"Good man. I'll tell Nellie to take care of you." Peter
stepped down from the brougham, being careful to avoid the
muck in the street.

Upon his entering the establishment, which to most would
appear a common tavern, Nellie immediately caught sight of
him. "Ah, good sir, how very lovely to see you again." She
curtsied and offered Peter her hand.

"My Nellie, how good to see you as well." Peter kissed the
hand of the woman who had taken his virginity so many
years before.

"Monsieur Rennard, isn't it somewhat early in the day to
be seeing you here? It is not yet five o'clock."

"Pamela has completed her schooling and is coming home
today. We are meeting her train shortly." Jack had followed
Peter into the tavern and stood off to the side. "Is there by
chance anyone here who might fancy Jack?"

"But of course." Nellie took Jack by the arm and led him
behind the bar to a curtained doorway. "Go in here and ask

for Sally. Tell her you are Nellie's special guest." She turned back to Peter. "And, now you, monsieur . . ."

"Nellie, please, no formality. We know one another better than that."

"My dear Peter, what would you like today?" She came over and threaded her arm through his. "Your favorites are not here just yet. But I am sure I could find someone who would please you."

"What about you?"

"Oh, my good sir, you know I do not take clients these days."

"Not even for an old friend?" Peter ran the back of his hand across Nellie's cheek.

"You would want an old woman when I have younger ones waiting?"

"Nellie, you are not old."

"Sir, by anyone's standard, I am old."

"I am thirty-five. You cannot be more than ten years my elder."

"And how many gentlemen do you think ask for one such as myself?"

"I do." He rested his hand on her shoulder. "You are just as beautiful as the first day I saw you."

Nellie studied him for a moment, then went behind the bar and picked up a bottle with two glasses. "Who am I to refuse the most sought-after barrister in London?" She turned to the barkeep. "Henry, look after things until I return."

Nellie led Peter through the curtained door into the inner world of Nellie's Tavern. Only those considered her clients were escorted into her sanctum. Walking up a dark flight of stairs, she led him to her personal quarters. "I'm honoured, Nellie. It's been some time since I have had the privilege."

"It's been some time since anyone has had the privilege." She set the bottle and glasses on her desk and poured them each a drink.

"Those pink curtains around the bed, they are new?"

"That is my French canopy. It is the most beautiful thing I have ever owned! I love sleeping inside the colour. It makes me feel safe."

Peter smiled as he looked at the gaudy strips of pink cloth hanging in a circle around the bed. "They are nearly as colourful as you are! Your canopy bed suits you very well."

"You have not come to see me to chat about my bed." Handing Peter the glass, she asked, "Are you going to tell me why you are really here?"

"For some female companionship, of course." Drinking the brandy she gave him in one swallow, he held out his glass for more.

Before refilling his glass, Nellie lifted the corner of her skirt and tucked it into her belt. She watched him as she poured the brandy. He did not take his eyes off of her legs. "Female companionship you will have, but not before you tell me why it is me you want."

He looked directly at her. "Because you are a woman, because you know me, and because you know what Sir George did to me." Peter downed the second glass of brandy.

"Sir George Kingston made you a very wealthy man. He named you as his successor and the guardian of his daughter."

"And I am to remain her guardian until she is married. No matter what her age, she must continue to live with me until she has a husband. It is in the will. If I refuse, I forfeit everything."

Nellie poured him more brandy, and then sat down on his lap. "Ah, *mon cher*, I know what troubles you."

"I have never asked you, why do you speak French? You have lived in London your entire life."

"Ah, but French whores raised me and gave me my name. I learned more than my trade from them, I learned their language."

Peter slid his hand under Nellie's skirt. "You learned your trade very well. *Tu es éternellement belle.*"

"You see with your heart, not with your eyes. For my very handsome Peter, I have no trouble remembering what I have learned." She slid her hand along Peter's hard length. His breath caught. "You do not know about yourself what I know."

"And what would that be?" He cupped Nellie's ample breast in his other hand and squeezed.

"I know you come to visit me more when Pamela returns on holiday. I know she tempts you and you resist. There is now no escape and no reprieve."

Peter squeezed Nellie's breast harder, his fingers sinking deep into the soft flesh. "You know much more than you should."

Nellie pushed Peter's hand away and stood. "You will not bruise me." Her eyes flashed fire. "No man bruises Nellie Flambeau!"

Peter stood as well. Being taller and stronger, he had no trouble pulling her tightly against him. "I will not hurt you, but I will have you." His engorged cock strained in his trousers. He lifted Nellie's skirt and petticoat.

Nellie is dominant, continue reading
Peter is dominant, turn to page 11

Nellie smiled. "Would you not rather watch me disrobe? My girls tell me how you will pay just to watch, as you once did with me."

Peter released her. "Nellie, I must have relief before I see her. You know what to do. Please, do it. I haven't much time."

"*Mon cher*, you must sit and watch then. You must not

touch until I tell you to. You know the penalty if you do not do as I say."

"I know well. I will never forget when you refused me because I touched too soon. Please understand. I only have an hour before I must leave."

"You will have your pleasure before then." Nellie undid the buttons down the front of her dress and stepped out of it. "Now, that we have begun, you will tell me more."

"More of what?"

"More of your desire for Pamela."

"I have no desire for Pamela."

"*Mon cher*, I know differently." She lifted her petticoat to expose her legs, watching his eyes follow her movements. She held the folds of material thigh high for a few moments, letting him take her in, before she let it fall to the floor. "Sir George first brought you to me when you were his apprentice. He knew you needed to learn. I taught you much."

"I remember. It seems a lifetime ago."

"My dear Peter, you have come to me for a reason. We have known one another for many years. I know your heart." She slowly began to unhook her corset. "I know your desires." The corset popped open and she let it fall to the floor. "I know why you sent Pamela to boarding school."

"Nellie, do not do this."

"*Mon cher*, it is why you are here. You have come to me because I know."

Peter's hand involuntarily moved toward his erect cock. "Nellie, I must!"

"You will not!" Her sharp tone stopped his hand before he touched his throbbing organ. He gripped the sides of the chair until his knuckles turned white, the bulge in his trousers straining for release. "Tell me, Peter, tell me what you feel for her!"

As obediently as a schoolboy being admonished, Peter blurted out, "I cannot control myself when she is close. My organ stiffens and I want to touch her. It has always been this way, and has only become worse with time."

Nellie came over to him and ran her fingers through his thick brown hair. Then she stood directly in front of him and pulled her chemise over her head, baring her breasts. "Show me your nob."

Peter undid his trousers and gingerly pulled his rock-hard cock free of the material. Nellie only had on her drawers, which had an opening between her legs for her toilette. Pulling them open wide so Peter could plainly see her privy parts, she straddled him. She lowered herself onto his throbbing head.

"*Mon Dieu*! Nellie, I cannot stand it!"

With Peter's full length inside of her, Nellie kissed his forehead. "This is why you have come to me, so I would be Pamela for you. It is why you have always come to me. Close your eyes, *mon amour*, and feel a woman's heat around you." She slowly rocked back and forth on his lap. "Your prick is a good one. Pamela is a woman now. She is ready for you."

Peter moaned loudly and grasped Nellie's bum. "Nellie, I cannot, she is my ward."

Ever so slowly, she raised and lowered herself onto him. "Do you not think she wants this, too?" With Peter buried deeply inside of her, she leaned over and whispered to him, "She is a woman, *mon cher*. Do not underestimate the daughter of Sir George."

Then, with speed which belied her age, Nellie rode him. She took him deeply inside of her again and again. Peter thrust upward each time Nellie's cunt gripped him until he could no longer endure. He bellowed as his lust exploded inside of her. She let him bury his face between her breasts and heave his groin into hers.

When finally he quieted, she lifted herself off of him, their combined juices soaking her drawers. She took them off and stood bare before him. She gently cleaned him with the cloth, so there would be no stain left on his trousers. After tossing the sullied material to the side, she picked up a dressing gown from the chair beside the bed.

He had just tucked himself back into his trousers when

someone knocked. A female voice said, "Mademoiselle Flambeau, Monsieur Rennard, Jack says it is time."

Peter looked at his pocket watch. "Tell Jack I will be right there." He went over to Nellie. "You are beautiful beyond words. I am grateful for what you just did."

"*Mon cher*, you can come to Nellie whenever you are in need. You know you will be welcomed."

"I must go now. Please take this. It should be a proper recompense for both myself and Jack." He pressed a guinea into her hand.

"*Merci*. Remember, *mon cher*, she is a woman now."

"I will remember, Nellie." With that, he left to meet Pamela.

Go to page 15

"Ah, *mon cher*, if you want what Nellie has to offer, then you will be a gentleman?"

"I will be a gentleman." He reached into the folds of cloth under her dress, wanting to feel her moist warmth against his hand. Nellie's words lingered in his mind. "Why did you say Pamela tempts me? How could you know this?"

"*Mon cher*, I have already angered you. I do not wish to cause you any more distress."

Frustrated with her silence as well as with the layers of petticoat that prevented him from touching her, Peter stepped away. "Pull up your skirt, Nellie, so I can touch you."

Nellie lifted her skirt and petticoat to the middle of her thigh. "My Peter is being quite bold today."

"Perhaps if I touch your cunt, I can convince you to tell me more." Again he reached under her skirt, this time finding the opening in her drawers. Cupping the soft flesh of her privy parts in his hand, he gently squeezed. "Tell me, Nellie, tell me why you think Pamela tempts me."

"You do not know you are so bold today because your Pamela will soon be here?"

Pressing his fingers inside the folds of skin, he massaged her clitoris. "I know nothing of the sort. I am here today to have the pleasure of your company once again."

Nellie pulled her skirt up higher, exposing the toilette opening in her drawers to Peter's hungry eyes. "You would not like to see Pamela raise her skirt for you as I do?"

"Nellie, you are wading into dark waters with this."

Nellie jumped when Peter's finger slid inside of her. Still, she spoke her mind. "But you must swim in the dark waters, *mon amour*. How else will you be able to live with your sweet Pamela?"

"Take off the dress, Nellie. Do not bring Pamela into your fancy bed with us."

"I do not have to bring her here, *mon cher*. You have already done so." Nellie unbuttoned the front of her dress and pulled her arms out of the sleeves.

"It is not something I care to dwell on. I would much rather linger on the bed with you." He took hold of Nellie's skirt and pulled the dress off. He then picked her up and carried her to the bed. "I want to watch you take off your corset and your petticoat."

"Shall I talk of Pamela while I do so?" Nellie smiled as she began undoing her corset.

"And if you were to talk of Pamela, what would you say?" Peter stroked his stiff cock through his trousers. The very idea that they should be talking of Pamela here, in this place, both repelled him and inflamed him.

Nellie slowly undid the remaining hooks on the front of her corset. "I would say you have desired Pamela for many years. I can see you do not remember what you told me after you sent her away."

"I remember saying nothing to you of Pamela."

"Ah, *mon amour*, you had too much brandy one evening. When I raised my skirt for you, you thought me to be her and told me of your desire. You called me by her name as you spent inside of me."

"I did no such thing!"

Nellie's corset dropped to the floor. She lifted her chemise, revealing her voluptuousness. "Ah, but you did. You have wanted Pamela in your bed for many years."

Peter closed his eyes and took a deep breath. He had the urge to harshly reprimand her for talking to him in this way. A lesser man might have backhanded her. But he could not deny that her words held truth. He did remember the night of which she spoke, but did not realise he had spoken his secret aloud. As he undid his trousers to have her, he asked, "Did I say anything else?"

Nellie removed her chemise and petticoat, leaving her only in her drawers. She pulled them wide open, showing Peter her hidden treasures. "You told me she could never live with you, that you could not keep yourself from her bed."

Exposing his stiff cock, he stood silently for several moments, staring at Nellie. He stroked himself as he looked at her. Peter lowered himself onto her, forcing her legs wide apart with his knees. "I cannot do with her what I do with you."

"And why not, *mon cher*? She is a woman now. You have a good prick. She would welcome it between her legs."

Peter rammed his cock into Nellie's cunt, causing her to gasp at his abrupt entry. "*Mon Dieu*, monsieur! You stretch me so! I am like a virgin again."

"You are no virgin, *ma chérie*." Peter stuffed himself deeply into her moist opening. "Do you think I could do this to innocent Pamela?" He pulled out and slammed back into her.

Nellie lifted her bum and met his thrust. "You will do it to her. She will welcome it as I do."

Again and again, Peter slammed into the velvet glove that swallowed his organ. Again and again, Nellie met each thrust. As he felt the wave of his desire about to overtake him, he called out, "Sweet fuck, yes!" His body went rigid. The scalding fluid moved through his throbbing nob into Nellie's belly.

Peter buried his head between Nellie's breasts as he quieted. Stroking his hair, Nellie whispered softly, "She is a woman, *mon cher*. Do not underestimate the daughter of Sir George."

Their combined juices had soaked Nellie's drawers. When Peter rolled off of her, she removed them and gently cleaned him with the cloth so there would be no stain. After tossing the sullied material to the side, she picked up a dressing gown lying at the bottom of the bed.

He had just tucked himself back into his trousers when someone knocked. A female voice said, "Mademoiselle Flambeau, Monsieur Rennard, Jack says it is time."

Peter looked at his pocket watch. "Tell Jack I will be right there." He leaned over and kissed Nellie on the cheek. "You are beautiful beyond words."

"*Mon cher*, you can come to Nellie whenever you are in need. You know you will be welcomed."

"I must go now. Please take this. It should be a proper recompense for both myself and Jack." He pressed a guinea into her hand.

"*Merci*. Remember, *mon cher*, she is a woman now."

"I will remember, Nellie." With that, he left to meet Pamela.

Chapter Two

Pamela could see the spires of London Bridge in the distance. She knew the train would arrive at the railway depot soon. Gathering together the few things she had brought on board with her, she readied herself for departure.

The guard knocked on the glass door of the coach she shared with an elderly gentleman. Opening it, he announced, "London Bridge is the next and last stop on this train." Looking directly at her, he inquired, "Is someone meeting you at the depot, miss?"

"Why, yes, thank you. A carriage will be waiting."

"Give the driver your baggage claim, and tell him your luggage will be unloaded from the last car."

"Thank you, sir. I will tell him."

Pamela smiled at the thought of Jack stuffing her heavy trunks into the carriage. They would take most of the space, leaving very little room for two passengers. She fancied the thought of having to sit close to Peter in the crowded carriage. Since he always took care to keep a respectable distance between them, she would need to make sure the trunks were properly placed.

The train lurched as it slowed to enter the depot, causing her hat to slip over her forehead. She quickly adjusted it, hoping it hadn't mussed her hair. She had taken great care choosing her traveling attire. When Peter saw her, she wanted to impress him as a proper lady. Pamela had seen the sort of women he took to parties or to the opera. She envied both the way they looked and how Peter looked at them.

Now, however, it would be different. Peter had no choice but to notice her. In his will, her father clearly stated he wanted her to live with Peter until she married. Having completed her formal education, she had now returned to take up residence in Peter's town house.

Her obsession with Peter began long before her father died. Peter had been a regular guest in their home. Peter and her father would drink cognac together and discuss the details of her father's estate.

Often, they would be in the library well into the night debating the law and how best to manage her father's assets. She would sit on the stairs outside the door and listen, wanting to hear Peter's voice. Almost in spite of herself, she also learned. She understood her inheritance because of what she overheard.

Sometimes, they would ask her to play the piano for them. She adored it when Peter watched her play. Whenever he watched her, the music flowed through her body into the piano. Once he sat on the bench beside her and watched her play. His leg pressed against hers and she thought she might swoon.

She had felt his arms around her only once. Peter held her through the funeral. Even in her grief, she felt stirrings inside from his closeness. Save for a brief kiss on the cheek, he had not held her again.

Pamela knew what she wanted to learn could no longer be taught in the classroom. The lessons that waited were more suited to the bedchamber. She wanted it to be Peter's bedchamber. She had rebuffed more than one suitor, holding on to her chastity—not for marriage, but for Peter.

The older man sitting across from her stood as the train rolled alongside the platform. He held the door open for her as they exited the coach.

"Thank you, sir. How very lovely to ride with you." The fellow had been the perfect seatmate. He had slept nearly the entire trip.

"You as well, miss. Now, mind your step getting off. There is a nasty gap between the train and the platform."

"I will be careful." She stepped into the aisle, and then allowed the gentleman to lead the way to the nearest door. They joined the line of passengers waiting for the guard to open the door.

Pamela saw Jack before she saw Peter. He stood one car-length away, looking in the wrong direction. She made her way through the crowd and stopped behind him. "Boo!"

Jack spun around and nearly bumped into her. "Miss Pamela, excuse me, ma'am."

"Hello, Jack. How very good to see you." For a moment, she feared Peter had sent Jack to fetch her and had not come himself. But then she saw him, standing a little further down the platform. He stood there, tall and dignified, looking every bit a barrister in his black waistcoat. Pamela's stomach fluttered at the sight of him.

She wanted to drop all of her things and run to him. Instead, she stood still and waited for him to come to her. He kept his eyes on her as he walked, not paying attention to the passengers filing off of the train around him. A large woman carrying an equally large bag bumped right into Peter as he walked past her. He stumbled, catching himself before he completely lost his balance. Pamela smiled, watching him politely bow in apology to the woman who had very nearly knocked him down.

With only a few meters left between them, she could no longer contain herself. She set her bags down beside Jack and went to him. They stood face-to-face on the platform, oblivious to the jostling crowd. For a moment, they simply drank each other in, not saying a word. Peter broke the silence. "Welcome home, Pamela." He gave her a short kiss on the cheek.

"Thank you, Peter. I am glad to finally be here."

"I must say, you are looking quite lovely."

"I'm pleased you think so. It is so terribly good to see you again." Pamela opened her bag and retrieved the claim ticket. Turning to Jack, she said, "My boxes will be unloaded from the last car. A porter should help you get them to the carriage." Jack took the ticket and gathered the bags she had left on the platform.

Jack then left to find a porter, leaving Pamela alone on the platform with Peter. Taking hold of his upper arm, she asked, "How have you been, Peter?"

"Splendid. Everything is very good indeed." Then he surprised her. Rather than standing rigidly while she held his arm, he reached across and covered her hand with his. "Shall we go to the carriage and wait for Jack to bring round your boxes?"

"That would be fine." They walked through the railway depot together, his hand holding hers as they walked. She could hardly believe it when she felt his fingers rubbing the back of her hand almost in a caress.

"Did you ship most of your things on the luggage van, as I thought best?"

"Yes. I brought two boxes with me, to have enough clothing until the rest of my things arrive."

"I had Lucy prepare your room. It does occur to me that since you are moving back to the house permanently, you may wish to consider changing your bedchamber to the larger room across from mine. It would be more comfortable and put you closer to the water closet."

Even though his suggestion startled her, she managed to sound calm. "That would be lovely, Peter, thank you." She could not explain this change of his attitude, the implications of which did not escape her.

"The mahogany bed and cupboard from your father's house are still in storage. If you wish, we could have them brought round for you."

"Let me consider that. I may want a canopy bed."

Peter smiled. "I understand they are quite fashionable."

Pamela giggled, not believing she could be talking about her bed with Peter. "Oh, my, yes, and so wonderfully feminine."

They had reached the carriage before Jack. Noticing an empty bench off to the side, Peter led Pamela to it. "Why don't we sit here and wait for Jack?" Peter continued to hold her hand as she sat down, only releasing it when he sat beside her.

"Have you found a young man that takes your fancy?"

"No. I've told you, I am in no hurry to sell my soul to a husband."

"Pamela, finding a suitable husband is hardly selling your soul."

"It is if all that is mine is given to a husband."

"What makes you say that?"

"Peter, I know all the property Papa left to me will be handed to my husband on a silver platter. If I marry, I lose everything."

"You will not lose everything. I manage your holdings and will continue to do so once you are married."

"And who will receive the earnings if I am married?"

Peter folded his arms across his chest and looked away for a moment. Turning back to her, he said, "I see you have learned much in the last years."

"I have learned enough to know I am at the mercy of my husband's generosity for income that is rightfully mine."

Just then, Jack and the porter came into view with the boxes. "We will continue this conversation later, my dear. Matters of such importance should not be discussed at a railway depot."

"To be sure," Pamela snapped back. Peter stood and again took hold of Pamela's hand, helping her to her feet. This time, Peter wrapped her arm through his and held it there, as before.

"Jack, will those sit on top of the brougham?"

Pamela smiled as Jack answered, "No, sir, they are too heavy. They will have to sit inside the cab if we are to take them with us."

Pamela feigned concern, saying, "I do really need them now. I so want to change this dusty dress once we are home."

"And so you shall. Jack, see if you can get them both in the cab." Jack and the porter loaded the two boxes and the small bags into the cab.

"Shall we?" Peter helped Pamela into the carriage and then climbed in beside her. Just as she had hoped, the boxes gave them very little room to sit.

Peter tried to wedge himself in beside her. "Pamela, perhaps I should sit on top with Jack or ask the porter to call me another carriage."

"Don't be silly, Peter. There is room for both of us." She pulled her dress tightly against her, giving him just enough space to squeeze in.

"If you say so and do not mind that I am practically sitting on you."

"I don't mind at all." Feeling bold, she once again put her arm though his. "Might I ask if you are still seeing Constance?"

"Not for some months now. I began to find her company a bit tiresome."

"Really! I'm surprised."

"You shouldn't be. As I recall, the last time you came home on holiday, you asked me what in the name of heaven I saw in such a persnickety prig."

"Well, I honestly could not understand your attraction for her. I've never met such a humorless whinge."

"And what sort of woman do you think would suit me?"

"Someone younger, someone..." Pamela stopped just short of saying "someone like me."

"Go on."

"Someone who is fun and lively." She didn't know what else to say. Just then, the carriage wheel hit a hole in the street and bumped enough to cause Pamela's valise to fall over on top of her trunk. The latch came open and several books spilled out onto their laps.

Before Pamela had a chance to scoop them up, Peter picked up a periodical that had fallen with the books. "What is this, *The Pearl—A Journal of Facetiae and Voluptuous Reading*?"

He opened the journal and skimmed a few pages, then read a passage aloud. "'I'll fuck you this time from behind, in what is called dog fashion. He then got up, and knelt between her legs, and drawing apart the white cheeks of her bottom, pushed his prick into her cunt. Then holding her hips, he worked his article rapidly in and out, telling her to push back her bottom to meet each thrust of his prick.'"[1]

Peter closed the journal and waved it in the air. "Is this what you have learned going to University? You paid seven shillings and sixpence for this rubbish?"

"Peter, that is my personal property. Give it back to me."

"Not until I have a closer look, to see exactly what kind of literature you enjoy reading."

"I am well beyond the age of consent. It is my business if I choose to read such things."

"And I am still your guardian, granted enduring privileges by Sir George until such time as you marry. That being the case, I will keep this journal and read it. We will discuss the contents once I have thoroughly reviewed it."

Pamela sat pressed up against Peter's side, absolutely seething. She grabbed the books lying on Peter's lap. As she did so, her fingertips brushed against his trousers and hit something rigid inside. She pulled her hand away as if she had been burned. "Peter!"

"My dear Pamela, why should you be shocked by my condition? Your education has included this!" He held up her copy of *The Pearl*.

[1] *The Pearl*—No. 11 – May 1880

"Peter, I do not know of such things in my experience. I have never . . ."

"It seems perhaps it is time you did." He took her hand and stroked himself with it. She tried to pull away, but he held her tightly. "That, my dear, is a real prick. You have made it hard, you and your literature. You should know the effect you have on me, since you are now the lady of my house."

"Peter, why are you being so coarse with me? I do not understand!"

"Pamela, matters of the flesh always make a man coarse, without regard to his breeding or education. It is the reality of being a man." He relaxed his hold on her hand, giving her the freedom to remove it from his lap. "It is not something easily controlled."

Instead of pulling her hand away, she continued to touch him. "I do not know of such things, but I have read it is uncomfortable for a man to be in this state. Are you in pain?"

Peter exhaled loudly though his nose in utter exasperation. "My God, Pamela, you do not know this sort of pain. It is an ache, a throbbing, a need that is overwhelming."

"If I caused this, I want to ease your discomfort." She continued to stroke him.

Peter closed his eyes and said through clenched teeth, "Sweet Lord, you are driving me mad. I am your guardian, I cannot allow this." Even with his spoken conviction, Peter made no attempt to stop her caresses.

"I want to do this." Having read many accounts of ways to satisfy a man, Pamela knew how to stroke him. "Peter, I really do want to touch you."

"Pamela, listen to me. I am very close to spending and will make an embarrassment of my trousers. If you are willing, allow me to spend into my handkerchief."

"Yes, of course." Pamela watched with shocked fascination as Peter opened his trousers.

He reached inside and covered himself with his handkerchief. "Now, give me your hand." She obediently held out her hand to him. He pushed it inside of his trousers. "Now, continue what you were doing."

Pamela grasped his cock in her hand and rubbed him. "Faster, my dear, faster and harder." She did as Peter asked and watched him transform before her eyes. His breath came in rapid bursts, his chest rising and falling inside his vest. Suddenly, his body shook and he groaned. The hot fluid burst from him in spurts, his organ pulsing against her hand. She felt the cloth grow damp as he spilled himself into it.

She quietly waited until he had softened. Too shy to ask him if she should take the handkerchief, she removed her hand and left the kerchief. Peter did not say a word. He reached inside his trousers and pulled out the soiled cloth. Crumpling it into a ball, he discarded it onto the floor of the carriage. Then he arranged his clothing and put himself right.

Her copy of *The Pearl* had fallen between them. Pamela reached for it, but Peter grabbed it first. "I will take that."

"Please give it back to me, Peter! It is not something I ever meant for you to see."

"Nor did I ever intend to have your hand upon me. It is evident your education has been extensive. Perhaps this journal will give me an indication of how much you have learned."

"This is all a tempest in a teapot!" Frustrated and angry, Pamela folded her arms across her chest and tried to turn away from Peter. She only managed to wedge herself tighter against him, his body as unyielding as his temper.

They rode in silence. Pamela struggled with her own pain, the pain Peter spoke of earlier. The burning would not go away, the feel of him against her causing an ache inside she did not understand. She wanted to scream at him, but knew she should best hold her tongue. They were almost home. Nothing would be gained by having a row in front of Jack.

Remembering Peter had offered her the room across from his provided some solace. Tomorrow, she would see to the move.

Chapter Three

By the time they rounded the corner from Regent Street onto Piccadilly, the lamplighters were lighting the gas lamps. Peter could feel the heat from Pamela's body against his. Even worse, he could smell the fragrance of her skin. They had to reach the house soon, before he lost control again.

The carriage stopped at the corner of Bolton and Piccadilly, in front of the iron gate surrounding Peter's town house. Jack jumped down from the carriage to open the gate. Not waiting for the formality of having the door opened for him, Peter quickly exited the carriage. He stuffed the confiscated periodical into his inner coat pocket, and then turned to help Pamela. Taking her hand, he tried not to notice when she lifted her skirt to step down to the ground. The effort proved pointless, as the very thought of lifting her skirt made him stiff.

Pamela had said nothing to him for the remainder of the trip, not one word. He could see her fuming. Moments like this showed him, without question, that Sir George lived inside of her. She had inherited her father's temper as well as his fortune.

Once inside, he immediately barked orders to the staff. "Jack, take Pamela's boxes to her room and make sure her new lamps are working properly. Lucy, please see to Pamela's comfort, and help her unpack. And tell May we will each be taking dinner in our own rooms."

Pamela appeared visibly angrier. "Peter, why aren't we dining together on my first night home? I am sure May prepared a special meal. She always does!"

"Because, my dear, I have something I must read before we sit down together again." With that, he went up the stairs for the night, leaving her standing alone in the foyer.

Follow Peter to his room, continue reading
Follow Pamela to her room, turn to page 33

Peter knew he had just behaved abominably, but saw no other way to escape. He needed some time alone to think, and to digest what had happened. Sitting across from Pamela at dinner would have been impossible under the circumstances.

He threw the journal onto the chair, wondering how on earth she came to have such a thing. This sort of literature flourished in certain circles, but Pamela should not have been aware of this. He thought he heard the rumblings of Sir George turning over in his grave.

What happened between them in the carriage could not be excused. He had lost control and allowed her hand on him. As he took off his coat and vest, he muttered aloud, "My God, what have I done?"

Someone knocked on his door, startling him. He growled, "Yes, what is it?"

Lucy answered. "Sir, Miss Pamela would like a bath and wants to know if you have need of the water closet."

He went over and opened the door. "Tell her she is welcome to a bath. I have no need at the moment."

"Thank you, sir."

"Oh, and Lucy, make sure she has some dinner. Tell her I will see her at breakfast. "

"Yes, sir. When would you want dinner, sir?"

"An hour from now would be grand. Bring me some brandy as well."

Lucy nodded her understanding. Peter watched her walk down the hall toward Pamela's room. Glancing at the closed door across the hall, he realised if Pamela accepted his offer, she would soon be much closer to him. He had offered her that room because of Nellie. Now, the full import of Nellie's words raged inside his mind. *She is a woman now.*

After removing his clothing, Peter poured water into the washbowl. Splashing cold water on his face did not wash away the unease of being close to Pamela, nor did it remove his self-recrimination for being weak. Somehow, he had to come to terms with the disquieting reality that she lived with him now. He would see her every day, and he would know she had touched him.

Peter put on his dressing gown. He turned up the flame on his gas lamp and settled into his overstuffed armchair with *The Pearl*. He read from the beginning, thinking all the while that Pamela had read the same words as he. Only that afternoon, he had called her an innocent when speaking of her to Nellie. Now he realised his Pamela had shed her innocence, at least of the spirit. He believed she still held her chastity, but obviously understood the matters of the flesh.

The stories in *The Pearl* spoke openly and explicitly of pricks and cunts, sucking and fucking, bare bottoms and breasts, spanking and caning. While reading the bawdy prose, Peter heard Pamela running her bath. His cock, already stiff from the indecent stories, hardened even more at the thought of Pamela disrobing in the next room.

He opened his dressing gown and rubbed his aching organ with the palm of his hand. Loathe to satisfy himself while thinking of Pamela, he brought to mind images from the stories. But visions of Pamela reading those stories overshadowed any other thought.

Before he could stop himself, he saw her curled up on her bed in a lacy nightdress, drinking in the impassioned tales. He hid in the closet of his mind's eye and watched. She lightly caressed her full breast through the cloth of the gown. As she read more, her fingers kneaded the soft flesh, no doubt imagining the hand of a man on her.

Being quite alone in her own bed, she lifted the hem of her gown. He watched her slide her hand underneath and find the opening in her drawers. His own hand gripped his cock tightly as he thought of Pamela brushing the hair between her legs. Surely her female curls were the same lush chestnut brown as the hair on her head.

He wanted to see her disrobe, to have her naked beauty revealed to him. He thought of her in the bath, feeling the warmth of the water cover her body. Her feminine treasures were no longer hidden from view. Much like David watching Bathsheba bathe on the roof, Peter drank in her loveliness. The clear water hid nothing. He saw her fingers tickling the curly mound between her legs, before they disappeared inside her secret place.

Peter lost himself in voyeuristic pleasure, watching her in his mind's eye. Her body tempted him as no other did, or ever had. His prick throbbed as he thought of her touching herself, her fingers sliding deeply into her virginal cunt. Now that she had touched him, she would remember how his cock felt in her hand, and imagine how it would feel sliding in and out of her.

Without warning, Lucy knocked on the door, shattering his reverie. "Sir, I have your dinner." For a moment, Peter couldn't speak. "Master Rennard, are you there?"

"Yes, Lucy, I need a moment." Peter tied the cord around his dressing gown and went to the door. Lucy brought in a tray with his food and a decanter of brandy. As she bent over to set the tray on the table beside his chair, her bottom caught his attention. Peter quietly closed the door.

It had been some time since he had made an advance to her. She had resisted him then, but he convinced her to acquiesce. She twittered like a bird when he squeezed her bubbies. She did not allow him to lift her skirt, but did permit him to bump against her arse until he obtained his pleasure.

Peter approached her from behind. "Lucy . . ."

"Yes, sir?" He slipped his arm around her waist before she could turn around.

"I am very hungry tonight, the sort of hunger the dinner you have brought will not satisfy." He pressed his rigid cock against her bum.

"Oh, my, sir!" She tensed and stood very still.

"Now, do not be frightened. I mean you no harm and will do nothing more than you allow." She relaxed against him. "Do you feel my trouble?"

Lucy nodded. "I need your help, Lucy. Miss Pamela is home now. I do not want her to know this happens to me. Will you help me keep it a secret?"

"Master Rennard, it is indecent!"

"No one will know, Lucy." He fondled her breasts. She did not resist. "Remember what we did before?" Lucy nodded. "That's all I wish from you, to help me control my urges while Miss Pamela is here."

Lucy said nothing. Her consent to Peter's lewd request came when she wiggled her bum against his prick. Peter wasted no time. He opened his dressing gown and exposed himself, knowing she could see nothing. "Lucy, lift your skirt so I can rub against your petticoat. When I spend, I will soil your dress."

This made sense to the girl. She obediently lifted her skirt, taking her petticoat up with it, too. Peter did not wait for her to adjust herself. He held her tightly against him and pressed himself into her bum cheeks. He moaned aloud as his prick sunk into her soft bottom, her warm flesh welcoming him through the opening in her drawers.

She struggled, but he had her firmly around the waist. "Now, now, Lucy, settle yourself. I will not enter you. You do trust me, don't you?"

She quieted. "Yes, sir. I do."

Peter wedged himself between her fleshy cheeks. "Lucy, if I touch you in front, it will feel very good to you. Has a man ever touched your privy parts?"

She hesitated. As Peter reached under her skirt, she blurted out, "Jack has."

"Has he now?" Lucy pulled her skirt up a little higher to allow Peter access to her front. "Did you like it?" Peter rubbed more insistently against her bum.

"Yes, sir, I liked it better than a drop of gin, I did!" She wiggled against his fingers as he separated her moist lips. The sensation of her hips rotating against him made his breath catch.

"That's right, Lucy, move against me." He tickled her clit with his fingertips and she moaned.

"You like that, don't you, Lucy?"

"Oh, yes, Master Rennard. It is good, it is."

Her gyrations became more rhythmic. He moved with her, allowing her to pleasure herself against his hand. He very much wanted to push his cock into her wet cunt. He thought better of forcing himself on her, knowing he would need her cooperation in the days ahead.

It excited him terribly knowing Jack had pleasured the girl. "Does Jack touch you often?" He hoped the licentious mist they floated in would loosen her tongue.

"When I let him, he does!"

"And how often do you let him?"

"When he brings me a pint, he can touch my bubbies. When he gives me his gin, he can lift my skirt."

Peter slid his finger into her cunt and pushed hard inside of her. Lucy gasped. "Does he touch you here?"

"Oh, sir . . ." Lucy did not answer his question as she squirmed forcefully against him and began to shudder. Peter clutched her breast and rammed himself deeply into her bum crack. He pushed again and the tip of his prick exploded with hot fluid. Lucy continued to writhe against him, still in the throes of her own release. Peter moaned and whispered, "Pamela," as his thick juice dripped down Lucy's arse.

Lucy had released her skirt. When Peter stepped back to tie his dressing gown, both her petticoat and her skirt fell to her ankles. Once he had composed himself, he picked up the copy of *The Pearl* lying on his chair. "Lucy, I have something else I want you to do for me."

"Yes, Master Rennard." She turned around, but avoided looking directly at him.

"Do you see this journal?"

"Yes, sir."

"When you are helping Miss Pamela unpack her luggage, I want you to tell me if you see any more of these." He knew the girl could read simple words. "If it says *The Pearl* on the front, I want to know how many volumes she has. But you mustn't let her know I have asked you this. It is another secret we will have between us. Do you understand?"

"I understand." She timidly pointed to his dinner tray. "Sir, your food is probably stone cold. Would you like May to warm it?"

"Thank you, Lucy, but no. I am sure it will be fine." Peter thought he should reward the girl for her extra duties. He went to his desk and opened a small purse he kept there. Handing Lucy five shillings, he said in his most conciliatory voice, "If I need you again, will you help me?"

Lucy tucked the coins into her pocket. "Oh, yes. I am of a mind to help you, sir." Peter smiled, knowing he would not have to visit Nellie quite so often now.

Peter escorted her to the door and opened it. Reconsidering the wisdom of seeing Pamela in the morning prior to appearing in court, he gave Lucy a message for Jack. "Lucy, please tell Jack to have the carriage ready at half past seven tomorrow morning. I shall be leaving early for chambers."

"You told Lucy to tell me you would see me for breakfast." Pamela's voice cut through him like a razor. There she stood, in her nightdress, outside the door of the water closet. "Has that changed?"

Lucy awkwardly curtsied to Peter. She muttered, "I will tell him, sir," and hurried down the hall.

Pamela called to her, "Lucy."

Lucy stopped and turned around. "Yes, miss."

"I will need some help with my things. I would like my clothes unpacked and put in the cupboard in this room." Pamela indicated the room across from Peter's. "I will be moving everything there tomorrow."

Lucy glanced at Peter, waiting for his consent. "It is all right, Lucy. I have offered the room to Pamela if she cares to have it."

Pamela glared at Peter. "I have accepted the offer." Turning back to Lucy, she softened her voice. "Lucy, I will have my dinner now."

"Yes, miss." Lucy left them standing in the hall.

Peter turned to go back into his room. "Peter, you did not answer my question. Are we taking our morning meal together?"

Rather than answer her question, he snapped at her, "Have you no modesty? It is quite unseemly to be standing in the hallway in your nightdress."

Without hesitation, she replied angrily, "No more unseemly than your standing there in your dressing gown."

The colour in her cheeks had risen. Her hair had come partially undone. A long chestnut strand hung below her shoulders. Everything in him wanted to hold her, to see the rest of her hair fall, to touch her. His inner struggle threatened to split him in half. Instead of reaching for her as he so wanted to do, he said, "I will be taking my meal at ten past seven, if you care to join me." He stepped back into his room and closed the door.

Go to page 45

Pamela stared at the empty steps for several moments, trembling with anger. The utter audacity of the man infuriated her! He left her standing alone in the foyer on her first night home, without so much as a good night!

She suddenly realised both Jack and Lucy were standing behind her, waiting on her instructions. Collecting herself, she took off her hat and laid it on the hall table beside the lamp. "Lucy, tell May I wish to bathe before dinner, but would very much like a cup of tea and some biscuits now. Jack will help me upstairs with my cases. Oh, yes, and ask Master Rennard if he is in need of the water closet, as I will be occupying it."

"Yes, miss."

"Jack, if you would be so kind?" Pamela pointed to the luggage stacked on the floor.

Pamela knew Jack had the strength to lift the heavy cases. During Christmas holiday, after imbibing a bit too much rum, he had picked her up and spun her around. She blushed, remembering he had also kissed her several times under the mistletoe.

She had purchased a large bundle of mistletoe at Covent Garden and hung it in the doorway of the dining room, hoping Peter would be carried away by the holiday spirit. Peter never paid it any mind, but Jack did. It became a game between them, with Jack catching her under it more than once. Had Peter seen him, there would have been hell to pay.

Standing off to the side, she watched him lift the larger of the two trunks. "After you, Miss Pamela." He nodded toward the stairs. She led the way upstairs to her room. Jack set the case down in the hallway, going in first, to check the lamps. Pamela followed him in.

"Thank you for helping me, Jack. I do appreciate it."

"It is my pleasure, Miss Pamela." After checking the gas flow on the lamps, he brought in the first case. "I won't be but a minute with the rest, miss."

True to his word, he brought the rest of her luggage into the room within a few minutes. "Will you be needing anything else, Miss Pamela?"

Still chafing from Peter's rudeness, Pamela decided she did need something more from Jack. "Actually, Jack, there is one more thing I need."

"What would that be, miss?"

"A proper welcome home. I have yet to receive one."

"Miss Pamela, don't pay him any mind. He's probably tired."

"I wasn't talking about Peter." Jack looked at her, but did not move from the spot where he stood. Coaxing him along, Pamela added, "Sorry to say, I don't have any mistletoe."

Without saying a word, Jack came up to her and put his arm around her waist. He pulled her tightly against him and kissed her, not the playful kiss from under the mistletoe, but a kiss that said he understood what she wanted from him.

Still holding her close to him, he put his hand on her bum and kneaded it with his fingers. "Miss, Master Rennard would have my head if he knew I kissed you."

"Jack, he won't find out. He never knew about the mistletoe, now did he?"

"No, miss, he never did, him being in chambers all day."

"Jack, I promise, he will never know."

"Miss Pamela, I do like kissing you." He hugged Pamela tightly and kissed her again, this time brushing her breast with his thumb. The hard ridge in his trousers pressed into her belly.

"I can tell." She brazenly wiggled against him to let him know she knew how much he liked it. "You better go now. Lucy will be bringing my tea soon. But I will need your help tomorrow. I am moving to another room, the larger one across from Master Rennard's."

"Yes, miss. May will know where to find me."

"Thank you, Jack. And thank you for a proper welcome."

"Thank you, Miss Pamela." He hesitated and then added,

"If you would need help with these lamps during the night, or with anything at all, tell Lucy to fetch me."

"I will do that. Good night, Jack."

"Good night, Miss Pamela."

Her coquettish behavior with Jack excited her. She craved the tingles from his kisses and smouldered with the burning it left in her belly. If only Peter would kiss her like that. What had happened in the carriage strengthened her resolve. She would find a way to break though the wall he kept between them. Peter would be her first. Somehow, she would find a way.

While waiting on Lucy to bring her tea, Pamela set about unpacking. Taking the bag of books and papers to her desk, she emptied it. She had brought her favorite volumes of George Sand and Mary Wollstonecraft, her personal correspondence with Richard and Emmeline Pankhurst and several copies of *The Pearl*. The rest had been shipped with her other things.

Considering Peter's reaction to *The Pearl*, Pamela thanked the heavens that most of her favoured reading remained concealed in her bag. Thankfully, only one volume of her collection had fallen, Lord have mercy, right into his lap! He had not paid any attention to the books once he opened the journal.

He shocked her with his reaction and with forcing her hand on him. She had read about hard cocks and had occasionally felt a young man pressing into her when they danced. Once she had even allowed a young man to briefly rub himself against her leg. But never, ever had she held one, or ever witnessed a man spend!

To have the first man she touched be Peter she could hardly imagine. But it had happened! Maybe Peter's taking a copy of *The Pearl* would prove a stroke of luck. Perhaps he would start to think about touching her the way she wanted to touch him.

Pamela stacked her books and the remaining copies of *The Pearl* on the desk, beside the bundle of letters from the Pankhursts. Some years before, Richard Pankhurst qualified as a barrister at Lincoln's Inn and during his tenure there, made acquaintance with her father. After her father's death, Richard sent a letter of condolence. Knowing of Pamela's inheritance, he offered his legal advice, if Pamela should be in need.

Through a series of letters, Pamela learned that by law, she would forfeit her property to a husband if she married. Richard and his new wife, Emmeline, advocated to change the law to protect a married woman's right to own property. They promised to keep her informed of their progress.

Emmeline had personally written to Pamela after her marriage to Richard. They discovered they were the same age and shared like minds. Even though Emmeline tended more toward political activism than Pamela, they had become friends. Pamela found hope knowing Emmy had married the older barrister and they were expecting their first child. If the law did change, perhaps it could be the same for her with Peter.

Lucy knocked on her door. "Miss Pamela, I have your tea."

Pamela opened the door. "Thank you, Lucy. Does Master Rennard have need of the water closet?"

"No, miss. He says you are welcome to a bath and he will see you at breakfast, miss."

"Splendid. Tell May I will be having dinner when I am finished."

"Yes, miss. Will there be anything else, miss?"

"No, Lucy, that is all for now." Lucy tapped her toe behind her in an abbreviated curtsy and left Pamela alone.

Pamela sipped her tea. Opening one of her trunks, she found a suitable nightdress. Taking her tea and biscuits with her, she went to have a bath.

She paused outside of Peter's door and, for a moment, considered knocking. Quickly dismissing the idea as foolish, she instead opened the door to the room that tomorrow would be hers. In the dim light from the hall, she saw that the large room looked like a man's study with a bed. "Well, this will certainly change," she muttered to herself.

Pamela wasted no time shedding her clothes. She filled the

enameled cast-iron tub with warm water and settled in for a soak. After finishing her refreshment, she closed her eyes and thought of Peter in the carriage. She had suspected his passions ran deep. Now, she knew firsthand how deep.

She had always thought Peter handsome. He never slicked back his sandy brown hair the way most men did. He didn't need to; his wavy hair stayed in place naturally. Even though his work with the courts did not require physical prowess, his muscles were as developed as Jack's. She loved it when he took off his jacket and she could see his shirt cling to his arms.

Thinking of him caused her privy parts to throb. She burned as she had in the carriage. Trailing her hand between her breasts, she reached down to the pulse-beat between her legs. Lightly stroking herself, she remembered holding Peter's prick in her hand, of watching his chest rise and fall with his breath. She had seen him in the throes and immersed herself in the memory of his excitement.

His cock came alive in her hand, the blood vessels hard and ropey in her palm. The closer he came to spending, the more his cock came to life. It actually moved in her hand, of its own accord! Her own hips moved in the warm water, as she stroked him again in her mind.

Pamela started. She thought she heard Lucy's voice. For a moment, she thought Lucy had called to her, but then realised she had brought Peter his dinner. Pamela sat quietly and listened. She did not hear Lucy leave, and in fact heard voices from the next room. She could not distinguish words, but knew, without question, that Lucy had remained in Peter's room. A sense of unease flooded her as she realised what could be happening.

Washing herself quickly, Pamela finished her bath and dressed. Still listening for any sounds that might confirm her suspicion, she waited. Then she heard Lucy's voice, a muffled "Oh, sir," and then another barely audible sound that had to be Peter. She might be chaste, but she knew what she had heard. Peter had groaned!

Gathering herself to her full height and remembering that her father had been Sir George Kingston, she went outside to the hall. Peter did not even notice that she stood outside the water closet when he opened his door and escorted Lucy out.

"Lucy, please tell Jack to have the carriage ready at half past seven tomorrow morning. I shall be leaving early for chambers."

Pamela barely controlled her fury when she interrupted. "You told Lucy to tell me you would see me for breakfast. Has that changed?"

Lucy awkwardly curtsied to Peter. She muttered, "I will tell him, sir," and hurried down the hall.

Pamela called to her. "Lucy."

Lucy stopped and turned around. "Yes, miss."

"I will need some help with my things. In the morning, I would like my clothes unpacked and put in the cupboard in this room." Pamela indicated the room across from Peter's. "I will be moving everything there tomorrow."

Lucy glanced at Peter, obviously waiting for his consent. "It is all right, Lucy. I have offered the room to Pamela if she cares to have it."

Pamela glared at Peter. "I have accepted the offer." Turning back to Lucy, she softened her voice. "Lucy, I will have my dinner now."

"Yes, miss." Lucy left them standing in the hall.

Peter turned to go back into his room. "Peter, you did not answer my question. Are we taking our morning meal together?"

Rather than answer her question, he snapped at her, "Have you no modesty? It is quite unseemly to be standing in the hallway in your nightdress."

Without hesitation, she replied angrily, "No more unseemly than your standing here in your dressing gown!"

"I will be taking my meal at ten past seven, if you care to join me." He stepped back into his room and closed the door.

Pamela stood in the hall for several minutes, invoking her

father's spirit to help her control herself. She wanted to beat on Peter's door with her fists, call him every obscene name she had ever heard or read, and if he should open the door again, slap his face.

But that was not what her father taught her. Sir George had presented himself to the world as a gentleman and always, no matter what he truly felt, carried himself with dignity and grace. She would do the same.

As she walked down the hall to her room, a long forgotten memory bubbled to the surface. After her mother died, her father employed a series of nannies for her. The last one stayed with her until her father died.

Pamela would often wander through the dark house late at night, holding a candle, looking for ghostly specters she hoped to catch unaware. She never found any, but she did discover another secret.

As she walked past her father's room one night, she found the door ajar. Peeking into his room, she saw her father and her governess on his bed. Her governess laughed and said, "Sir George, you are such a rogue."

Her father had replied, "And you, dear Clarissa, are more of a temptress than this old man can resist."

Pamela stood in the hall then as she had now, listening. Hearing things she did not understand, and that had actually frightened her much more than the ghosts she hoped to find, she crept back to her room. Now she understood. And she had no fear.

Once back in her room, she put her dressing gown on over her nightdress. Lucy would be along directly with her dinner. How she would face the girl given the situation, she did not know. But she would. She had to.

Several long minutes later, Lucy knocked. "Miss, your dinner."

Pamela went to the door and let Lucy in. "Just put it on the desk, Lucy."

Lucy walked past her without looking up, pushed aside

the stack of books and journals, and set the tray on the desk. "Will that be all, miss?" She still did not look up and continued to stare at Pamela's desk.

"Lucy, you appear flustered. Is everything all right?"

"Very fine, miss. Will that be all?"

"I need to discuss with Jack the retrieval of my father's furniture. Will you please send him to my room when you leave?"

Lucy turned and looked at her for the first time since entering the room. "Now, miss?"

"Yes, Lucy, now. Please find him and tell him to come to my room."

"Yes, miss." Lucy glanced back at the desk and adjusted the tray. "Anything else miss?"

"No, that will be all." Lucy left her alone.

Pamela checked the tray Lucy had brought. May always prepared her favorites, and Pamela knew on her first night home, the tray would be loaded with delicious treats. But somehow, even May's expertly prepared delicacies would not satisfy her. She wanted something more.

After she waited impatiently for several more minutes, Jack knocked at her door. "Miss Pamela, you wanted to see me?"

Pamela untied her dressing gown before opening the door. It excited her knowing how terribly improper it would be to invite Jack into her room. At this hour, dressed as she was, Pamela knew it to be positively scandalous.

She opened the door. "Please, come in, Jack." He came in and Pamela closed the door behind him.

Jack had combed his dark hair and put on a clean shirt. "You wished to see me, miss?"

"Indeed I did, Jack." He fidgeted a bit, shifting from one foot to the other. Pamela tried to put him at ease. "Jack, tomorrow, I am moving to another room and I wish to have some of my father's furniture brought to the house. Master

Rennard suggested I retrieve my father's bed from storage. Could you do that for me?"

"Of course, miss. I will do it in the morning, I will."

"That would be splendid. Perhaps I will accompany you. There might be other things there that would suit my new room."

"Of course, miss."

Pamela could see Jack's discomfort. She needed him to relax with her. "Jack, I remember at Christmas, you carried a flask of rum in your back pocket. I don't suppose you have a flask now?"

Jack smiled broadly. "Oh, I do indeed, miss. 'Cept it is gin and not up to your refined taste."

"Let me see if it is. I expect it is delicious."

Jack pulled his flask from his back pocket and handed it to Pamela. "Miss Pamela, it is rotgut, not fit for a lady such as you."

"Nonsense, Jack." Pamela took the flask and opened it. Bolting back a healthy swallow, she shivered as it went down. "Oh, my, that does have a kick, doesn't it?" She shivered again and handed the flask back to him.

"I told you, miss. It isn't meant for refined ladies like you."

Pamela took a moment before she spoke, to let the burn in her throat subside. Then she said, "Jack, it is better than the finest liquor I have ever tasted."

"Really, miss?"

"Really, Jack."

"Would you like another?" Jack handed her the flask again.

Hoping her stomach would accept another bolt, Pamela took the flask. "Yes, I would like another." Pamela took another swallow with the same reaction. Jack took back the flask and also took a swallow himself, before he capped it.

"Will that be all, Miss Pamela?" Jack didn't move. But he made no pretense of not looking at her breasts, then moving his eyes lower.

The hidden desire in Pamela, given a voice by the gin, spoke the words she could not. "Jack, there is something else."

"Yes, miss." Jack moved closer to her.

Pamela took off her dressing gown and let it fall to the floor. She stood in front of Jack in her nightdress and nothing else. "Kiss me again."

Jack did not hesitate. He took hold of Pamela and kissed her, forcefully, deeply. Pamela responded in kind, digging her fingernails into Jack's back as she returned his kiss.

When the fusion of their mouths broke, Pamela gasped for air. Jack immediately attempted to capture her mouth again. "Jack, wait."

He stepped back, obviously with some effort. "Yes, miss."

"Jack, you must understand, I am untried." Pamela paused for a moment, collecting herself, and then continued. "I know you have experience. What can we do together that will leave me intact?"

"Miss Pamela, I am not of a mind to compromise you."

"I know that, Jack." Pamela closed her eyes and took a deep breath before she continued. "But I have feelings, things that will not go away. I do not know how to keep the wolves away from the door."

"Miss, if you like, we can do something about it without busting your maidenhead."

"What, Jack? Tell me what!"

Jack took her hand and led her over to her armchair. "Sit on my lap, miss, and we will see to it."

He sat down and Pamela sat on his lap. "Jack, you will have to show me. I don't know what . . . I have never . . ."

"Miss Pamela, if you let me, I can show you."

"Please, Jack, show me."

Jack palmed her breast. "Miss Pamela, your bubbies are so nice. I've thought about licking them more than once, I have."

"You want to lick my breasts?" Pamela never dreamed any man would want to lick her breasts.

"Yes, miss, I've wanted to lick them for a long time."

Pamela unbuttoned the front of her nightdress. "Do it, Jack, lick my breasts."

Jack slipped his hand inside Pamela's gown and lifted a breast out. Bending over her, he first kissed the mound, and then he licked it. Pamela shuddered as his tongue swept the surface of her titty. Then he lingered on her nipple. He sucked the nub into his mouth and circled it with his tongue.

Pamela's hair had fallen around her shoulders. She took out the few remaining pins, so that her hair could cascade over her. Jack reached into her gown and exposed her other titty. He kissed and licked it as he had the first. As he sucked on the second nipple, Pamela's head lolled backward, pushing her breast deeper into Jack's mouth.

Jack broke the suction on her breast long enough to say, "Miss, my prick is hurting."

"Take it out and let me touch it, Jack." Jack undid his trousers and freed his aching prick. Pamela stared down at his engorged cock, and then gingerly ran her finger over the tip.

"Have you ever seen one, miss?"

Too inflamed to care about revealing her innocence, Pamela admitted, "I've never seen one so exposed."

"Touch it, miss. Feel how hard it is."

Pamela did touch it. She ran her finger over the tip. Jack had not been cut, so his foreskin crinkled at the base of the head. The loose skin easily slid back and forth as she studied this hidden male treasure.

"Miss, we can take care of business together. I can do you while you do me. It is a way to keep you chaste."

Before Pamela could say yes or no, Jack had his hand underneath her gown. The throbbing became unendurable as his hand connected with her privy parts. She moaned, "My God, Jack, I am dying."

"You ain't dyin', miss, you just want to be fucked good."

As he said that, he jammed his fingers into her cunt. Pamela gasped and lifted her hips. "I feel it, miss, your maidenhead. I won't be poppin' it, but I will be makin' you squeal."

Jack rammed his fingers into Pamela's hungry cunt again and again. Each time, his fingers grazed her chastity, but never hard enough to break through. Pamela held on to Jack's prick, squeezing harder every time he pushed into her.

"Oh, yes, miss, that's right, let those pretty titties bounce. You and me, we're both goin' to cream tonight."

Pamela writhed on Jack's lap, his ministrations to her wet cunt merciless. Just when she thought she would lose her mind with need, something exploded inside of her and consumed her. Her entire body shook uncontrollably. Jack's arm caught her as she threw herself backward and went rigid.

Wave after wave of sensation washed through her, annihilating all sense of propriety and identity. She still had hold of Jack's prick and pulled his shaft hard. Without warning, he, too, went rigid, shooting white liquid onto her hand and nightdress.

They sat together on the chair, Jack supporting her with his arm, her hand still on his now softening cock. She tried to right herself, but found she could not manage it. Without bothering to tuck himself back in his trousers, Jack picked her up and carried Pamela to her bed.

"Jack . . ."

"Shhh, miss. It is time for you to sleep." He pulled back the blankets and tucked her into the clean sheets.

Pamela watched as he put himself back into his trousers. "Jack, I . . ."

Jack put his fingers over her lips, the same fingers that had been inside her only a few minutes earlier. She could smell herself as he brushed her lips. "Miss Pamela, give Master Rennard some time. He will come round."

With that he turned down the gas lamp and let himself out, closing the door behind him.

Chapter Four

Sunlight shining in her eyes woke Pamela. She bolted from her bed, hoping to heaven she had not overslept. The clock showed three quarters past six. She had enough time to make herself presentable for breakfast with Peter.

After cleaning herself in the washbowl, she selected a fashionable forest-green day dress from her trunk. When she wore it at Christmas, Peter had commented that she looked lovely in it. Shaking out the wrinkles as much as possible, she put it on over her chemise and petticoat. After quickly pinning up her hair, she hurried down the hall, hoping to be comfortably seated in the dining room before Peter came in.

May had set out the tea and muffins. The smell of bacon wafted in from the kitchen. When her stomach growled in a most unladylike fashion, Pamela remembered she had not touched her dinner the night before.

Sitting at her usual place, she poured herself a cup of tea. Within a few minutes, Peter came into the dining room. "Good morning, Peter."

"Good morning, Pamela." Peter sat opposite her. "Would you mind passing me the teapot?"

Rather than passing him the tea, she stood and poured it for him. "It appears to be a lovely day. The sun shining in my window woke me."

"Yes, indeed it does."

Pamela sat down and looked at him. He avoided looking back. "Peter, I've asked Jack to retrieve my father's bed from storage. I do believe I will have a canopy built for it."

"As you wish." His rigid jaw said much more than his words.

"Peter, for Lord's sake, I live here now. Do you plan to never have a conversation with me again?"

"And what would you care to discuss, Pamela? Perhaps the literature you have been reading lately?"

"What I read is my own affair."

Peter sipped his tea. "Interesting choice of words, my dear. How many of your own affairs have you had?"

"Not nearly enough to suit me." Pamela took a muffin and spread some jam on it. Sparring with Peter on this subject pleased her for some reason. She waited for his move.

He leaned forward and also took a muffin. "And what would suit you?"

Pamela gauged her answer carefully. She had him talking and didn't want to set him off again. "I don't know what would suit me. Or perhaps I should say who."

"I understood you to say marriage would equate to selling your soul."

"I'm not talking about marriage." Just then Lucy brought in a platter of bacon and eggs and set it down between them.

Peter smiled. "Good morning, Lucy."

"Good morning, sir." Nodding at Pamela, she simply said, "Miss."

Remembering her place in the household, Pamela responded, "Good morning, Lucy." Helping herself to some food from the platter, she continued, "After Master Rennard has left for the day, I would like to move to my new room. I trust that will not be a problem?"

"No, miss."

"And please tell Jack that later this morning, I will be going to the building where my father's furniture is stored, to see what I care to bring back for my room."

"Yes, miss. Will there be anything else?"

Peter sharply interjected, "Lucy, I would like to see you before I leave. Please wait for me at the door."

Lucy's face flushed and she wiped her hands on her apron. "Yes, sir, as you say, sir." She quickly turned and nearly ran to the kitchen.

"Peter, what is the point of rattling the girl so?"

"I did nothing to rattle her."

"Yes, you did! Anyone spoken to in that tone would think they are about to be caned!" Pamela got up from the table. "I'm going to make sure she knows everything is all right."

"Pamela, sit down!"

Pamela stood beside the table, her small fists clenched at her sides. Had she been a man, she would have connected one of those fists to his jaw. "Peter Rennard, you may speak that way to the hired help, but you will not use that tone of voice with me! I live here now. I will do what I wish when I wish to do it."

Peter stood as well and threw his napkin on the table. "And Pamela, whether you like it or not, I am still your guardian and master of this house. As long as you live here, you are answerable to me. Do you understand?"

"I understand you have been a brute since I arrived. I do not know why, nor do I care for it one bit! And whether you like it or not, I am a woman now! I have my own mind and fully intend to use it!"

Before Peter had a chance to stop her, she grabbed hold of her skirt and went through the door that led to the kitchen. He leaned on the table and closed his eyes, hissing, "Damn that girl," through clenched teeth. She had done it to him again. As he watched her fire rise and her temper flare, his cock voiced what he could not.

Peter sat down and tried to focus on his food. His stiff prick stretched uncomfortably against his leg, a constant reminder that Pamela had come home to stay. How in the name of God could he endure this? No other woman had ever done this to him, not one! Only Pamela. He had sworn to Sir George on his deathbed that he would protect his daughter. And who would protect Pamela from him?

Knowing he would be in chambers shortly helped Peter regain his control. It also helped that Pamela had not returned. No doubt she had taken the back stairs up to her room. For some insane reason, that disappointed him. Now, he wouldn't see her again until his day ended.

He finished his meal and went to find Lucy. She stood in the foyer waiting for him. "Lucy, does Jack have the carriage ready?"

"Yes, sir."

"Good. Let's step outside for a moment." She followed him to the stoop. "Lucy, there is no need to be anxious. I am sorry if I spoke too sternly in the dining room. I only want to know if you have anything to tell me."

"Sir?"

"Remember I asked you to keep your eyes open when Miss Pamela unpacked?"

"Yes, sir, I remember."

"Did you see anything?"

"Yes, sir. She has more volumes of that *Pearl* journal on her desk, with some books and letters."

"Does she now! Did you see how many?"

"Not exactly, sir, maybe six or eight. I couldn't be sure."

"Lucy, you do me a great service with this information." Peter hesitated for a moment, and then asked, "Did Miss Pamela say anything to you about me when she came into the kitchen?"

"No, sir, just that . . ."

"What, Lucy?"

"Just that I shouldn't let you scare me into doin' nothing I don't want to do."

"Are you scared of me, Lucy?"

She said very timidly, "Not usually, sir. But sometimes, when you get riled up, I do catch a bit of fright."

"Like in the dining room?"

"Yes, sir."

Peter could see Jack sitting on the carriage waiting for him. He didn't want to draw attention to the fact that he and Lucy were talking. "Lucy, I have to go to chambers now. But I want you to know, I am not angry with you, not at all. It is Miss Pamela that has me riled, not you."

"Sir?"

"Yes, Lucy?"

"I beg your pardon, not to speak out of turn, but if you and Miss Pamela don't get on, why is she moving into that room? You'll be seeing her all the time." Lucy put her hands on her hips and in a rush of words, blurted out, "You called me by her name last night, you did!"

The urge to reprimand her for her indiscretion welled up in him. But continuing this conversation on a public stoop would only make matters worse. "There are reasons for it I can't explain to you. I have to go now. Good day, Lucy."

With a quick curtsy, she tersely replied, "Good day, Master Rennard."

When Jack saw Peter walking down the cobblestone path from the house, he jumped down to open the gate. "Good morning, sir. It is a fine one, it is."

"Good morning, Jack." Peter stopped beside the carriage and waited for Jack. Jack came round to open the door. "Jack, I understand Pamela wants you to retrieve some furniture for her today and that she wants to go with you."

"That's what she told me, sir."

"Make sure you stay close to her. She shouldn't be wandering around a storage room alone."

"I will make sure she is safe. I surely will."

"Good man." He pulled a crown from his vest pocket. "Here, Jack. Contract for a wagon to carry anything she wants to bring. The bed alone will require a wagon."

"Yes, sir. I'll see to it, sir."

"And Jack, could you please tell May that Miss Pamela and I will be taking dinner together tonight, at the usual time? Tell her to set up the small table in the library, in front of the fireplace. We will need some privacy."

"Yes, sir."

Jack closed the brougham door. With images of Pamela reading those journals for many months now threatening to overtake his concentration, Peter forced his attention to the day ahead.

Pamela stood at the window in the parlour and watched the carriage pull away from the house. Once it disappeared down Piccadilly Street, she immediately rang for Lucy.

"Yes, miss?"

"Lucy, I need your help moving my things."

"I know, miss." Lucy nervously twisted her apron.

"I saw Master Rennard speaking to you. Did he upset you again?"

"No, miss."

Pamela pressed for more information. "Lucy, I heard something last night. Did Master Rennard take liberties with you when you brought him his dinner?" Lucy did not answer. "Lucy, please, I need to know. Did he?"

Lucy answered coldly, "No more than Jack did with you, miss."

Pamela weighed her words carefully. "Lucy, are you and Jack fond of each other?"

"We have tipped a pint now and again, miss."

"It might help you to know I fancy Master Rennard, not Jack."

"Master Rennard fancies you, too, miss."

"He does? How do you know that?"

"I can't say, miss. I just know."

Pamela motioned to the sofa. "Lucy, come here and sit beside me for a bit." Obviously flustered, Lucy followed Pamela and sat down beside her. "I want to explain something to you."

"Yes, miss."

Knowing the indelicacy of speaking of such matters with a servant, Pamela nevertheless continued. "For a long while, I have hoped Master Rennard would see me as a woman. I think he is beginning to, but it is upsetting him."

"He told me, miss."

"Lucy, please, what did he say?" Pamela heard the pleading tone of her voice. She didn't care.

"He said you had him riled, not me."

"I know he is angry with me."

"It's not just that, miss."

"Please, Lucy, what else?"

"Last night, he wanted you, Miss Pamela, not me."

Pamela closed her eyes and took a deep breath. Trying to keep her voice steady, she asked, "Then he did take liberties with you."

"He doesn't want you to know about his state, Miss Pamela. He is hiding it, he is. Miss, that's all I can say. Master Rennard is good to me. I won't speak badly of him."

"All right, Lucy, I understand. Let me show you what I would like moved."

Pamela led the way upstairs to her room. She told Lucy what to move: her clothing, her books and a few of the pictures. When Lucy picked up the pile of books from the desk, Pamela noticed her interest in the journals. "Lucy, leave those. I will take care of them myself."

Lucy put them back on the desk. "Miss, if I may ask, what are they?"

"It is a publication, Lucy, with stories and poems. Why do you ask?"

"I saw Master Rennard reading one last night, when I brought him his dinner."

"That journal is why Master Rennard is so angry with me. The stories are about men and women being together."

Lucy's eyes opened wide. "Miss, you mean indecently?"

"In a manner of speaking, yes."

"Oh, my, Miss Pamela. He didn't tell me that!"

"No, I don't suppose he did."

"You have so many of them! That's why he . . ." Lucy stopped short.

"Why he what, Lucy?"

"He just wanted to know if you had more."

Pamela went over to her desk and picked up the stack of journals. "I have six here. There are four more in my boxes that will arrive in a few days. You have my permission to tell him I have ten of them. Plus the one he already has makes eleven."

"Yes, Miss Pamela."

"Lucy, I am not angry with you. This is between Master Rennard and myself. I do not want you caught in the middle. Now, could you go and see if Jack has returned yet? I am anxious to get my furniture." Lucy hurried from the room, taking the stack of books with her.

Pamela hugged the stack of journals to her chest. Peter had read one. He now understood her yearnings. Somehow, she had to find a way to have him come to her instead of to Lucy or to anyone else!

She took the journals and her letters to her new room. Jack would have to dismantle the present bed and store it in the attic. The sparsely furnished room needed more furniture and some bright colours. Pictures and a looking glass on the wall would brighten it, as would some new wallpaper. She would manage that later. Right now, she wanted to be as close to Peter as possible.

Not having eaten dinner yesterday nor much breakfast today, Pamela felt a bit peckish. She took the back
stairs down to the kitchen. May always had something
cooking. She would fix Pamela a plate of whatever she had
on hand.

At the bottom of the stairs, she heard voices coming from
the servants' quarters at the other end of the hallway. Then
she heard a crash and glass breaking. She heard Jack yell,
"Calm down, Lucy, I'm telling you, nothing happened!"

"The devil nothing happened! She's been reading indecent
books. Master Rennard knows about it, too. He's bloody
frigged off, he is!"

"And how the bloomin' 'ell would you know he's frigged
off?"

"I know, is all, I just know."

Pamela crept closer to the door, which they had left ajar.
She saw a broken ale bottle on the floor. Lucy and Jack stood
beside the bed. "You had better mind yourself, Lucy. You
could cost us both our employ. Throwing that bottle at me
could've woke the dead!"

"You don't need to worry about that, now do ya? Miss
Pamela will be taking care of you, I'm sure."

"Leave Miss Pamela out of this."

"And what do you think Master Rennard would say if he
knew you went to her room last night?"

"Now, you wouldn't be thinking of telling him?" Jack
took hold of her arm.

"I might be. He's asked for my help, letting him know
what Miss Pamela is doing."

"I don't think you'll be wanting to tell him, Lucy. You really
don't want the guvner to be throwing me out on my arse,
now do ya?"

"I'll have to be thinkin' about that." Pamela could hardly
believe her eyes when she saw Jack reach out and openly rub
Lucy's breasts.

Jack confronts Lucy, continue reading
Lucy confronts Jack, turn to page 57

"Maybe this will help you make up your mind." Jack pushed Lucy back on the bed and pushed up her skirt. She made no attempt to stop him.

"You bugger. You think your prick will keep me quiet?"

"I think you need reminding of what you lose if the guvner sacks me!"

"Miss Pamela is waitin' on you. She wants to get her furniture."

"She won't mind waitin' a few more minutes."

"And just what have you been doing that makes her so agreeable?"

"Bloody 'ell not what I've been doing to you!" Pamela stifled a gasp as Jack pulled off Lucy's drawers and left her bare. "She's saving herself." He undid his trousers and pulled his pud. "Seems the guvner has a bit of something waiting for him."

Lucy laughed. "She's got more than a bit of something waiting for her, too. He's got a big one, he does."

Jack snapped at her, "And how the 'ell would you know how big it is?"

"Wouldn't you like to know?" Lucy squirmed on the bed and opened her legs wide.

"Seems you need a reminder of our agreement. Roll over."

"Jack, you're getting yourself all riled over nothin' at all."

"I said roll over." Jack did not wait for Lucy to respond. He grabbed her and flopped her over on her belly. Then he straddled her legs.

"Jack Sims, get off of me!"

"I ain't doin' nothin' of the sort, not until I'm ready."

Before she realised what she was doing, Pamela was stroking her breast as she watched them on the bed. Jack had his back to her. She saw him raise his hand a moment before she heard a loud smack. Lucy squealed. "What the bloomin' 'ell are you doing?"

Jack smacked her again. "You need reminding that you promised your cunt to me and nobody else."

"He ain't had my cunt!" Jack smacked her again.

"Then what's he done that he's told you so much?" Lucy squealed as Jack's hand came down on her again, and again.

Lucy clutched the quilt in her hand. At first Pamela thought her in pain. But when Lucy moaned again, Pamela realised the thrashing from Jack had caused another kind of pain, the exquisite pain Pamela knew from the night before.

"I don't believe you. He had your cunt, didn't he?" Jack's hand came down again and Lucy moaned.

"No, I swear, he ain't had me. He rubbed against my bum, is all. Miss Pamela makes him hard and he doesn't want her to know. He even called me by her name when he creamed, he did!"

Pamela froze. Lucy's words rang in her ears. She stared at Jack's back and watched as he knelt behind Lucy. "Lift up your arse." Lucy raised her bum into the air. He pushed her legs wider apart. "The guvner wants her all right. Let him pop her jewel, she wants him to. He sure as 'ell ain't havin' you!"

Jack lunged forward, burying himself inside Lucy. He pulled out and lunged again, smacking his groin against Lucy's bum. "You won't be wantin' him when you can have this!"

Pamela heard Lucy's muffled groan. Jack pounded her with a forcefulness that shocked Pamela and made her stomach feel queer. He had hold of Lucy's hips, holding her still. "That's it. Let your cunny grab me. I want to feel your fanny milk me dry."

Jack continued to pound Lucy. Suddenly, Lucy moaned, "Jack, oh, Jack . . ."

"Oh, ya, doll, that's right." Jack slammed into Lucy one

more time. Pamela saw him spend inside Lucy as he had in her own hand the night before.

Not wanting to be discovered, Pamela hurried down the hall to the kitchen.

Go to page 59

Lucy pushed his hand away. "If you don't want me to tell the mister, then you have to tell me what you did with Miss Pamela."

"Nothing happened! She ain't been broke yet."

"Is that so! I suppose she told you that."

"She did."

"What else?" Lucy stood with her hands on her hips, her face flushed red. "Miss Pamela being in her nightdress and asking you to her room, somethin' happened!"

"All right, have it your way. She sat on my lap and I put my fingers up her cunny. I know she ain't broke. I felt it."

Pamela stood in the shadows of the hall, nearly holding her breath for fear of discovery. Lucy had a peculiar look on her face as she came up to Jack. "Did you make her squirm for you?" Lucy put her arms around Jack's neck.

Jack pulled Lucy up against him. "She did more than squirm, she did. Her cunny wanted it bad. She creamed against my fingers."

Lucy slid her hand down Jack's chest to his belt. "Did she, now?"

"She did." Jack squeezed Lucy's breasts. "Her bubbies are plump ones. They bounced real nice when I touched her up."

Quite unconsciously, Pamela stroked her own breast. As Jack spoke about Pamela's arousal the night before, Lucy changed. She pressed against Jack and rubbed against him. "Did she go off for you?"

"She wants cock in her real friggin' bad. I made her go off till she nearly fainted."

Lucy's head lolled back as she muttered, "The mister will like that, he will."

"What did you do with the guvner?"

"I've been very naughty. I let the mister rub off against me bum."

"You promised me your cunt, only me. You didn't give it to him, did you?"

"He didn't want my cunt, he wants hers. She makes him

hard, he told me so. He even called me by her name when he spent."

Pamela's heart beat so rapidly in her chest, she thought she might swoon. Lucy's words pierced her. Unable to move, her body filled with heat as she watched Lucy raise her skirt.

"Jack, I should be punished for being so wicked. Don't you want to warm my bum for letting the mister rub against it?"

Lucy raised her skirt and stepped out of her drawers. She bent over the bed. Pamela had full view of her privy parts for a moment, before Jack came up behind her. When his hand connected with Lucy's bum, Lucy moaned and grabbed the quilt. Jack slapped her bum with the flat of his hand over and over. Each time, Lucy moaned and writhed against the bed.

Pamela caressed her own breast, mesmerised by the sight of Lucy's abandonment to the thrashing. Jack suddenly stopped and opened his trousers. "Lift your sweet arse, Lucy."

Lucy spread her legs wide and lifted herself up, her opening visible to Pamela. Jack pulled his pud several times, staring at Lucy's cunt. "Lucy, you've got the sweetest cunny I've ever seen." He positioned himself behind her and in one stroke, entered her. "I'm not stopping until you milk me dry."

Pamela could feel each thrust in her own privy parts as Jack slammed into Lucy. Suddenly Lucy made a ragged sound as though she couldn't breathe. "Oh, God, Jack . . ."

"That's it, doll, go off for me, squeeze my prick." He slammed his pelvis against Lucy several more times before he went rigid. As he had the night before into Pamela's hand, he spent inside of Lucy. Dragging himself out of her, he slammed again. "Oh, ya, milk me, pet."

Not wanting to be discovered, Pamela hurried down the hall to the kitchen.

Chapter Five

B efore going into the kitchen, Pamela stopped to compose herself. So many images flashed in her mind, too many thoughts. She took a deep breath as dizziness threatened to overtake her. Tea, she needed a cup of tea.

Pamela opened the door to the kitchen. May stood at the stove, stirring something in a large pot. "May, could I have a cup of tea and a biscuit, please?" Her voice trembled a bit.

May turned around. "Good Lord, child, what is wrong with you?"

"I am feeling a bit peaked. Having a cup of tea will bring me around."

May led her to a chair. "Sit down before you faint. You must be ill. You didn't touch your dinner last night."

"I'm not ill, May, just terribly excited to be home. I will be fine once I have some tea."

"You know I always have a kettle on the stove." May poured a cup of tea and prepared a plate of biscuits. "Here, child, sip this. I will make you an egg."

Pamela gratefully took the cup. "May, I don't want an egg."

"Nonsense! You must have some nourishment."

Pamela picked up a biscuit and nibbled at it. More than food, she wanted the comfort of the warm tea. It calmed her, as she knew it would.

A few minutes after May had set a plate with a fried egg in front of her, Jack came into the kitchen. He kicked the door open with his foot, hands in his pockets, whistling a merry tune. He stopped short when he saw Pamela.

"Miss Pamela! What are you doing here?" He took off his hat and ran his fingers through his hair. "Lucy went upstairs to tell you I'm back and ready to take you for your furniture."

Pamela gripped her teacup tightly to still her trembling hands. When she spoke, her voice sounded calm and natural. "I felt a bit peckish. Before making the trip, I needed some tea and biscuits."

"Of course, miss. I'll wait at the carriage." He turned to go out the back door, then remembered Peter's message. "May, Master Rennard says to tell you he would be taking dinner with Miss Pamela tonight in the library. You should set the small table in front of the fireplace." Glancing at Pamela, he added, "He wants some privacy." Saying nothing else, he went to the carriage.

Gathering herself, Pamela finished her tea and took a small bite of the egg, which her stomach promptly rejected. May stood across from her, with her arms crossed over her ample bosom. "Pamela, I have known you for many years. When I worked for Sir George, you would visit me in the kitchen, just as you are now. You would tell me your troubles. Do you want to tell me what is bothering you or should I guess?"

"May, it is not something I am free to discuss."

"Then, let me tell you something. Since Christmas last, Master Rennard has had a sour temper. After you left, he dined with no less than five different ladies in as many weeks, none of which took his fancy for more than a few days. Miss Constance has sent him messages, which he has not returned. They sit on his desk, unopened."

May came over and put her arm around her. "Pamela, your father might not have seen it, but I did. You had stars in your eyes for that man long before you knew why they were there. Now you understand."

The emotion inside Pamela boiled over. She hugged May around the waist and cried, tears flowing for all the years she had waited. "There, there, child, it will be all right."

May took the tea towel she had tucked under her belt and handed it to Pamela. "Dry your tears. He will come around. He just doesn't want to face up to how he really feels."

"How does he really feel, May? Sometimes I think he hates me and blames me for his never marrying."

"Pamela, dear, perhaps you are the reason he never married, but it isn't because he hates you."

"I'm not so sure."

May stroked her hair. "I am."

Pamela gave May an affectionate squeeze, "What would I have ever done without you? I never knew my mum, and Papa preferred the law to raising a daughter."

May laughed. "Master Rennard ended up with both of us, dear. Sir George saw to that."

"May, you and I both know that Papa hired a governess more for himself than for me. You are the only constant in my life."

"Not the only one, my dear. Sir George saw to that as well."

"You really do believe Peter doesn't hate me?"

"Sweet girl, no man in his right mind could hate you! Perhaps you should stand in front of the looking glass and pay attention!" May helped Pamela to her feet. "Now, you find yourself a pretty dress to wear at dinner. I'll make sure everything is ready in the library as the guvner asked. He will have his privacy with you."

Pamela kissed May on her fleshy cheek. "You are the mum I never had."

"Dearie, I don't know that your real mum would be encouraging this romance." May had a twinkle in her eye. "Master Rennard is older, and more experienced, than you."

"But won't catching up be a bit of fun!" Pamela grabbed a

few more biscuits from the plate and stuffed them in the pocket of her dress.

Running back upstairs to grab her bonnet and bag, Pamela bumped into Lucy in the hall outside her new room. "Oh, Miss Pamela, there you are. I come to tell you Jack is back."

"I know. He is waiting for me at the carriage. Could you bring me my bag and green bonnet, please?"

"Yes, miss." Lucy disappeared into the room.

It seemed inconceivable to Pamela that Lucy could be so passionate. Never would Pamela have imagined this about her. Rather than that being a cause for concern, Pamela decided to approach it as her father would. He always maintained that any liability could be turned into an asset if intelligence prevailed.

Lucy brought out her things. "Lucy, will you help me with something?"

"Yes, miss?"

"Master Rennard left a message for May to set a table in the library for our dinner this evening, so we could have some privacy. I want to look pretty for him. While I'm out, could you please prepare the rose dinner dress I brought with me, the one with the lace bodice?"

"The one I unpacked this morning, miss, the party dress with the low front?"

"That's the very one. When I return, I will need your help getting dressed and doing my hair."

"Yes, miss."

"Do you think Master Rennard will like that dress, Lucy?"

"I wouldn't know, miss."

"You know more about his likes and dislikes than you are telling me."

"Miss, I won't speak badly of Master Rennard!"

"Nor would I expect you to speak badly of him. May told me how unhappy he has been. You told me yourself he is hiding how he feels from me." Pamela took Lucy's hand and held it. "Lucy, I want to know how to please Master Rennard and make him happy. Help me with this. Tell me how you please him."

Pamela continued to hold Lucy's hand and waited. In a barely audible voice, Lucy whispered, "He likes to be rubbed, miss."

Pamela squeezed Lucy's hand tightly. "Say it again, Lucy, what does he like?"

"He likes to be rubbed. And he likes to look at and squeeze my bubbies."

"What else, Lucy? Tell me everything."

"Miss Pamela, he's never had me, he hasn't. I promised Jack."

"Then tell me what he does instead. What did he do last night?"

"He rubbed against my bum, miss. I told you, he fancies rubbin'."

"Does he fancy rubbing you, too?"

"Yes, miss. Sometimes, he'll lift my skirt."

"If I wear that dress, do you think he will want to lift my skirt?"

"If he don't, miss, he ain't normal!"

Pamela smiled for the first time that day. "Lucy, thank you."

Much to Pamela's delight, Lucy smiled back. "You're welcome, Miss Pamela."

Pamela tied her bonnet under her chin. "I have to go now, Lucy. The morning is getting on."

"Yes, miss."

Pamela lifted her skirt and practically ran down the stairs. She had learned more during the last day than she had the whole semester at University. The clock in the foyer read half past ten. This day had only just begun!

Jack helped her into the carriage, discreetly patting her bum as she climbed in. When she felt his hand on her again, some wonderful tingles moved through her privy parts.

Before he closed the door, he pointed to the sky. "Miss, there are some dark clouds moving in. Looks like we might be gettin' some rain."

Pamela looked out of the window. "You are quite right, and it was so sunny this morning. Do you think we will be able to hire a covered wagon? I don't want the furniture to get wet."

"I expect so, miss. Master Rennard gave me a crown to contract what we need."

"How very kind of him."

Jack smiled. "He also told me to stay close and make sure to keep you safe. I hope you won't be minding that too much."

"No, Jack, I won't mind."

The carriage rolled down Piccadilly toward Shaftesbury and Charing Cross Road, where they would round the corner to Old Compton Street. Pamela understood Peter's concern. The storage building sat adjacent to several alehouses and pubs, places that attracted many men. It was not a street she should be on alone.

However, being in the company of Jack, she felt quite safe. She had no doubt he could handle himself in a brawl and would certainly make sure no one threatened her. He had never told her his age, but she guessed him to be somewhere between twenty-five and thirty years. That made him younger than Peter, but still older than herself.

The carriage hit a rut in the street and bounced, making her stomach roll. She took a biscuit out of her pocket and ate a few bites of it. Closing her eyes, she saw Peter sitting beside her in the carriage. Lucy had confirmed what she already knew from yesterday—he liked to be rubbed. It pleased her to know Peter allowed her to touch him. She had waited for him and now, it seemed, the wait might be nearing its end.

It seemed inconceivable to her that she had touched both Peter and Jack on the same day. She heated up all over again when she remembered how they each felt in her hand, how their manhood came alive with her ministrations. Having held each cock in her hand, she thought them to be similar in size, although Peter had a thickness to him that Jack did not.

She had only ever felt a man's organ once before, through his trousers. A classmate's brother, while visiting his sister, had escorted Pamela to a party. While dancing with her, he became quite amorous. They slipped out to the garden, where he quite boldly pressed his hardened organ against her leg. Her curiosity overcame her fear and she allowed the intimacy.

For several minutes, they stood silently in the shadows. He touched her breasts while he rubbed his organ against her. Only when other couples came into the garden did they stop, for fear of being discovered. They had no other opportunity that evening to be alone. He returned to London the next day.

They corresponded briefly, but had not seen each other again. Pamela did not want to encourage his attentions, because she so wanted to be with Peter. Without question, her father would approve of this suitor. As the eldest son, Charles would inherit the title Earl of Essex from his father and his seat in the House of Lords. If they were to marry, she would be a countess.

She did not want Peter to know about Charles. If he thought she had a suitor with a peerage, she knew he would do everything in his power to have her marry into the line. It was what Sir George had wanted, to have his heirs titled. Pamela had no desire to fulfill her father's ambition. For as long as she could remember, she had only wanted Peter.

Pamela drifted in a drowsy haze as the carriage rolled along. She had her hand on Peter again, while he kissed her neck and fondled her breasts. He whispered to her how he wanted to touch her and be touched by her, and how he wanted to spend inside of her. But Peter had Jack's voice. Jack whispered to her, Jack touched her.

"Miss Pamela, miss, wake up. We're here to get your furniture."

"Furniture?" Pamela sat up, disoriented.

"Miss, are you awake?" Jack reached in and took her hand.

"Yes, of course, my furniture." She allowed Jack to help her out of the carriage. "Where are we?" The street did not appear to be Old Compton Street.

"We are on Greek Street, miss, around the corner from the storage house." He pointed across the street to an area where several freight wagons were parked. "That is where I will hire the wagon and over there," he said, pointing to a large doorway, "is the dock where they will load your furniture."

"How very good of you, Jack, to handle this for me."

"It is my pleasure, Miss Pamela. Wait here and I will ask about a wagon."

Jack ran across the street. Gesturing toward Pamela, he spoke briefly to a large man leaning against one of the wagons. The burly fellow nodded agreeably. Coming back to where Pamela stood, Jack told her, "That bloke will bring his wagon around to the dock and wait there for the furniture. We best be getting inside, miss. The rain is coming."

A light drizzle fell as they entered the building. Jack made sure he stayed directly behind Pamela as they made their way to the office. Men working inside would notice a genteel woman walking through.

After explaining to the foreman why they had come, Pamela and Jack were led to a padlocked room on the second floor. Once inside, Jack lifted the drop cloths, so Pamela could see the furniture underneath.

"Jack, here is the mahogany bed I want. It belonged to Papa. I want to have a canopy made for it."

They quickly found the matching pieces: a bureau, a cupboard and a night table. Jack told the foreman which pieces to load onto the wagon. A bright floral love seat and chair also caught her attention. "Please take these as well."

Pamela found a box of trinkets and a clock. "Do you see this, Jack?" She held up a small wooden clock, carved with an intricate design, with a brass dial. "This is a rosewood bracket clock with eight chimes. Papa gave it to my mum on their first Christmas together. He told me she adored it." She ran her hand over the rich wood. "Papa kept it by his bed. He said my mum spoke to him from heaven whenever the bells chimed." Pamela had almost whispered the last words.

"Miss Pamela, are you all right?" Jack came up close to her out of concern.

Blinking back the tears that had welled up in her eyes, she smiled up at him. "Yes, Jack, I am quite well, thank you." She held the clock tightly to her chest. "I will take this in the carriage with us. And that box. The rest can be brought in the hired wagon."

"Yes, of course, miss." Jack picked up the box of trinkets and led the way out of the room. At the loading dock, he spoke to the wagon driver and instructed him to take care that the furniture did not get wet, as the rain had begun in earnest.

"Jack, he knows where to deliver the furniture?"

"Yes, miss. He intends to wait for a bit, until the rain lets up. He will deliver everything this afternoon."

"Splendid! Will you be able to set up the bed for me today?"

"I expect so, miss. There's not much in your new bedroom. I'll pay that bloke to help me carry it all upstairs and put it right in your room."

"Thank you. I do appreciate your help with this."

Jack and Pamela went to the door. "Miss, it is really raining. Do you want to wait here until it stops?"

"I would much prefer being in the carriage."

"As you wish, miss."

Jack ran out in the rain and opened the carriage door. Pamela ran out after him and quickly climbed inside. Jack followed her in and put the box he held on the floor. As he turned to go back outside, Pamela grabbed his arm. "Jack, sit here with me. You'll catch your death if you sit outside in this rain."

"It wouldn't be proper, miss, for me to sit inside with you."

"And who will know? Look at the street, it's deserted. No one in their right mind would be out in this. Come, sit with me."

Jack closed the carriage door and sat down beside Pamela. "Miss, Master Rennard would not like this."

"Master Rennard does not like many things." Pamela threaded her fingers through Jack's. "Jack, I have a very big favour to ask of you."

"Miss Pamela, you know I will do whatever it is you need."

"This is personal, Jack, very personal." Pamela summoned all of her courage. Squeezing Jack's hand tightly, she blurted out, "I want to know how to please a man. I want to know how to please Peter."

"Miss Pamela, if you be saying what I think you're saying, it will come natural to you. I know it will."

"Jack, that simply isn't good enough. Master Rennard is worldly, and experienced. I am neither. You know that from last night."

"Miss, the guvner must know you are chaste."

"He does. That part of it I will learn from him, when the time comes. But that isn't what I am talking about." Pamela placed her hand high on Jack's thigh. "I want to know what a man enjoys, how he likes to be touched, how to give him pleasure."

Pamela could see Jack's response to her suggestion. The bulge growing in his trousers nearly grazed her fingertips. "Miss, Pamela, what do you want to know?"

Pamela moved closer to Jack. "I want to know what a man and a woman can do together, how they can please each other. Show me things, Jack, so I don't feel foolish and awkward with Peter."

*Pamela pleasures Jack, continue reading
Jack pleasures Pamela, turn to page 74*

Without his asking, Pamela stroked his hardened cock through his trousers. "I have read that men like to be licked. Is that true, Jack?"

"Oh, Miss Pamela, there ain't a man alive that don't want to be licked."

"Would you show me how?"

"Yes, miss, if you really want to know."

"Jack, I do want to know."

"Miss Pamela, I'm not sure . . ."

"Not sure about what?"

"Miss, you will have to kneel on the floor in here to do it. It's beneath you to be doing that, it is."

Pamela immediately knelt on the floor of the carriage, eye level with the lump in his trousers. "Jack, I want to learn. I want to know what will please you. Tell me what to do."

Jack closed his eyes for a moment, his own hand involuntarily stroking his prick. The rain pounded on the roof of the carriage, creating an impenetrable curtain of water outside the carriage window.

When he opened his eyes, they had a sharpness Pamela had never seen. "Miss, I like your bubbies. If you want to know what I like, I like to look at your bubbies."

Pamela felt the razor's edge of his eyes on her. She caressed her own breast, watching him follow her hand. "Would you like to see them now, Jack?"

"Yes, miss. I would like that very much."

Pamela undid the buttons down the front of her green

dress, opening it to her waist. Undoing the string on her chemise, she pulled it wide open.

Jack gripped his prick in his hand. Closing his eyes for only a moment, he softly moaned, "Friggin' 'ell, your bubbies are nice."

"Do you think Master Rennard will like them, Jack? Do you?"

"Miss Pamela, if he don't, the guvner ain't the man I think he is."

Pamela shamelessly massaged her own breasts as Jack watched. "You like it when I touch them, don't you?"

"Yes, Miss Pamela, but it's friggin' vulgar for a lady such as yourself to be doin' it for the likes of me. It's something you would see in a bawdyhouse."

Pamela leaned forward, resting her full breasts on Jack's knees. She moved his hand away from his prick and replaced it with her own. "Does Master Rennard go to bawdyhouses, Jack? Have you ever taken him to one?"

"Miss, you be askin' me something I can't answer." Pamela undid Jack's trousers and reached inside. She stroked his hard prick as she had Peter's the day before. Jack slid forward on the seat, spreading his knees open wider. Pamela's face hovered over his crotch.

Pamela carefully untangled his prick from his clothing and exposed it. Continuing to stroke it, she asked him again, "Jack, please tell me. I have to know his habits, so I can be to him what they are, those ladies I know he must visit."

Jack pushed his groin forward, the tip of his cock bumping Pamela's chin. Pamela instinctively leaned over and licked the tip. He moaned loudly. "God almighty, miss, lick me some more."

"Tell me, Jack, where does Master Rennard go?" She lightly licked the tip again.

Jack grimaced and pushed forward, trying to find Pamela's mouth. She pulled back, not letting him find the opening. His breath came in short gasps as he said, "Nellie's, he goes to Nellie's. He went there yesterday, before we come to fetch you."

Pamela fondled his bollocks. "Only yesterday, he went yesterday?"

"He needed to spend before he saw you. He has always done that when you are home."

"Where is Nellie's, Jack?"

"By the Thames, past Blackfriars Bridge." Pamela licked the tip of his cock again.

"Put it in your mouth, Judas Priest, suck me."

Pamela opened her mouth wide and enveloped the tip of his cock, taking as much of the length as she could manage. It tasted salty, with a hint of sulfur. The smell of him hit her spot on. Rather than being repulsed, she found his scent exciting, even intoxicating.

"Use your tongue, Miss Pamela. Keep licking me in your mouth."

Pamela slid her tongue back and forth in her mouth, licking him as she would a melting chocolate. Jack stopped her and pulled himself out of her mouth. "Miss, you best be taking off your hat. I nearly grabbed onto it."

"Yes, of course." Pamela quickly discarded her bonnet. Before she could resume, Jack instructed her.

"Now, Miss Pamela, you want to learn to do it right?"

"Yes, I do."

"Listen close, now. Take it full in your mouth and keep licking. Don't move your head. I'll be doing the moving, not you. When I spend, you have to swallow it. The guvner will like that, he will, if you swallow his cream."

Pamela nodded her understanding. Jack reached out and squeezed her breasts. "Another thing the guvner would like is if you let him spend rubbing against your bubbies." He pinched her nipples. "You have real fine bubbies, you do."

"It feels good when you touch them." He pinched her nipples again. She pushed her chest forward onto his lap. "I want to lick you, Jack, but rub your prick against my breasts first."

Jack slid forward and wedged himself between her breasts. "Squeeze your titties together, miss. Hold me tight between them."

Pamela did as he told her. His stiff cock slid between her breasts. Jack held her shoulders and shoved his organ forcefully into her flesh. He held her tightly and frigged her bubbies as he would a cunt. When his thrusting became more insistent, she feared he would leave bruises. "Jack, let me suck you now. I want to suck you."

He released her shoulders and slid his hand up into her hair. Pushing her face into his groin, he hoarsely whispered, "Suck me, miss, suck me till I spend."

Pamela took his throbbing organ in her mouth. The blood pulsed against her tongue as she licked him. As he said he would, he held her head still and used her mouth as a cunt, rapidly moving in and out. She kept her tongue moving, in circles, up and down, in as many different directions as she could manage.

To keep him from thrusting too deeply and gagging her, she held the base of his prick in her hand. Even when he shoved hard into her mouth, her hand kept him from ramming himself too deeply into her throat. Having seen him in the throes the night before, she knew he would spend at any moment.

Suddenly, he closed his fists in her hair and liquid hit the back of her throat. She automatically swallowed to keep from choking. Each squirt of his hot cream hit her palette and she swallowed, until he spent completely. He held her head and pulled himself out of her mouth. He sat for several moments with his eyes closed, catching his breath. Pamela remained kneeling.

Forgetting her dress remained open, she watched him, fascinated by the incredible power she felt at giving him such pleasure. When he opened his eyes, he looked down at her still kneeling.

"Miss Pamela, you should cover yourself. It is unseemly for you to be hanging out like that." As he said it, he reached out and cupped a fleshy breast in his hand. "They are lovely bubbies. The guvner will like them, he will."

"Thank you, Jack." Feeling randy as she laced up her chemise, she said, "I don't know what I like more, when you look at them or when you touch them."

"Miss Pamela, I am fond of doin' both." He picked up her bonnet. "You best be putting this back on and keeping it on. Your hair is mussed."

"I will." Pamela looked out the window. The rain had lessened. "We should be getting on now, Jack, before anyone notices we are still here."

"Yes, miss, quite right." Before opening the door to go to the driver's seat, Jack reached out and pulled Pamela to him. He kissed her, deeply and passionately. "Miss Pamela, once the guvner opens you, if you ever have a mind to lay with me, I would be honoured."

Before Pamela could answer, he opened the door and jumped down to the street. The carriage jolted forward as Jack took them home.

Go to page 78

"Miss Pamela, men want women, no matter how they can have 'em."

"But how do they want them, Jack? I've read about it, but I don't understand what it is that attracts them, or what they want to do."

"Well, miss, men fancy the way a woman looks and smells." Jack reached out and caressed one of Pamela's breasts. "I fancy looking at your bubbies."

"The way I fancied looking at your prick last night?" Pamela leaned back in the seat, while Jack aggressively kneaded her breasts.

"Miss, a lady like yourself shouldn't be using words like 'prick.'"

"When I say indecent words to you, I tingle all over."

"Do you now? Do you tingle when you show me your bubbies?"

"I did last night." Pamela's privy parts throbbed as Jack fondled her breasts.

"Then show them to me now. It's raining so hard. No one is on the street." The rain pelted the carriage, fogging the carriage windows. "No one can see, even if they walked by."

While taking off her bonnet, Pamela glanced at the windows, to reassure herself they had privacy. The bulge in Jack's trousers encouraged her to do as he asked. She unbuttoned her green dress and unlaced her chemise. Jack pulled the dress and chemise wide open, exposing Pamela's full bosom. "Miss, they are good bubbies, they are."

Jack leaned forward and kissed her titty. Pamela's tingles surged through her privy parts until they throbbed more. Jack clamped his lips around a hard nipple and pulled it into his mouth. He suckled her, without mercy, pinching the ripe bud with his teeth. He moved to the other titty and did the same.

Pamela could hardly breathe as he squeezed her nipple in his mouth. What should have caused her pain instead sent fiery sparks though her privy parts. He had to touch her there, like he did the night before. She managed to gasp, "Jack, touch me again, like you did last night."

He released her titty and put his hand under her skirt. "Are your drawers open?" Before she could respond, his hand connected with the hair between her legs. Pamela moaned and squirmed on the seat.

"Miss, you want it bad, you do. The guvner better take care of business soon, because if he don't, I will."

"God in heaven, I want him to, Jack. I really want him to, but I don't know if he wants me."

Jack slowly massaged her clitoris. "Miss Pamela, the guvner went to Nellie's yesterday before meeting you at the train. He wants you all right. Whenever you are home, he goes to Nellie's and spends to keep from touching you."

In her aroused haze, Pamela tried to make sense of what Jack had said. "Who is Nellie? I don't know any Nellie."

Jack laughed. "Miss, Nellie runs a bawdyhouse, by the Thames, just past Blackfriars Bridge. The guvner has been going there for years."

Before Pamela could ask anything else, Jack knelt in front of her and pushed up her skirt. She managed to say, "No," and tried to move away. Jack held her still.

"Now, miss, I'm not doing nothing to pop you open. I swear I won't." Pamela quieted. "Has any man ever kissed you here?" He slipped his hand under her skirt and diddled her clitoris.

"No, of course not." Pamela wanted to stop him, but could not do it. The throbbing overpowered whatever sense of propriety she retained. She wanted to know what he could do to give her relief.

"If you let me, I want to kiss your privates."

"But, you will see!"

"Men like to see, miss. You wanted to know how to please the guvner. When he wants to see, you spread your legs and let him look. His prick will stiffen like a brick when you do."

"But it's so common and vulgar."

"Pull up your skirt, miss, and give me a look. You'll see. It will give you palpitations to know I'm looking."

Pamela slowly dragged her skirt up her thighs, exposing her drawers. She felt like a trollop giving herself over in a gentleman's carriage. When a rush of something she had never experienced before moved in her belly, she realised Jack spoke the truth. She wanted him to look at her. She wanted him to see her spread wide.

"That's real fine, Miss Pamela. Spread your legs and let me see."

Pamela opened her knees as wide as she could. Her drawers gaped open, exposing her feminine parts to Jack's lecherous gaze. With her titties hanging out of her dress and her cunt uncovered and open, she thought she would be consumed with the wanton fire burning inside her womb.

"Miss Pamela, your cunt is so wet and beautiful." Jack slipped his finger inside. "The guvner will pop you, I know he will. He likes cunt too much not to want this." He jabbed at Pamela's maidenhead and she moaned.

The next thing Pamela knew, Jack had his head between her legs, clutching her pelvis to his face. The sensation of his mouth sucking her clitoris made her swoon. When his tongue swept across the hood of her hardened nub, she pushed herself against his face. She had never known such feeling was possible. Her entire body melted like hot wax on a candle.

Without warning, her sense of identity disappeared, replaced by a scorching heat that started between her legs and enveloped her entire body. She shook and moaned, while Jack continued to lap at her like a cat drinking milk. Wave after wave of glorious feeling washed through her, until finally she dissolved into a limp puddle on the carriage seat.

When she opened her eyes, she saw Jack had opened his trousers and exposed his stiff prick. Still fearful he would penetrate her, she tried to cover herself. "Miss, please. I need to spend. Let me look at you whilst I do my business."

Opening her legs to give him a clear view, she watched,

fascinated, as he pulled at himself. He crept a bit closer and tugged harder, the tip of his cock pointed at her parted lips. Within minutes, he made the sound of a man dying from a dreadful wound and sprayed his cream onto her. Each spurt hit her already wet lips spot on. Never had she seen anything like a man spending by his own hand.

When Jack recovered, he took out his handkerchief. Before he tucked himself back into his trousers, he wiped Pamela clean and pulled down her skirt. She laced up her chemise and buttoned her dress.

While putting her bonnet on, Pamela looked out the window. The rain had lessened. "We should be getting on now, Jack, before anyone notices we are still here."

"Yes, miss, quite right." Before opening the door to go to the driver's seat, Jack reached out and pulled Pamela to him. He kissed her, deeply and passionately. "Miss Pamela, once the guvner opens you, if you ever have a mind to lay with me, I would be honoured."

Before Pamela could answer, he opened the door and jumped down to the street. The carriage jolted forward as Jack took them home.

Chapter Six

Pamela and Jack arrived home well before the hired wagon with the furniture. That gave Pamela time to wash and tend to her hair. Jack dismantled the old bed and readied the room for the new furnishings.

When the wagon arrived, it took some time to get everything inside and up the stairs. Fortunately, two men came with the wagon, which spared Jack most of the lifting. Once they had the bed assembled, Pamela decided to use the mattress from the dismantled bed, it being in better condition than the older one from storage. Lucy fetched the bedding from Pamela's newly vacated room.

By the time Jack had to leave to pick up Peter, the room looked like Pamela's room. She wanted to have new curtains made, with a matching canopy for the bed. And certainly, new wallpaper to replace the cheerless paper Peter had selected for the walls. She carefully placed the rosewood clock on her night table and set it to the correct time. Now, she had to think about getting dressed for dinner.

"Lucy, I don't have much time. Jack will be back with Peter in less than an hour. Does May have everything set for dinner?"

"Yes, miss. The table is set. While you were out, she sent me to the fishmonger to get some fresh cod." Lucy grinned.

"I got a fine one, I did. Master Rennard fancies the way May cooks up fish."

"I remember. He asked for it on Christmas Eve. I'm surprised he allowed the Christmas goose. I thought perhaps we would have the Christmas haddock instead."

"May says she thinks he should have been a fisherman, the way he fusses about fish. He sometimes goes to the fishmonger himself, to see what they have. He'll bring home too much and May has to dry it before it goes bad."

Pamela steadied herself against the bedpost as she said, "Lucy, I didn't know that about him."

"Miss Pamela, are you all right? You look a bit drawn."

"I'm fine, Lucy. Hearing about Peter's habits, the things about him I know nothing of, makes me sad. There is so much I don't know."

"But, miss, you're home now. You'll find out soon enough about his habits."

"I hope so, Lucy." Pamela shook off the feeling of melancholy. "Help me to dress. I want to look beautiful tonight."

Lucy laid out Pamela's clothes on the bed. From the petticoats Pamela had in the trunk, Lucy had selected the laciest one. Even the camisole and knickers had lace.

Picking up the frilly undergarments, Pamela had to ask, "Lucy, are these for me or for Master Rennard?"

"Why, for both of you, miss. You did say you hoped he would lift your skirt tonight."

"You are quite right, I did say that."

"Miss Pamela, don't be scared about it all. He'll do right by ya. The mister is an honourable man."

"Sometimes, too honourable, Lucy. That's why he won't touch me."

Lucy giggled. "Miss Pamela, in that dress, he'll be on you like flies on treacle."

"From your mouth to God's ears. He'll be home soon. Help me with all of this."

Pamela quickly removed her day dress. Lucy helped her lace up her chemise. "Miss, don't tie it too tight. You don't want the mister to have to fuss with it to undo it."

Pamela smiled at Lucy's lack of modesty. "How would you know about that, Lucy?"

"I just know, miss. Men don't like to fuss with strings."

After pulling the dress over her head and fastening it properly, Lucy worked on Pamela's hair. Lucy noticed her reflection in the looking glass. "If you don't mind my saying so, miss, you look pale."

"I am simply a bit peckish. I haven't eaten much today. I'll be fine once I have some dinner."

They heard the door across the hall open and then close. Pamela's skin went from pale to flushed. "Lucy, he's home. What time is it?"

"It's half past six, miss."

"Oh, my. We have to finish here. My jewelry, where did we put the necklace I want to wear?"

Pamela jumped up from the dressing table stool, nearly knocking the brush from Lucy's hand. She turned to apologise for her abrupt movement. She only said, "Lucy, I'm . . ." and her legs turned to jelly. The room spun for a moment and then, nothing.

As Peter unbuttoned the last button on his shirt, he thought he heard Lucy's voice across the hall shouting Pamela's name. He stopped for a moment and listened. He did hear Lucy shouting. Before he could reach his door, Lucy pounded on it.

"Master Rennard!"

When he opened the door, Lucy seemed frantic. "Miss Pamela!" She pointed to the open door across the hall. What he saw made his heart stop. Pamela lay sprawled on the floor.

"Lucy, what happened?" He ran into the room and knelt beside Pamela's motionless body.

"Sir, I don't know. I was fixin' her hair and she jumped up to find her necklace. Then she fell to the floor." Lucy almost sobbed.

"Lucy, go to the kitchen and fetch May. Tell her Miss Pamela fainted and to bring some brandy."

"Yes, sir, right away, sir." Lucy ran out of the room, yelling for May.

Peter took no notice of Lucy's hysterics, his only concern being Pamela. He scooped her up and carried her to the bed. After gingerly putting her down on the quilt, he sat down on the bed beside her. "Pamela, can you hear me? Pamela?" He shook her. She did not respond. Lightly slapping her face also brought no response.

He quickly went over to the washbasin and poured cold water over the face flannel in the bowl. Wringing it as he walked, he went back to the bed and wiped her face. Pamela softly moaned.

"Pamela, can you speak? This is Peter." She didn't answer him.

"Good Lord, what happened to her?" May came into the room with Lucy following.

"I think she fainted. Did you bring the brandy?"

May handed Peter a glass. "It's your cognac, good and strong, it is."

Peter put the glass under Pamela's nose. Pamela turned her head away. Peter followed her with the glass. "Breathe, Pamela." She raised her hand and tried to push the glass away. Peter dipped his finger in the cognac and put it in Pamela's mouth. She coughed.

Lucy whimpered in the background, stifling another sob. May said sternly, "Hush, child. She'll be all right. The foolish girl has hardly eaten anything since she's been home. A good meal will bring her around."

Peter again gave Pamela a taste of cognac on his finger. "What do you mean she hasn't eaten? Why hasn't she eaten?"

"She says she's excited about being home. At least that's what she says."

Peter turned and scolded May. "You are to see to her meals. Why haven't you?"

"Miss Pamela is a grown woman. I can't make her eat if she refuses food."

"Peter?" Pamela faintly spoke his name.

"Pamela, are you all right?"

"What happened?"

"You fainted, dear heart. Went down like a stone, from what I can tell."

"I did?"

"Yes, you did." Peter handed May the face flannel. "Could you wet this again?" May wet the cloth and handed it back to Peter. He folded it and put it across Pamela's forehead.

"Take a sip of this. It will help bring you around." Peter put his arm underneath her shoulders to support her. To balance herself, she reached out and put her hand on his bare chest.

He had forgotten about his open shirt. Her hand rested on his skin as he tipped the glass to her lips. She sipped the cognac and coughed again, pressing her hand against his chest. He thought surely she was branding his skin with her handprint, the heat of her palm searing his chest.

"Why haven't you eaten anything today?"

"I did eat. I had some biscuits."

"May says you haven't eaten a meal. She says you've been too excited."

"I am excited. I'm home."

Pamela didn't seem to realise she had her hand on his bare chest, but Peter certainly knew. He could feel himself stirring, at a completely inappropriate and undesirable time.

Even in a dead faint, her femininity took his breath. Now, seeing her in this exquisite dress, lying on the bed, with her hand on him, he again questioned his capacity to control himself with her.

"May, perhaps you should bring Pamela her dinner on a tray."

"No!" Pamela tried to sit up. "I want to take our meal together in the library."

May stepped in. "Master Rennard, I think if you help her down the stairs, she will do better to have dinner in the library. I have the table set and the fire is stoked."

Peter removed Pamela's hand from his chest and held it for a moment. "As you wish, Pamela. I must finish dressing. You are not to leave this room without having me at your side. Do you understand?"

"I will wait for you to come back. Could I have a glass of water?"

Lucy stood closest to the pitcher. She picked it up, but Peter came and took it from her. After pouring the water himself, he took it back to Pamela.

He set the glass on the night table and helped her to sit up. "Drink it slowly, dear heart."

His shirt remained open as he leaned over her. She reached up and lightly touched his chest, sliding her hand the full length to his stomach. Her eyes moved lower than her hand. He could not hide his reaction to her touch. She smiled and simply said, "I will, Peter. Thank you."

"You are welcome." He turned to go back to his room. "May, we will be ready for dinner in ten minutes. Lucy, stay with Pamela until I come back. I do believe she will want her hair fixed when she sees herself in the looking glass. It has come undone."

Peter went back to his room and closed the door. He had to decide how to handle this situation once and for all. Pamela could not help but see the stiff ridge in his trousers. Even with the vapors, she responded to him as a woman would. In that revealing dress, she obviously wanted him to know of her charms.

He took off his shirt and washed himself, and then dressed

for dinner. Seeing that Pamela had formally dressed for dinner, he did as well. He selected a white ruffled shirt with a black ribbon bow tie, a grey waistcoat and a black tailcoat. The narrow trousers hid nothing. Any reaction he might have would be clearly outlined.

Within ten minutes, he had readied himself for dinner, and he had made his decision. When he knocked on the door, Lucy opened it. Pamela sat at her dressing table about to fasten her necklace. Coming up behind her, he said, "Let me do that, my dear." He took the necklace. "How do you feel?"

He saw Pamela watching him in the looking glass. "Much better, thank you."

Lucy spoke up, "She still looks peaked to me, Master Rennard."

"I agree with you, Lucy." Peter carefully fastened the necklace. Resting his hand on her shoulder, he looked at her reflection. "Isn't this the necklace I gave you two years ago for Christmas?"

"Yes, I am quite fond of it. It is lovely."

"As are you this evening. Your dress is stunning. I've not seen it before."

"I only bought it a few months ago, for a party to celebrate our finishing University."

"Then we should go to dinner. It would be a shame for this lovely dress to be crumpled on the floor again, if you should once more succumb to your empty stomach."

"Thank you, Peter. Your concern for my dress is commendable."

Peter smiled, noting the typical cheekiness in Pamela's retort. She had always answered him with sass. As she matured, her tone with him became saucier, tinged with a familiarity no one else shared with him. "Come, let me help you down the stairs. I am quite sure May is waiting dinner."

Pamela stood. Peter noted a slight wobble as she took a step. "Slowly, dear. Lean on me." He put his arm around her waist and steadied her as they walked down the hall. When they reached the stairs, Pamela wrapped her arm around his waist. He cautioned her as they went down the stairs. "One step at a time, Pams."

"I'm not inclined to slide down the railing, Peter, which is what I did the last time you called me Pams."

"As I recall, you nearly knocked me onto the floor, sliding down that railing as if it were a greased pole. I believe your father scolded you for not conducting yourself as a lady and sent you to your room for that incident."

"I'm surprised you remember. Of course, you know I wanted to knock you down. At least I hope you learned never to stand with your back to the railing."

"I've learned much more than that from being with you."

They reached the bottom of the stairs. Peter turned her around to face him, still holding her around the waist. "Pamela, you must promise me you will not allow this to happen again. Such folly, not eating properly. Had you been on the stairs when you fainted, it could have been disastrous."

Pamela stepped closer to him and touched his face. "I am surprised, Peter. You have not shown concern for me to this degree in some time."

"Pamela, we have much to discuss about who we are to one another, but this is not the time. The first point of order is to feed you!" Peter stepped back and quite deliberately threaded Pamela's arm though his, as though making an entrance to a formal ball. "Shall we?"

When they entered the library, May stood waiting to serve. Peter led Pamela to her chair. "May, Lucy could do this."

"Poppycock! I am going to stand right here until I see her put some nourishment inside her belly!"

As Pamela sat down, Peter leaned in close to her ear. "I do believe she means it. I suggest you eat something before she takes that wooden spoon she's holding to your bottom."

"If anyone takes a wooden spoon to my bottom, I expect it would be you."

"As I have been sorely tempted at times!" Peter went around the table to his chair. Pamela's comment indicated she had taken to heart some of her newly discovered literature. However, he could not speak of that until they were alone.

May handed Pamela a freshly baked roll. "Now, missy, you start on this bread while I serve your meal. You need a cushion so this fish doesn't upset you more."

"May, for Lord's sake!"

"Don't you be taking that tone with me, young lady! You have Master Rennard cross with me because of your foolishness."

Peter folded his arms across his chest and enjoyed watching May take Pamela in hand. "May, Sir George certainly understood the need to send you along with Pamela. You are the only one who has ever been able to discipline her properly."

"Why, Master Rennard, I thought Sir George meant that to be your job, he did!"

"Perhaps so. I could always get the original will out of the safe and review who has proper authority to discipline her."

Pamela sat across the table, chewing a piece of bread. "In case the two of you have forgotten, I'm sitting here!"

Peter picked up his fork to sample his fish. "We haven't forgotten that, Pamela, have we, May?"

"No, sir, we haven't. You're well within your rights to take her over your knee and paddle her for puttin' us all through what she did."

"May!"

"Thank you for the suggestion, May. I'll consider the necessity for it later." Peter tasted the fish. "As always, it is perfection. If you would be so kind as to pour us some wine, I will supervise Miss Pamela's meal. I promise you, she will finish what is on her plate."

"Make sure that she does. I've had quite enough for one day." May poured the wine, leaving the bottle beside Peter.

"Ring for me if you be needing anything." As she left, she gave Pamela a pat on the back.

"May set a lovely table, didn't she?" Pamela poked at her fish with her fork.

"She always does. She also prepares fish better than the finest chefs in London. If you taste it, you would better appreciate what I'm saying."

"Peter, the smell, I don't know if I can."

"Of course you can. Lift your fork and put it in your mouth. It's really quite simple."

Pamela ate another bite of the bread, and then tried the fish. Peter watched her roll it around in her mouth before she swallowed. "What is that flavour?"

Peter tasted another bite and smiled. "This is my favourite. She marinates the fish in wine and spices, usually dill, coriander and a hint of anise. Then she puts the fish and marinade in an iron skillet and cooks it until the liquid is nearly gone. The remaining sauce coats the fish, as you see here. It is superb!"

Pamela appeared incredulous. "You know how May cooks fish?"

"Of course I do. Perhaps she should teach you. Then you could cook me a fish dinner."

"It seems you know the cooking method so completely, you should be cooking me dinner instead."

"Not very likely, dear heart. It is more likely May would throw us both out of her kitchen if we tried to pick up a frying pan."

"That's the God's honest truth. I remember she tossed Papa out when he tried to tell her how to season a pot of stew. She told him he could season his own plate at the table. When we sat down to dinner, she lined up every spice bottle in the kitchen on the table and told Papa to season it any way he liked. He never interfered again."

"Very wise man."

"He was, wasn't he? I wish I could know him, now that I am older. It is difficult to accept I never knew him as you did."

"Pamela, you never would have known him as I did. Sir George did not care to include women in his conversations."

"Do you?"

"It depends."

"Depends on what?"

"On the woman."

"And what women have you included?"

"Yourself. There are few others."

"Lately, you have distanced yourself from me. I don't think you could say I am included."

"Pamela, our situation is difficult. We must discuss subjects of some delicacy this evening. However, your plate must be cleaned before we begin."

"Bargaining with me, Peter?"

"It is how I spend my days, bargaining. It comes naturally to me."

"I will remember that when we have our discussion."

Peter ate his meal, quietly monitoring Pamela's progress. She ate slowly at first, taking a small bite and sipping her wine. As the colour returned to her cheeks, the food disappeared more quickly, until she had finished the plate which May had heaped full.

Peter lifted the lid on the serving platter. "There's more here, if you care to have a second serving."

Before Pamela could decline his offer, Lucy knocked on the door. "Master Rennard, I must see you for a moment."

Obviously irritated, Peter pushed back his chair. "Excuse me, Pamela, while I find out what is so important as to interrupt our meal."

Peter opened the library door. "Lucy, I left very clear instructions that we were not to be disturbed."

"I know, sir. I am sorry, sir. It is Miss Constance. She is here and refuses to leave until she speaks to you."

"Constance! What the bloody devil is she doing here?"

"I don't know, sir, but she threatened to have me dismissed if I didn't come fetch you."

"Lucy, no one can dismiss you but myself, and I certainly will not do that." Peter turned back to Pamela. "I apologise, Pamela. I have to see to this."

"Of course, Peter."

Peter followed Lucy to the foyer, where Constance sat rigidly in a chair. When she saw Peter, she stood. "Good evening, Constance. Might I ask why you have come unannounced? As you can plainly see, I am otherwise engaged."

"I understand Pamela has finished her schooling and is returning here to live with you. Is this true?"

"What concern is that of yours?"

"I thought we had an understanding."

"Constance, I have not spoken to you in well over three months! How in God's name could you assume there is any sort of understanding?"

"My father told me you spoke of me to him in chambers, that you had a fondness for me. My father took that to mean you have intentions toward me."

"Your father is a fool. I never said anything to him other than what would politely be said to a father regarding his daughter."

"Is she here now?"

"Constance, I must ask you to kindly leave. This conversation is over."

"It is a scandalous disgrace, your living here with an unmarried girl! Has she become your courtesan? Is that why you keep her?"

"Peter does not keep me, Constance. This is my home."

Peter turned to see Pamela standing behind him. "Pamela, this does not concern you."

"Oh, but Peter, I think it does." She handed Peter several unopened letters tied in a bundle. "May told me you had left these on your desk. I thought perhaps you might wish to return them."

"Those are my letters! How dare you!"

Pamela walked directly up to Constance, absolutely regal in her rose ball gown. "You will see, Constance, they are unopened. I have not read them. Nor has Peter. It seems unlikely there is any sort of intention if your many letters go unopened and unread."

"What sort of concubine have you become? Sir George would be ashamed of you in that dress!"

"I am no one's concubine. It might interest you to know that my father not only took great pride in me, he also left me his fortune. I am a very wealthy woman, Constance. I do not need any man to keep me. I could buy and sell most wealthy men three times over."

"Who do you think you are, speaking to me in this fashion?"

"I am Sir George Kingston's daughter. You have come into my home, debased my character, threatened my chambermaid and made slanderous accusations. My father certainly would not tolerate such an invasion into his home, and neither will I. Please leave now, before I am forced to have you bodily removed."

"Peter, are you going to stand there and allow this impudence?"

Peter handed Constance the bundle of letters. "Constance, you do not understand. I am the one Pamela would ask to have you removed, and I would honour her request. Good evening."

Peter calmly walked over and opened the door. Constance stuffed the letters into her bag and went back to her carriage waiting on the street.

Turning back to Pamela, Peter noticed her hands balled into fists at her sides. "My dear, it seems you have recovered from your fainting spell."

Pamela still had a head of steam up. "I told you six months ago I thought her a persnickety prig. How on earth could you bear to be with her? She is utterly infuriating!"

Peter came over and lifted Pamela's fist. Unfurling it, he kissed the back of her hand. "I couldn't, which is why I stopped seeing her."

"It is totally beyond me what could have attracted you in the first place! Her blonde hair and blue eyes do not change the fact she is hateful as a toad!"

"If you must know, her father is a member of my chambers. He asked me if I would escort her on a few occasions, and I did. The old man read too much into the situation. Wishful thinking, I suppose."

"You did not see her of your own volition?"

"No, only as a favour to her father. Once I saw her true colours, I severed the connection."

"I think she would have shattered like glass had you touched her!"

Peter laughed. "If you are implying her passions are not as fiery as yours, you are correct."

"What would you know of my passions?"

"Considerably more today than I did yesterday. That conversation is yet to be had. Let us sit by the fire and have some brandy." Peter escorted her back into the library.

The remains of their dinner still sat on the table. Peter rang for Lucy.

Lucy cautiously poked her head in the door. "Yes, sir?"

"Could you clear the table and tell May we are finished with dinner?"

"Yes, sir. She said to tell you she made Miss Pamela's favorite honey almond cake, if you care to have some."

Pamela clapped her hands together. "Oh, how delightful! That is the cake she would make for me on special occasions. She would let me lick the bowl and I would wipe it clean."

"Yes, miss. She made it yesterday, to welcome you home."

"Oh, Peter, we must have some. It is wonderful!"

Pamela's enthusiasm for the cake diffused the tension created by Constance. "Lucy, tell May we will have some cake and brandy in here, by the fire."

"Yes, sir." Lucy quickly cleared the table and took the tray to the kitchen.

After stirring the embers a bit, Peter tossed another log into the fireplace. He then took Pamela's hand and led her to the sofa beside the fire.

"Peter, will the situation this evening with Constance compromise your position in chambers?"

"Hardly. Others have come forward and warned me of Constance and her incessant hysterics. I am not the first, and most probably, will not be the last to have discovered she is not what she seems."

"Does she sustain social connections?"

"You are concerned she will speak of us together?"

"Actually, I am hoping she will."

"Pamela, you are an enigma. You always have been to me. Why would you hope that she does?"

"Because if she does, and others accept that there is something between us, then perhaps you will come to accept it as well."

"You present me with a serious dilemma, Pamela, both moral and emotional."

"Peter, if you could try for only a moment to see me as someone other than Sir George's daughter, would there still be a dilemma?"

"Perhaps not as severe, but yes, there would still be the difficulty of age."

"There are those who find a way to bridge a larger gap than ours."

"Perhaps so. But that does not negate the fact that I am your designated guardian. Your well-being was entrusted to me by your father."

"Peter, I am of age. Your guardianship now is only of my

estate, not of me. What will it take to have you see me as a woman and not that girl sliding down the banister so many years ago?"

"My dear Pamela, you have no idea."

Lucy knocked on the door. "Master Rennard, I have your pudding here."

"Indeed." He got up to open the door. Lucy brought in a tray with the cake, a decanter of brandy and two snifters. A pot of tea and two cups also graced the pudding.

"Thank you, Lucy. That will be all for tonight. The cleanup can be done in the morning."

"Yes, sir. Good night."

Peter poured them each some brandy and served the cake. "It is good to see the colour back in your cheeks."

"Thank you. I am feeling quite fine now." Pamela took a substantial mouthful of cake, and then another. She cleaned her plate in a few minutes.

"It is also good to see your appetite has returned." Pamela nodded, unable to speak as she savoured the sweetness in her mouth.

"Shall we now talk about *The Pearl*?"

Chapter Seven

Pamela swallowed her remaining cake and sipped her brandy before she answered. "All right, if you care to, we can talk about *The Pearl*."

"I read the entire journal last evening. It is coarse and vulgar, certainly not something you should have. Where did you get it?"

"From a classmate."

"Do you have more of them?"

"Why are you asking me that? Lucy told you I do."

"All right then. Have you read them all?"

"Yes. And if I have the opportunity, I will continue to read them."

"Why?"

"Because I enjoy them, because they make me burn inside, because they talk of things I want to learn."

"Haven't you learned enough?"

"No, certainly not! One does not learn about such things by reading. Experience is the true teacher."

Peter turned and stared into the fire. "Is that what you want from me, experience?"

"I can gain experience from anyone. What I want is you."

Peter turned to face her. "Earlier you asked what it would take to have me see you as a woman. That has never been my problem."

"I don't understand."

"My problem has been not seeing you as a woman. Even while Sir George still lived, I enjoyed your company more than any of those who sought my attention."

"Peter—"

"Pamela, let me finish. I sent you away because I did not trust myself with you in the same house. To protect you, and to honour the trust that Sir George placed in me, I enrolled you in the finest school I could find." Peter paced in front of the fire and sipped his brandy. "I thought you would meet someone and marry, that I would never have to face the moment of your sharing this house with me. But here we are. It is now your home."

"Peter, why is that so horrible? Why do you still push me away?"

"I promised your father, Pamela. I promised him I would care for you and see to your marriage. To do otherwise is to betray an oath I swore to him on his deathbed."

"Papa lives with the angels now, he is with my mum. He cannot judge you."

"Yes, but I can judge myself."

"And what about us, Peter? What about what I want and what you want?"

"What do you want, Pamela?"

"I want you, any way I can have you."

Peter set his glass on the table. He sat down beside Pamela and pulled her close to him. He whispered, "Lord Christ in heaven, forgive me for what I am about to do."

Pamela brushed his cheek with her lips. "Darling Peter, there is nothing to forgive."

Then Peter kissed her, giving the searing heat so long inside of him a voice. To his astonishment, she ardently returned his kiss. With mouths open, they tasted the sweetness of the other's tongue, the flavours of cake and brandy mingling in an ambrosial nectar.

The kiss opened Pandora's box. Peter wanted to overpower her, to consume her, to ravage her. He forced himself to pull back. But he had to know. "Have you ever been with a man, Pamela?"

She put her hand on his chest and leaned in close to his ear. "No. I have waited for it to be you."

Peter kissed her hair and held her tightly. "Pamela, for that, we will wait. I want you to be sure. If it is to be so, then it should not be done here, in a library."

"I am sure, Peter. I have wanted it to be you for many years."

"We will explore other things for a time, until you have a chance to consider the full import of giving yourself over to me. Once done, it can never be undone." Peter brushed her lip with his fingertip. "Pams, tell me what you want to do with me now. I will do nothing more than you ask."

Pamela touches Peter, continue reading
Pamela does as Peter asks, turn to page 102

"I want to touch you again, like yesterday in the carriage."

Pamela slid her hand up Peter's leg, stopping just short of his thickening bulge. "Peter, let me touch you again, except this time, I want to see you."

"You are a wonderment! You speak of such personal matters with the same enthusiastic delight which greeted May's cake."

"And why shouldn't I, Peter Rennard? Isn't it just as delicious, in its own way?"

"All right, my dear. It would be equally delightful for me to touch your bosom for the first time."

"Shall I open my dress?"

"Pamela!"

"Oh, Peter, stop being such a Mrs. Grundy. You said we can explore other things. I have read of all sorts of things I want to explore."

"Have you read of these adventurous things in *The Pearl*?"

Pamela playfully reached up and undid his ribbon bow tie. "Mostly. Some of the things I've read were borrowed and had to be returned."

"Such as?"

"There is a book, *Fanny Hill*. Do you know it?"

"John Cleland, 1749. Yes, of course I know it." Peter reached out and caressed her breast with the back of his hand. "The fact that you know it intrigues me."

"Why is that?"

"It tells me more of your curiosities, and perhaps your cravings."

"Does that please you?"

"I would say so, yes." He slid his hand under her breast and allowed the weight of it to fall in his palm. "Your bosom is lovely, Pams. If you care to show me, I would like to see."

"First you have to show me." Pamela slid to the edge of the sofa and stared directly at his bulging prick.

"Dear heart, I must adjust to your lack of modesty about such things."

"Oh, Peter, I've waited so long for this. Don't make me wait any longer."

Feeling rather like a fly being lured into a spider web from which he could not escape, Peter opened his trousers. It brought him some relief when he freed his stiff prick from the constricting cloth. Pamela reached to touch him.

"Oh, no, my dear. Now, it's your turn. Undo the bodice of your dress and show me your lovely mounds."

Staring wide-eyed at Peter's thick cock, Pamela slowly unbuttoned her dress. Peter wanted to touch himself while he watched, but remembered the pleasure/pain at Nellie's when he held back from touching.

Pamela undid her dress to the waist and slipped her arms out of the sleeves. Now, only her camisole covered her. Peter's eyes burned a hole in the cloth as she slowly exposed the flesh underneath. When finally her breasts tumbled free, she closed her eyes and whispered, "Yesterday you said I did not know the ache and the throbbing need." She opened her eyes and looked into his. "You were wrong."

Peter took off his tailcoat and vest. "Come, sit on my knee and we will help one another manage it all."

Without hesitation, Pamela wedged herself between Peter's legs and sat on his knee. Now that she could see it, she realised Peter's endowment exceeded Jack's both in length and thickness. She squirmed on Peter's knee thinking of how it would feel inside of her.

Peter shifted and pulled her in closer to his chest. "Are you comfortable, Pams?"

"Sitting on your knee is quite fine, but I am certainly not comfortable."

Peter lightly caressed her breast, with a veneration that caused a tremor in his hand. "And what would it take to make you comfortable?"

For the first time that evening, Pamela hesitated. Her cheeks blushed fiercely as she dried her palms on her skirt. Without saying a word, she clutched the rose material of her skirt in her fists and pulled. The skirt lifted a few centimeters from the floor.

In utter disbelief, Peter watched as she repeated the motion several more times, until the full skirt lay rumpled on her lap. Still holding her breast in one hand, Peter rested his other hand on her bare thigh. "Pams, are you sure?"

"If you don't, I will have to touch myself. I am on fire!"

Peter needed no other encouragement. Sliding his hand further up, he felt the lace of her knickers. "Are they open, dear heart?"

Pamela nodded and opened her knees further, causing the opening to gap. Peter could never have imagined the sensation of touching her for the first time. The wet curls covering her privates moistened his fingertips like dew on grass. He brushed them, marveling at the lush softness of the hair.

Pamela moaned and put her head on his shoulder. Reaching up to the buttons on his shirt, she opened them, scraping her fingernails down his chest as she moved toward his groin. Peter continued brushing her curls, not knowing if he should do more.

Then, she touched him. Without any warning or modesty, she gripped him in her warm hand. As she did, her pelvis slid forward on his knee and his fingers slipped inside her velvet lips. Her slippery juice coated his fingers as he traced the inner edges of her crevice. As she had yesterday, she rubbed his prick in the curve of her hand.

Peter nuzzled her hair, whispering, "Tilt your head back so I can kiss you again." As her lips parted to receive his tongue, his fingertips found her clitoris. She moaned into his mouth as he massaged her nub, her hips undulating on his lap. All the while, her hand never stopped moving on his cock.

He kissed her roughly, passionately, thrusting his tongue into her mouth the way he wanted to put his prick into her cunt. Firm in his resolve to not take her this evening, he frigged her mouth and diddled her clit. The heat rising from her exceeded anything he could have imagined.

Pamela broke the suction of their mouths, practically panting. "Sweet mercy, Peter, I cannot stand it."

Peter did not heed her call for mercy. "You will endure the exquisite suffering, Pamela, just as I am." He continued rubbing her clit with his thumb as he slipped his middle finger inside of her, hitting her barrier. "It is true, then, you have waited."

"I would not lie to you." She squeezed his prick tightly. "You will break me with this. It is what I want."

The movement of Pamela's bum on his lap and the pressure of her hand on his cock brought Peter to the edge. "I am going to spend, Pamela. I cannot stop it."

Pamela threw the hem of her petticoat over him and rubbed him vigorously through the cloth. Peter grunted loudly and thrust himself into the lacy folds. A dark stain formed as he spilled into the fabric. Even through her petticoat, she could feel the ropey veins pulsing as his organ emptied itself into her hand.

She held him until he began to soften. Taking a dry piece of her hem, she wiped him clean. She thought he would immediately cover himself. He did not. "Lie back, Pamela, and let me help you be more comfortable, too."

Peter gently cradled her in his arms, helping her lie back. Kneeling on the floor beside her, he lifted her skirt and pulled her knickers down. She closed her eyes and gasped when his hand connected with her flesh.

"Have you ever spent, dear heart?" He pinched her nipple between his thumb and forefinger and squeezed while massaging her clit.

Clutching a pillow, she answered in a throaty whisper, "Yes."

"By your own hand or another's?"

"Both."

"Will you tell me who?"

She opened her eyes. Even in this compromising position, she challenged him. "Only if you tell me whose hands have been on you!"

Without a doubt, the beautiful woman lying here, exposed and heated, could only be his Pamela. No one else would dare be this cheeky with him. "One of these days, my dear Pamela, your sass will get your bottom paddled. But as with the other things we will explore together, that will wait."

Peter leaned over and captured a nipple in his mouth and suckled her. Pressing harder on her clitoris, he felt the hard core, that point of contact he knew to be as sensitive as his own prick. He focused on that secret button, circling and pinching.

Muttering incoherently about how she would soon die of

need, Pamela lifted her hips from the sofa and rubbed against his hand. He watched with absolute fascination her abandonment to pleasure. She kicked off her knickers and spread her legs wide, arching her back to press into his hand. He saw the signs of spending closing in, and allowed her to rub as she needed. Within seconds, she grabbed his shoulders and lifted herself up against his chest, her bare breasts pressing into his skin.

"Sweet Jesus, Peter!" She dug her fingernails into his skin, piercing the flesh and surely drawing blood. He did not break contact with her clitoral nub, rapidly stroking it. She clung to him and spasmed, her chest flushed as deeply as the rose gown crumpled at her waist. Gasping, she fell back on the sofa cushion.

Peter waited until her breath came normally. Only then did he say what he felt in his heart. "Pamela, never in all my days of witnessing women in the throes have I ever seen such rapturous passion." He leaned over and kissed her breast. With a trail of small kisses, he traced a path to her ear. There, he whispered to her, "If, after considering the implications, you decide it is what you want, I will be your first."

Damn the morality, damn the promise to Sir George, damn his very soul. Peter wanted her in his bed.

Go to page 107

"Peter, I want to do things with you and explore with you."

"Do you want to explore the things you read in *The Pearl*?"

"Yes, and things I've read in a book called *Fanny Hill*. Do you know it?"

"John Cleland, 1749. Yes, I know it. The fact that you know it intrigues me."

"Why?"

"Because it tells me your curiosities have matured, and so have your cravings."

"Peter, tell me what you like to do. I want to please you."

Far beyond caring about propriety or morality, Peter wanted more from her. "Pamela, how much do you want to please me?"

"More than anything, Peter. I swear to you, that is the truth."

"I very much like watching beautiful women disrobe. Will you let me watch you disrobe, everything except your petticoat?"

"Even my drawers?"

"Even those."

"Will you take me tonight?"

"No. As I told you, that will not be in a library. But we can explore, as you have asked."

"Will you let me see you, too?"

"What would you like to see, dear heart? Tell me outright. You've certainly read enough to know the words."

Pamela closed her eyes and took a deep breath. When she opened them, she looked directly at the bulge in his trousers. "I want to see your prick. I felt it yesterday, but I want to see it."

Peter found her willingness to be both intoxicating and irresistible. "I am certainly willing to show you what you wish to see, on one condition."

"What is that?"

"That you not take your eyes off of it while you disrobe, so you can see the effect you have on me." Peter opened his trousers and for the first time, exposed himself to Pamela. His prick throbbed in his hand as he stretched it the full length for her to see.

Pamela reached out to touch his organ. He grabbed her hand and kissed her palm. "No, Pamela. No touching. Until I say so, you can only watch."

Peter scrutinised her carefully, to see if she showed any signs of timidity. In answer to his unspoken question, she stood and began undoing the buttons of her dress.

"Are you going to open your shirt, so I can see your chest?" Pamela had always been a straight arrow, speaking her mind in any situation. He had never considered she would also be this way about matters of the flesh.

"If you wish." As Pamela opened her dress, he took off his tailcoat and vest. "Do you want it open or completely off?"

"Open. It is what I saw when I woke from my faint. I thought I might have dreamed it."

"You did not dream it, dear Pamela, just as I did not dream your hand touching me when you woke."

"Will you let me touch your prick again, like I did yesterday?"

"Perhaps." He stroked himself as he adjusted his organ on his belly. "Or perhaps I will have you watch me stroke myself."

Pamela stepped out of her dress, leaving her in her camisole and petticoat. "Do you want me to continue?" Her eyes never left his prick, which had thickened even more while watching her.

"Your bosom is lovely, Pamela. I have always wanted to see it bare. Please show me."

She took hold of the camisole and pulled it over her head. Her breasts tumbled free. Peter's cock twitched as he drank in the beauty of her plump bosom. She surprised him when she asked, "Do you like them, Peter? Do my titties please you?"

"Yes, Pamela, your titties please me very much. But what sort of common language have you grown accustomed to using?"

She stood there proudly, defiantly, with no sign of modesty or embarrassment. "It is language appropriate for your sitting there touching up while staring at me!"

Peter felt the laughter in his belly before it came out of his mouth. It took a moment to compose himself. She remained standing in front of him, a perfect marble statue of beauty and grace. "My dear Pamela, not only are you a beautiful woman, you are an absolute delight. You are quite right. It is language appropriate to the situation."

"Then I shall use whatever language I deem appropriate to what we are doing."

"What language will you use when you take off your knickers for me?"

"Whatever comes to me."

Pamela lifted her petticoat from the back, obscuring Peter's view. She undid the string holding up her knickers and they fell to the floor. After stepping out of them, she kicked them aside. "Do you want to see my privy parts?"

"Not just yet. We must prolong the ache. Then the release is much sweeter." Peter picked up her knickers from the floor and caressed his organ with the damp material. "These are lovely, as is your petticoat. Either is enough to turn any cock to stone."

"Is your cock stone?"

"Come here. You can see for yourself."

Pamela came over to Peter. Bending over to examine his cock, her breasts fell forward. Peter caught them in his hands and squeezed them together. "You have glorious titties, Pams." He took hold of her hands. "If you hold them together, you can feel my cock between them."

"Show me how."

Peter slid to the edge of the cushion. "Kneel in front of me and lean over." He positioned his cock between her breasts. "Now, use your hands to squeeze them together and hold my cock between them."

Pamela's face rested against his belly as he frigged her cleavage. As he thrust into the soft flesh, she kissed his belly. He thought he would go mad with desire, the feel of her so close to him nearly making him lose control. He pushed her away.

"Peter, have I done something wrong?"

His breath coming in short gasps, he steadied himself. "No, my sweet lady, you have done nothing wrong."

"Then what is it?"

"Pamela, I am feeling such an intense longing for you. I will not take your chastity in a fit of lust."

"What can I do, Peter? Please let me do something."

"There is something, if you are willing."

"Tell me. I am willing."

"Have you ever spent?"

"Yes."

"By your own hand?"

"Sometimes, before I sleep."

"Lift your petticoat and touch yourself now until you spend, while I do the same."

"But you will see."

"As will you." Peter saw her indecision. "Pamela, listen to me. If I touch you, I may lose control and do more than either of us wants to do tonight. If we spend by our own hands, we have intimacy while protecting your chastity until the time is right."

Pamela nodded and stood in front of him. Slowly, she lifted her petticoat. Peter followed the hem of her petticoat up her thighs, until finally, he saw the first wisps of curly chestnut hair. Pamela stared at him, watching him watching her.

His arousal grew more apparent as his breathing changed. In a hoarse whisper, he asked for more. "Tuck your petticoat into the waistband, show me everything, Pamela. I want to see."

With a stance worthy of a seasoned streetwalker, Pamela tucked the garment up high, revealing all of her privates to Peter's hungry eyes. His hand pumped his organ with increasing speed. He watched her fingers graze the hair between her legs, and then disappear into her secret place. She rubbed delicately at first, but as her own fire grew, the speed of her hand soon matched his.

"Peter, I am so close." In complete abandon, she squeezed her own breast and pinched her nipple, harder than he ever would have. The other hand worked furiously between her legs, which she had spread wide apart.

"Let it happen, Pamela, let yourself find release."

"Oh, sweet God in heaven!" She clutched the chestnut triangle between her legs full in her hand and thrust her pelvis forward. Her fingers closed so tightly around her breast, they were sure to leave bruises. No less than three times did she thrust herself forward, each time moaning in lustful delirium.

Peter grabbed her knickers and covered his prick just as his cream sprayed out of the tip. The hunger for his Pamela had finally found release.

Pamela sat down on the sofa beside him. Peter waited until her breath came normally. Only then, did he say what he felt in his heart. "Pamela, never in all my days of witnessing women in the throes have I ever seen such rapturous passion." He leaned over and kissed her breast. With a trail of small kisses, he traced a path to her ear. There, he whispered to her, "If, after considering the implications, you decide it is what you want, I will be your first."

Damn the morality, damn the promise to Sir George, damn his very soul. Peter wanted her in his bed.

Chapter Eight

Pamela rolled over in her bed and looked at the clock on her night table. When she saw the time, she bolted out of bed. Running to the window, she saw the carriage disappearing down the street, with Peter inside.

She couldn't believe she had overslept, and that no one had awakened her. What if, with the new day, Peter pushed her away? She wanted to see him, to reassure herself that the door they had opened the night before had not slammed shut again. Of course, he had to leave at his scheduled time. He had an appearance in court that morning. But why hadn't he sent Lucy to wake her?

Last night, they made an ineffective attempt to put themselves in order before leaving the library. Peter suggested, with utter devilment, that since the help had settled in for the night, they might dash up the stairs as they were. He bundled her dress and drawers with his tailcoat and vest. In only her camisole and petticoat, she ran for the stairs. Peter followed in his open shirt, their clothing tucked under his arm.

He handed her the dress. Then he kissed her good night in a way he never had before, revealing his passion once again. The lacy petticoat provided the thinnest of barriers between her and the hard ridge that grew in his trousers. He declined the invitation to come into her room, bidding her a good night and sweet dreams at the door. Only after she had hung up the dress did she realise he had not returned her knickers. She giggled, wondering if he had intentionally kept them.

Since Peter had already left, she took her time dressing. It being Friday, she knew Peter would have more time tomorrow to spend with her. She couldn't help wondering what that might mean.

When she opened the cupboard to select a dress, she saw Lucy had done a fine job of organizing her clothing. After some thought, she picked a blue day dress, with a ruffled bodice. The rest of her clothing should be arriving today, with the other things she had shipped. It would be good to settle in and truly establish something of a daily routine.

Lucy knocked softly on her door. "Miss Pamela, are you awake?"

"Yes, Lucy. You may come in."

"Miss, May sent me to fetch you. She wants to make sure you eat something this morning. If I might say so, she still seems a bit cross with you. She says Master Rennard told her this morning that she has to watch you put the food in your mouth and swallow it, he did!"

Pamela smiled. "Did he say anything else?"

"Yes, miss. I thought to wake you and he told me not to disturb you. He wanted you to rest after not feeling well yesterday." Lucy reached in her pocket and took out a small envelope. "He also said to give you this after you got around."

Pamela took the envelope and opened it. What she read made her heart leap.

Dearest Pamela:

I am pleased you are able to rest so well after our evening together. I, too, slept most comfortably.

It seems as though we have rounded a corner with one another. Perhaps over dinner this evening, we might further discuss this unexpected turn of events and what it means for both of us. I would also suggest that per-

*haps tomorrow, we do a bit of shopping. Would a new
dress or other finery please you? Perhaps some lingerie
would make you smile.*

I will be home by mid-afternoon.

Until then,
Peter

Folding the note and putting it back in the envelope,
Pamela turned to see Lucy watching her. "Miss, is everything
all right? You have a queer look, you do."

"Oh, yes, Lucy, everything is quite fine, quite fine indeed!"
Lucy smiled. "Very good, miss. You might fancy knowing
Master Rennard whistled this morning."

"He whistled? I don't understand."

"A merry tune, miss, as he sat for his morning meal. In all
my days in his employ, I have never once heard him whistle."

"I didn't even know he could whistle!"

"Nor I, miss. He seemed mighty cheerful, he did."

"Thank you for telling me, Lucy." As Lucy picked up her
petticoat and camisole from the floor, Pamela blushed. "Those
will need to be laundered, Lucy. I should have put them in
the basket when I dressed for bed."

"Yes, miss." Lucy shook the petticoat. "Your drawers,
miss, should they be laundered? They're not here." Pamela's
face went from warm to hot. "Oh, miss!" Lucy turned away,
to hide the giggle that she forced herself to swallow.

Pamela considered how much she should share with her
chambermaid. "Lucy, do you gather Master Rennard's clothing to be laundered?"

"Yes, miss."

"My drawers may be with his."

Lucy's eyes met Pamela's for only a moment, but in that
moment they exchanged an awareness of the other. "Yes,
miss. I understand."

Pamela picked up a copy of *The Pearl* from the stack sitting on top of her books. "When you go to Master Rennard's

room to gather his clothes, could you please leave this on his pillow? He will know it is from me."

"Of course, miss. Oh, and miss, I found something last night you might want to have." Lucy went to the cupboard. "I cleaned the cupboard while you had dinner. There's a bundle of letters in a tiny drawer at the bottom."

Lucy went to the cupboard. She put her hand underneath the bottom and sure enough, a narrow drawer pulled out, running the full width of the cupboard.

"Well, isn't that odd. This cupboard belonged to my father. I thought everything had been removed when he died."

"The handle is broken, Miss Pamela. It's hard to see that it's a drawer unless you scrubbed it like I did."

"Thank you for telling me about this." Pamela scooped out the letters. "I'll take a look at them while I have some food."

"Miss, if you don't mind my saying, May will box my ears if I don't fetch you to the table soon."

"Of course, Lucy."

Pamela left Lucy at the door to Peter's room. "Miss, do you want to leave this journal on his pillow yourself?"

"I certainly want to, Lucy. But I will not enter Master Rennard's room without an invitation."

Lucy smiled. "Miss, I think you would be getting that soon enough!"

Remembering Lucy with Jack the day before, Pamela couldn't help being envious. Without thinking, Pamela took Lucy's hand. "Lucy, there is so much I don't know. Peter has years of experience that I do not have. Oh, my, I am so afraid he will think me young and foolish compared to the other women he has known."

"Miss Pamela, it all comes natural, it does."

"Lucy, how did you learn?"

"I didn't so much learn it, miss, as felt it. The feelings are what taught me. You just have to listen to the feelings and you know what to do."

"You're right. Last night, I didn't think about it, I simply felt it."

Lucy's face turned a bit pink. "Miss, the guvner will show you what he wants. All men do. They have a real strong drive in them to do what they want."

"And what about what we want, Lucy? Do we tell them what we want, too?"

"Miss, Jack likes it when I tell him what I want. I can't speak for the guvner, but I don't think he'd mind one little bit if you spoke up and told him you want something special."

"You really don't think so?"

"Miss, I don't want to speak out of turn, but you know now as well as I do that the guvner has a taste for it. If there's something that takes your fancy, tell him! I'm thinkin' it might be gettin' you that invitation to his room a bit sooner than you think."

Both Lucy and Pamela started when they heard May shout from the other end of the hall, "Missy, you get your fine arse down to the table right this minute. I have to get some food in your belly or the guvner will have my head when he comes home tonight!"

Pamela squeezed Lucy's hand and pointed to Peter's door. "Leave the journal on the pillow for me. We'll talk more about this later." With that, she ran down the stairs to the dining room.

The tray May set in front of her had enough food for a starving man. Pamela looked at the bowl of porridge, alongside the bacon and eggs interspersed with mounds of bubble and squeak, wondering how on earth she could manage it all.

May stood there, with a stern expression Pamela remembered from her younger days. May had once caught her sampling the Christmas pudding, even before dinner had been served. Had it not been Christmas Day, May would have taken a wooden spoon to her bottom. Pamela wondered if the same fate might befall her today if she did not clean her plate. Not wanting to take the risk, she ate.

The letters lay beside her on the table. She didn't want to read them with May standing over her, so she waited, and ate her food. Only after Pamela had finished most of the food on the tray, did May finally say to her, "The mister told me to watch you eat. Now I have. You best be minding yourself, missy, or the mister will be having me watch you every meal." With that, she went back to the kitchen.

Pamela poured herself another cup of tea from the pot and unbundled the letters. The stylised handwriting on the envelopes had the look of calligraphy, with her father's name written in loops and swirls. They had no return name, but had certainly all been written by the same hand. On the back of each envelope, she found a date, in penmanship she recognised to be her father's. He bundled the letters oldest to newest, with the oldest dated ten years prior.

Pamela opened and read the first one, the oldest.

26 April 1870

Mon cher *George,*

I trust you are well. It has been a bit of time now since we have seen one another. That being so, I have asked the charming young man Peter Rennard to deliver this letter to you. He tells me he sees you often. I am envious.

It has been some ten years now since we first met, and nearly five years since you brought Monsieur Rennard to me for his initiation. You are both honest men, and knowledgeable about matters of the law.

One of my profession has to consider what will happen with the passing years. For some time, I have been tucking away earnings for the days when men no longer come to me. There is a chance now to acquire a tavern on Upper Thames Street, between Blackfriars Bridge and Southwark Bridge. Since I know nothing of legal matters, I am at a loss to understand what I must do. I do not

*know how to put forth a purchase offer, or even if my
meager savings would allow me the opportunity to
make the attempt.*

*I would ask out of the kindness of your heart, and in
deference to what we have been to one another over
these many years, that you would assist me in this matter. To be the proprietress of a tavern would secure a future for me that could not be had otherwise.*

Avec toute mon affection,
Nellie Flambeau

Pamela read the signature three times, before laying the let-
ter on the table. Jack said Peter had gone to Nellie's on Thames
Street before meeting her at the train. Her father had known
Nellie and had introduced Peter to her? How could this be?

As Pamela worked her way through the letters, the fact
that Nellie and her father sustained a relationship over many
years became increasingly apparent. Within two years, Nellie
owned the tavern, with both the legal and financial help of
her father.

21 October 1872

Mon cher gentilhomme,

*It is with great joy I tell you that your gift has been
received. The sign you had made now hangs over the
door. The tavern on Thames is now* Nellie's.

*Without your help, I could not have managed. I truly
thought all had been lost when the owner's asking price
far exceeded what I could manage. Your willingness to
supplement my savings to meet the cost came on the
wings of a prayer.*

I assure you, mon cher, *your generosity will be remembered to my last breath.*

Affectueusement,
Nellie Flambeau

Throughout the letters, Nellie made reference to Peter. Not only did he deliver the letters to her father, he assisted Nellie by acting as an ombudsman with her solicitor. More than once, Nellie told her father that Peter had spoken on her behalf to negotiate a fair purchase price.

The last letter brought Pamela to tears. Written during the final weeks of her father's life, Nellie's words spoke of a love that could never be realised.

10 January 1874

Bien-aimé *George,*

> *Peter brings me such very sad news. He tells me you are soon to leave this world and move on to a better one, better than we will ever know here. My heart breaks knowing you will leave, but my soul sings with gratitude that I have known you as I have.*
>
> *You have been to me what no one else ever has, you have been my love. I say this to you knowing that you shared with me what you could, and have cared for me as no other man ever has.*
>
> *Mon cher, carry my love with you as you prepare for the final crossing. May God receive you with grace.*

Adieu, mon amour,
Nellie

Pamela sat for many minutes, holding the letters as tears slid down her face. These letters spoke of a man she never knew. Her father had deep feelings for Nellie, as Nellie had for him. Peter had seen her only two days before, continuing a relationship that had started with her father twenty years ago.

Carefully stacking the letters in the proper order, Pamela bundled them once again. She rang for Lucy.

"Yes, miss?"

"Has Jack returned?"

"Yes. He is tending to the carriage. Is everything all right, miss?"

"I have to call on an old friend of my father's today. I will need Jack to take me. Could you please tell him to ready the carriage?"

"Yes, miss." Pamela took the letters and went to her room to prepare herself for the trip.

Pamela stood waiting at the gate when Jack brought the carriage round. He jumped down from the driver's seat to open the door.

"Is everything all right, Miss Pamela? Lucy said you seemed upset."

"Jack, take me to Nellie's."

Jack looked at her as though she had lost her mind. "Miss Pamela, I can't do that! Master Rennard would serve me my head before he tossed me out on the street!"

"Jack, either you will take me or I go onto Piccadilly and hail myself a hansom cab to do it. I am going to Nellie's."

"Miss Pamela, why in God's name do you want to do that? Is it because of what I told you yesterday?"

"No, Jack. This has nothing whatsoever to do with what you told me. This is about my father."

"Miss, you ain't making sense. Nellie's is no place where you should be going! She don't even open till noontime."

"Jack, I'm not going to stand here and argue." Pamela started walking down Piccadilly, looking for a cab. Jack ran after her.

"All right, you got your mind made up. But I'm telling you, Master Rennard will go right through the roof, he will. This could cost me my employ."

"Jack, I will not allow Peter to hold you responsible. He will no doubt thank you for accompanying me, when he realises I would have gone there myself." Pamela took the bundle of letters from her bag and held them up for Jack to see. "This is why I am going. Not you, not Peter, not the Archbishop of Canterbury nor anyone else will stop me from meeting Nellie Flambeau."

"Yes, miss." With his jaw set in resignation, Jack helped her into the carriage. Pamela settled in for the ride to Thames Street.

When they arrived at Nellie's, Pamela opened the door to get out of the carriage before Jack had fully stopped it. "Miss Pamela," Jack yelled at her as he jumped down. "Breaking your bleeding neck isn't going to get you in the door any faster!"

Pamela ignored his chastisement as he took her hand and helped her step down to the street. Stepping over the grime in the gutter, she marched right up to the door of the tavern. She tried the door and found it locked, so she knocked. When no one came, she knocked again and shouted, "Hello, is anyone there?"

"Miss, Pamela, hush!" Jack came up beside her. "You'll draw attention to your being here. You don't want that, I'm sure of it."

"Jack, I'm not leaving until I meet her, if I have to sit on the steps until she opens!"

Jack threw his hands up in the air. "Miss Pamela, if the guvner were here, he'd carry you back to the carriage and give you a good wallopin', he would!"

"Well, Peter isn't here, and I'm telling you right now, if you value your bollocks, you won't try carrying me back to the carriage!"

"Miss, making a fuss in the street is not seemly for a lady." He took off his hat and ran his fingers through his hair. "Miss Nellie has a side door the guvner sometimes uses. Let me see if anyone answers there. You wait right here and mind yourself!"

Jack slapped his hat back on his head and rounded the corner into an alley alongside the tavern. Pamela stood and stared at the sign she now knew her father had given to Nellie. Her eyes welled. The grief she felt at never having known this part of the man she loved so dearly choked her. She struggled to compose herself.

A few minutes later, Jack returned. "Henry is coming round to open the door."

"Who's Henry?"

"The barkeep, miss. A good gent, he is."

Henry opened the door. "May I help you with something, miss?"

"I'm here to see Nellie Flambeau."

"May I tell her who is calling, miss?" Henry seemed a bit bewildered by this early morning intrusion.

"Tell her Pamela Kingston has come to call, Sir George Kingston's daughter."

Henry's eyes grew as wide as teacups. "Yes, miss, right away, miss." He hurried through the curtained door.

Pamela walked into the tavern, with Jack following. She wandered around the tavern while she waited, running her hand across the backs of chairs, looking at the pictures, tracing a path with her finger the entire length of the bar. She stopped at a nutcracker, made to look like a squirrel. Picking it up, she pumped its tail and watched its jaws move, as though jabbering a tall tale.

"*Bonjour*, Mademoiselle Kingston. At last we meet." Pamela turned around so quickly she almost dropped the squirrel.

"Miss Flambeau?"

"Yes, I am Nellie Flambeau." Pamela set the nutcracker on a nearby table. She stood silently, taking in this woman who had to be at least twice her age, but looked no more than ten years her senior. She wore a lavender day dress with a high lace collar, gathered tight at the waist. Pamela knew only the tightest of corsets could draw her in so small. The bustle ended in a train, which lay in a colourful trail on the wooden floor.

With her dark, braided hair done up neatly on the back of her head, she looked more like a governess than the owner of a tavern. "Henry, could you make some tea, please? I am sure

Mademoiselle Kingston would find a cup of tea most refreshing."

"Is there someplace where we could talk privately, Miss Flambeau?"

"Yes, of course."

Pamela turned to Jack. "Please wait here for me while I talk to Miss Flambeau."

"Yes, Miss Pamela."

"Come with me." Nellie led Pamela through the curtained door and up the narrow stairs to her private sitting room, next to her bedroom. Nellie had decorated her sitting room as she had her bedroom, in pink. The pink floral fabric of the French side chairs matched the elaborately carved settee. Hand fans, painted with scenes of French ladies and gentlemen at a costume ball, hung on the wall.

"Please, mademoiselle, sit down." Pamela sat down in a chair across from the door to Nellie's bedroom. The adjoining door stood open. She had a clear view of Nellie's canopy bed. She forced herself to look at Nellie, and not at the bed, which both her father and Peter had most probably seen.

Pamela cleared her throat. What she said was not what she meant to say. "Is the sign hanging over the door the one my father had painted for you?"

Nellie gave her a queer look. "Why, yes, it is, but how would you know about that? Peter wouldn't have—" Nellie abruptly silenced herself, obviously aware she had inadvertently spoken of Peter.

Pamela's voice remained steady, even as she felt the tears sliding down her face. "No, Nellie. Peter didn't tell me." Not trusting herself to say more, Pamela opened her bag and took out the bundle of letters. She handed them to Nellie.

Nellie took them. In a voice barely above a whisper, she said, "My letters! Where did you get these?"

Pamela took out a handkerchief and dabbed at her nose. "From a drawer in my father's cupboard. It had been in storage until yesterday."

"Did you read them?"

"Of course I did! They belonged to my father. I didn't know they were from you! When Jack spoke of Nellie's, I thought it only a quaint name for a tavern. I didn't know you existed until I found those letters."

"Which, mademoiselle, is how it should have remained."

"But it is too late for that, now isn't it, Nellie? I do know about you."

"Why have you come here, Pamela? What do you hope to accomplish by being here?"

"I want to know my father, Nellie. I want to know who he was." Pamela had to stop for a few moments, as the tears took her voice. She fought for control, her need to understand at odds with her grief. "Nellie, I loved him, and I didn't know him. He died when I was only sixteen. You knew him in a way I never did, or could."

"Does Monsieur Rennard know you found these?"

"No, I only just read them this morning. He had already left for chambers. I should also tell you I know Peter still comes here. I know he came here before he met me at the train two days ago."

"You have learned much, my dear Pamela, in the short time you have been home."

"And you intimately know the two men most important in my life. How could I not come here? How could I not meet you? How could I not want to know what you know?"

"You are certainly the daughter of Sir George. You have his brash nature, his fearlessness, his honesty. My dear, you even have his eyes, his beautiful brown eyes."

Henry knocked at the door. "Miss Nellie, I have your tea."

"Yes, Henry." Nellie got up to open the door. "Please put the tray on the table."

Nellie poured them each a cup of tea and handed one to Pamela. "Sip this, Pamela. It will help settle you."

Pamela didn't argue. Tea had always comforted her. She needed that now, staring into the face of her father's past, and the legacy he left to Peter. Glancing into the bedroom again, she noticed a flimsy piece of lingerie tossed over a chair. She put her cup back on the saucer and set it on the table. Almost in a trance, she got up and walked into Nellie's bedroom.

"Pamela, where are you going?"

Pamela stood in the centre of the room, in the same place Peter had stood two days prior. "This is a brothel, isn't it?" She turned and stared at Nellie as though she had two heads. "You run a brothel."

"My dear girl, this is a place where gentlemen come to find female companionship. It is how I met your father, and also how I met Peter."

"You've been with both of them, haven't you?"

"It would be indiscreet of me to answer that question, Pamela."

"You don't have to, because I know you have. In one of your letters, you speak of initiating Peter. You were his first, weren't you?"

"Your father brought him to me and entrusted me with teaching him. I did what Sir George asked of me."

"And Peter still comes here. He came here only two days ago, to see you before meeting me." Pamela slowly walked over to the bed and stared down at it. "Does Peter love you as my father did? Is that why he still comes here?"

"You foolish girl, Peter Rennard does not love me, he loves you!"

"How can you say that? You could not know such a thing!"

"Oh, but Pamela, I do know. And now you shall. You came here wanting to know of your father. What there is to know you have already read in my letters. What you do not know is how Peter Rennard suffered these many years since your father died."

"I don't know what you are talking about. Suffered how?"

"He suffered with his hungers, and his struggle to protect

you from the cravings of a man. He came to me to help him preserve your innocence."

"But, Nellie, I want him to be my first, as you were his! I wanted that even before Papa died." Pamela sat down on Nellie's bed and ran her hand over the pink quilt. "Last night, he finally agreed to it. He said he would be my first."

"Thank the heavens above. I told him you were a woman now and would be ready for him."

"You told him that?"

Nellie came over and sat down on the bed beside her. "Pamela, Peter is a complex man who values his privacy. But given his longing for you, he needed someone to help him control his urges. He came to me because I knew Sir George, and through your father, I knew you."

"My father spoke of me to you?"

"Oh, my dear, many times. Your spirit delighted him, although I doubt he ever told you so. I heard many stories about your antics."

"I didn't think men would talk of such things in this place."

"You would be surprised what men wish to tell. Their hearts, and their mouths, open when they are satisfied with a woman and a glass of gin."

"Has Peter spoken of me?"

"There is only one word he has spoken here which you should know." Nellie took Pamela's hand. "Dear girl, he has mistakenly called me Pamela on more than one occasion."

Pamela closed her eyes. "Dear God, please let that be so."

"It is so, Pamela. The first time, you had just left for boarding school."

Pamela stifled a sob. "Nellie, he sent me away! I had no one except him, and he sent me away."

"I do not mean to betray my dear Peter, but I must tell you, Pamela, the night you left, matters of the flesh did not concern him. He came here only to soothe his soul, as he had no one else who understood."

"And all the other times he has come here? What of them?"

"Peter Rennard is a commanding man, Pamela, in all matters. He comes here when he needs release."

"How can I hope to be to him what he finds here? He will think me callow compared to you."

Much to Pamela's surprise, Nellie laughed. "Oh, dear Pamela, it is your innocence that appeals to him so. He wants you, my lovely girl, much, much more than he wants me!"

"But I want to please him. Nellie, I want him to come to me, not to you."

"And he will, Pamela. I am sure of it."

"Then help me."

"Help you with what?"

"Help me know what to do to please him." Nellie still held Pamela's hand. Pamela turned to face her and took hold of her other hand. "Nellie, you know his habits, you must! He's been coming here for so many years."

"Pamela, you ask much of me."

"As you did of my father. He did not refuse you."

Nellie stood and walked to the window, overlooking the street. "Pamela, a woman such as I am knows much about men. I am privy to their secret desires. It is true, I know some of what Monsieur Rennard finds pleasing."

"Will you tell me of his desires, Nellie? I so want to know."

"If I tell you some of his inclinations, you must be careful how you use this knowledge, Pamela. He is exceptionally protective of you and of your innocence. You cannot be to him what I am. That is not what monsieur needs from you."

"Nellie, I do not understand."

"He must always feel he is the one guiding and teaching you. Now that I have met you, I see clearly why he has given you his heart. You are quite charming and lovely, but that is not all that draws him to you." Nellie gestured toward the sitting room. "Come, Pamela, let us have some more tea and we will talk." Nellie led Pamela back to the sitting room.

"Are you going to tell me what you meant?"

"Yes, but first allow me to help you settle a bit." Nellie went to a cupboard and took out a decanter. "A bit of brandy will soothe you and you will hear me better for it." Nellie added a healthy dollop of brandy to Pamela's tea. "There, now. Sip that while we talk."

Nellie added brandy to her own cup before continuing. "Pamela, your father told me many stories of his daughter, who had the spirit of a bird in flight."

Pamela smiled. "He often called me 'Little Bird.' He said I flitted about like a hummingbird."

"The delicacy of a hummingbird does not describe your soul, Pamela. The daughter of Sir George is as adventurous as a gull flying over the sea. What Peter Rennard responds to in you, my dear, is the flight of your spirit, the fearlessness of your nature, the openness of your heart."

"I want him to respond to me as a woman. Until last night, he had not."

"What happened last night?"

"He touched me intimately for the first time."

"Did you respond to his touch?"

Despite her timidness about speaking to Nellie of such things, Pamela answered honestly. "Yes, I responded. He excited me terribly."

"Peter enjoys watching women who are not afraid to show their arousal. Did he ask to look at you?"

The blood rushed to Pamela's face. "Yes, he wanted to watch me."

Nellie smiled. "If he asked you that, he is well on his way to accepting you as you would like, Pamela."

"Nellie, I wanted to show him, and I wanted to see him as well."

"Did you touch him?"

"Yes, he likes to be rubbed."

"Are you listening to yourself, Pamela? You are asking me to tell you of his hungers. You are the one telling me."

"Nellie, I don't know anything."

"Child, you will learn. Peter is the one to teach you. You must also tell him what you wish. He will be open to hearing, especially now."

Pamela took a large swallow of tea, to bolster herself. "Even if I wish for him to spank me?"

"My dear girl, where on earth did you come by that? I know your father never once laid a hand on you."

"I saw a spanking, and it stirred me."

"Provoke him enough, and I am sure he will oblige."

"Do you know if he would be inclined to it? Spanking me, I mean."

"Peter is inclined to most activities of the flesh. I am sure taking you over his knee and slapping your bare bottom would please him greatly."

Pamela had the nearly uncontrollable urge to squirm in her chair at the thought of Peter taking her over his knee. "I have read about such things. It is only Peter whom I would allow such a liberty."

"As it should be, Pamela. No other man has the right to take such liberties with you."

"You say that when you have known many men in your lifetime?"

"Pamela, it is my profession. It is not yours. You must always protect yourself against those who would take advantage of you."

"I have, Nellie. Always. I only want it to be Peter."

"Your father did not understand how locking the two of you together as he did would play out as you became a woman. You have both struggled against that which naturally pulls you, one to the other. It is time to allow the fires inside to burn brightly."

"You loved my father, didn't you?"

"Your father treated me with kindness and generosity. Love is an indulgence I could not afford."

Pamela pointed to the letters. "You wrote to him of your feeling. He would not have kept your letters if he had not felt the same."

Nellie picked up the bundled stack. "Please, take these with you."

"But Nellie, they belong to you."

"No, dear, they belong to you." Nellie's eyes filled with tears. "Pamela, I cannot look at these, they would torment me. But you saw your father in them. For that, they should remain with you."

Pamela took the bundle and tucked them in her bag. "Do you still have his letters to you?"

"No, I burned them after I read them. Letters such as he wrote to me should never be left for others to read."

Pamela jumped when someone knocked on the door. They heard Henry's voice a moment later. "Miss Nellie, Jack says it is getting late. Master Rennard left instruction to be called for early today."

"Very good, Henry. Pamela will be there momentarily."

"Nellie, may I come visit you again?"

Nellie hesitated. "Pamela, I doubt Peter will allow it."

"Stuff and nonsense! Peter does not tell me what to do!"

Nellie smiled broadly. "My dear, you are the daughter of Sir George. If you wish to visit me, you certainly may. I must say you will no doubt receive that spanking you want because of it."

"Might I tell you of it when it happens?"

"If you wish. That will get you another walloping, I suspect."

Nellie took Pamela's arm to escort her to the door. Rather than walk ahead, Pamela turned and embraced Nellie. "Thank you for receiving me. If my father loved you as I believe he did, you are an exceptional woman. I am most pleased to have met you."

Nellie held Pamela tightly. "And, dear child, I am most pleased to have met you. You have grown into a beautiful young woman. Sir George would be proud."

Pamela wiped the tears from her face, as Nellie dabbed her own eyes with her handkerchief. Together, they walked down the dark, steep stairs to the tavern proper.

Jack immediately stood when he saw Pamela. "Miss Pamela, are you all right?"

"I am very fine, Jack. Miss Flambeau is a most gracious hostess."

"I'm sorry for interrupting, miss, but the mister will have me arse if I'm late fetching him. He asked I call for him at two o'clock."

"That's fine, Jack."

"Thing is, miss, there isn't time to take you to Piccadilly first. I have to go straightaway to fetch the mister."

Pamela glanced at Nellie and smiled. "And won't he be surprised when I am in the carriage to greet him!"

Nellie patted her hand. "I am sure he will be very surprised. Make the most of it, dear."

"Thank you, Nellie, I will."

Chapter Nine

Peter stood at the corner of Gray's Inn Road and Holborn Lane, waiting for Jack to bring round the carriage. He glanced at his pocket watch yet again. Fifteen minutes past two. Tucking the watch back into his vest pocket, he felt a vague sense of unease move through him. He had never known Jack to be anything less than punctual. To be as much as fifteen minutes late meant that something of a serious nature must have detained him.

Just as Peter considered flagging a hansom cab to take him home, he saw his own brougham coming toward him. His concern heightened when he saw Jack coming from the wrong direction, driving the horse much too quickly for the busy street. As the carriage slowed and stopped in front of him, Jack jumped down to open the door.

"Jack, is everything in order? You are late."

"Yes, sir, so sorry, sir. Everything is all right. Miss Pamela had me drive her, making me late to fetch you."

"Pamela? Where the devil did she want to go?"

"Sir, it ain't up to me to tell you. She will if she likes." Jack gestured toward the carriage door.

"Are you telling me Pamela is inside?"

"Yes, sir, that's what I'm telling you."

Peter didn't wait for Jack to open the door. He jumped up

on the step and pulled the door open himself. "Pamela, what the bloody hell are you doing here?"

"Hello, Peter."

Peter hoisted himself into the carriage and sat down beside Pamela. "What are you doing here? Jack said you asked him to drive you. Where did you go?"

"To visit an old friend of Papa's." Jack stood outside the open door, waiting for instructions. Pamela leaned across Peter's lap. "Jack, could you drive us around a bit? I would like some time to speak to Peter before going back to Piccadilly."

"Certainly, miss." Before Peter could counter Pamela's request, Jack slammed the door shut and climbed up to the driver's seat. The carriage lurched as it rolled down Holborn Lane.

"Pamela, tell me what on earth you've been doing. What friend of your father's did you visit?"

Pamela gave Peter an inscrutable look before she opened her bag. Pulling out the bundle of letters, she handed them to him. "Do you recognise these?"

Peter took the letters. For a moment, he didn't understand. Then, the full realisation of what he held swept through him. "Where in the name of God did you get these?"

"From Papa's cupboard, the one we claimed from storage yesterday."

"That cupboard has sat empty for six years! I checked it myself before they took it away!"

"Papa had them in a drawer at the bottom. He either took the handle off or it fell off. Lucy found it when she scrubbed the cupboard before storing my things."

"My God, Pamela, you didn't go to see her, did you?"

"Yes, Peter, I did."

"Have you lost whatever good sense I thought you had? I will have Jack's hide for taking you there!"

"Peter Rennard, you will do nothing to Jack! He took me only because I made my way onto Piccadilly to hire a cab. He had no choice."

"Pamela, you have always been strong willed and fool-hardy, but this is beyond anything someone with intelligence and breeding would do! Taking it upon yourself to enter Nellie's establishment is sheer madness!"

"Peter, I think you mean her brothel." Pamela glared at him. "I know you went there before meeting me at the train."

Peter threw the packet of letters on the floor. "Did Nellie tell you that?"

"Nellie told me nothing of it. Someone else saw you there." Pamela bent down and picked up the letters. "Have you read these?"

"Of course, I haven't. They belonged to your father, not to me."

"I read them, all of them. Some of them I read twice." Pamela gently ran her hand over the bundle. "Papa loved her. And she loved him. How could I not want to meet her, Peter? How could I not?" Pamela's voice trailed off into barely a whisper. "Peter, I understand why Papa loved her."

"Pamela, she is a whore."

"And she is the woman who gave Papa love after my mum died."

"You do not seem to understand, Pamela. She has loved many men."

"No, Peter. You do not understand. She has given herself to many men, but she has only loved one. She told me so today when we spoke. Even before I met her, she told me so in her letters to Papa."

"Whatever you read in those letters does not justify what you did, Pamela. I hope to God Jack stayed with you the entire time."

"He accompanied me into the tavern. I wanted to speak to Nellie privately. We went to her sitting room."

"Upstairs?" Peter hit his knee with his fist. "She took you upstairs?"

"Yes, where I am sure you have been enough times to know the way."

"I do not have to explain my behaviour to you."

"Nor do I have to explain mine to you! I don't believe you are angry because I went to see Nellie. I think you are angry because I caught you red-handed! The secret you had with Papa is not a secret any longer." Pamela tucked the letters back into her bag. "When you are ready to discuss this in a civilised manner, you might care to read what Nellie had to say about you in these letters."

"Pamela, I don't give a damn what Nellie says about me in those letters. I also don't give a damn that you know I frequent her establishment. What I do give a damn about is your well-being. The utter stupidity of putting yourself in jeopardy as you did makes me want to lock you in your room and throw away the godforsaken key!"

"I did not put myself in jeopardy."

"Bloody hell you didn't! A beautiful young woman, dressed as you are, in a location frequented by men from the docks and God knows who else? Pamela, you stood ripe for the picking!"

"Jack protected me."

"Jack couldn't protect you with a knife between his shoulder blades, now could he?"

"Peter, we were never in any danger."

"And how would you know that? If you were being watched, it would be by the grace of God you're sitting here beside me."

"Why are you being so unreasonable about this?"

"Unreasonable? Is that what you think I'm being?" Peter grabbed Pamela's wrist and held it tightly. "Do you have any idea how it feels to me to know you could have been in danger, that in an instant, I could have lost you?"

Pamela tried to free herself of Peter's hold. "Let go of me."

"Like hell I will!" Peter pulled her roughly against him.

Pamela made a fist and struck him hard against the chest. "Let me go."

"Pams, I'm not letting you go, not now, not ever!" Peter gripped the back of Pamela's neck and forcefully pulled her head toward his. Pamela struggled to free herself. Her bonnet fell onto the floor of the carriage and her hair tumbled down around her shoulders. When his lips met hers, his fury at what she had done fused their mouths together. He kissed her harshly, his fingers digging deeply into the flesh of her neck.

Peter overpowers Pamela, continue reading
Pamela seduces Peter, turn to page 137

Pamela tried again to push him away, but Peter held her too tightly. As he continued to kiss her, his hand found her breast. He fondled her, squeezing and massaging the soft flesh. Running his fingers up her neck into her thick hair, he made a fist, holding her head still by the roots of her hair.

Pressing his cheek against hers, he whispered into her ear, "Did it excite you, Pamela, to see where I've been? Did you think about what I might have done there?"

Peter felt her heart racing as he palmed her tit. Loosening his hold on her hair so as not to hurt her, he asked her again. "Did it stir you, Pamela? Tell me. I want to know."

Pamela dug her fingernails into the back of his neck, surely breaking the skin. "Perhaps if you tell me what you have done there, I will tell you if it stirs me."

"But my dear Pamela, you're read about all that goes on in a bawdyhouse. I am certain you entertained those thoughts while sitting with Nellie."

"I saw her bed, the one with the canopy. Have you been in it with her?"

Peter did not answer. Instead, he tugged at her skirt, pulling it up above her knees. Pamela could do nothing to stop him. Peter had her pinned to the seat of the carriage. He felt the cloth of her knickers and forced his hand between her legs. Pamela gasped as his fingers touched the downy tuft between her legs.

"I will see for myself if you are stirred." His middle finger slipped inside her secret place. Warm honey coated his hand as he probed deeper. "My dear Pams, you are quite stirred. Perhaps you would like to hear what I do at Nellie's now, while I touch you."

Pamela's breath noticeably quickened. Rather than struggle, she opened her legs wider. "Tell me, Peter, what do you do? I want to know."

"Ah, my curious little cherub wants to know." Peter stroked her clitoris. "Nellie calls this '*La Praline*.' It is the sugared almond all women want licked."

"Have you, Peter? Have you licked her?"

"Nellie taught me many years ago how to please a woman. Would you care to know what she taught me?"

Pamela tried to reach between them to pull her skirt up higher. She couldn't manage it. "Peter, for God's sake, I'm burning up."

"As am I, Pams. It is a hard lesson to learn, that the fire never goes away. It smoulders and it flares, and it always, always burns."

Peter shifted his position and opened his trousers, exposing his stiff cock. "You see, Pamela, this is the curse of being a man. When it hardens, it demands urgent attention, either by my own hand or, preferably, with a woman." He knelt on the carriage floor. "You are beginning to understand the pain of needing release."

He pushed her skirt and petticoat up to her waist. "Spread

your legs wide so I may see the beauty of your womanhood."
Pamela did as he asked. Her knickers opened, revealing all of
her hidden charms. He adored looking at women, at seeing
their private parts glistening with feminine dew. The beautiful rosebud between Pamela's legs made him heady.

As much as he wanted to look, and in fact, study her
beauty, he wanted to taste her more. Lowering his head, he
nuzzled the chestnut nest framing her beauty. Her scent made
his head spin, as though he had indulged in too much gin.
"Pamela." He spoke her name softly, so softly she could not
have heard.

Supporting his forearms on her thighs, he used his fingers
to spread her wide and hold her open. The evidence of her
arousal ran in the crimson valleys on either side of her clitoris. With a volatile mix of reverence and randiness, he penetrated her slit with his tongue. She shuddered and grabbed
his head.

As many women as he had tasted in his life, none tasted as
sweet as Pamela. Her nectar coated his tongue like honey
syrup. His cock bumped the edge of the carriage seat as he
lapped at her. He allowed the rocking carriage to control the
rhythm, his organ rubbing the seat every few seconds. The er-
ratic motion made the movement of his tongue unpredictable,
jabbing one moment and licking the next.

Pamela abandoned herself to his ministrations, writhing
on the seat as he lapped at her. Her heat washed through him
as he intensified his invasion of her private parts. He sucked
her clitoris with a hunger he felt in his belly, a desire to have
her that had gnawed at him for years.

To his utter amazement, she drew both legs up and put her
heels on the edge of the seat. Her movement broke the suction he had sustained and he lifted his head. For a moment
their eyes met. The fire he saw burning in them cemented his
resolve. She would share his bed. They were destined to be
lovers.

Pamela grasped her shins, holding her propped legs wide open. "Peter, for merciful heaven, let me finish."

Before he returned to the treasure between her legs, he leaned forward and kissed her, knowing she would taste herself in his mouth. He left her breathless as he again bowed at her feminine altar. With a singular focus, he sucked her, creating a vacuum with his mouth that made her squeal. He sustained the suction, using his tongue to torment her.

She signaled her climax when she cried his name and tried to lunge forward. He held her still and continued to suck with an intensity he could not control. She spasmed and shuddered while he held her, until finally, she collapsed onto the seat, sated.

Slowly lowering her legs, she struggled to get her wind. Even before she had caught her breath, she reached for his organ.

Catching her hand, he kissed her fingertips. "Pamela, there is no need. I can manage."

"Peter, do not deny me! Let me touch you!"

"Why do you want to, Pams? If it is to prove to me that you are willing, you have already done that."

Before Peter could shift and sit back on the seat, Pamela caught his face in her hands. She kissed him, not the kiss of a virginal young lady, but the kiss of a woman wanting a man. Without meaning to acquiesce, Peter instinctively returned her kiss. He felt her again reach for him. This time, he did not stop her.

She had already begun to understand how he liked to be stroked and touched him with confidence. Still kneeling in front of her, his organ fully exposed, he seemed to be praying to a goddess and offering himself as a sacrifice.

Peter knew he would soon spend. He reached inside his jacket pocket and took out his handkerchief. "Here, Pamela, so we do not muss our clothing."

Pamela folded the cloth over the tip of his cock and rubbed

his cock with a finesse beyond her experience. "Please, Peter, squeeze my bubbies. It feels so good when you touch them."

Peter lost all sense of propriety as he kneaded her titties. As Pamela rubbed him, without warning, she reached under his prick with her free hand and fondled his balls. "My God, Pams, I'm going to spend." Bracing himself against her chest, so as not to fall forward, he filled his handkerchief with his cream. Her fingers continued to tickle his balls until he had fully spent.

He lifted himself up and fell back on the seat beside her. "Sweet God in heaven, Pamela! How did you know to do that?"

"I love the way they dangle, Peter. They are so deliciously soft and fleshy. I simply had to touch them."

"Young lady, you are a complete mystery to me! From a girl sliding down banisters to the woman you have become, how did this happen?"

"I grew up, Peter. You know, it does happen from time to time. The reading I do has taught me more than you know."

"You have only read this? If I didn't already know you are chaste, I don't know that I would believe you."

"Darling Peter, you know I have waited for you. Why do you doubt me?"

"Because, dear Pamela, you have the touch of a professional. Perhaps you should speak to Nellie about obtaining a position in her establishment."

"I will be sure to mention it the next time I see her."

"Do not even entertain the notion you will be going back there. It will not happen."

Pamela laughed. "But how am I to be a professional if I am forbidden to entertain such thoughts?"

"Dear heart, I will see to it you are paid very well for keeping your services at home." Peter took his handkerchief and wiped himself clean before tucking himself back into his trousers. "Pams, you best fix your hair. It is in complete disarray." Peter smiled. "Not that I mind, I rather fancy it down. But I do not think you want to be seen looking as though you just left your bedchamber."

"Or, rather, that I just left your bedchamber."

Peter laughed. "It seems that is a distinct possibility."

As Pamela made herself presentable, Peter leaned forward and unlatched the small window below Jack's seat. "Jack, we are ready to return to Piccadilly now."

Jack turned the carriage around and headed for home.

Go to page 142

Peter held her tighter, sliding his fingers up her neck and into her hair. He closed his hand, immobilizing her by pulling her hair's roots. He kissed her again, fully expecting her to resist. Instead, she went limp in his arms.

Rather than struggling, she relaxed. The fist she had used to thump him opened and her fingers dug into his chest. She returned his kiss with ardor. Realising he had her hair bunched tightly in his hand, he loosened his hold so as not to hurt her.

When he released her mouth, she didn't move away. She gently kissed his cheek, tracing a path of kisses to his neck. She whispered into his ear, "Peter, don't be angry with me. Jack would not have allowed anyone near me. You know that to be true."

"It is dangerous to have been there, with only your coachman as a companion. Not only that. You do not belong in a place with whores."

"Peter, you go there. You've been going there for quite a long time."

He wrapped both arms around her and buried his face in her hair. "Pams, how could you know what it's been like, to be here without you? Yes, I went to see Nellie. I went to see her because I could not have you."

Pamela held him tightly. "Nellie told me. She said you called for me while with her."

"Pams, you just don't know."

"I'm beginning to know, Peter, but you must tell me of your needs. Nellie would not. She said you are the one to teach me, and to show me how."

"She said that to you?"

"Yes. She said you are inclined to most activities of the flesh and that I should ask you to teach me."

In spite of his anger, Peter smiled. "She would say that. She told me the very same."

"Told you what?"

"That I should teach you, that you are ready."

"Peter, I want you. I have always wanted you. She is right. I am ready."

"Pams, I don't know if she is right. I only know that having you this close to me is driving me mad." He caressed her cheek and followed the line of her neck down to her breast. "You are so incredibly beautiful."

"Dearest Peter." Pamela rested her hand on his upper thigh. "Will you let me touch you again, like you did the day I came home?"

She didn't wait for him to answer. Her hand found his organ, already thick in his trousers. "Peter, I want to taste you. Please let me."

Peter closed his eyes and groaned. Her hand on him sent shards of glass into his belly. "How can you ask me such a thing, Pamela? It is what a common trollop would do. It is beneath you."

She leaned in close to his ear, pressing herself into him. "I am only asking to please you, my darling. I want to give you pleasure." The softness of her breasts against him drove him to the brink of control. He wanted her, more than he had ever wanted any woman.

Silently, deliberately, he removed Pamela's hand from his cock and undid his trousers. Before exposing his cock, he asked her once more, "Pamela, are you quite sure you want to do this?"

Pamela slid off the seat and knelt on the carriage floor. "Yes, Peter, I am sure. I want this."

Opening his trousers fully, Peter freed his prick. It twitched in his hand when he saw Pamela lick her lips. The carriage bumped and lurched as Jack drove them aimlessly through the streets, allowing them both privacy and time.

He watched her prepare to take him in her mouth. She looked at him closely, as though memorising every contour and vein. Never had he seen such innocent curiosity. Knowing her as he did, having seen her grow from girl to woman, he knew this to be her nature. He had never expected her inquisitiveness to transfer to such carnal matters.

When her mouth finally closed around his organ, he allowed the sensation to consume him. Her tongue circled the tip of his cock, but she did not move her head. Only the more experienced whores he had paid for the pleasure knew to stay still and let him move. Slowly, he pulled himself out of her mouth and slid back in. Still, she did not move her head, only her tongue, all the while keeping the suction steady and even.

Had he not been in such a state of need, he would have stopped her and insisted she tell him how she had learned this. But the sheer bliss of having her mouth on him put those thoughts at bay. Reaching down, he threaded his fingers through her hair, the silken strands scattered on his lap. Finally, he had her here, with him.

As his arousal grew, so did the pace of his thrusts. Pamela stayed steady, allowing him to control the movement. She continued to lap at him, and circle his prick with her tongue. She loosely held the base of his cock in her hand, preventing him from thrusting too deeply into her throat.

Suddenly, she stopped. Being close to spending, he tried to force himself back into her mouth. She moved away. "Pamela, what are you doing? I am very close. Do you not want me to spend in your mouth?"

"Darling Peter, I want you to know I can give you the kind of pleasure you want." She stroked his bollocks as she spoke and Peter shuddered. Bending over him, she gently lifted the soft flesh of his testicle and licked it. Before he had a chance to recover from the shock of her tongue on him, she sucked his bollock into her mouth and rolled it around. Surely, he would go mad! The flame in his groin shot through his entire body.

As she had with one testicle, so she did with the other. Taking it into her mouth, she rolled it around. When she once again captured his cock between her lips, he leaked his first drops of cream.

Again, she covered him with her mouth. All sense left him as he thrust deeply into her throat. Only her hand at the base of his organ prevented him from choking her. With one final thrust, liquid fire boiled from his balls. She drank every drop that he spilled, not releasing him until he had spent completely.

Pamela sat down on the seat next to him. Leaning in close to his ear, she whispered, "How do you feel?"

Peter still had his eyes closed, not yet having recovered from her expert ministrations. He managed to whisper back, "My God, Pamela, where did you learn to do that?"

"It is quite amazing how much I have learned from the reading I do."

He opened his eyes and looked squarely at her. "You have only read this? If I didn't already know you are chaste, I don't know that I would believe you."

"Darling Peter, you know I have waited for you. Why do you doubt me?"

"Because, dear Pamela, you have the touch of a professional. Perhaps you should speak to Nellie about obtaining a position in her establishment."

"I will be sure to mention it the next time I see her."

"Do not even entertain the notion you will be going back there. I absolutely forbid it!"

Pamela laughed. "It is very difficult to be intimidated by your pronouncements with your business lying in your lap."

"You seem to have also learned impudence, my brassy tart!" Peter tucked himself back into his trousers. He then leaned over and kissed her. "I am serious, Pamela. I do not want you going back there."

Pamela playfully tickled his side. "But, darling Peter, perhaps Nellie will let us a room for the night. I could be your hired girl."

Peter tugged her skirt up to her knees and slid his hand underneath. "I have no need to go anywhere except across the hall in my own house." He found the opening in her knickers and brushed the soft curls.

Pamela opened her legs, inviting him to further explore her hidden charms. "And may I come to your room as well?"

"If you wish. My door is open."

Pamela squirmed as Peter slipped his finger inside her wet crevice. "As is mine."

"I am aware." Peter rubbed her clitoris and Pamela sighed. "You are even lovelier when you are heated, my dear. I enjoy watching you in your pleasure."

"It stirs me when you watch me." Pamela pulled her skirt up around her waist. "I want you to look at me."

Peter cupped her vulva in his hand. Leaning forward, he kissed her while roughly stroking her clitoris. She lifted her arse to increase the pressure of his hand. "Oh, Peter, please!"

"Pams, rub against my hand." She did as he said, sliding her throbbing clitoris against his fingers. "That's right, show me your passion. Let me watch you in your pleasure."

Practically delirious with need, Pamela pushed against his hand. Peter slipped his arm around her waist to support her. When her climax struck, her entire body shook violently. Peter held her until she quieted.

Before letting her go, Peter kissed her and whispered, "We should go home now, Pams."

As Pamela made herself presentable, Peter leaned forward and unlatched the small window below Jack's seat. "Jack, we are ready to return to Piccadilly now."

Jack turned the carriage around and headed for home.

Chapter Ten

Once back at the house, Peter escorted Pamela to her room. They both had to refresh themselves for dinner. Leaving her at her bedroom door, he gave her an affectionate kiss on the forehead.

Pamela feigned indignation. "I expected a bit more than that, considering the current state of affairs!"

"Young lady, some decorum please!"

Pamela seductively ran her finger down Peter's chest and hooked it in the same pocket with his watch. "We are home. There is no one here but the two of us. Why shouldn't I want more?"

"Because, there is a time and a place for such things. The hallway is certainly not the proper place for a liaison."

"All right then, Mr. Stuffy, I'll see you at dinner."

"Indeed." Peter smiled as Pamela sashayed into her room and closed the door. He could hardly believe this unexpected change in Pamela. She had become a beguiling siren seemingly overnight.

He had to consider the implications of this situation. Under the terms of Sir George's will, he still retained guardianship of Pamela. However, according to the law, Pamela had long since come of age. Certainly at twenty-two years, she could make her own decisions about such matters.

Of course, the gossips' tongues had already begun wagging, fueled by the jealous venom of Constance. Only today, a colleague had inquired about Pamela being at his home and the perceived impropriety of the situation. He had dismissed the inquiry with a wave of his hand, saying Pamela could stay in his home as long as she cared to stay, as Sir George had asked of him.

He could certainly stand in the face of any and all scandalous rumors. The legacy of Sir George left him with his own personal fortune and a respected position in the courts. However, he had to consider Pamela's reputation. He did not want the vipers near her. He would not allow them to debase Pamela's character in any way.

An unsettling thought occurred to him. What would happen if Pamela were to marry? That is what he had been wanting all this time. Now, that had all changed. They had discovered their feelings for each other. How could he let her go?

In all his days, he had never fallen under the spell of any woman as he had with her. She positively bewitched him. When he thought of her voracious curiosity about carnal matters and of everything he could teach her, his prick turned to stone.

Even with her reckless decision to go to Nellie's today, Peter had to smile. He tried to resist the underlying urge to be amused, as a parent is loathe to smile at the actions of a mischievous child. But Pamela's brash, fearless nature had always appealed to him. To have that impetuous spirit transfer into such a beautiful woman absolutely captivated him.

As he started to disrobe in order to wash up before dinner, Peter noticed something on his pillow. When he saw another copy of the *The Pearl* lying there, he chuckled. He picked up the journal, went back to Pamela's door and knocked.

"Yes?"

"I have something that belongs to you." Pamela opened the door wearing nothing more than her camisole and petticoat. "Do you always open the door in your dainties?"

"No, but since it is you, I fancied doing it." She glanced

down at his bare chest. "I see you have come into the hall with your shirt undone."

"It seems I have at that. Do you mind?"

"Of course not. Do you mind that I am only in my camisole and petticoat?"

"I should mind, but it is difficult to say so in the face of such beauty."

Pamela blushed, turning pink down her neck onto her chest. "Thank you, Peter. It means everything to me to hear that from you."

"I think this belongs to you?" He held the journal up for her to see.

Pamela giggled. "I had Lucy leave it on your pillow for bedtime reading."

"I see. Do you think I should study this scholarly bit of literature to increase my knowledge?"

"Perhaps. I do not yet know about such things, or if you need to study more."

"It seems you know much more than I had anticipated." With one last look at her bosom, Peter tucked the journal under his arm and returned to his room.

Before returning to her room, she laid her hand on Peter's closed door. She whispered, "Soon, my love, soon."

Even though she would have preferred a nap at that moment, Pamela set about preparing herself for dinner. She had only a few dresses left from those she had carried on the train. Thankfully, Lucy would soon be unpacking the clothing she had shipped. With those, and Peter's promise to take her shopping, her choices would be plentiful.

Needing help with her hair, she rang for Lucy. Within a few minutes, Lucy knocked on her door. "Miss Pamela?"

Pamela opened the door, still in her camisole and petticoat. "Hello, Lucy. Could you please help me dress for dinner? You always manage my hair much better than I am able myself."

"Certainly, miss."

Pamela sat at her vanity. She watched Lucy in the looking glass as she pinned her hair. "Lucy, may I ask you something?"

"Of course, miss."

"How do you manage when Jack is not with you?"

"Manage what, miss?"

Pamela's face grew warm as she continued. "Lucy, I am having difficulty controlling my urges. I thought perhaps you could tell me how you manage them when Jack is not with you."

Lucy giggled. "Miss Pamela, such a thing to ask!"

"I'm sorry, Lucy, if you would rather not speak of it . . ."

"Oh, no, miss, I don't mind a bit. You and the mister have some hankerings, all right. I've seen them, I have."

"Oh, Lucy, sometimes I simply want to scream with the cravings." Pamela closed her eyes. "What do I do when I want to scream with it?"

Pamela felt Lucy's hand on her shoulder. "You touch yourself, miss. It's what I do."

Pamela reached up and put her hand over Lucy's. "I do sometimes, Lucy. But it's not the same."

"No, miss, it isn't. But, if you do it right, it can still be plenty satisfying."

"What do you mean, Lucy, do it right?"

Lucy slid her other hand down Pamela's shoulder to the top of her camisole. "Your bubbies, miss, do you touch them?"

Lucy touched the lace covering the top of Pamela's breasts. Pamela's breath quickened. "Sometimes I do, but mostly I touch further down."

Lucy quietly slipped her hand fully inside Pamela's camisole and cupped her breast. "You have to touch both, miss, at the same time, like this." She massaged Pamela's breast, then rolled her nipple between her fingers.

Pamela squeezed Lucy's hand and sighed. "That feels good, Lucy."

"You have to use one hand like this, on your bubbie and

the other hand between your legs." Lucy pinched her nipple and Pamela moaned. "See, touching your bubbie makes it better."

Pamela shifted on the stool. Leaning back, she rested her head on Lucy's belly and opened her legs slightly. Lucy continued to massage her breast. "My God, Lucy, I want to touch myself."

"Go ahead, miss. It's just the two of us. I don't mind."

Pamela tugged her petticoat up and found the opening in her drawers. She found the throbbing pinpoint between her legs and rubbed it. Lucy lowered Pamela's camisole to her waist and stared at her breasts in the looking glass. "Oh, yes, Miss Pamela, your bubbies are fine ones, they are."

Lucy guided Pamela's free hand to her breast. Lucy stroked one breast and Pamela massaged the other, all the while caressing the throbbing heartbeat in her privy parts. Squirming on the stool as her passion increased, Pamela thought of Peter.

Her belly ached with wanting to feel his thick prick inside of her. She thought of him lying on top of her and in that moment, everything stopped. All sense left her as she called his name. "Peter, oh, sweet Peter." Lucy held her steady as her body shook with desire.

Somewhere, in the sensual haze that surrounded her, Lucy softly murmured, "That's good, miss. Think of the mister when you spend."

Images of Peter swirled in her head, his cock, hanging thick and heavy. His shirt undone, exposing his chest. His eyes while he watched her. She burned with an unquenchable thirst for him.

Lucy supported Pamela until she quieted. With her usual matter-of-fact efficiency, Lucy restored Pamela's camisole to its proper place and smoothed her petticoat over her lap. "Now, miss, we must see to your hair. You don't want to keep the mister waiting."

"No, Lucy, I certainly do not want to keep him waiting."

Lucy finished Pamela's hair and helped her into a dark purple evening dress. "Did all of my crates arrive today?"

"Yes, miss, they are in the back hallway. I'll be asking Jack to open them up in the morning."

"Splendid. I hope I have enough room for everything."

"I'll see to it, miss. There is room for another cupboard if we should need it."

"Lucy, I don't know what I would do without you. Thank you."

"Miss, I enjoy being in your employ. You and the mister have been awful good to me."

"I'm pleased you want to stay here, Lucy. We are quite fond of you."

As Lucy fastened Pamela's necklace, they both heard Peter's door open. He knocked. "Pams, are you ready for dinner?"

"Yes, Peter. I'll be there in a moment." With one final glance in the looking glass and a squeeze of Lucy's hand, Pamela opened the door.

"You are exceptionally lovely this evening, Pams." When he saw Lucy standing inside the room, his tone became more formal. "Won't you accompany me to the library? I believe we have time for a glass of wine before dinner."

"I would be delighted." Pamela slipped her arm through Peter's. They walked together down the stairs as though they were entering a grand ballroom.

Pamela sat on the sofa while Peter poured them each a glass of wine. "Pams, I have a bit of news to tell you."

"What would that be?" She noticed Peter seemed serious. "Is everything all right?"

"Nothing to be alarmed about, but I do have to leave London for a few days."

"Peter, why?"

"I received the annual report from Samuel Lamton today, along with a letter. Do you remember him?"

"Of course I do. He is the solicitor Papa appointed as the resident agent of his estate in Gloucestershire."

"He has asked me personally to tend to matters of some import that have arisen. I am taking the train on Sunday to meet with him. I may be there all week, depending on the outcome of my review."

"Peter, what has happened that demands so much of your time? That property has always been self-sustaining and profitable."

"I am surprised you would know that."

"It is my land, isn't it?"

"Yes, of course it is. But I have never known you to show any inclination toward your business affairs."

"You have always sent me the reports!"

Peter chuckled. "Yes, I had to, by law. You are the owner until you marry. However, I never thought for one moment that you read them."

"What a bloody pompous thing to say! Of course I read them. I have studied every single report you sent to me, and in fact, have on occasion, discussed them with others."

"Is that so? And who would you trust with the private matters of your financial affairs?"

"Richard Pankhurst. He is a barrister who knew Papa. I have had correspondence with him, and his new wife, Emmeline. They are good friends."

Peter looked into his wineglass for several seconds before he spoke. "Pankhurst is a radical in the Liberal Party, Pamela. He is notorious for his activities there."

"Peter, his 'radical activities,' as you call them, are the best chance I have of keeping the inheritance Papa left to me. He is trying to change the law, so that if I marry, I do not forfeit to my husband everything that is rightfully mine."

"So, Pankhurst is the one who has educated you about property law. Pamela, I will protect your holdings. That is why I am making this trip."

"Peter, have you suddenly gone deaf?" Pamela stood and paced across the room. "As the law now stands, the moment I marry, my husband controls my holdings. You cannot change that. Richard is advocating changing the law, and is on the very brink of doing so."

"And if he succeeds?"

"Only then will I consider marrying."

Peter swallowed his entire glass of wine in one gulp, and went to pour another. "You also lose everything if you leave my guardianship before you marry. Your father saw to that detail."

"I know."

"So, if Pankhurst fails in his mission to change the law, you intend to live with me until your hair turns grey?"

"It seems those are my options. Now, are you going to tell me why you have to go to Gloucestershire?"

"Lamton tells me he has been approached to lease the rights for collieries. There is a large vein of coal running through the property, extending from the adjoining estate. They cannot mine it, because the vein cuts a path directly across your property."

"Peter, that land has always been farmed. If I recall, one section of it is leased to a man who raises Cotswold sheep."

"You continually amaze me, Pamela. You are correct on all counts."

"You were not going to speak to me about this decision?"

"Before any decision is made, I have to speak to Lamton and audit the accounts."

"The last report you sent to me showed the profits from the land up from the previous year. I have not seen the current report you received, but the indications were that the land would prove even more profitable this year."

"Yes, and—"

"Peter, do not condescend to me! I understand the implications of this decision. Unless there is a loss reported on the books, I want the land to remain as it is. I do not want it mined."

"My dear, you do not have to convince me. I am inclined to the same decision. However, Lamton sees it differently. He is convinced that the collieries are necessary."

"But why, Peter? How on earth can he justify that recommendation?"

"That's what I'm going to find out. Something is amiss there. I have a suspicion he is being offered a handsome sum to convince me to allow the mining operation to proceed."

"And what will you do if that is the case?"

"No doubt dismiss him. I need . . ." Peter paused and studied her. "Correction, we need to have an agent we can trust to oversee the property as we want it managed. If that is not this chap, I will find someone else. That is why I do not know how long I will be there."

Pamela set her glass down and came up to him. "Would you have informed me had your decision been to mine the land?"

"Before this conversation, I would have to say no. Perhaps I would have mentioned it after the fact, but I would have singularly made the decision."

"And now?"

"It seems your education is much broader than I could have imagined. I expect I will involve you as much as you care to be involved. However, I would expect you to defer to my considered opinion on matters where we disagree. I have managed your holdings for six years. There are many things of which you have no knowledge."

Pamela put her arms around Peter's neck. "What I do not understand, you will explain. I learn very quickly."

"I am counting on it." Peter set his glass down beside Pamela's. He held her tightly against him and kissed her, with passion beyond any he had ever known. She returned his kiss, with her own passion meeting his.

Pamela broke the kiss. The thickness of his organ pressed into her side. "Peter, please, let it be tonight. I want to be with you."

"Pams, I have agreed to what you have asked of me. But it will not be tonight. The first time only happens once. I want it to be special, to be a memory you will hold in your heart forever."

Tears welled up in Pamela's eyes. "You are leaving on Sunday. If I can't be with you tonight, at least let me come with you to Gloucestershire."

"This is not a holiday, Pamela. I must have my wits about me to properly conduct the business at hand. There may be some unpleasantness before it is all settled."

Pamela wiped the tears from her face. "You are absolutely correct. I would be a distraction."

Peter caressed her cheek with the back of his hand. "I am pleased you understand."

"It doesn't make it any easier, but I do understand." Another tear slipped down her face. Peter brushed it away with his thumb.

"Tomorrow, we are going shopping. I know of a shop that imports the latest fashions from Paris. We will be sure to pay a visit."

"Peter, dresses are not what I want. You are what I want."

Peter smiled. "This shop imports more than dresses. I understand it is where the most sought-after courtesans purchase their lingerie."

"Now, how would you know that?"

"Word of mouth, of course. How else would I know?"

"If we walk in there and they address you by name, I will expect a full explanation."

"I will keep that in mind. Now, shall we see if May is about to serve dinner?"

"Peter . . ."

"Yes?"

"When you return, will you promise me you will not make me wait?"

"When I return, we will see if you still feel as you do tonight. If that is the case, we will take the appropriate action."

Pamela kissed him on the cheek. "I will hold you to that."

"Something tells me I will fancy being reminded of this promise. But you must promise me something as well."

"Anything, Peter."

"While I am gone, you must consider the consequences of this liaison. Rumors about us are already spreading. The longer you live in my home, the more scandalous it may be perceived. I also expect you will wish to marry eventually. You will not have your chastity to give to your husband."

"Unless, of course, I marry you. No one would speak ill of us if we are married."

"Pamela, get that thought out of your foolish head this instant!"

"Oh, pooh! Emmeline married Richard. She tells me they are expecting their first child. There are twenty-four years between them. There are only thirteen between us. Why couldn't we marry?"

"They are hardly an example to follow, Pamela. Your father wanted his daughter to marry into a peerage. That is where you shall find a husband."

"We will see." With that, Pamela gathered her skirt and went to check on dinner.

Peter followed her into the dining room just in time to see her disappear into the kitchen. A few minutes later, she came in carrying a tureen of oxtail soup.

"Pamela, what the devil are you doing? May will serve us our dinner."

"She is busy finishing the main course. I'm famished and want to have some soup now." Pamela ladled soup into each of their bowls before she sat across from Peter.

Peter shook his napkin and spread it on his lap. "I trust you will mind yourself while I am gone? No visiting Nellie's or anything of the sort."

"Why, Peter, I will promise not to visit Nellie's if you will do the same."

Peter shook his spoon at her. "You are an impertinent young woman."

Pamela sipped the soup from her spoon. Flipping it over, she suggestively licked the spoon's bowl. "If I am so impertinent, perhaps I should be spanked."

Peter coughed, and wiped his mouth with his napkin before he spoke. "My dear Pamela! That can certainly be arranged! If you continue to push me, it could be sooner rather than later."

Pamela stifled a giggle watching Peter's composure slip with her suggestion. "Promises, promises."

"How did this happen to you?"

"How did what happen to me?"

"How did you become a woman with such appetites? I am dumbstruck by the changes in you."

"Peter, it has been there all along. Nellie told me you have always tried to protect my innocence. You have been so busy protecting the girl you remember that you haven't seen the woman I've become."

"You had quite the talk with Nellie, it seems. I would like to know what else she told you about me."

"She said you are a complex and commanding man, in all matters. She also said I should tell you what I want, that you would be open to hearing."

"What do you want, Pamela?"

Just then, May pushed the dining room door open and carried in a platter of roast loin of mutton, surrounded by potato croquettes and brussel sprouts. "What on earth have you two been doing in here? You haven't finished your soup and I'm here to serve your meal!"

"We've been talking. If you leave the platter, I am sure Pamela will not mind serving the meal. She did a splendid job with the soup."

If Pamela had been able to reach Peter's leg, she would have kicked him. "Peter is quite correct, May. I served him his soup without spilling it on his lap. If he trusts me not to drop his dinner on the floor, I would be happy to serve the mutton."

After putting the platter in the middle of the table, May gave Pamela a stern warning. "I expect you will eat a proper dinner, missy."

"Oh, I promise you she will, May. I will take her over my knee if she doesn't."

"Well, if you don't, I surely will. She won't be getting any raisin pudding unless she cleans her plate!"

Peter gave Pamela a look that curled her toes. "That will be fine, May. I will take care of the spanking and you can withhold the pudding."

"Mind him, missy. He means it." May took the empty tureen and returned to the kitchen.

"If that is supposed to encourage me to eat my meal, I think you should reconsider your threat."

"Quite the contrary. I think you should reconsider the full import of the suggestion."

"You asked me what I want and I am telling you."

"Indeed. Perhaps we should eat now and ruminate upon this matter."

"I have ruminated upon it. I'm about to burst with rumination!"

Peter chuckled in amusement. "You have obviously given this some thought. Eat your dinner. We will retire to the library to have our pudding and discuss it a bit more."

"Then, allow me to serve you your dinner." With grace and poise worthy of royalty, she walked around the table and stood at Peter's side. Reaching for the platter, she deliberately brushed his shoulder with her breast. She served the food slowly, making sure she pressed into him each time she reached for his plate.

She could feel Peter watching her as she served her own food. Reclaiming her seat across from him, she picked up her wineglass. "Would you care to offer a toast?"

Peter picked up his glass and raised it in the air. "To Sir George and his legacy. May the angels carry to him news of his daughter, so he knows the beautiful woman she has become."

Pamela's eyes filled as she said, "To Papa. May he also know I am happy with you."

Chapter Eleven

Lucy removed their empty pudding bowls and closed the library door as she left. Peter stoked the fire and poured himself more brandy before sitting down beside Pamela.

Putting his arm around her shoulders and pulling her close, he whispered into her ear, "Are you still ruminating?"

"Peter Rennard, I've been ruminating for many years."

"As have I, my dear."

"I still don't understand why it can't be tonight. Why can't we be together right now?"

"Pamela, I will not have you give me your virginity on a sofa. It is tawdry and beneath you."

"We could go to your bedchamber. Peter, please!"

"No, Pams, not tonight. I want you to be very sure it is what you want. Once done, it cannot be undone."

"I am sure it is what I want."

"We have waited this long. We can wait another week. My absence will give you a chance to settle in here and think about all we have discussed. I will keep my promise. When I return, the door to my bedchamber will be open to you if you still care to walk through it."

"Then, if I cannot share your bed tonight, tell me what we can do."

"Anything you want to do that will not compromise your chastity."

"Do not say such things unless you really mean it."

"Pams, I do mean it. You have had me in a state all evening."
Peter picked up her hand and kissed her palm before laying it
on the hard bulge in his trousers. "Do you think I would jest
about this?"

Pamela lightly caressed his cock. "I want to know of your
habits with Nellie."

"Pamela, do not speak of Nellie now."

"Why shouldn't I? I want to know what you do with her.
She says you are inclined to many things."

"You are not only invading my privacy with that question,
but also being quite disrespectful. My dear, that spanking
you mentioned is much closer than you might expect."

Peter indulges his appetites, continue reading
Peter's hunger consumes him, turn to page 163

"Do you think me a naughty girl?" Pamela breathed the
words into his neck, sending a shiver down Peter's side.

"You have been more than naughty, Pamela. Visiting a
bawdyhouse in broad daylight is a seriously wicked offense,
one that quite demands discipline."

Pamela kissed his neck and then licked it, sliding her tongue
to just below his ear. "Isn't that why you go to Nellie's, to keep
the company of wicked girls?"

"Perhaps it is time you understand what happens to wicked
girls who live in my home." Peter grabbed Pamela's wrist and
yanked her over his lap.

"Peter! What are you doing?"

"I presume exactly what you want to happen."

Wrapping one arm across her back, Peter held her down.

He roughly pulled up her skirt and petticoat with his other hand.

"You're going to tear my dress!" Pamela tried to get her footing on the carpet. She slipped and sprawled across Peter's lap, her legs spreading wide. Before she could try again to stand, Peter clamped his leg over hers.

"If I tear it, dear Pamela, I will buy you another tomorrow. I will also buy you another pair of drawers. There is no question they will be torn."

No sooner had he stated his intention than he found the opening in the crotch of her knickers. To pull them off properly, he would have to release her. Of course, that would be out of the question, as he had her exactly where he wanted her. So, he jerked the material upward until the seam gave way. Her knickers opened to the waist, revealing a gloriously round bum.

"My God, Peter, you ripped my pants!" Pamela squirmed again. He clamped her in tighter, this time making sure her side pressed against the rock-hard ridge in his trousers.

"Yes, my dear, I did. You want to know of my appetites? You are about to discover one of them." With that, he raised his hand high and brought it down full force on the smooth flesh of her arse. Pamela yelped and tried to raise herself. He held her fast. Again, he slapped her bum and again she resisted.

"Peter!" Even as she gasped out his name, he saw her legs spread wider.

"Are you enjoying yourself? Let's see if you are." Peter wedged his hand between her legs and curled his fingers deeply into her body. When he felt her maidenhead, he knew he could go no further. A soft, guttural sound escaped from her throat as he slid his fingers out and back into her.

"Are you ready for it, Pams? Are you ready to take me inside of you?" He pushed harder against her chastity. "Are you ready to let me break it, dear Pamela, and take your virginity?"

Pamela writhed on his lap, her arse pushing backward to increase the pressure inside her cunt. "My God, yes, I want you to do it now, tonight."

"Not tonight, Pams, but soon." He withdrew his fingers from her pussy and traced the crack of her arse with his slick finger. With no warning, he raised his hand and slapped her again. He continued until her bum turned pink under his hand. Each smack cracked loudly in the quiet room.

Pamela pressed her pelvis into Peter's leg, trying to find some relief. "Peter, I am on fire. Please, rub me! Let me spend!"

"I think not, sweet Pams. I want the fire to grow hotter." Peter caressed her warm bum as he spoke. "I will help you to spend, but not just yet."

Peter noticed Pamela's dress buttoned down the back. Making sure he had her pinned tightly with his leg, he reached up and undid each button, opening her dress.

"I'm going to give you a choice, Pams. I will let you stand and take your dress off, or I can pull it off as you are. If I allow you to stand, you will remove it and then return to your current position."

"I will take it off. There is no need to risk tearing it."

Peter moved his leg so Pamela could stand. She wobbled a bit as she got her balance, but regained her poise quickly. She lowered the dress from her shoulders and let it fall to the floor. She picked it up and tossed it over the back of an armchair.

"Do you have stockings on under your petticoat?"

"Of course I do."

"Leave those on. It would please me if you removed everything else." Pamela removed her clothing, first her camisole and then her petticoat and drawers. Peter opened his trousers as he drank in her loveliness. "Would you take pleasure in knowing that you rival any of the girls I've seen at Nellie's? They quite enjoy showing themselves as you are now."

Looking at his exposed organ, she licked her lips. "I would also enjoy watching you take everything off."

"Not tonight, dear heart. We will save that for my return."

"At least open your shirt for me. I want to feel your skin against mine."

"You may open it yourself before you resume your position across my lap."

Pamela slinked toward him like a cat stalking a mouse. She stopped directly in front of him. With deliberate care, she slowly unpinned her hair, letting it fall around her shoulders. Her stockings stopped mid thigh, held in place by her garters. She had nothing else on.

With no hesitation, she came up to him, straddled his lap and sat down. His exposed erection lay on his belly, only a few centimeters from the tight curls between her legs. Pamela methodically opened his waistcoat, taking care to unhook his pocket watch and tuck the chain fully into the pocket. Then, she undid his shirt buttons.

He stroked her breast with the back of his hand. She slid even closer to him. He could feel her feminine heat against his groin. Pamela pulled his shirt open wide. She leaned forward and kissed his chest, pressing her moist crevice against his cock. Peter pushed her back.

"Pamela, you only had permission to open my shirt."

"I fancy being naughty with you. I thought you fancied it, too."

Peter reached around and dug his fingertips into her still warm bum. "This naughty girl is courting another spanking."

"Am I?"

"It seems you have a taste for it."

"It seems so."

Peter reached down and brushed her moist curls. "What else do you want to do with me?"

"Everything, Peter, simply everything!"

Peter chuckled at the enthusiasm only Pamela could bring to such matters. "Pamela, that is a tall order. Perhaps we best start slowly."

"I thought that is what we are doing?"

Peter massaged her clitoris and watched her reaction. She grabbed his shirt and arched her back, her breasts begging to be licked. "You think this is starting slowly? Dear Pamela, starting slowly is sitting in the parlour having tea, chaperoned by May. This is not starting slowly."

Putting his arm around her waist, he bent Pamela backward. Capturing her nipple with his mouth, he suckled her. Pamela's hips undulated on his lap, the need in her belly great. Burying his face between the inviting mounds, he licked the valley between her breasts. Covering her chest with kisses, he worked his way up to her neck. Bringing his mouth close to her ear, he whispered, "It is time. I want you across my lap."

Pamela's eyes had the look of someone who had taken too much laudanum. With her voice thick with arousal, she whispered in turn, "Peter, I will split in half I ache so. Please, I need to spend."

"Lay across my lap, Pams. I will see to it."

She did as he told her. Immediately, she pushed against his leg, desperately needing relief. Peter also needed release, the throbbing in his cock unendurable. But he would see to Pamela first. He wanted to send her higher than she had ever been and savour her moment of release against him. Pulling her in closer, he lodged his prick in the soft flesh of her side.

The pink flush on her bum had faded. He smiled, knowing that would not be the case for long. Raising his hand, he brought it down with a loud crack against her bottom. Pamela yelped in surprise. "Perhaps I should have done this years ago." Pamela squirmed on his lap. He smacked her arse several more times. The squirming quickly became thrashing.

Opening her legs, he penetrated her virginal cunt with two fingers. Pamela lifted her arse in the air like a cat in heat. He finger-fucked her, bumping her maidenhead with each thrust. Pamela humped his leg with desperate need, her climax close. Peter reached under her and found her clitoris. Holding her tightly around her waist, with his leg over hers, he pinched her clit and twisted it between his fingers.

Pamela's breath caught in her throat and she convulsed on his lap. He pinched her clit harder and a strangled scream escaped as she tried to say his name. Peter unhooked his leg from hers, to let her move. With the fury of her climax freed, tremors seized her body. She thrashed against his prick. He drove his organ into her side, sinking it into her flesh. His cream shot from him, spraying her bare skin. His trousers would be stained with the residue of their evening. He didn't care.

Go to page 167

"But Peter, I only want to know of your appetites. Nellie told me to ask you. That's what I am doing."

"Nellie is now your confidante, and your advisor? I remind you again, Pamela, she is also a whore."

"And Peter, might I also refresh your memory? According to her letters, you have been keeping her company for at least fifteen years. It seems she is also your confidante and advisor."

"You want to know of my appetites? Disrobe for me and you will find out more."

Pamela studied him for a moment before making up her mind. "All right then, I will!" Turning around, she said to him, "This dress has buttons in the back. Will you undo them for me?"

"Of course." Peter unbuttoned her dress. As he did, Pamela asked, "What would you have me do?"

"Disrobe and I will tell you."

"Shall I leave my petticoat on?"

"Oh, no, Pamela. You will display yourself for me fully. I wish to see all of your charms this evening."

Peter knew he challenged her. He wanted her to fully appreciate what he would ask of her. Better she understood now, before deciding to share his bed.

He watched her carefully. He saw no hesitation as Pamela stepped out of her dress and carefully draped it over an armchair.

"Do you have stockings on under your petticoat?"

"Of course I do! Do you think I go barelegged?" Her fiery sass made his prick twitch.

"With you, dear Pamela, one never knows." As she watched him, he slowly opened his trousers. Her eyes followed his every move. "Take the stockings off next."

She did as he told her, lifting her petticoat so she could hook her fingers under the garters. "Are you going to undress for me as I am for you?"

"No need, at least not this evening. You want to know of my appetites. I am showing you what I like."

Pamela pulled off a stocking. "What about what I like?"

He stroked himself, watching her remove the other stocking. "Sweet Pamela, by your own admission, you do not yet know what you like."

Pamela threw her stocking in his face. "How the bleeding devil did you get to be so cunting arrogant?"

"Now, now, your common tendencies are showing. You are a child of class and privilege. You should act as if you are." Peter took the stocking she threw at him and caressed his face with it, before he held it under his nose to smell her on it. "You smell of being in a brothel."

Pamela lifted her camisole and pulled it over her head. Her breasts tumbled free. She stood there, in full view of him. "Just how does a brothel smell, Peter? I wouldn't know."

"Of course you know. You spent the better part of today at Nellie's, even being in her private quarters."

"I didn't smell anything!" With her hands on her hips and her breasts hanging in all their weighted glory, Peter didn't know if he should laugh or pin her to the floor and fuck her until she couldn't walk.

"Pamela, the smell of a brothel is full of a woman, that penetrating musk that only a woman can produce. Surely you noted it today, as you were in the very heart of Nellie's world."

Pamela lowered her petticoat to the top of her drawers. Before continuing, she quite emphatically stated, "Peter Rennard, you have spent years absorbing the nuances of a brothel. Obviously, the atmosphere appeals to you." Pamela slowly, with excruciating unhurriedness, lowered her petticoat, taking her knickers with it. "Perhaps, that is what you really want."

"Now who is being arrogant?" Peter did not take his eyes off the flesh being revealed to him.

"Stating the obvious is not being arrogant."

The first glimpse of the chestnut hair covering her feminine beauty had come into view. Peter, without any sense of propriety, stared at the softness between her legs. "Pamela, it seems being a privileged child has caused you to miss your calling."

"Which is?" The petticoat and drawers both fell to the floor. Pamela kicked them aside leaving her completely bare. She stood with her hands on her hips, challenging him, without the least bit of modesty.

"Which is . . ." Peter stood and exposed his engorged cock. "Which is being a déclassé trollop on the streets."

Pamela's face and chest flushed equally pink. "Do you know you are a son of a bitch?" Peter thought she might spit at him.

"Pamela Kingston, what kind of language is that for the daughter of Sir George to use?" Peter grabbed her and pushed her over the back of the same chair on which she had draped her dress. He gave her bare arse a resounding slap. "I think your father would approve of the spanking I am about to give you."

Peter slapped her arse, with the intensity and voraciousness a starving man would bring to a wedding feast. Her voluptuous loveliness, bare and enticing, swept though him as would a gust of wind through autumn leaves. Pamela's squeals, be they of ardor or pain, fueled his zeal for her flesh.

He slapped her with the palm of his hand, feeling the sting of his flesh against hers. She begged him to stop and take her, but he did not heed her cries. When he could no longer endure, he grasped her hips in his hands and wedged his prick in the crease of her arse.

"Dear God, Peter, please, put it inside of me. I want you inside of me." She pushed herself into him. He held her firm.

"No, Pamela! I said not tonight and I meant it!" He thrust himself between her arse cheeks, and squeezed her breasts like a drowning man clutching a piece of driftwood. "I will spend against you, but not in you. It is not yet time."

Like a man possessed by demons, Peter rubbed. He held Pamela's titty and pushed his engorged prick into the crack of her arse. She arched her back and wedged him deeper into her bum.

"Peter, I'm dying!"

"No, sweet Pamela, you are living!"

Peter reached around to grasp her vulva in the palm of his hand. The sound that came from her neared a scream, but she swallowed it before it erupted from her throat. Pamela thrashed in his grip, but he held her. His cock, wedged in her arse cheeks, throbbed and pulsed, aching for release. But he wanted her to spend before he did.

He gripped her, the viscous evidence of her arousal coating his hand. Without regard to any decorum or modesty, she rubbed against his hand, her climax being the only thing that mattered to her. "Peter!" The demand and the plea in his name drove him to the edge.

"Pamela, I know what you want. You are my whore and my virgin. I will have you, you belong to me." Peter wedged himself so deeply into her bum cheeks, he nearly penetrated her from behind.

"Sweet Mary, I am his!" Pamela pushed herself back into Peter, so forcefully the tip of his prick did find her arsehole.

She pushed back again, his rigid cock poking her more deeply. Peter squeezed the vee between her legs with the palm of his hand. Pamela shuddered and whimpered, "Peter!" Her naked body vibrated in his arms. Peter held her as she shook with the uncontrollable power of her own release.

As his passion for her seized him, Peter's liquid fire moved. The desire he felt for Pamela spurted from him, coating the crack of her arse in his milky torment. With their bodies still pressed tightly together, back to front, Peter held her. He had his face in her hair, the fragrance making him giddy. His cream and her juice ran down her bum onto his trousers. He didn't care.

Go to the next page

Once they had both settled, he helped her to stand. Holding her naked body against him, he marveled again at this beautiful woman in his arms. "Pams, are you all right?"

"Oh, yes, Peter, I am quite all right. Perhaps a bit chilled at the moment, but certainly all right."

"Come, stand by the fire." He led Pamela closer to the fireplace. "There is an afghan coverlet on the chair in the corner. I'll get it for you."

"I could put my clothes back on."

"Yes, you could. But I would much rather wrap you in a blanket and hold you for a bit longer." Pamela waited by the fire while Peter retrieved the afghan. He wrapped the large blanket May had crocheted around her shoulders. "May gave this to me for Christmas two years ago. Do you remember?"

Pamela leaned back against him. "Of course I remember! She told me it took her the better part of a year to make it."

Hugging her, Peter brushed his cheek against her hair. "I have used it several times when I slept here on the sofa."

"Why on earth would you sleep on the sofa? Did you have too much gin to make it into your bed?"

"I suppose that is a reasonable guess, but it is not the true reason."

"Then, why?"

Peter kissed the top of her head. "Because I didn't want to sleep in my bed alone. Some nights, it is easier to stay here with my books."

"Oh, God, Peter . . ."

"Pams, I am not one to wear my heart on my sleeve. But I want you to know, for as many times as I have tried, I have yet to meet someone I can abide."

"May told me."

"Did she now? And what does dear May have to say about the ladies who have kept my company?"

"Nothing about them, only about you. She said you have been in a sour state since Christmas last." Pamela turned around. When she put her arms around Peter, the afghan opened, once again revealing her femininity to him. "Peter, May thinks it is because of me. Is she correct?"

Peter wanted to deny the observation, both to Pamela, and to himself. But as he looked at her loveliness and saw her unguarded eyes, her acceptance of him so forthcoming, he could not lie to her. "It is true that when you returned to school after your last holiday, I may have been a bit sour."

"As I understand it, you went through companions faster than a cobbler uses nails!"

"We should retire for the night."

"You are changing the subject."

"You are correct." Peter pulled the afghan closed around her. He knew the evening had to end before temptation bested him.

As he gathered her clothes, she stood quietly behind him. But Pamela would not be Pamela if she didn't have one more thing to say. "Peter . . ."

"Yes?"

"Might I sleep beside you tonight?"

"No."

"But why?"

The contradiction of her standing there wrapped in nothing more than a crocheted blanket and the naiveté of her puzzlement confounded him. "Pamela, I have explained, tonight is not the night."

"But I only wish to sleep next to you. That is all."

"I am not strong enough to lie next to you in the same bed and safeguard your virtue. Do you understand?"

"If you are determined to wait, I understand. But Peter Rennard, I am telling you right now, do not expect me to stay out of your bed once you return from your trip! You have offered me the invitation. I intend to accept it!"

"Pamela Kingston, I want you in my bed, but with your eyes open. This is not a game for children. If we stay this course, we will face considerable obstacles. The speculation and gossip will not stop. It could compromise your reputation and my career. There is also the difference in our ages, the terms of your father's will that precludes your leaving my home until you marry, and my management of your estate. All of this must be considered before you lay your head on the pillow next to mine."

"Do you think I haven't considered all of this?" Pamela held the afghan tightly in her fists. "I have spent many restless nights thinking about it all and have often cried myself to sleep wanting to be here with you." Pamela's voice caught. She closed her eyes and took a deep breath. With staid control, she continued. "You sent me away, without even asking me what I wanted. In all the years I have been your ward, you never once asked me what I wanted."

"What do you want, Pamela? I am asking you now, tonight, what do you want?"

"You. It's all I have wanted for many years, even before Papa died. I want you."

"Do you know why I sent you away, Pams?"

"Not until today. Nellie told me you wanted to protect me."

Peter dropped the bundle of Pamela's clothes onto the sofa. He walked over to where she stood, opened the afghan, and let it fall to the floor. He put her hand on his stiffening prick. "Do you feel this? When I would sit beside you on the piano bench in your father's house, this would happen. When you would grab me around the neck and give me a hug hello, this would happen. Even when you slid down the banister and nearly knocked me flat, this happened."

He picked up the afghan and again placed it around her shoulders. "You were seven years old when I met you. I watched you grow, and mature into a lovely woman. I struggled with these unholy feelings even before your father died.

Yes, I sent you away. I had to. If I hadn't, your maidenhead would have been broken long ago."

Wiping the tears from her face, Pamela asked, "Can you see me for what I am now, Peter? Can you see how I want to be with you?"

"What I see is the most beguiling woman I have ever known." Peter took her hand. "Come now. Let us retire for the night. We have a shopping trip tomorrow."

Chapter Twelve

Pamela unfolded the telegrams and laid them out across her bed. Peter had sent one every day, with the first one arriving on Monday, saying only that he had arrived safely. Each day, the messages became progressively more poetic. On Tuesday, he quoted from the "Song of Solomon."

> *"Thou hast ravished my heart. I sleep, but my heart waketh: it is the voice of my beloved that knocketh, saying, Open to me."*

On Wednesday, he used the words of Francois duc de la Rochefoucauld.

> *"Absence diminishes little passions and increases great ones, as wind extinguishes candles and fans a fire."*

On Thursday, Shakespeare.

> *"Love is a smoke rais'd with the fume of sighs;*
> *Being purg'd, a fire sparkling in lovers' eyes;*
> *Being vex'd, a sea nourish'd with lovers' tears:*
> *What is it else? a madness most discreet,*
> *A choking gall, and a preserving sweet.—"*

And on Friday, the words were his own.

Dearest Pamela—Matters in hand, new agent hired, farmland preserved. Will return tomorrow, arriving on four o'clock train London Bridge. Meet me.

> *Until then my love. Peter*

Of all the beautiful words he had sent, none meant more to her than the last four. Touching the last line with her fingertip, her heart filled with promise and hope. Peter would be home this afternoon. Tonight. It would surely be tonight. He had promised.

She went to the cupboard and took out the peignoir and negligee Peter bought for her a week ago. The moment she saw it at the shop, she swooned. The clerk told her it had been imported from a Parisian couturiere, the price reflecting that exclusivity.

Pamela had never seen anything so elegantly beautiful and feminine in her entire life. The layers of creamy silk fell to the floor, ending in a crinkled ruffle, edged in lace. Embroidered pearls decorated the sleeves and the peignoir closed with satin-covered buttons. The sheer negligee underneath had a scandalously low neckline, with hardly enough gauzy silk to cover her breasts.

Bringing to mind the flimsy negligee she had seen in Nellie's boudoir, Pamela watched Peter as he looked at it. Wondering if he also thought of Nellie's dressing gown, she brought it to him for his opinion.

He examined it closely, saying he wanted to be sure the workmanship and material warranted the high price. But, as his hand lingered on the gown, his reaction became evident. He quickly closed and buttoned his coat, to hide the ridge growing against his leg. Calling the clerk over, he asked that Pamela be allowed to try it on.

Seeing herself in the looking glass wearing this ethereal gown, Pamela knew that no matter what the cost, it had to be hers. She would wear it for Peter, and he would not be able to refuse her.

When she told him it fit her well, he immediately asked the clerk to wrap it up with the dress she decided to buy. She wore that dress today, to meet him at the train. The peignoir and negligee would be worn later tonight.

They had spent the entire day together, shopping and sampling sweets at three different bakeries. Peter could not have been more of a gentleman, seeing to her every need and buying her anything she wanted.

He made a particular point of taking her to an elegant lingerie shop. Apparently, the shop mistress had become accustomed to gentlemen bringing in young ladies to buy intimate apparel, for she hardly blinked an eye when Peter helped her select new drawers. He also picked up several other bits of finery for her, all with lace and satin.

By late afternoon, Pamela's energy waned. Peter noticed she appeared peaked and suggested they go home. She didn't want the day to end, but her belly didn't feel quite right. Once back at Piccadilly, she discovered her ailment. Her cycle had come upon her, earlier than she had anticipated.

That evening, she found herself indisposed. She cried when Lucy brought a hot-water bottle to her bed. She had so wanted to spend the evening with Peter, but simply could not. Sitting with her for a short while before she fell asleep, Peter explained that, never having lived with a woman, he knew little of such things. He asked about her ailment, about her discomfort and about her timing. After explaining they would speak more about these matters on his return, he kissed her good night and told her to sleep.

He left the following morning. This time, he awakened her to say goodbye, kissing her gently and promising to return as soon as he could. Pamela spent most of Sunday in bed feeling unwell. By Monday, the worst had passed and by Thursday, her menses had finished.

She spent the week resting and organizing her things. With

all of her belongings in their proper place, she truly felt as though she had come home. Reading in the library helped to pass the time. In there, she felt close to Peter. By week's end, she even took her meals with his books.

Last night, she slept on the sofa under the afghan coverlet he had wrapped around her a week ago. She lay awake for several hours, thinking of him and the ache of his loneliness. The palpable emptiness of being alone eased when she was curled up on the soft sofa, surrounded by his books. She understood why he slept there.

In a few hours, Peter would be home. After serving Pamela her luncheon, May began preparing dinner. Once she'd eaten, Pamela made a nuisance of herself in the kitchen. She wanted to know every detail of the meal. All of Peter's favorites had to be included. She wanted dinner served in the library at half past six, no, better at seven.

Grumbling that the next thing would be the wedding cake, May turned to go to the stove and ran right into Pamela. Shaking a wooden spoon at her for getting in the way and for being a bother, May chased her out of the kitchen.

That was when she decided to go back to her room and read the telegrams again. While reading them, Pamela suddenly realised she'd forgotten to tell Jack when to bring round the carriage. She heard the water running in the toilet and knew Lucy must be there.

Going to her door, she yelled down the hall, "Lucy?"

Lucy came into the hall. "Yes, miss, is everything all right?"

"Quite all right, Lucy. I forgot to tell Jack to bring round the carriage at half past two."

"He knows, Miss Pamela. You told him yesterday when Master Rennard's Friday telegram came."

"I did? I don't recall."

"You seemed a bit flustered, miss. You said at two. Then you figured that would be too early for a four o'clock train and changed it to half past two."

Pamela felt her face flush. "I suppose I am excited about Peter coming home."

Lucy grinned. "I would say so, miss." Lucy had a pile of clean towels in her hand. "As long as you have your door open, let me put a fresh towel by your washbowl."

"Lucy, that won't be necessary . . ."

Before Pamela could stop her, Lucy walked into her room. There, on the bed were all the telegrams and her lingerie, in full view. "Miss Pamela, oh, my heaven!" Lucy stood by the bed and stared down at the peignoir. "That's the most beautiful gown I've even seen!"

"It is lovely, isn't it?"

Lucy brushed it with her hand. "My word, it's all silk, isn't it?"

"Yes."

"You're thinking of wearing it tonight, ain't ya?"

"Yes, Lucy, I am."

"Does the mister know you have this?"

"Yes, he bought it for me last Saturday."

"I knew something special had happened when I found your clothes in the library on Saturday morning last. Did he break ya, miss? Is that why the curse came on you early?"

"Lucy!"

Doing an awkward curtsy, Lucy muttered, "Pardon me, miss, if I spoke out of turn."

""No, Lucy, you didn't speak out of turn. I thought Peter had my dress under his arm when we went to bed. I didn't know you found it."

"Yes, miss, bundled up on the sofa, with your drawers."

In spite of her mortification at Lucy's unseemly discovery, Pamela had to laugh. "You've known this all week and didn't say anything?"

"No, miss, it wasn't my place." Lucy sheepishly added, "But I have wondered what happened. I didn't mean to blurt out my thinking like I did."

"It's all right, Lucy." Pamela gathered the telegrams. "Master Rennard is considering what is best. We will decide tonight."

"Then, you have good reason to be ruffled by him coming back." Lucy pointed to the telegrams in Pamela's hand. "Seems he missed you a bit, he did."

"It seems he did."

"Ring for me if you need any help getting ready for tonight."

"I will. And could you remind Jack to be ready at half past two?"

"I surely will, miss."

Pamela tucked the telegrams into her night table drawer. She left the lingerie on the bed where she could see it. Glancing at the clock, she realised she still had half an hour before Jack brought the carriage to the front gate. Pamela opened the drawer, retrieved the telegrams, and read them all again.

Jack brought the carriage round on time. Pamela already stood at the gate, waiting. "Miss Pamela? Am I late?"

"No, Jack. Not at all. I'm a bit restless. I thought I would wait here for you."

Jack opened the door for her and helped her into the carriage. After she sat down, he leaned inside the door. "Nervous like a cat is closer to the truth." He patted her leg. "No worries, miss. We'll be there before his train arrives."

"I know we will."

He reached into his back pocket and took out his flask. "Here, Miss Pamela, have a swallow. You look as though you need it."

Pamela didn't argue. She took the container and took a healthy swallow. The gin burned her throat and she coughed.

"Easy, miss. That's strong rotgut."

"That's the God's honest truth." Pamela capped it and handed it back to Jack.

"You hang on to it, miss. Give it back at the station."

"Jack, really, I don't need it."

"Miss Pamela, Lucy told me what might happen tonight. Keep it, just in case you start feeling jittery."

"Thank you, Jack. I'll give it back later."

"Righty-oh. Let's get cracking."

He slammed the door shut. A few minutes later, the carriage rumbled down Piccadilly.

As Jack predicted, they arrived at the station well before Peter's train. She waited in the carriage until just before the train arrived. Jack accompanied her to the platform, where they found a bench. Pamela handed him his flask. "Thank you for this. I did take one more swallow. It settled me."

Jack grinned. "I knew it would, miss." He tucked it in his back pocket. "Miss Pamela, if I might say so, the mister is a lucky sod to be coming back to you."

"I'm equally lucky to be waiting on him to come back, Jack."

Pamela heard the train whistle before she saw the train. She leaned forward and strained to see down the track. "Jack, there it is. There's Peter's train!" She jumped up and nearly ran across the platform.

"Miss Pamela!" Jack bolted after her. "Miss, you have to wait. We don't know which car he's in. And you surely don't want to trip and fall."

"No, of course not." Pamela smoothed her skirt, drying her sweaty palms.

"Do you want another swallow of gin, miss?"

"No, Jack. I'm all right."

Pamela took a deep breath and steadied herself. She would greet Peter as a woman of refinement, not as an overly zealous schoolgirl. Even with that conviction firmly in mind, her stomach did somersaults when the train finally came to a full stop. As the doors opened the length of the train, passengers streamed out onto the platform. Jack stood closer to Pamela so she would not be buffeted by the crowd.

"Jack, do you see him?"

"Not yet, miss. He's probably hanging back to avoid all of this."

"No doubt."

They waited and watched. Pamela clutched her bag, panic welling up in her as she realised he could have missed the train. Feeling movement behind her as Jack stepped to the side, she jumped when someone put his hands on her shoulders.

"Hello, Pams."

"Peter!" Pamela spun around like a dreidel and grabbed him, all thoughts of refinement and sophistication disappearing in a blur of spinning colour. Hugging him tightly, she whispered, "I'm so glad you're home."

"I am glad to be home." He held her at arm's length. "Let me look at you! That's your new dress, isn't it?"

"Yes, it is. I thought you would like to see it."

"It is lovely, as are you." Peter gave Jack his claim ticket. "We'll meet you at the carriage. Is it in the usual spot?"

"Yes, sir, sitting right where we did when we met Miss Pamela."

As Jack hurried down the platform to the luggage car, Peter turned back to Pamela. "Do you know how much I want to kiss you?"

Pamela slipped her arm through his. "I expect not nearly as much as I want to kiss you. But that cannot happen here. You are a known barrister in London. We might be seen."

"Well, that is uncharacteristically sensible of you." Pamela dug her fingernails into his arm. "Ouch! What was that for?"

"For being patronizing, and arrogant, and pompous."

"The last two are redundant."

Digging her fingernails as deeply into his arm as she could, Pamela added, "And bloody infuriating!"

Unhooking her fingers from his arm, Peter affectionately chided her. "Unclench your teeth, Pamela, and open your claws." Pamela relaxed her grip on his arm. "Thank you."

"You are quite welcome."

"Now, getting back to my original point . . ."

Pamela assumed a haughty tone. "Which was? I've forgotten."

"Which was, how much I want to kiss you."

"Peter Rennard, you aren't impulsive enough to kiss me in the middle of a railway station!"

"Is that a fact!" He stopped and swung her around to face him.

Pamela giggled. "You wouldn't!"

"Yes, I would." Holding her tightly against his chest, he opened his mouth and covered hers. Pamela melted into him, and returned his kiss. The London Bridge station disappeared inside that kiss. Nothing existed for her in that moment except Peter.

The kiss ended slowly, their lips touching even after the kiss had ended. With more concern for Peter's reputation than for her own, Pamela stepped back. "Peter, we might be seen here. Let's go home."

"You are quite right, Pams. You can be sure the wags are already talking. At least we are helping them tell the truth."

"Do you mean that?"

"Yes, I do mean it." He took her arm and they continued walking. "I've given all of this considerable thought during this last week, Pamela, as I hope you have."

"Peter, it's the only thing I've thought about."

"I did not have that luxury. But in the evenings and before sleep, when I had quiet time at the inn, I thought of you."

"The telegrams you sent told me as much."

They had reached the carriage. Before Peter opened the door for her, he reached into his pocket and pulled out an envelope.

"What's this?"

"Open it."

Pamela broke the seal. "These are telegram forms. There must be at least a dozen of them in here."

"Those are the telegrams I wrote and didn't send. The one on top may interest you the most."

Pamela removed the first form and read aloud, "'I think of you constantly, bordering on obsession. Every day here alone is a struggle. Going back to a life without you is unimaginable. God preserve us from ourselves, I am hopelessly in love with you.'"

She stared at the paper in her hand, not knowing if she should laugh or cry. "Why didn't you send this to me?"

"Because I wanted to see you when you read it." He opened the carriage door. "Come, let us sit inside."

Peter helped her into the carriage. They sat quietly for several minutes as Pamela absorbed the words he had written. The question that formed in her mind could not be held back.

"Nellie said you loved me. She said you have suffered for many years because of it. May said I am the reason you never married. Peter, tell me the truth, are they right?"

"Pams, I think you're holding the answer to that question."

"I don't want to read it, Peter. I want to hear you say it to me outright. Are they right?" Pamela's voice quavered, but she held her gaze steady as she looked into his eyes. "Peter, are they right?"

"Yes, Pamela, they are right."

She leaned back in the seat and closed her eyes. "Dear God, how long I've wanted to know this, how long I've dreamed of this."

"Pamela, do not think this to be an answer to a prayer. My finally admitting these feelings to myself, and to you, may mean more hell for us than heaven."

"Peter, how can you say that?"

"Because, Pamela, our lives are not meant to play out as lovers. I am your guardian, entrusted by your father to find you a fitting husband. Having feelings for you as I do is an abomination, and an insult to your father's trust in me."

"Having feelings for me is not an abomination! That is saying love is a disgrace, and it certainly is not! And what my father planned for me is not what I want. I will not marry, Peter, and forfeit all that is mine to some sniveling pantywaist with a title."

Peter chuckled. "I am sure there are young men of the peerage with a bit more virility than that."

"Those I have met are coddled and insufferably smug. Keeping their company is unbearably tedious. I would not trust any of them with one shilling of Papa's inheritance."

Peter raised an eyebrow. "Just how many of these young men have you met?"

"A few, enough to know they do not please me."

"And I please you?" Peter wrapped his arm around her waist and pulled her close to him.

"You please me more than anyone else." Just as their lips touched, Jack knocked on the carriage door.

"Pardon me, sir, I have your box and parcels here."

"Of course, Jack."

Jack opened the door. Peter slid close to Pamela, to fit his luggage onto the seat. He piled several parcels on top.

"What are those?" Pamela leaned across Peter's lap to get a better look. "That looks like a hatbox and that one a dress box."

"You mind yourself now. Those are for later."

"You brought me something, didn't you?"

Peter ignored Pamela's question and turned to Jack. "Do you see how she assumes I brought her gifts?"

Jack played along. "Yes, sir, I see that plain as day."

"Now why on earth would I want to bring her gifts? She is petulant, impulsive and sasses me every chance she gets! Why should such behaviour be rewarded?"

"I wouldn't know, sir."

"And there is one more thing."

"Yes, sir?"

"She tastes of gin. You wouldn't know anything about that, would you?"

Jack grinned. "No, sir, not a thing."

"No, I didn't think you would. Take us back to Piccadilly. The last thing I want is to have May after me for being late to dinner."

Still smiling, Jack closed the door. Pamela pinched Peter's arm through his coat. "You think you are quite amusing, don't you?"

"I do have my moments." Wiping his mouth, he grimaced. "I can still taste Jack's Old Tom. You've never heard the rhyme, 'Little nips of whisky, little drops of gin, make a lady wonder where on earth she's bin'?"

"No, I never have. I've led a sheltered life, thanks to you."

"Your taste in spirits certainly demands some refinement. I'll see to that."

Pamela slipped her arm through Peter's. "What else will you see to?"

"Your well-being. It is my duty."

"Well, if I am ever a burden to you, I am sure you could find a way to break Papa's will and put me out."

"No, I think it best you stay with me until you marry. There is no telling what would become of you left to your proclivities."

Pamela laughed. Doing her best cockney, she retorted, "I've done awright, I 'ave! Been on me own for six now and I'm no worse for it, guvner!"

"You've obviously been spending too much time with Lucy."

Pamela breathed into his ear, "I thought you fancied common girls."

"I fancy you." With no fanfare and no warning, he turned and put his hand behind her neck. Pulling her head toward his, he once again opened his mouth and covered hers. This time, the kiss had an edge and a potency that surprised her. Peter assaulted her mouth with his, roughly pushing his tongue between her teeth. His hand found her breast and closed around it.

His virile insistence continued as the carriage rolled on toward Piccadilly. Pamela could do little more than allow him to touch her. He had her wedged into the corner and his weight prevented her from moving. He kissed her neck and licked her ear. The hand that had been on her breast moved lower. Tugging at her skirt, he pulled it up high enough to reach underneath.

His voice thick with arousal, he asked, "Your cycle is over, isn't it?"

"Yes, for a few days now."

He reached further under her skirt, following the smooth thigh upward to her vestal treasure. Slipping his fingers inside of her, he audibly moaned, "God in heaven, I've wanted to touch you all week. I've spent by my own hand every night, thinking about touching you."

Still trapped in the corner, Pamela could not move. She pushed against him. "Peter, let me move. I can't stand it!"

With his fingers still inside her, he sat upright, allowing her a bit of space. Pamela immediately reached for his cock. He grabbed her hand. "No, Pams, not yet. I want to watch you spend before I do. I will tell you when." He continued to tickle the swollen flesh between her legs with his fingertips.

"You're driving me mad, Peter!" Pamela pulled her skirt higher, and twisted on the seat, trying to push his fingers in deeper.

"Pamela!" He barked her name so harshly she froze. "Be still, you will break yourself by bearing down as you just did. Neither of us want that."

Forcing herself to be still, Pamela acquiesced. Breathing heavily, she managed to spit back, "No, I want you to break me with your cock, tonight!"

"Which I have every intention of doing. That is why you must control yourself. If you do that again, there may not be anything left to break."

"But I need to finish."

"As do I. Now, behave and allow me to see to it." He reinserted his fingers into her cunt and stretched his thumb to reach her clit. Using his hand as if it were a claw, he opened and closed his fingers, two on the inside, one on the outside.

The rhythmic pinching had the desired effect. Pamela lifted her arse off the seat as her cunt clutched at Peter's fingers. She lost herself in the delirium of her arousal. Stifling a scream, the sound she made turned into a husky grunt as once again, she bore down on his hand. The need to be penetrated came upon her in earnest as she climaxed. Peter removed his fingers and cupped her in his palm. Pamela rubbed against his hand until she had spent fully.

Even before her breathing had slowed, Pamela again reached for him. "Peter, let me see to you." She gasped for another breath. "We will be at Piccadilly soon."

Peter quickly opened his trousers. Handing Pamela his handkerchief, he closed his eyes and leaned back against the seat. When Pamela untangled his organ from his underpants, she gasped. Peter opened his eyes. "Are you all right?"

"I might ask that of you! Peter, it's purple!"

Peter glanced down at his erection. "So it is."

"Is that normal? I've only ever seen it red!"

Peter rubbed his forehead in exasperation. "Pamela, dear, I am very aroused. If you please, could you give me some relief and I will explain later."

Pamela quickly covered his cock with the handkerchief and began tossing him off. She knew now when to apply pressure and when to ease off. Allowing him to thrust into her hand, she slowly squeezed. Knowing he would soon finish, she removed the hankie and bent over into his lap.

Before he could react, she had him in her mouth. Within seconds, he shuddered with the onset of his orgasm. As she sucked the purple tip, his cream hit the back of her throat. She swallowed just as another spurt filled her mouth, some trickling down her chin. She swallowed again, managing most of it one gulp. Before he finished, he squirted twice more. She drank it all.

The carriage stopped before Peter had the chance to gather himself. He quickly tucked himself back into his trousers. Pamela wiped her chin with Peter's handkerchief just before Jack knocked on the door.

"Master Rennard, Miss Pamela, in case you don't already know, we're home."

Chapter Thirteen

———————

May outdid herself with dinner. The Robert May's salmon with oranges in wine sauce, garnished with sweet and sour onions could have been a Christmas Eve feast. The stuffed dates in honey she served as pudding also tasted of Christmas.

When Peter asked why the celebration, May winked at Pamela and said, "Why, you're home, ain't ya!"

Pamela took the snifter of Napoleon cognac Peter offered to her. "You still haven't told me why it turned purple!"

"That's the third time you've asked me that question!"

"I would stop asking if you would answer me."

Peter sat down beside her. "It happens sometimes."

Pamela snorted in disgust. "That's not an answer! It's an evasion."

"And that is not a ladylike sound you just made."

"There will be a few of those tonight, I expect."

Peter shook his head and laughed. "Is there anything you won't say?"

"Not usually. Papa always said I had a mouth bigger than my head."

"Little did he know!"

"Why did it turn purple? I will ask until you answer."

"Because I am intact. When I am aroused for a period of time without relief, I have a tendency to go from red to purple. It has something to do with the blood pooled under the skin."

"Then it's normal."

"Yes, Pamela, it is normal. Did you think me ill?"

"No, not ill. You looked bruised. I didn't know if something had happened during your trip."

"I suppose when I sacked Lamton, he could have pummeled me. But he didn't. My colouration is because of you, not because of any injury."

"I rather fancy that."

"Do you?"

"Yes, I do. If I am stirred thinking about you, why shouldn't you also be stirred thinking about me?"

"I remind you, dear heart, yours doesn't show as mine does."

She giggled. "You are quite correct about that." Pamela sipped her cognac and let the warmth spread though her. "Will we retire soon?"

"I expect so. First, I want to speak to you about what we are about to do."

"Peter Rennard, I don't want to talk about it! I want to do it!"

"Pamela, are you sure this is what you want to do? By saying yes, you forfeit the pleasures and joys of your wedding night."

"We have already discussed this. You know my feelings on the subject."

"Yes, I do. But you do not know mine."

"Yes, I do. You want me to marry some limp-wristed boy with a title."

"Perhaps I have reconsidered."

"What do you mean?"

"Pamela, would you consider marrying me?"

Pamela looked at him as though he had suddenly grown two heads. "Did I hear you correctly?"

"I'll say it again. Pamela, will you marry me? Isn't it what you want?"

"Is that why you are asking me, because it is what I want?"

"I am asking you because no other woman has ever been to me what you are. I am asking you because I want to be with you and no one else."

"What about Papa's will?"

"There is nothing in the will that says we cannot marry. Sir George would never have thought it possible and did not create a contingency for it."

"And if I say to you I want to wait until the law is changed to marry, would you agree to it?"

"Why on earth do you want to wait? I have been protecting your property for six years. Our marriage would not change that."

"Yes, it would. Once we wed, you would be protecting your property, not mine."

"Pamela, I would do nothing without your knowledge or consent."

"Peter, my property rights are controlled by English common law. If we marry, all that is now mine becomes yours." She could not hold back her tears. "Peter, please, don't make me choose between you and my inheritance. It would tear me in half!"

"Don't you trust me to protect what is yours?"

"Of course I do! But what if you had decided that the land in Gloucestershire should be mined and I opposed that decision? Since that land is legally mine, I could have overruled a decision I did not want by refusing to sign the legal papers giving my authorization as landowner. If we marry, I have no say, no land, nothing."

"You have my promise that I will always consult with you."

"And who will have the final word, Peter? Tell me, who?"

Peter stood and paced across the library and back again. "I

never expected this conversation to take this turn, but since it has, let me ask you this. If you could have exactly what you wanted, what would that be?"

"To marry you and to keep my inheritance."

"And what if the law doesn't change?"

"But the law will change! The Married Women's Property Bill, the one Richard Pankhurst helped to draft, is being considered by Parliament. Prime Minister Gladstone supports it. Peter, it will pass, it simply must pass."

Peter continued to pace. "This legal battle has been raging for many years, Pamela, and has yet to become law. I am aware of the current bill. There is still considerable opposition, although support for it may be growing."

"Do you support it?"

"I am not in Parliament, Pamela. I have nothing to say about the matter."

"Nonsense! You are influential in all areas of the law. Your voice in support of this bill could well sway those who do vote. They are your friends and colleagues."

"I do not concern myself with such matters."

"Even if it means our marriage?"

Peter shot her a look that struck her like a lightning bolt. "You are mixing my professional and my personal life, Pamela. That is not acceptable."

Pamela deliberately set her glass on the side table and stood. "Nor is it acceptable that I should be required to give up all legal rights to marry." Biting back the sob that pushed its way into her throat, she gathered her skirt in her hand. "You have given me your answer and now I will give you mine. I cannot marry you if you do not believe I have a right to keep what Papa gave to me." She turned to leave the room.

"Pamela!" Peter grabbed her before she reached the door.

With tears streaming down her face, she turned to face him. "You are a master at the law. I expect you will find a way to break Papa's will so I can leave here."

"Is that what you want?"

"I told you what I want. You didn't hear me."

"Yes, I did. And I am telling you again I do not want you to leave. I want to marry you."

"Are you willing, then, to allow me to stay in your home until I can marry you on my terms?"

"Yes, if you are willing to accept my proposal of marriage, deferred until the law passes. And, you must also realise there will no doubt be consequences to this pact."

"There already are." A choking sob escaped. "My heart is breaking. I thought we would be together tonight, that I would be in your bed and wouldn't have to wait any longer."

Peter gave her his handkerchief. "I didn't say we have to wait."

"But didn't you say this should be my wedding night?"

"I said you would forfeit your wedding night. If you agree to marry me and swear that promise is binding, this can be our wedding night. No one need know we have already married in our hearts. When the time comes, we will have it sanctioned by the church. Until then, it will be our secret."

Pamela searched his eyes for any doubt. "Peter, are you sure?"

He kissed her hair. "Pamela, I have never been as sure of anything in my life."

Throwing her arms around his neck, her sobs and laughter mingled with her words. "Oh, Peter, darling Peter, yes, dear God in heaven, yes!"

He hugged her tightly. "Does that mean you accept my offer?"

She pulled back so she could look into his eyes. "I accept and I swear the promise is binding. I will marry you in my heart tonight and in the church when Parliament votes the bill into law."

Peter kissed her nose. "There is one more thing we must consider before we act on this promise."

Pamela saw a shadow of something in his eyes. "Peter, what is it?"

"Children."

"Pardon me? Children?"

"Pams, we cannot have children until we marry. We must take precautions to see that you do not conceive."

"Oh! I hadn't considered the possibility."

"I have. For tonight, I have both rubber and sheepskin sheaths." Peter chuckled. "Nellie calls them little English riding coats."

"Is that a fact?"

"That is indeed a fact!"

"I thought they were called French Letters!"

"Perhaps by the English. Not by Nellie!"

"What else has Nellie taught you?"

"Enough to know what to do and what not to do. There is also something called a womb veil, made of rubber. She has them for her girls."

"Perhaps I should ask her for one?"

"I think not! We will find a proper doctor to have one fitted for you."

"Won't that be difficult if we are not legally married?"

"I'll simply tell him that I am your guardian and your virtue has been compromised. Given your reckless nature, I want to be sure you are protected from conception."

"And if I were to go myself and ask for this shield, so you do not have to make up stories?"

"Pams, it would be easier if I manage it."

"You mean they would probably not see me without a husband or guardian of some sort."

"Probably not."

"Peter, it isn't right. None of it is."

"Pams, laws do not change overnight and attitudes may not change at all. But we can manage it, together, if you are willing."

"How does Nellie do it, then? How does she manage what I cannot?"

"There are ways, Pamela. She has friends who are willing to help."

"The way you helped when she bought the tavern?"

"Sometimes, one must work around the rules if they cannot be changed."

"And this from a barrister!"

"It's what we do. If we can't work with the law, we learn to work around it."

"Peter, I will do what is necessary to postpone conception until we marry. But are we in agreement that we will eventually have a family?"

"If you are able to raise our children so they are more obedient than their mother, yes, we will have a family."

"Well, they will certainly be more spontaneous than their father, to be sure!"

"That's the second time today you have implied I am stiff-necked."

"Well, aren't you?"

"You think so?"

"Prove me wrong."

"That would be better accomplished upstairs, don't you think?"

"Perhaps so." Peter opened the library door. "Wait . . ." Pamela ran over and picked up both brandy snifters. "Could you get the decanter, please?"

"Are you expecting to need this tonight?"

The reflex to put her hands on her hips nearly made her tip the brandy snifters. Peter's amused expression didn't help her exasperation. "Peter Rennard, I am about to be deflowered. Wouldn't you want a stiff drink before being broken?"

Peter's laughter rang through the quiet library. "Pamela Kingston, you are a joy, an absolute joy." He picked up the decanter. "After you, my saucy strumpet."

With a defiant look, Pamela put the glasses back on the

side table. Picking up the hem of the new dress Peter had given her, she tucked it into her belt. She saw his nostrils flair ever so slightly as he stared at her legs. Again gathering the snifters, she sashayed out the door and up the stairs. After turning off the lamp, Peter followed her.

He left her in the hall. "When you are ready, come to my room. The door will be open."

"I won't be long." She handed him one snifter. "I'll keep mine."

With the decanter in one hand and a glass in the other, he couldn't manage the door. "Would you be kind enough to open the door for me?"

"Of course." She pushed it wide open. "Now I know the door will be open."

"Pamela, after tonight, it may never be closed again."

She went to her room, where her lingerie still lay on the bed. Quickly taking off her new dress and everything underneath, she freshened herself at her washbowl. Taking the pins out of her hair, she brushed it so that it lay in wavy strands around her shoulders. Only then did she put on the negligee.

Before putting on the peignoir, she had a tentative glance in the looking glass. She stood awestruck as she viewed her reflection. What she saw could not possibly be her own image looking back at her! She picked up the silk peignoir and slipped in on. The layers of silk and lace cascaded around her, transforming the reflection into a gossamer sylph.

She pulled herself away from her reflection and picked up her cognac from the night table. She took a healthy sip and swallowed. It burned her throat going down. But as it warmed her, she felt braced for the moment she had so long wanted. With one last look at herself, she left her room to cross the threshold into her future.

Peter had his back to her when she came in. He stood at his cupboard, having just taken out his dressing gown. He had on striped silk pyjama bottoms and no top. Pamela shivered, seeing his bare back for the first time. She knew his

be broad and strong, but seeing the bare skin
ss them for the first time took her breath.

ning around, he slipped his arms through the
gown sleeves and tied it at the waist. Only then did
ne turn. When he saw her standing in the door, he stopped,
his eyes riveted upon her. Slowly, he came toward her. She
still held the snifter, her hands trembling around it. When
Peter reached arm's length, he took the glass from her hands
and set it on the bureau. Still standing in the open door, not
knowing what to do next, she waited.

He came back to where she stood and once again fixed his
eyes upon her. With unabashed admiration, he quietly said,
"My God, Pamela, you are stunning!"

Pamela's face grew instantly hot. She flushed with timidity,
all of her bravura disappearing in a cloud of self-consciousness.
She looked down at her trembling hands and whispered,
"Thank you, Peter."

"Come." He took her hand. "Darling Pams, you are shaking like a leaf in the wind."

"Peter, I am frightened."

"Oh, my beautiful Pamela, do not be frightened." He
pulled her close and held her against him. His dressing gown
opened just enough for her to feel his bare skin against the
top of her breast. "We will go very slowly. If you change your
mind at any point, tell me and we will stop." Pamela nodded
her understanding. "Would you like a sip of cognac?"

"Yes, please."

He led her to the side of the bed. "Sit down and I will get
it for you." He refilled her glass from the snifter and brought
it to her. He sat down beside her. "Drink it slowly; it is very
strong."

She took the glass and drank. "This is your special bottle
isn't it? It's the cognac Papa gave to you our last Christmas
together."

"Yes. I can't think of a more appropriate time to drink it,
can you?"

"Peter, why am I so afraid? I want this, I really do. But I can't stop shaking."

"Pams, it is understandable. What we are about to do only happens once in a woman's life." Peter took the glass and put it aside. "Let me help you. I want you to enjoy tonight."

"Have you ever done this before, I mean, been the first for anyone?"

"No. You are the only one."

"Then how will you know what to do?"

Peter smiled and ran his fingers through her hair. "Pamela, do you really think I won't know what to do?"

"I'm being silly, aren't I? Of course you will know what to do."

"You need to relax." He lifted her hair and kissed her neck. "Will you let me help you to relax?"

"Yes."

He surprised her by crawling on the bed behind her. When she turned to see why, he stopped her. "No, you stay still. I'm going to massage your neck." He lifted her hair and pressed his fingertips into the top of her spine. Making small circles as he moved, he gently traced a line outward on both sides of her neck and then came back to her spine. Still using the circular motion, he slid his fingers into her hair and massaged her scalp.

"Peter, that is wonderful."

"Drop your head forward, Pams, so your chin is on your chest."

When she did as he asked, he lifted her hair and kissed the back of her neck, sending chills down her side. "Oh, Peter, I feel that down to my toes!"

He continued to kiss her neck as her head lolled forward. Lowering the peignoir, he kissed her shoulders. As he bent over, he pressed his hardened organ into her back. Trying to make a joke, Pamela asked, "Is it purple yet?"

"I don't know. Perhaps we should check."

In spite of her nervousness, Pamela giggled. "Do you know

your door is still open? If Lucy should walk by, you'll give her quite a start, especially if it's purple!"

"Perhaps you should go close it then."

Peter tickled her side and she yelped. After jumping up to get away from him, she darted across the room and closed the door.

Pamela entices Peter, continue reading
Peter guides Pamela, turn to page 202

When she turned around, she saw Peter had removed his dressing gown. It lay in a crumpled heap on the floor. He still knelt on the bed, looking at her. She took in his bare chest, this being the first time she had seen him uncovered. Brown hair covered his pectorals and followed the line of his sternum down to his belly. She forgot her nervousness as she studied the masculine lines of his body.

"Pams, take your peignoir off for me."

His voice broke through her concentration. Realising her curiosity about him had been obvious, she apologised. "I'm sorry, I didn't mean to stare."

"Pamela, dear Pamela, nothing pleases me more than to have you stare at me. It is quite satisfying to know you want to look at me as much as I want to look at you."

"I've never seen you without a shirt. It is quite a revelation."

Peter smiled. "As I am unexpectedly spellbound seeing you as you are this evening?"

"I would suppose so."

"Let me see more. Take off your peignoir."

Pamela took a deep breath and slipped her arms out of

the sleeves. Keeping her spine straight and her head high, she walked across the room and draped the silk robe over the back of the chair. Feeling Peter's eyes on her, she turned to find Peter stroking his cock through his pyjamas.

The gaslight burned brightly in the room. Not knowing how she managed the control, she slowly walked over to the lamp on the wall and turned down the gas. The dim light flickered behind her, giving the room an ethereal glow. Peter still knelt on the bed with his hand on himself, seemingly transfixed by the sight of her.

His eyes burned into her. Standing under the lamp, a picture flashed in her mind. She saw a harlot standing under a street lamp, enticing men to look at her. He had called her his virgin and his whore. In this moment, she had become both.

With the heat of that realisation surging through her, she raised her arms and placed her hands under her hair. Sweeping her hair up onto the top of her head, she swiveled her neck to the side, and then back. The sensual movement obviously affected Peter. She heard a sigh trail off into a moan.

Her breath deepened as her belly filled with heat. Again, she rolled her head, before letting her hair tumble down around her shoulders. The intoxication of watching him watch her overcame any remaining anxiety.

She slowly walked to the bureau, where he had left his cognac. She picked up Peter's snifter and took a sip. Running her tongue across the rim of the glass before taking another sip, she watched him. In a shameless state of excitement, he followed her every move.

After carefully setting the glass down, she glided back to the circle of light under the lamp. She traced the line between her breasts with her finger. Peter pulled the string holding his pyjama bottoms in place. They sagged open and the very tip of his cock poked out.

The pulse-beat between Pamela's legs caused her hips to undulate. She heard Peter's breathing across the room. Clutching her breast in her palm, she flexed her fingers. She pinched

her nipple, this time her head rolling to the side unintention-
ally.

Peter stood, kicking his pyjamas completely off. Coming
over to where she stood, he wrapped his arms around her.
"Come back to the bed. I want to touch you."

Pamela pressed her pelvis into his prick. "Is it purple yet?"

"I don't know. Why don't you tell me?"

Pamela slid down the length of his naked body, her silk
gown caressing his bare skin. Peter groaned as her breasts
bumped his cock. She didn't stop until she had fully knelt in
front of him and examined his organ. Kissing the tip of his
prick before she stood, she grabbed onto his forearms and
pulled herself up.

"It's purple."

Peter took her hand. "Thank you for the report. It's my
turn to have a look."

He led her to the bed. "Are you still frightened?"

"No. I am too stirred to be frightened."

"That's what is supposed to happen. I am pleased you are
enjoying yourself."

"Are you?"

"Pamela, you are a siren Odysseus would have been unable to resist. Yes, dear heart, I am enjoying myself."

Peter took his place beside Pamela. He put his hand on her
belly and she tensed. "Is it time?"

"Pams, we have all night. There is much pleasure to be
had before the evening ends."

Taking a deep breath, she relaxed. "I'm delighted I am finally seeing you nude."

"Perhaps it is time to allow me the same pleasure."

Pamela giggled. "Then we will be naked at the same time."

"That is what usually happens."

She sat up. "Will you help me?"

"It would be my extraordinary pleasure." Peter pulled the
silky skirt up to the top of her thighs. "Lift your bottom."
She did and Peter dragged the material underneath. With one

smooth motion, he bunched the gown in his hands and pulled it over her head. She had nothing on underneath.

He threw the gown across the room onto the same chair with the robe. He then lowered her onto the bed. Lying down beside her, he bent over and kissed her breast. With no hesitation, he slipped his fingers between her legs and found her clitoris.

Leaning in close to her ear, he quietly explained what would happen. "Pams, you are very wet. That is good. Before I penetrate you, I will make sure you have enough lubrication to make it easier." He massaged her clitoris as he spoke.

"Peter, will it hurt?"

"I expect it will a bit. I don't know for sure, Pamela. Remember, I will be gentle. If you are in any discomfort, I will stop and wait until it passes. Do you understand?"

"Yes. Peter . . ."

"What is it, Pams?"

"We should pull back your quilt and get a towel. Some girls at school told me they bled afterward."

Peter quickly went to the washbowl and retrieved a towel. Once back at the bed, he dragged the quilt to the bottom. He resumed his position beside her and immediately inserted his finger inside of her. "Pamela, you are tensing. Try to relax, my love."

Pamela closed her eyes and concentrated on the sensation between her legs. Within a few minutes, she had the impulse to push against his fingers. "Peter, that feels wonderful."

"Good, Pamela. That's what we want."

She continued to bump her maidenhead against his fingers. When she pushed too forcefully, he pulled back. Spreading her legs wider, she thrust upward. Peter withdrew his hand completely. "Peter, don't stop! Oh, God, I want it deeper."

"Does that mean you are ready, Pamela? We can do whatever you have a mind to do."

"Yes, dear God, yes. I am ready."

Peter did not give her time to change her mind. He rolled

on top of her and pushed his prick between her scarlet lips. Pamela pushed herself upward, trying to lodge his cock into her cunt. Suddenly, Peter stopped and moved off her.

"Peter!"

"Pamela, I am so sorry, I forgot the sheath."

He took a small box from his night table and removed a thin sack. Rolling the sheath onto his engorged cock, he carefully tied the string to hold it in place. As he lowered himself on top of her, he checked the sheath again. She dug her fingernails into his back. "Peter, merciful heaven, do it!"

He found her entrance and pushed. The tip of his prick slid in easily. Slowly, he pushed further. When he hit the membrane that defined her chastity, he stopped. Pamela gasped for air, her breath rasping out of her in excitement and anticipation.

Without warning, Peter lunged and pinched her nipple at the same time. Her body convulsed in sensation. She screamed and clutched his back, nearly choking trying to inhale. Somewhere, in a hazy mist of pleasure/pain, she heard him. "Pamela, breathe. You are holding your breath. You must breathe."

Peter held her. She took a strangled breath and heard him say, "Again, do it again." She gasped and took in more air. Peter stroked her hair. "Shhhh, now. It is all right. You are broken. It is done."

The reality of his words penetrated her senses. She rasped out, "Is it over?"

"Yes, my beautiful Pamela, it is over."

As her mind began working again, she realised he lay atop her, his prick fully imbedded in her. "Are you inside of me?"

"I am."

"Oh, sweet Jesus, you are inside of me!" The pain had eased enough for Pamela to feel Peter's thick prick filling her.

"I won't move, Pams, until you tell me the pain has subsided."

She still held on to him. Her body relaxed as her breath became more regular. "Try to move. I can't tell otherwise."

Ever so slowly, Peter slid his prick out and back into her. Pamela winced, but did not tell him to stop. He did it again. This time she felt the urge to move herself. Tentatively, she pressed her pelvis into his.

"Oh, yes, Pams, that's it. Meet me when I push."

"Peter, do it a bit harder."

The next push became a full thrust. Pamela moaned. "Pamela, did I hurt you?"

"Oh, no, darling Peter, no. The feel of you so deep inside is heaven." Sweat dripped off Peter's face onto Pamela's cheek. She opened her eyes and saw the strain etched in Peter's face. "Peter, I am ready. Please fuck me!"

His startled expression at her pronouncement transformed into a smile. With her permission, he thrust harder, the rhythm of his movement guiding her. She moved with him, her cunt slippery with fluid. He rode her as he would a woman of experience. She responded in kind. He fucked her in earnest, until his prick exploded with lust. He poured himself into the sheath as she undulated underneath him.

Go to page 208

When she turned around, she saw Peter untying his dressing gown.

"Oh, my!" She nervously hugged herself, trying to remain calm.

"Pamela, it is all right. This is no different than what we have already done together. There will simply be more of it."

"I know that, Peter. But my stomach is full of butterflies."

Peter took off his dressing gown and tossed it on the floor. "Now take off your peignoir."

"I don't know . . ."

"Pamela, isn't this what you want? We can stop right now, if you have changed your mind."

"I haven't changed my mind. It is what I want."

"Then, take off the peignoir."

Pamela focused on his bare chest and did as Peter asked. The flimsy material fell away from her shoulders, revealing the negligee underneath. Peter still knelt on the bed, his eyes fixed on the deep valley between her breasts. She slipped her arms out of the sleeves and stood there, allowing him to drink her in.

"Put your peignoir on the chair. I want to see you walk in that gown."

Pamela again did as he asked. She slowly walked over to his favorite armchair and carefully draped the costly robe over the back of the chair. Trying to gather herself, she took a deep breath.

"Pams, turn around." When she did, she saw Peter had untied his pyjamas. "Pamela, I know you are nervous and a bit frightened, but remember, we have already enjoyed each other in this way. Try to relax and take pleasure in what we are doing together."

She watched as he lowered his pyjamas, completely exposing himself. She had calmed sufficiently to really look at him. His naked body took her breath. He had brown hair everywhere, covering his pectorals, his arms, even his belly. His cock hung heavily from his groin, also surrounded by hair.

His maleness, his incredible virility sparked something inside of her. The fear subsided enough for her to realise she felt her pulse beating between her legs. "Peter, I've never seen you without clothes before." Suddenly aware she had been staring, she looked away.

Peter stood and discarded his pyjamas. Completely nude, he said, "Pams, look at me. I want you to look at me."

She looked into his face, and then allowed her eyes to drift down his torso. "Peter, you are beautiful!"

"As are you, Pamela, quite astonishingly so."

He came over to where she stood. "That gown clings to you like a second skin." He ran his finger down the crevice between her breasts. "You are as beautiful as Aphrodite rising from the foam of the sea, a concubine for the gods."

Pamela could tell the sight of her affected him deeply. "You enjoy looking at me, don't you?"

"Yes, darling Pamela, looking at you gives me tremendous pleasure."

"I want to please you, Peter. Tell me what you want me to do."

"The light is too bright. Could you turn it down for me?"

"Certainly." Pamela walked across the room to where the gas lamp hung on the wall. Reaching up, she turned the knob, lowering the flame. The light instantly dimmed, creating shadows where before there had been none, and casting a golden circle where she stood.

"Pamela . . ."

"Yes." She turned to see Peter stroking his cock.

"Lower your bodice and touch your breasts."

As she watched him stroke himself, the throbbing between her legs intensified. Watching him watching her bedeviled her, as though an incubus had entered her body. The pulsebeat between her legs now pounded in her ears.

With her eyes fixed on his cock, Pamela lowered her gown. Her breasts hung as heavily from her body as Peter's prick did from his. She lifted one breast and squeezed. With her thumb and forefinger, she pinched her nipple, feeling the sensation all through her belly. The ripple of pleasure caused her hips to undulate ever so slightly.

"That's right, Pams, feel it, really feel it! Let me see you feel it."

She pinched both nipples, caressing her breasts at the same time. The ripples of pleasure once more surged through her groin. Clenching her thighs, she tried to increase the pressure between her legs. It didn't help. "Peter, please, touch me."

"Take off your gown, Pams, and I will touch you."

Drugged with arousal, Pamela pushed the gown down and stepped out of it. She scooped it off the floor. After coming back to where Peter stood, she put it on the chair with the robe.

"Peter, I need to be touched."

He took her hand and led her to the bed. "Lie on your belly, Pams."

"What are you going to do?"

"I'm going to touch you. Lie on your belly and you will see."

Pamela stretched out flat on the bed. After lying on his side beside her, Peter patted her bum with his palm. He then slipped his middle finger between her legs and tickled her cunt. Her bum lifted from the bed.

"Does that feel good?"

She murmured, "Yes."

Peter tried to push two fingers inside of her. She felt the tight resistance. "You need to relax, Pamela. It will make it easier if you loosen."

"I'm trying, Peter. Please, touch me some more. It will help."

"My beautiful Pams, raise up your bottom and open your knees wide."

"Peter, that is indecent! It is what a bitch in heat does!"

"Oh, yes, Pams, it certainly is."

Pamela heard the arousal in his voice, the low tone thick

with it. She knew he wanted to see her kneeling, with her arse in the air. Slowly, she pulled her knees up and apart. Heated moisture oozed as she opened herself for him.

"That's right, Pamela, open wide." She felt his palm on her arse. "Have you been a naughty girl, Pamela?"

She knew what he meant to do. Rather than telling him no, to stop him, instead she said, "Peter, I have been a very naughty girl."

"Do you think I should spank you for being naughty?' He lightly caressed her bum, making her itch for more contact. She rocked on the bed, moving her arse under his hand.

"Yes." It was all she could say, her breath coming too quickly to say more.

Peter's hand came down on her arse with a loud smack. Pamela moaned. He slapped her again and she lurched on the bed. "Now, let's see if you are looser."

This time, his two fingers slid in without resistance. "Much better. But I don't think you are quite ready." Withdrawing his fingers, he spanked her several more times.

Pamela bunched the quilt up in her hands and moaned, "Peter, please, I'm ready. I want you inside."

"Not yet, Pamela. I'll know when you are ready and it isn't just yet." Again he pushed his fingers inside of her. "Show me, Pams. Show me how much you want it."

As she pushed back against Peter's hand, her fear and nervousness evaporated in a delirious haze of carnal longing. Modesty and respectability had been replaced by lust and need. Neither the coarseness of her actions nor the lewd performance for Peter mattered to her.

Pushing back against his fingers, her body's need to satisfy the burning inside intensified. Peter reached under her and pinched her nipple. She yelped. She then heard him say, "Roll over, Pamela."

Without hesitation she rolled over onto her back. She barely had awareness of Peter going to the washbowl and getting a towel. When he returned to the bed, he pulled back the quilt and shifted her onto the sheet. Taking his place beside her, he muttered something unintelligible and stood back up.

"Peter . . ."

"It's the sheath, Pams. I have to put it on." He picked up the sheath he had left on the night table. He rolled it onto his length and securely tied the string.

Again lying down on the bed beside her, he massaged her belly. "Pamela, listen to me."

"Yes?"

"Dear heart, it is time."

"God in heaven, I am ready."

Before she had a chance to change her mind, Peter lay on top of her. In the next moment, she felt the fullness of him sliding into her. The exquisite sensation of being filled by him disappeared in a flash of blinding pain. Peter had forcefully pinched her nipple while pushing his full length into her. She moaned and shuddered underneath him.

He whispered, "Oh, yes, Pamela, feel me inside of you."

Peter lay atop her, his prick enveloped in her flesh. He did not move. Stroking her hair, he whispered, "It's all right, Pamela, the pain will go away. Then you will enjoy it as I do."

When she had enough breath to speak, she managed to ask, "Peter, is it done?"

"Yes, dear Pams, it is done."

"Are you going to fuck me now?"

"Do you want me to?"

She clutched his back, digging her fingernails into his shoulders. "Yes, slowly."

Peter pulled out and slowly pushed back in. Stopping again, he asked, "Did that hurt?"

"It burned a bit, but no, it didn't hurt like before. Try it again."

"Pamela, I must spend soon. If I try again, I will need to continue until I finish."

Pamela touched his face. Sweat ran down his temples and

covered his forehead. "Oh, darling Peter, yes, I want you to spend inside me. I've waited so long."

Peter pulled back and pushed again. The strain in him apparent, he still stopped. "Pams, are you all right?"

"Yes, Peter, please, fuck me."

He did not ask her again. Filling her with his cock over and over, he claimed her completely. Pamela picked up the rhythm, the fluids running inside her coating the broken flesh. The pain stopped. The joy of having Peter inside of her overwhelmed her senses. At the moment of his climax, she held him tightly. His body tensed and he shouted her name, a sound that filled her, body and soul.

Go to the next page

When he had recovered his wind, he very gently extracted his prick.

"Peter, get the towel, I feel something running."

He found the towel and pressed it between her legs. "Are you in pain, Pamela?"

"Not exactly. It burns a bit, but my monthly pain is much worse than this."

"I thought I might help you spend before we finish." He pulled the towel away and checked it. "There is some blood, but not significant."

"I would rather wait a bit, if you don't mind. I need some time."

"Of course. When you are ready, I will see to it." Peter took the sheath off and placed it on the night table, being careful not to spill its contents.

"Thank you for remembering the sheath. I'm afraid my preoccupations did not accommodate such practical concerns."

"Nor did mine. However, I did remember in time."

"I am a bit cold. Could you cover us with the quilt?"

"Certainly." Peter dutifully spread the quilt over both of them. With the towel wedged between her legs, Pamela rolled over and snuggled in closer.

"I am so sleepy."

Peter put his arm around her and gently kissed her. "Sleep then, my beautiful bride-to-be."

Pamela closed her eyes and drifted into blissful sleep.

Chapter Fourteen

Peter woke to Lucy frantically pounding on the door. "Master Rennard, wake up! Master Rennard!"

Opening his eyes, he immediately squinted from the sunlight coming in the window. Pamela still slept, although with Lucy shouting outside his door, that wouldn't be the case for long.

He found his dressing gown by the bed and quickly made his way to the door. Opening it, he found Lucy near tears. "Lucy, what on earth is the matter? Is someone hurt?" Fearing something might have happened to May or Jack, he stepped into the hall and closed the door. He did not want Pamela to overhear any unsettling news.

Lucy pointed to Pamela's open door. "It's Miss Pamela! Her bed hasn't been slept in. She's not in the library or anywhere in the house." Her voice cracked. "Something must have happened to her. Where could she be?"

The awkwardness of the situation made Peter uncomfortable, but the humor did not escape him. He smiled in spite of his discomfiture, knowing the impossibility of keeping this a secret within his own house. "It's all right, Lucy, she's with me."

"Pardon me, sir, she's what?"

"She's with me." The utter shock on Lucy's face actually made Peter laugh. "You don't believe me?" Peter opened the door, to find Pamela awake and staring wide-eyed at the door, the quilt pulled up to her chin.

"Peter!" Pamela blushed a lovely shade of pink when she saw Lucy standing in the hall.

"Pams, Lucy thought you had disappeared. I had to prove to her you are alive and well in my room." Peter crossed his arms over his chest. Looking from one redfaced female to the other, he found he quite enjoyed this licentious moment.

"Peter, for Lord's sake, close the door!"

Rather than closing the door, he stepped in front of it, blocking Lucy's view of the room. "Lucy, perhaps you should draw Miss Pamela a warm bath. She may want to freshen herself before breakfast."

Lucy curtsied. "Yes, sir."

"And Lucy . . ."

"Yes, sir?"

"Bring us a tray to my room. We will have our morning meal in here, once Pamela has bathed."

"Yes, sir. Very good, sir." Lucy curtsied again. As she left to draw Pamela's bath, she strained to see in the room one more time. Peter obliged by stepping aside. He rather fancied the idea of Lucy seeing Pamela in his bed. Still chuckling over Lucy's panic, he closed the door.

"Peter, what the bloody devil were you doing?" Pamela sat up in his bed, still holding the quilt under her chin.

"Lucy thought something had happened to you. Your bed had not been slept in and she couldn't find you."

"So you opened the door? Peter Rennard, I am naked in your bed!"

"I know." Peter smiled as he took off his dressing gown. "I'm naked as well."

Still obviously peeved, Pamela allowed herself to be distracted by Peter's bold maneuver. "Peter, I am overcome by your modest reserve." Even as she spoke, her eyes followed his torso down to his groin. His prick responded to her visual touch just as surely as it would to her hand.

"Pams, you do realise, what we are to one another has changed. I am no longer here to replace your father. We are lovers."

Pamela relaxed her hold on the quilt. It sagged, revealing first the deep cleft between her breasts, and then falling to her waist, exposing them. He stared at her voluptuous beauty, his cock thickening at the sight of her.

"You told Lucy to draw me a bath?"

"I did. I thought perhaps the warm water would both soothe you and clean you, after being broken last night. Are you in any discomfort this morning?"

"I have some burning, but nothing terribly uncomfortable." Pamela again focused on his groin, now heavy with a full erection. "I would rather freshen myself before we are again intimate. Perhaps you will join me while I bathe?"

Peter smiled. "Much as David looked upon the beauty of Bathsheba?"

"You do seem to take pleasure in seeing me." Pamela threw back the quilt, allowing Peter a full view of her nakedness.

Without thinking, Peter stroked himself while taking her in. "Oh, yes, Pams, looking at you pleases me."

"Then, come with me and look upon me as I bathe."

Retrieving his dressing gown, he carefully concealed his prick and tied the sash securely. He gathered Pamela's peignoir from the chair and brought it to her. Standing, she turned so Peter could help her slip her arms into the sleeves.

"Oh, dear!"

"What is it, Pamela?"

"I've soiled your bed." Pamela pointed to a bloodstain beside the crumpled towel lying on the bed. "The towel must have dislodged once I fell asleep. I am so sorry."

Her obvious embarrassment touched Peter. Wrapping his arms around her, he leaned in close to her ear. "Darling Pamela, I have never before had anything so beautiful grace my bed. That is a symbol of our connubial commitment. The law may not yet recognise our marriage, but the marriage of our spirits has been consummated."

"Peter, do you mean that?"

"With all my heart, Pamela. No other woman has ever been to me what you are. To finally be able to say that outright is a blessing from heaven."

"It is also a blessing from heaven, dear Peter, to know you desire me as much as I desire you."

"Pamela, I daresay, more. Much, much more."

"Let it always be so."

"Considering over the last six years, I have lived with it every day, I do not expect it to diminish anytime soon!" Peter hugged her tightly. "Now, my lady, let us see to your bath."

Peter escorted Pamela to the water closet. The door stood open. Lucy knelt over the tub, stirring scented salts into the water.

"Thank you, Lucy. That will be all."

Lucy started when she heard Peter. Quickly standing, she wiped her hands on her apron. "Sir?" She turned to see Peter standing in the door, with Pamela beside him. Her eyes fixed on Pamela wearing nothing but her peignoir. "Miss?"

Pamela tried to explain. "Lucy, Peter will help me with my bath today." Lucy stood immobilised, rendered speechless by the situation.

Peter again dismissed her. "Lucy, that will be all."

"Peter . . ." Pamela's chastising tone surprised him. Hugging her peignor tightly around her, Pamela walked across the room to where Lucy stood. "Lucy, things have changed. Master Rennard has asked me to marry him."

Lucy's shocked expression softened and a smile formed. "Miss, is it really true? You and the mister will be married?" Realising Peter still stood in the door, Lucy corrected herself. "Pardon me, miss. I spoke out of turn."

"It's all right, Lucy." Pamela took her hand. "Yes, it is true. However, there are certain legal matters that must be addressed before we can marry. The wedding may not happen immediately."

"Yes, miss." Still smiling, Lucy curtsied. "I'll be going now. I'll tell May to fix a tray."

Lucy hurried from the room, dodging Peter as she went through the door. Peter closed the door behind her.

"You know, she's going to run to the kitchen and tell May."

"And why shouldn't she?" Pamela bent to test the water temperature. "Unless of course, you intend to withdraw the proposal."

"Pamela, you know better than that. If I had my way, we would be arranging the church today."

"Then why are you concerned? May will be happy we are marrying."

"You don't think Lucy will tell her about finding you in my room? I doubt May will be happy to know we have consummated our marriage before having the ceremony."

"Oh."

"You do have a remarkable gift for understatement." Peter came over to where Pamela stood. "Your bath is cooling. You should take advantage of the warm water to soothe your soreness."

Pamela put her arms around Peter's neck. "You have to take off your dressing gown first."

"And why is that?"

"You aren't the only one who likes to watch."

Peter smirked and shook his head. "Pamela, no one would believe that you could be so brazen."

"I have always been this way with you."

"Perhaps that's why I fell in love with you years ago."

"That's the first time you've said you loved me."

"I told you in that unsent telegram you read."

"You wrote it. You have never said it."

"Pamela Kingston, I do love you. Otherwise, I would not

have asked you to be my wife." Peter kissed her nose as he untied his dressing gown. "Of course, you also affect me in other ways."

Pamela stepped back to better see him. "I am happy about that."

"It is inconceivable to me, Pamela, that a woman of your breeding should be so lusty. I have only ever encountered this with common women, such as those at Nellie's."

Pamela opened her peignoir. Boldly, she walked up to Peter. Putting her arms around his neck, she pressed her naked body against his and kissed him. Without any reservation, Peter held her tightly against him and ardently returned her kiss.

Breaking the kiss, Pamela stepped back and allowed her gown to fall to the floor. With poised delicacy, she slowly stepped into her bath and lowered herself into the water. Peter picked up the peignoir and draped it over a chair in the corner. Coming back to Pamela, he knelt beside the deep, clawfoot tub.

Dipping his hand in the water, he rubbed her belly with his palm. "How do you feel, my lady? Do you have any pain?"

"There is no pain. The warm water is quite soothing."

Peter slid his hand lower and lightly caressed the curls between her legs. "Then, might I help you spend? I did not see to you last evening and would quite enjoy doing so now."

"What about you, Peter?"

"We will see to my needs later. It would give me tremendous pleasure to watch your excitement build in your bath." Peter considered for a moment if he should tell her the whole truth. "Pamela, there are also things I have not yet done."

Pamela feigned surprise and giggled. "Go on! A gentleman such as yourself? Why, captain, it seems by now there should be nothing you wouldn't have done!"

Peter splashed her with water. "Yes, you silly moo, there are still things I have yet to do. Sharing a bath with a lady is one of them."

"You really have never shared a bath?"

"No, I really haven't."

Pamela sat up, wrapped her wet arms around his neck, and playfully kissed him. "Then, I can be the first for you with some things?"

Caressing between her legs, he said softly, "Oh, yes, darling Pams, you certainly can."

Pamela lowered herself back into the water and closed her eyes. "Peter, your touching me as you are is wonderful."

"Show me how much you enjoy it, Pams. Let me see your arousal."

Pamala murmured, "Nellie told me you like to watch women in their arousal."

Peter rubbed her harder and Pamela squirmed. "Did she now? You learned much from Nellie."

Pamela sighed. In a barely audible whisper, she said, "I want to learn more."

"What you want to know you will learn from me, not from Nellie." Peter carefully inserted his finger into her recently violated space. Pamela moaned. "Is there pain?"

"Oh, my, no! It is not pain I am feeling."

Peter smiled and slowly slid his finger out and back into her. "Then show me what you are feeling, Pams."

Pamela pressed down on his hand, wedging Peter's finger in deeper. "Peter, get into the water with me."

"Pamela, there isn't room for both of us."

"Nonsense! This is a sizeable tub. If you sit behind me, I can lean against you. Please, Peter, it will be wonderful."

Doubtful that it would work, Peter reluctantly agreed. "Slide forward and we will try."

Pulling her knees up to her chest, Pamela slid forward. Stepping into the tub behind her, Peter realised he did have enough space to lower himself into the water. Stretching his legs out on either side of Pamela, he settled back against the porcelain, still warm from Pamela's skin.

"Are you properly in?" Pamela remained huddled in the centre of the tub.

"Dear Pams, last evening I was properly in. Now, I'm sitting behind you."

Giggling, Pamela put her hands flat on Peter's thighs and pulled herself backward. "See, I told you this would be simply grand."

Peter wrapped his arms around her waist and kissed her hair. "You are introducing me to pleasures I had never before conceived."

"You see, I've learned much from what I've read."

"Indeed. It seems so. Would you hand me that sponge floating in front of you?"

"Why, of course." Pamela reached for the large bath sponge. She handed it to Peter, then again leaned back against his chest.

With deliberate care, Peter traced sensual circles around Pamela's breasts before slowly moving down her belly. He felt Pamela's breath change as he caressed her vulva with the sponge. As he squeezed her breast with one hand, he swabbed between her legs with the other.

Moving the sponge with a slow up-and-down motion, he could feel her respond. She picked up his rhythm and pressed back against him as he massaged her vulva. Never had he experienced anything quite like the sensation of her wet back rubbing against his thickened cock.

Leaning in close to her ear, he whispered, "Pamela, tell me about what you have read. Perhaps there is more we can do together."

"Peter Rennard, you were ready to lock me up and throw away the key for reading such things. Now, you want to know what I've read?"

"Yes, I certainly do! Now that I understand you are such a curious woman, I want to know what interests you." Peter opened his hand and the sponge floated away. Holding her tightly against him, he dipped his fingers into her fleshy crevice and rubbed. Pamela strained against his arm, trying to move. "I want you to spend, Pamela, I want to feel you spend."

Pamela gasped as he continued to stroke her clitoris. She squirmed and thrashed, splashing water onto the floor. When her climax came, she shouted, "Peter!" and lifted her hips high in the water, her breasts floating above his arm. Her body shook with the force of her genital contractions. She quieted for a moment, and then her muscles contracted again, causing another wave of spasms.

The bath water had grown tepid. Peter could feel the gooseflesh on Pamela's arms as she settled and leaned back against him. "Pams, you are getting chilled. Let us finish here and go back to my room."

"But I want to satisfy you as you have me."

"And you will, after we both warm ourselves." Peter grabbed the sponge. "We must finish your bath."

He quickly washed her back. Squeezing the sponge so that the water would rinse her, Pamela shivered. "The water is cool."

"That is why I want to wrap you in a very warm towel. Stand up." Pamela stood and Peter washed her legs. Kneeling behind her, he caressed her bum before he sponged it down. Even in the cool water, his erection hung heavily from his groin.

He stood behind her and put his arms around her waist. He pressed his cock into the crevice between her arse cheeks. "Pams, might I spend against you?"

"I would rather it be inside of me."

"My dear, we will enjoy one another intimately often, I am sure. Now, it would please me to rub against you." As he spoke, he pressed into her more forcefully, the soft cushion of her bum urging him on. "Push back, Pams. Move with me."

With no hesitation, Pamela clenched her buttocks and swiveled her hips. Picking up his rhythm, she helped him along as he bumped against her. "Peter, I adore how you feel against me. Your member is so thick."

Being too far gone to respond, Peter simply held her tighter and rubbed harder. As he felt the surge of hot fluid move in his bollocks, he grabbed her tit with one hand and held her tightly against him with the other.

Without regard to who in his house might hear him, he bellowed, "Sweet Christ! Yes! Bloody hell! Yes!" as he slammed himself into Pamela's arse. She held steady while he unloaded his balls onto her backside.

Once Peter had his wind, he again found the sponge and finished cleaning both of them. Helping Pamela out of the tub, he noticed the pool of water on the floor. "I'm afraid we've made a bit of a mess in here. Lucy won't be happy."

Pamela smiled coyly. "Oh, I think she might be happier than you think."

Peter wrapped a large towel around Pamela's shoulders. "Perhaps so. Sorry to say, I doubt that happiness will spill over to May."

"How angry do you think she might be?"

"Honestly, Pams, I do not know. We'll have some food, and then speak to her."

"Peter, perhaps I should speak to her alone. She is like my mum, after all."

Peter picked up a towel for himself and wrapped it around his waist. "Pamela, I know you have always thought of her as such, understandably so. But I want you to remember, she is not your mum. She is our cook and housekeeper. She does not dictate what I do in my home. Nor does she have authority over you."

"Nonetheless, I would like to speak to her alone. She will say to me privately what she would not say with you standing beside me."

"I will agree to allow you a few minutes alone while I wait in the dining room. Then, I will join you in the kitchen. I do not want an eruption of emotion over this, from either of you."

"What on earth do you think will happen?"

"I will not allow May to upset you, Pamela. If she wants to continue her employ in my house, she will accept our relationship and not judge it. Nor will I allow her to use your history together to sway your opinions."

"Peter . . ."

"Pams, enough about this for now. Come, I expect Lucy has our morning meal waiting." Peter picked up his dressing gown. "Put this on. It is warmer than the peignoir." He held it open as Pamela slipped her arms though the sleeves.

Peter picked up Pamela's robe. Grateful to find the hallway empty, he escorted her back to his room. Pamela started when she walked through the door. Only then did he see Lucy changing the bed.

Standing behind Pamela, he simply said, "Lucy, that will be all. You can finish the bed later."

Lucy jumped and whirled around. "Sir?" When she saw him in his towel and Pamela wearing his dressing gown, her face turned scarlet. "Oh, my goodness!"

Again, he said, "Lucy, that will be all."

"Yes, sir, quite so, sir." Obviously flustered, Lucy grabbed the soiled linens from the bedroom floor and practically ran to the door. Pamela followed her.

"Pamela!" Peter tried to stop her.

"Hush, Peter." Pamela shook herself free of his hand. "Lucy, wait."

Lucy stopped just outside the door. "Yes, miss?"

"Lucy, it is all right. You were just doing your job." Pamela put her hand on Lucy's arm. "You're shaking. Lucy, truly, it is all right."

"Miss, I am so sorry. I saw the soiled linens when I brought in the tray. I meant to finish changing them before you and the mister came back. I never intended to intrude on your privacy."

"And you didn't. We will have our meal and then come downstairs. You may finish the bed then." Glancing back at Peter with a warning look to mind himself, Pamela gently asked, "Does May know I am in Peter's room?"

"Yes, miss."

"Do you know how she feels about that?"

"I really couldn't say, miss."

"Lucy, I want to know if she is angry at me. Is she?"

"Yes, miss, I believe she might be."

"Thank you, Lucy. You may go now. Oh, yes, you best take a mop into the toilet. I accidentally splashed some water on the floor." Lucy nodded her understanding, curtsied and hurried down the hall.

When Pamela closed the door and turned around, Peter stood there with his arms crossed over his chest, looking quite perturbed. "Pamela, what do you think you are doing?"

"What on earth are you talking about, Peter?"

"Lucy is our maid, a servant in our employ. You owe her no explanation."

"Lucy is also my friend and companion, and I will not have her be made apologetic for doing her job properly."

"You know she is on her way to the kitchen right now to give May a full report on what she has just seen. That will only add fuel to this already explosive situation."

"I told you, I will talk to May."

"And I told you, I will not permit you to be upset by May's view of what we are doing."

"Peter, stop trying to protect me. You told me our relationship has changed. It certainly has. You are no longer my guardian. You are my lover and will eventually be my husband."

"It would be easier for May to accept if we could tell her we will be married within the next month."

"Easier for May or easier for you?"

"Judas Priest, Pamela, you know I do not want to wait to be married. This preposterous idea you have about our marriage waiting until a law is changed is beyond reason!"

In an eerie reflection of her father, Peter saw Pamela's jaw set in the same manner Sir George's would when he intended to take the floor and win. "When we marry and you take control of all my holdings, how will I be any different to you than Lucy? Will I also be a servant in your employ?"

"Pamela, never as long as I have a breath in my body would I think of you in those terms!"

"Then stop thinking of my desire to be independent as preposterous. You do not love me because I sublimate to you. You love me because I do not."

Peter could not deny that what Pamela said was true. Her spirited disobedience had always intrigued him and, now, genuinely captivated him. "Pams, your capacity to be independent has never been in question. I cannot fathom your ever being subservient to anyone, especially to me."

"Then why do you think it foolish that I want to retain my financial independence and be self-reliant?"

"I do not want your money or your land, Pamela. I want you."

"The law says as a married woman, ipso facto, I lose all my rights to you as my husband. Therein, Peter, I lose my self-reliance and my self-respect. I cannot do that, not even for you."

"Even if I promise that privately, you will be the decision-maker about your inheritance and I will abide by your wishes?"

"Peter, you said I did not have to choose, that if I accepted your proposal, I could stay here on my terms. We made a pact last night. If you are not willing to honour that pact, how do I know you would honour your promise?"

"Sir George taught you well."

"Had I been born male, I would be a barrister, just as you are."

"Thank the Lord you were not born male. That would be a pickle, now wouldn't it?"

"Perhaps my body would not welcome yours as it now does, but my mind would be the same. The fact that I am a woman does not make me less than you."

Peter ran his fingers through Pamela's damp hair. "Pams,

there are few individuals, male or female, that have the capacity to meet me head-on as an equal. I daresay, you are certainly among the very few."

"Does Nellie?"

"Your fixation about Nellie is tiresome, Pamela. I do wish you would let it go." Peter turned away, took off the towel and went to the cupboard to retrieve his clothes.

"What about your fixation with Nellie?" Pamela snapped back.

"My what?" Peter turned to face her. "You think I have a fixation with Nellie?"

"Peter, why the fecking devil would you sustain a relationship with her for fifteen years if you did not have a fixation?" Pamela's cheeks flushed with anger. "I'm quite sorry if you find my interest in Nellie irksome. Pardon me if I am curious about a woman who has been a courtesan to both my father and my fiancé."

"Pamela, you have no reason to be jealous of a whore!"

Pamela clenched and unclenched her fists, glaring at him. "Your disrespect for her is disgusting."

Forgetting his clothes for the moment, Peter came closer to Pamela. "Why are you defending a harlot? Neither your father nor myself were her only lovers! She has had innumerable men throughout her life, and hasn't felt anything for any of them."

"I never expected to hear ignorance personified from you, Peter. You are speaking about the woman my father loved and who loved him in return. When she spoke of you, I heard near reverence in her voice." Pamela paused and took a few steps closer to Peter. "She has been your confidante for fifteen years. I only hope to gain the same intimacy with you as she has enjoyed for so long."

They now stood an arm's length apart. Pamela still wore his dressing gown. He wore nothing. The intensity of their exchange had stirred Peter. He could not hide the effect.

"Pamela, Nellie has never once affected me as you do. I

could not reveal my desire to you. I had to find release with someone." Peter spread his arms wide, fully displaying his erection for Pamela. "See what you have been doing to me for many years! There is no other woman that can do this to me. Only you."

Their eyes met for a moment. Pamela slowly lowered her gaze to see his erect cock. "How many years, Peter? How long has this been happening?

"I am ashamed to tell you."

"Tell me, I need to know."

"Since we sat side by side in your father's house playing piano. The first time, I made an excuse about feeling ill and left shortly after."

"You left to see Nellie, didn't you?"

"Yes. I had no one else."

"Did you tell her what happened?"

"Not that night. But I did speak of you on other occasions."

"Did you tell anyone else?"

"Certainly not! This is not something I am proud of, Pamela. I simply could not control it. Obviously, I still can't."

"Peter, there is no shame in our attraction. I, too, have wanted you for a very long time. It is why I waited."

"You've had other opportunities?"

"Yes. But I couldn't give myself to anyone but you. I've known that for many years."

"I'm grateful you waited."

Pamela shook her head. "Papa never knew, did he?"

"No, darling Pams, he never knew. Do you think he would have entrusted your guardianship to me had he known?"

"I suppose I would have been sent to a convent had he suspected."

"Probably so." Peter closed the gap between them and untied the sash on the dressing gown. Opening the gown, he pulled Pamela to him. "I cannot imagine you in a convent. I do not believe celibacy would agree with you."

"Nor do I."

Peter leaned forward and kissed her, gently at first, and then with increasing need. Pamela wrapped her arms around him, digging her fingernails into the flesh of his back.

He kissed her throat and her neck with long-held hunger. Saying it as much to himself as to her, he whispered into Pamela's ear, "God help me, Pamela, no woman has ever been inside me the way you are."

"Show me, Peter. All those times you went to Nellie instead of to me, sweet Jesus, come to me now. Please."

"Pams, are you able to take me inside again? I do not want to cause you any pain."

Pamela pressed her vulva against his leg. Her warm moisture coated his skin. "My body is ready for you, Peter. Please, love me."

"Take off the gown and lie on the bed." Peter opened the drawer in his night table and found a small box containing another sheath. He encased his cock in the sack. "Open your legs wide for me, Pams. You know I like to see."

Pamela spread her legs as he asked. As Peter stood over her, taking in her womanhood, Pamela slowly raised her knees and opened her legs wider. The lewdness of the pose made his cock itch with anticipation.

He lowered himself onto her, belly to belly. "This is rather like getting a bit of mutton from the back alley."

Pamela wiggled underneath him, tickling his prick with her cunt lips. "Why, guvner, I hear tell you be wanting a bit of cunny from a flagger now and again."

"It seems I don't have to go far to find a piece of trade now, do I?" Even as Pamela continued to squirm under him, he bore down on her. His prick entered her swollen flesh with a small pop, and then effortlessly slid in the full length. As his cock penetrated her, Pamela gasped and clutched his back.

Before fucking her in earnest, he had to be sure she had no pain. "Pams, am I hurting you?"

"No. This is glorious!"

"All right then, my sweet strumpet, I will give you a bit of hard for a bit of soft."

"And I'll give you a bit of mutton for a bit of beef!"

Peter laughed, something he had never done in this circumstance. "Pamela, you are truly a delight! It is a rare gift to manage witticisms while fucking."

Before she could come back at him with a sharp retort, he lifted his pelvis and drove himself back into her. Again she gasped and clutched at his back. With her knees in the air, the impact of his pelvis hitting hers caused her hips to tip. The motion escalated his desire.

With each thrust, her pelvis rocked, creating a wave of sensation like nothing he had ever experienced. She allowed him to control the motion, her body pivoting each time he embedded his cock inside her cunt. The night before, he had to hold back, for fear of hurting her. This morning, he finally allowed himself the freedom to fuck her as he had always dreamed of fucking her.

The momentum increased as his need burned in his balls. She stayed with him, keeping pace as he slammed into her. The fire between his legs erupted and a lightning bolt exploded from his cock. He ground his teeth and snarled as he once again claimed Pamela as his own.

Chapter Fifteen

Once they had eaten and dressed, Peter and Pamela went downstairs for their meeting with May. Pamela knew Peter would not allow her to be alone in the kitchen for long, so she decided not to waste any time getting to the point.

Leaving Peter in the dining room, she pushed open the kitchen door. May sat at the table, peeling potatoes.

"Good morning, May."

"Hello, Pamela."

May did not look at her. Pamela sat down in a chair directly across from her. "I want to talk to you about what has happened."

"We have little to say to one another, dearie."

"I think we do."

May continued peeling potatoes and did not look up. "Then say your piece."

Pamela's stomach rolled as she saw the rigidness in May's face. She remembered that expression from her childhood, when May took exception to hearing Pamela cuss at a playmate. Pamela forced that memory back as she said, "Peter has asked me to marry him."

"Is that so?"

"Yes, May, that is so."

"When is the wedding?"

"We haven't yet set a date. There are legal issues about my inheritance that must be handled before the wedding."

"Um-hmm."

"I know Lucy spoke to you."

"She did."

"May, I know you are angry with me."

"Pamela, I am in the employ of Master Rennard. I have no say in his private affairs."

"Perhaps not, but I care about what you think of me."

"Then perhaps you should have considered that before you did what you did."

"What I did, May, I did because it is in my heart. I love Peter and he loves me. There is nothing shameful about that."

May threw a peeled potato in the pot, splashing water onto the table and onto Pamela's dress. Raising her voice more than Pamela would have liked, May chastised her. "I suppose sharing a marriage bed before the marriage is something to celebrate? What do you think Sir George would have to say about that?"

Pamela heard Peter's voice behind her. "If Sir George were alive, he would give Pamela away at our wedding."

May glared over Pamela's head at Peter. "Master Rennard, I will be seeking other employ. There is no need to sack me."

Pamela felt Peter's hand on her shoulder. "May, I have no intention of sacking you."

May pushed back her chair and stood. Looking as intimidating as Pamela had ever seen her look, she spoke her mind directly to Peter. "Miss Constance once told me that if ever I wanted to work for her family, to let her know. I will be sending a letter to her telling her I am ready to move on, and ask if she will employ me."

Pamela started to protest. Peter interrupted her. "Pamela, allow me to handle this."

Pamela, being close to tears, simply said, "Peter, May is like my mum. Don't let her leave."

Everything stopped. A pot hissing on the stove made the only sound. Pamela felt tears slide down her face, but made no attempt to wipe them away. When Peter spoke, his voice held a quiet distance. "May, do you remember the Christmas before Sir George died?"

"Of course I do. I ain't feebleminded yet!"

"We had a conversation on Christmas Eve. Do you remember?" May gave Peter a queer look, but did not say anything. "I see you do remember."

"I do."

"Sir George told you the day before that you would be in my employ once he had passed. He also told you I would be Pamela's guardian."

Pamela looked from one to the other. She knew something had passed between them on that night that she knew nothing about. Glancing at May, she realised May had tears on her cheeks. She wanted to ask what in heaven's name they were on about, but thought better of it. Peter seemed to understand what needed to be done.

Peter continued. "We were all trying to come to terms with Sir George's illness, and that he would be leaving us soon. I came into the kitchen to speak to you privately about Pamela."

"You did." May brushed the tears from her face. Taking the tea towel from the waistband of her apron, she wiped her nose.

"Do you remember what you said to me?"

"I told you this is nonsense, that you would be her guardian. I saw you were in love with her. I told you to tell Sir George you would marry her and be done with it."

"May, that was six years ago. Pamela was only sixteen. You saw my feeling for her and wanted us to marry. Had we married, I would have taken her into my bed straightaway. But I waited."

"You didn't just wait. You sent her away."

"I had to send her away. I did not have the strength to have her under my roof and not in my bed. Now, that Pamela is grown and has had a proper education, I want her to be my wife, if she will have me."

"You have waited this long, why the bloomin' 'ell couldn't you have waited for a proper wedding night?"

"Because I am still not strong enough to have her under my roof and not in my bed. Our wedding must wait, for reasons that are private between Pamela and myself. Our love for one another could not wait any longer."

May studied Pamela for a moment and then sat down. Reaching across the table, she took Pamela's hand. "Missy, I know you've had eyes for this one since the first time he walked in the door. I often thought it a shame that God saw fit to make you so much younger. It seems God is wiser than the rest of us, 'cause He knew that what He joins together cannot be taken apart."

Pamela choked back a sob. She managed to say, "May, I love him with all my heart. I will be his wife legally. I already am in spirit."

Peter added, "We will keep our separate rooms until we are married. For the sake of discretion, we will not reveal our engagement until we have set a date. Until then, our love will remain private and inside this house."

"When do you expect that date to be?" May again wiped her nose with the tea towel.

"I hope soon. Pamela's inheritance is in question. We must make sure her bequest from Sir George is protected before we can legally marry."

"Is that true, missy? Your inheritance is why you are waiting?"

"Yes, May, it is true. It is too complicated to explain right now, but if I hope to keep what Papa left to me, I have to wait to marry."

"I didn't know."

Peter redirected the conversation. "May, if I remember correctly, you don't like Constance."

"She is a prig."

"I've heard that before." Peter squeezed Pamela's shoulder. "Then, I hope we can count on you to stay in our employ?"

"For now. Just don't take too long to have a church wedding."

"We will make arrangements as soon as we can. Pamela will be beautiful in a wedding dress, don't you think?"

May smiled. "I've always said she would be a beautiful bride. I just want to live to see it!"

Just then Lucy came into the kitchen from the back stairs. When she saw Peter and Pamela with May, she stopped short, and then turned to leave.

"Lucy, wait." Peter came around the table. "Do you know where Jack is?"

"Yes, sir. He is in the parlour cleaning the gas lamps."

Turning to Pamela, he asked, "It is such a beautiful summer's day. Would you like to go out and about? Perhaps we could walk though Covent Garden?"

"Oh, Peter, you know I adore Covent Garden. I haven't been there since Christmas last."

"Then get yourself ready. I will tell Jack to bring round the carriage."

Peter leaned over and kissed May on the cheek. "Are we four square, Miss May?"

"Oh, fiddlesticks. You know I ain't leaving. Someone has to have some common sense in this house."

Pamela jumped up and ran round the table. Wrapping her arms around May's neck, her relief poured out. "Oh, I just knew you wouldn't leave! You could never work for that namby-pamby Constance. She would drive you bats!"

May patted her hand. "You best be minding yourself, missy, until you and the mister here are married."

Lucy giggled and tried to cover it with a cough. Pamela kissed the top of May's head. "I'll mind myself. Perhaps you should say the same to the mister."

"There's no point in doing that! He does what he pleases; has ever since I've known him." May gave Peter a pointed look.

"You are quite correct, May. I do what pleases me." With that, he turned Pamela around and kissed her full on the mouth, in front of both May and Lucy. Not saying another word, he left the kitchen to find Jack. They heard him whistling as he made his way to the parlour.

Pamela stared at the door. "Well, isn't that something! He can whistle!"

Lucy grinned. "I told you, miss. Surprised the bejesus out of me."

"Lucy! Mind your manners." May's scolding did not temper Lucy's amusement. "Master Rennard is happy. Men whistle when they are happy."

"Yes, ma'am." Both Pamela and Lucy had to swallow hard to keep from giggling.

Pamela managed to say, "Lucy, would you please come to my room and help me with my hair? I did it myself today. I fear it may come down when I put my bonnet on."

"Of course, miss."

"May, I expect we will be back for dinner. I will check with Master Rennard and let Lucy know before we leave."

Pamela led the way up the back stairs, with Lucy close behind. When they entered the upstairs hall, they could no longer hold in the giggles. Running down the hall like schoolgirls, they burst into Pamela's room and closed the door.

When Pamela had enough breath to speak, she couldn't help but blurt out, "Master Rennard should be whistling a happy tune for quite some time to come!" That set off another wave of laughter, which took several minutes to fully subside.

"Lucy, I really do have to prepare to leave. Peter will be here at any moment asking what is taking so long."

Lucy wiped the tears from her face, now quite flushed from laughing. "Quite so, miss. Sit and I will pin it more securely."

Pamela sat at her vanity while Lucy skillfully rearranged her hair. "Lucy, you haven't said anything about what has happened."

"I told you, miss, I am happy about your engagement. It is meant to be."

"I know you are happy about our being married. That isn't what I meant."

"It is not my place to say more, miss."

"Lucy, I confided in you about my feelings for Peter and what I wanted to happen."

Pamela saw Lucy smile in the looking glass. "Yes, miss, you did."

"You know it happened last evening."

"I know, miss. I saw the stains on the mister's bed."

"Lucy, it is wonderful, more wonderful than I ever imagined."

"The way he is whistling, I suppose the mister thinks the same!" Their eyes met in the looking glass and they both burst out laughing.

Peter knocked on the door. "Pamela, what the devil is going on in there?" Without waiting for an invitation, he walked in.

Pamela spoke to his reflection in the looking glass. She saw him scrutinizing both Lucy and herself. "Do you always walk into a lady's boudoir during her toilette?"

"Not usually. However, it seems I have a licence to do so now, especially when I hear such carrying-on."

Pamela smiled. "I wouldn't let May hear you say that. She could well box your ears for such presumptuousness."

"She won't know I said it, unless, of course, one of you tell her I did."

"I'm not going to tell her. Are you going to tell her, Lucy?"

"No, Miss Pamela, certainly not."

"It seems you both are the mice that took the cheese, from the ribald laughter I heard. Might you share with me what the bloody hell is so amusing?"

"Peter Rennard, there are some female secrets not meant for male ears. Lucy, could you hand me my bonnet and parasol?"

"Yes, miss."

"Peter, will we be back for dinner?"

"Yes, I plan to be. Lucy, will you inform May we will have dinner at six o'clock this evening?"

"Yes, sir. The dining room or the library?"

"The dining room, I do believe. Then May will know all hands are on the table." Peter checked his pocket watch, as was his habit. "Are you ready, Pams? Jack should have brought round the carriage by now."

"I am ready." Pamela slipped her arm through Peter's, adding, "And very willing."

Peter patted her hand. "I am aware."

They rode quietly down Piccadilly, enjoying the day and each other. By half past twelve, they had arrived at the Covent Garden Piazza. They walked past the vendors with their carts, the wagons with flowers brilliant in the summer sun. The sights and smells of the market brought back fond memories for Pamela, of the days when her father would take her there to shop and to see the street performers.

Walking arm in arm with Peter, she remembered the acrobats, the jugglers, the mimes and her very favorite, the puppets. Their antics always tickled her. She chuckled remembering her curiosity about what they did together in the box under the stage.

Peter interrupted her reverie. "Did you see something amusing?"

"No. I simply remembered being here with Papa and watching the street performers." She smiled and squeezed

Peter's arm. "I always imagined the puppets having a secret life under the stage, where they would, shall we say, commit a few indiscretions."

"Pamela, your precociousness only increases with age." He laughed, adding, "Perhaps our circumstance will give us a glimpse of their life under the stage."

Pamela nodded in agreement. "You may be quite correct about that!"

A gentleman walking past Pamela touched her arm. "Pamela, is that really you?"

Lowering her parasol to see the man's face, Pamela recognised him immediately. "Charles? What on earth are you doing here?"

"I expect the same thing you are, enjoying the day."

Forcing herself to remain composed, she turned to Peter. "Peter, might I introduce Charles Capell, the brother of a classmate? Charles, this is Peter Rennard."

"Hello, Peter. How very fine to see you again."

"Hello, Charles."

Pamela, now quite bewildered, asked, "You know one another?"

"Quite so. We met at a party my cousin Constance hosted. Peter was her escort."

Pamela could see the tight line of Peter's jaw at the mention of Constance. She quickly deflected the conversation. "Oh, how charming, and such a coincidence! Peter, Charles graciously escorted me to a party in April. His sister Sarah attended Newnham with me. That is how we met."

"Indeed. That is a coincidence, now isn't it?" Pamela could see Peter's jawline ripple as he ground his teeth.

Conversely, Charles smiled warmly. "Are you back in London now?"

"Yes, I am. It is so good to be home."

Directing his next question to Peter, Pamela's heart sank to her toes. "I say, old man, would you mind terribly if I call on Pamela? I would so enjoy seeing her again."

With rigid self-control, Peter replied, "I daresay that is up to Pamela."

Fully understanding the familial connection to Constance and the need to maintain decorum, Pamela smiled and said, "Of course, Charles. Please drop by for tea tomorrow afternoon and we will talk. That would be one sixty-nine Piccadilly, at the corner of Bolton and Piccadilly." She felt nauseous and thought surely she would vomit.

"Marvelous. I shall do that." He took hold of Pamela's hand and kissed it. "It is delightful seeing you again." Almost as an afterthought, he nodded to Peter. "Good seeing you again, Peter."

Peter nodded in return. Pamela felt his fingertips sink deeper into her arm.

Once Charles disappeared in the crowd, Pamela felt the need to sit down. "Peter, could we find a bench? Or perhaps a café? I am feeling a bit faint."

"We passed a tea shop a few minutes ago. You do look as though you could use a cup of tea."

Pamela nodded, not feeling well enough to speak. Peter led her back through the crowd to the small tea shop, where they sat. He ordered them each some tea and crumpets.

Pamela sipped her tea and ate. As her stomach calmed, she felt more in control of the situation. "Peter, do you have an opinion about how best to handle this?"

"No," he answered flatly.

"You have nothing to say? I find that difficult to fathom!"

"What is there to say, Pamela? Charles will soon inherit his father's title and his seat in the House of Lords. If you marry him, you will be a countess and the wife of the Earl of Essex. Isn't that what Sir George wanted, and asked me to oversee in his absence?"

"Peter Rennard, you are the single most infuriating man God ever placed on the face of this earth!"

"And I am sure you could hire out as the town crier! Pamela, we are in a shop!"

"I wouldn't give a fig if we were in Westminster Abbey! I agreed to see him only because of our situation, for no other reason."

"Indeed!"

"And I intend to tell him the truth, that I am betrothed."

Peter's teacup froze halfway to his mouth. "You can't do that!"

Pamela stood, nearly knocking over her chair. "You just watch me!" She turned and left the shop.

Peter ran after her, nearly losing her in the crowd. Grabbing her arm from behind, he pulled her to the side. Keeping his voice low, he growled at her, "Pamela, what has gotten into you?"

"You did, in case you have already forgotten!"

"What the devil is that supposed to mean?"

"That means we are already married in spirit, at least that's what you told me. One chance meeting with a titled suitor and you are back to singing the same old song."

Peter glanced around, concerned they would be overheard. "Pamela, this is not something we should be discussing here."

"Just answer this for me, Peter. Do you want me to treat Charles as a suitor? Should I let him touch me as a lover?"

With fire in his eyes, he answered her. "If he lays a hand on you, I'll kill the son of a bitch."

"All right then, can you be home tomorrow for tea?"

"Probably. Why?"

"Don't you think I should have a proper chaperon when I take tea in the parlour with Charles?"

"Are you going to tell him about us?"

"I said I would tell him I am betrothed. I didn't say I would identify my intended."

"Do you realise you are courting a scandal?"

"Peter, realistically, whenever we announce our engagement, there will no doubt be gossip. Most of them will thoroughly enjoy being scandalised." Pamela kissed him on the cheek and whispered, "I would give a month's income on my properties to see the expression on Constance's face when she hears the news."

Peter smiled. "I would match that with a month's income on mine." He glanced at his pocket watch. "We still have an hour before meeting Jack at the carriage. Let me buy you some flowers."

Pamela napped during the carriage ride home. Peter woke her only when Jack stopped the carriage in front of the gate.

"Pams, we're home. Wake up."

"We're home?" Pamela lifted her head from Peter's shoulder and squinted when she glanced out the window.

"Yes, we are home. You might want to adjust your bonnet. Tipped sideways as it is, the neighbours will think you've had a bit too much gin."

Peter reached across her to open the door and Pamela swatted his arm. "Smart aleck!"

Jack came around and helped her out of the carriage. He winked at her as she stepped down. Pamela blushed and then returned his smile, knowing Lucy had shared her news.

Once inside, Peter leaned over and whispered in her ear, "We have some time before dinner. I want you to go into the library and wait for me. I will be in directly."

"Why?"

"You'll see." He swatted her bottom. "Tit for tat." Then, he ran up the stairs.

Pamela went into the library and took off her bonnet. She still held the bouquet of violets Peter had bought for her. She poured some water from the pitcher into a glass, then carefully arranged the flowers and put them on Peter's desk.

When he came in, Peter closed the door. He came around to the inside of his desk, opened a drawer, and took out a measuring ruler. Then he moved the glass with the flowers to the windowsill.

"What the devil are you doing?"

"Preparing to discipline you."

"What?"

"It seems you need to be shown what will happen when you have unseemly outbursts in public places. Bend over and put your hands on my desk."

Pamela didn't move. Peter stood with the ruler, lightly tapping it against the palm of his hand. "Pamela, I'm waiting."

"You aren't serious!"

"Oh, yes, I am! I told Lucy we are not to be disturbed, and that we will be out for dinner shortly. May is to hold serving until we are seated." He continued to tap the ruler against his palm. "Unless, of course, your preference will be to stand and take your meal. Now, are you going to bend over?"

Pamela could see he meant to do as he said. "We don't have much time. I don't want May to be cross that our meal is ruined."

"Then I suggest we get down to it. Bend over, Pamela."

With her heart pounding, Pamela put her hands on the edge of Peter's desk. Almost immediately, she felt him behind her, raising her skirt and petticoat. He tucked the hem of her garments under the sash of her dress to hold them up. After hooking his fingers into the waistband of her knickers, he pulled them down to her ankles. He raised each foot to pull them off.

The cool air against her bare skin made her shiver. Peter rolled her stockings down to her knees. "Why are you doing that? Aren't I bare enough for you?"

He answered her with a sharp swat of the ruler against her arse. The sting went directly to her clitoris. "Pamela, you are being disciplined. I am not required to explain my actions. However, you are required to comply with obedience." He tapped the inside of her thighs with the ruler. "I'm going to warm you. Spread your legs wider."

When she did, Peter slid the flat side of the ruler between her legs and rubbed her. She involuntarily pressed herself against the flat surface, trying to increase the pressure. He allowed her to masturbate against the ruler for several seconds.

In a hoarse whisper, she muttered, "My God, Peter, this is lewd."

"Deliciously so, Pamela, as it should be. It whets the appetite before the main course."

Without warning, he smacked her. She lurched forward and moaned. "Pamela! Stay still."

She straightened her back just as the ruler connected again. The wood bit into her flesh, the stroke burning, and then tingling. What had been pain became pleasure, as her already swollen clitoris throbbed with need. Again, Peter smacked her. This time she heard a sound from him that sounded as though he growled.

With each successive stroke, the pleasure and the need increased. "Peter . . ." She moaned his name, a plea for release.

"Tell me, Pamela, tell me what you want." This time the stroke lashed her thighs.

"I want you."

Her bum flamed with heat as he smacked her again. "No, Pamela. Tell me what you really want. You know the words. You have been reading them long enough."

Her breath now coming in short gasps, it took a moment to take in enough air to speak. "I want your prick in my cunt. I want you to fuck me until I scream."

He put the ruler down on the desk beside her. She realised he must be undoing his trousers. Gathering her wits, she asked, "Peter, what about the sheath?"

"Dear Pamela, why do you think I had to go upstairs to my room? I did not forget."

He positioned himself behind her. "Say it again, Pamela, what do you want?"

"Peter, have mercy! I want your cock! I need to spend!"

In the next moment, he buried his full length inside her aching cunt. Slamming his pelvis into her arse, he took her harshly, deliberately. Pamela pushed backward with every thrust, reveling in the sensation of his hardness rubbing her.

The need in her body controlled her. Peter held her hips

and thumped against her hot arse, while she rode his cock. As though possessed by demons, they savagely fucked. Her climax hit without warning. She squeezed her buttocks and thighs as every muscle in her lower body contracted. Peter continued to slam into her as she shuddered. When he shouted, "Yes! Fecking hell! Yes!" she knew Peter had also seen the face of God.

Barely taking time to get his breath, Peter slid out of her. He rolled her stockings back up her thighs and adjusted the garters. Once he picked up her knickers, he gently lifted each foot and threaded it through the leg hole. Before pulling them over her pink bum, he tenderly kissed each cheek. Only after he lowered her skirt and petticoat did he remove the sheath and see to his own clothing.

Once they were both presentable, he glanced at his watch. "Five minutes past six. I hardly think May should be cross. Our tardiness is negligible."

"Do you think she will guess why we are late?" Pamela smoothed her skirt once more, hoping the creases were not obvious.

"Well, sweet thing, if she does, my guess is she would approve of the spanking."

"To be sure, she would not approve of what followed."

"Unless she stood at the door listening, she would not know. Of course, Lucy might."

"I don't mind if Lucy knows."

"Is that so? You have intimacies with Lucy of which I am unaware?"

"Now, Peter, that would be telling." She smiled demurely as they made their way toward the dining room.

At breakfast, Pamela told May they would have a guest for tea that afternoon. Peter asked Jack to collect him at two o'clock, hoping to have a bit of time with Pamela before their guest arrived.

When Peter came home, Pamela had already prepared the

parlour for afternoon tea. May had made her special scones with Devonshire cream and jam, as well as a platter of finger sandwiches and petit fours. The tea would be served once Charles arrived.

Peter surveyed the table, set with his best china. "My, we have outdone ourselves, haven't we?" He reached for a scone.

Pamela slapped his fingers. "Mind yourself. You'll muss my arrangement."

"Pardon me? Isn't this my house?"

"Pardon me! I thought it our house now!"

"So it is." Peter carefully pulled out a scone and re-arranged the rest to cover the empty space. Holding up his prize, he teased her. "Now I have my scone in our house and you have your arrangement in our house."

"Wiseacre!"

"It's my job, to have more wisdom than most. Speaking of which, I had an interesting conversation today with a friend of Richard Pankhurst." He broke off a bit of his scone and handed it to Pamela.

She took it without paying attention or making any attempt to eat it. "What did he say?"

Peter swallowed a mouthful of scone. "You should taste this, it's quite good."

"Peter!"

Peter chuckled. "All right, I suppose you aren't hungry." He took the piece of scone back and popped it in his mouth.

With poise worthy of a fine hostess at an afternoon tea, Pamela walked up to him, gripped his bollocks in her hand and squeezed. Peter nearly choked.

"What the bloody hell are you doing?" Bits of scone fell from his mouth.

"Getting your attention."

Peter removed her hand from his crotch and put the rest of his unfinished scone in it. "You've made your point."

"I thought I might. Now, what did Richard's friend tell you?"

"Now that the Liberal party has won the election and the Grand Old Man is prime minister again, Pankhurst's bill is back on the table. Gladstone has been in contact with Pankhurst directly, asking for a new draft of the Married Women's Property Act. With Gladstone personally behind the legislation, it has a good chance of becoming law."

Pamela clapped her hands. "You see, Peter, I told you. Emmeline thought it would be soon."

"It is a bit of good fortune that Gladstone won the election and the liberals are back in power. Disraeli's conservatives would not have supported Pankhurst."

"I will write to Emmeline this evening. She will surely tell me what she knows about the progress of the bill. And I have yet to tell her I am to marry an older barrister, just as she did."

"Pams, might I remind you again, our engagement is a secret!"

"Emmeline is my friend. I trust her, Peter. She will not give us away."

"I hope not."

"Anyway, we may not have to keep our secret much longer."

"Pamela, Parliament does not act overnight. It may be a year or more before this issue is decided."

"Then, we will wait. In the meantime, you can use your influence to gain votes."

"It's that simple, is it?"

"Of course it is, darling Peter. You are an influential man. I inherited Papa's fortune. You inherited his reputation."

"And his daughter."

"To your good fortune."

"Indeed."

Lucy knocked on the door. "Pardon me, Miss Pamela. Lord Charles Capell is here to see you."

"Yes, of course. Show him in, Lucy, and then please bring in the tea."

"Yes, miss." Lucy curtsied as Charles entered the parlour.

"Charles, how very good to see you."

Charles bowed. "And you, Pamela." He took her hand and kissed it.

Peter had stepped to the side. Making himself known to their guest, he said, "Hello, Charles. Welcome to my home."

Charles, obviously startled, jumped a bit. "Peter! Yes, indeed, thank you." Regaining his composure, he added, "I'm sorry, I didn't see you. I thought you might still be in chambers."

"I excused myself early today, knowing Pamela had arranged tea."

"I see."

Pamela could see the tension between the two men. Assuming her role as hostess, she invited Charles to sit. "Please, Charles, have a seat and I will fix you a plate of May's dainties."

Pamela busied herself at the table, making small talk. "How is Sarah? I haven't seen her since we left Newnham."

"She is well. Doing a bit of writing now, poetry mostly. Father promised her he would find a journal that would take her work, although honestly, I can't imagine who would want it."

Pamela handed him a plate. "Why do you say that? My recollection is that she writes quite well."

"I find her work derivative. I've actually made a game of reading a piece she has written and finding the poet she has mimicked. So far, I am eight for ten. I am still working on the elusive two."

Pamela went back to the table to make a plate for Peter. "Perhaps she is still finding her voice."

"Perhaps so. I expect she will forget the whole business when she finally marries."

Lucy came in with the tea, creating a welcome distraction. Pamela handed Peter a plate, rolling her eyes as she did so. He got her message and engaged Charles in conversation. Pamela felt relieved until she heard his chosen topic. "What

244 P. F. Kozak

do you think of the Grand Old Man being prime minister again, Charles? Quite something, isn't it?"

Pamela gave Peter a cup of tea and a sharp look. She saw the smirk on Peter's face as he sipped his tea. "Peter, I'm sure Charles does not wish to speak of politics."

Charles spoke up behind her. "It's quite all right, Pamela. I don't mind expressing my family's view that his reelection is a travesty. The Queen is beside herself. She confided to my father that she is devastated by Disraeli's defeat."

Pamela muttered, "I'm sure she'll get over it." Peter heard her and chuckled. Fortunately, Charles didn't catch what she said. Without realising it, Charles had just made what she had to tell him infinitely easier.

Handing him his teacup, she sat down beside him. "Charles, I have something to tell you that I believe should be said straightaway."

"What is it, Pamela? You look so serious."

"Let me say it is wonderful to see you again and I hope we can remain friends. But, I have accepted a proposal of marriage from someone else."

"You have? I hadn't heard."

"It is not public knowledge as yet. For personal reasons, we have not yet announced our engagement."

Charles glanced at Peter, who sat quietly sipping his tea. He said nothing. "Do I know your fiancé?"

Pamela blushed. "It would be indiscreet for me to say. Please understand, Charles, I am bound by a promise to him to say nothing until certain private matters are resolved."

He addressed his next question to Peter. "Peter, do you approve of this engagement and give it your blessing?" Pamela held her breath, not knowing what Peter would say.

"Quite assuredly so! Sir George met him before he passed and considered him a prodigy."

"Well, then, Pamela, I offer you my sincerest of congratulations. Of course, I expect an invitation to the wedding."

"I will be sure to send you one, Charles, as I certainly will your cousin Constance. However, I would appreciate your keeping this a private matter until it is announced."

"Of course, Pamela. Anything for you." Charles stood, preparing to leave. Pamela stood as well. He took her hand and kissed it. "Pamela, I want you to know, if for whatever reason, you do not marry this man, I am at your service."

"Thank you, Charles. I will remember."

"Peter . . ."

"Charles . . ."

Pamela saw Charles to the door.

Chapter Sixteen

The Christmas tree stood outside the kitchen door at 169 Piccadilly, propped against the back fence. Peter had Jack put it there last evening after the old wooden tub meant to hold the Norway Spruce cracked when Jack filled it with sand. This being the first year they had a tree large enough to place on the floor, they had nothing else to stand it in.

Pamela asked Jack to get another tub and more candles for the tree, after dropping Peter at chambers. She also gave Jack a letter of permission and asked him to stop at the storage house on Old Compton Street to retrieve the ornaments from her father's house. Now that they had a bigger tree, she could display them. Having the familiar ornaments again would both comfort her and truly make it feel like home.

While they waited for Jack to return, Lucy and Pamela busied themselves hanging garlands of holly and ivy in the doorways and all around the parlour. The house smelled of gingerbread, as May was baking marvelous gingerbread men to hang on the tree. Cranberry stringing would be the next chore to tackle.

"Miss Pamela, where do you want to hang these?" Lucy held up a basket filled with bunches of mistletoe.

"Over every door, Lucy. I bought the whole lot from the vendor yesterday, basket and all."

"Miss, this is plenty of mistletoe, it is. You must be figurin' on a whole mess of kisses."

Pamela grinned. "I am."

Lucy held up a bunch. "Maybe I should hang a bunch in the kitchen and over my door."

"Do you think Jack will notice?"

"He will if he knows what's good for him!"

"Oh, I think he might know what is good for him. We'll see if Peter gets the hint."

"Miss Pamela, all this mistletoe should tell him something!"

"Do you know he has never kissed me under the mistletoe?"

"For Lord's sake, why?"

"Probably because he feared losing control if he did. Now, that isn't a concern."

"You and the mister have quite a time together, I see that!"

"Indeed, we do. He is a changed man."

"Miss, he's happier than I've ever known him to be."

"Lucy, hold the stool while I tack this up." Pamela took a bunch of mistletoe and hung it over the parlour door. They repeated the process over each door, with the library door being the last.

Pamela retrieved a bottle of rum from the library cupboard. "Lucy, run to the kitchen and get us some tea. We are going to have some Christmas cheer while we string the cranberries."

"Miss Pamela, the mister won't be happy you're taking Christmas cheer this early in the day."

"The mister isn't here now, is he?"

Lucy giggled. "No, miss, he isn't."

"And what's the worst that could happen if he did find out? I don't mind if he takes me over his knee!"

"Miss Pamela!"

"Lucy, you must know he enjoys that sort of thing."

Lucy blushed. "Miss, it ain't proper, me talking to you about the mister."

"After our first night together, you made up his bed and saw that he broke me. You've known we've been intimate for many months. I think you see more than you let on." Lucy wiped her hands on her apron, as she always did when her nerves were on edge. "Run and get us the tea now. We'll get on with the decorating."

Once Lucy had left, Pamela stopped at Peter's desk. He kept a tin of sheaths there, as well as several well-used paddling implements. After considering for a moment, she selected the hairbrush and a sheath to take to the parlour. Perhaps she would receive a special Christmas Eve present beside the tree.

Pamela smiled as she went back to the parlour. She discreetly tucked the hairbrush and sheath behind a picture frame on the piano. Certainly Lucy knew Peter spanked her. For several months now, Peter would call Pamela into the library and close the door. Sometimes, he would chastise her for some transgression; other times he would say he had lost patience with her sass.

He would spank her and then make amorous advances, often asking her to disrobe while he watched. His discipline made her burn and he knew it. Always, he would manipulate her into a lustful frenzy before allowing her to spend.

Several times recently, Pamela saw a shadow pass under the library door while she and Peter were enjoying one another. Fortunately, Peter hadn't noticed. Suspecting Lucy to be eavesdropping, Pamela decided she should somehow confront Lucy. Not wanting Peter to catch her listening, she wanted to warn Lucy that Peter could discover her secret. Today, she had the opportunity to offer a warning, if only she could persuade Lucy to speak of it.

An odd realisation came over Pamela while considering how best to handle this. Knowing Lucy might well be privy to these intimate moments excited her. Pamela remembered how it felt to her the day she accidentally saw Lucy and Jack together. Every time she thought of it, her clitoris itched. She wondered if perhaps Lucy felt the same.

She picked up a rosewood music box from the mantel and wound it. Peter had given it to her the Christmas before. It played "God Rest Ye Merry, Gentlemen." When Lucy came into the parlour carrying a tray with the tea, she caught Pamela humming along.

"Miss Pamela, you surely are in the Christmas spirit! You hum almost as good as the mister whistles."

"And isn't it a blessing, Lucy, that after these many months, he's still whistling!"

"Yes, miss, it is. You make him happy, as May said last summer."

"God willing, it will always be so."

Lucy poured the tea. "You can add the rum now. If anyone comes in, they'll just think we're havin' some tea."

"Unless they are close enough to smell our breath." Pamela opened the bottle and poured a healthy dollop of rum into each cup. Handing Lucy one and keeping the other, Pamela held up her cup in a toast. "Happy Christmas, Lucy."

"And a Happy Christmas to you, Miss Pamela. It is a pleasure being in your employ."

"Why, thank you, Lucy. I am quite happy to have you in the house. I need a woman my age here. I adore May, but she can be a bit sour at times."

"Don't I know it, miss. She is cross with me most of the time."

"Lucy, I know her very well. Her bark is much worse than her bite."

"It ain't troublin' me, miss. I know my job and I do it proper. If she sees something I should do better, I listen. Otherwise, I don't pay her no mind when she is sharp with me."

Pamela sat on the sofa and picked up a needle and thread. "Come, sit beside me and let's get to stringing." Lucy gingerly sat on the edge of the sofa and picked up a bowl of cranberries. "Lucy, for goodness sake, relax." She topped off Lucy's tea with more rum. "You obviously need some more Christmas cheer."

"Miss Pamela, you'll have me drunk as a fiddler!"

"I'm sure Jack shares his flask with you, doesn't he?"

"How do you know about that?"

"When I've needed it, he's shared some with me."

"Has he now?" Lucy sipped her tea.

Pamela could see a bit of jealousy bubble up. "I only thought the two of you, being as close as you are, would share a little more than a pint."

"That we have."

"Like the mister and I have?"

Lucy glanced at Pamela, no doubt weighing whether she should say more. After taking another sip of tea, Lucy nodded. "Jack fancies me like the mister does you."

Pamela continued threading her cranberries. Lucy leaned back on the sofa and began threading her bowl of berries.

"Lucy, does Jack ever spank you the way Peter spanks me?" Pamela hoped the matter-of-fact tone of her question would encourage Lucy to share her experience.

"Sometimes."

"Do you like it?"

Lucy blushed, but answered honestly. "Yes, miss, I do."

"So do I."

"I know, miss."

Pamela finally had an opening. "Do you hear us sometimes, in the library?"

"Sometimes."

"Then you know a bit of what we do." Pamela shifted on the sofa. The itching around her clitoris had intensified.

Lucy did not look up from her string of cranberries.

Continuing to pierce each berry with the sewing needle, she answered, "You and the mister do go on."

"He's very forceful in his ways."

"Do you like that, miss?"

"I do. He makes me tingle all over."

"So does Jack. He's quite the rooster, he is."

"I expect he is. If you don't mind my asking, what does he do that you like?"

Lucy giggled. "Miss Pamela, you shouldn't be asking such a thing."

"And why not? Peter asks me to do all sorts of things with him. I'm curious about what Jack asks you to do."

Lucy blurted out, "He likes to feel my bubbies, he does! He's all the time trying to squeeze them."

Pamela sipped her tea and slid closer to Lucy. "Do you let him?"

"Depends. If no one's around, I'll give him a bit of titty." Lucy glanced at Pamela's chest. "I'm expectin' the mister is fond of yours!"

Pamela giggled. "Lucy, he is a gentleman, but when it comes to getting a handful, I'd swear him to be a sailor from the docks!"

"I know he fancies bubbies, miss. Yours are fine ones, they are! He must be all over you."

"Jack also has an eye for them. It is no surprise he is after yours. They are quite beautiful."

"Thank you, Miss Pamela."

"Would you mind if I touch them?"

"Miss Pamela!"

"Do you remember? You touched mine the day I asked you how best to control my urges, before Peter broke me."

Lucy shifted on the sofa, moving a little closer to Pamela. "I remember, miss. You spent saying the mister's name."

"Lucy, could you please close the parlour door?"

"Certainly, Miss Pamela."

While Lucy walked across the room to close the door, Pamela poured more tea and added yet another dollop of rum to their cups. She also set both bowls of cranberries on the floor.

When Lucy came back to the sofa, Pamela patted the spot beside her. "Sit here, Lucy." Lucy sat next to Pamela, so close her apron draped across Pamela's leg. Reaching across Lucy's lap, Pamela picked up the teacup and handed it to Lucy. "I warmed the tea. Have a bit more."

Lucy took the cup and again glanced at Pamela's chest. "Miss, you can touch my bubbies if you want."

Pamela caressed Lucy's breasts with the back of her hand, as Peter had done to hers so many times over the last months. "And you can touch mine if you have a mind to touch them."

Lucy reached out and ran her finger down the crevice between Pamela's titties. "Miss, if I might ask, has the mister ever spent here, between them?"

"He did just last week, when I had my cycle." Pamela took Lucy's breast in her hand. "Does Jack with you?"

"He fancies rubbing almost as much as the mister." Lucy's face turned bright red and she pulled her hand away. "Oh, miss, it's the rum. I spoke out of turn."

Pamela put her arm around Lucy's shoulders and pulled her close. "No, Lucy, you didn't speak out of turn. I know Peter came to you for release before I came home." Pamela continued to caress Lucy's bosom. "I also know you sometimes listen to us. I've seen your shadow outside the library door."

Lucy looked horrified. Clutching her apron, she appeared about to cry. "Oh, miss, please don't tell the mister! He'll sack me for sure."

"Lucy, it's all right. I won't tell him. But you have to be more careful, so Peter doesn't notice."

"Miss Pamela, I won't do it anymore, I promise."

"I don't mind. I rather fancy the idea that you enjoy listening to us."

"You do?"

Pamela pinched Lucy's nipple through her dress and Lucy sighed. "Do you remember when I touched myself that day, when I spent in front of you?"

"Oh, yes, miss, I remember quite well."

"Do you ever touch yourself while you listen to us in the library?"

"I want to, but I wait till I get back to my room. I surely don't want to get caught!"

Pamela leaned quite close to Lucy's ear. "Do you ever tell Jack what you've heard?" Being so close to Lucy's neck, Pamela had the urge to lick it, as she would Peter's.

Lucy's breathing changed as Pamela continued to knead her breast. "If the mister really wallops you, I'll tell him. He likes to hear about when the mister takes the ruler to your bum."

Pamela gave in to the compulsion to run her tongue along the side of Lucy's neck, and then kiss her ear. "Does Jack spank you when you tell him the mister has spanked me?"

"Yes, miss. He gets randy when I tell him what I hear."

"Does he? What else have you told him?"

"I told him how the mister rubs against your bum, instead of always putting it in you, so you don't conceive. The mister gave Jack some sacks to catch his spunk, so we wouldn't conceive. But since Jack fancies rubbing on my titties and bum, I let him, knowin' I won't get with child that way."

Pamela sat up and began unbuttoning the front of her dress. "Sip your tea, Lucy." Lucy did as Pamela asked. "Would you do something for me if I asked?"

"Miss Pamela, you know I will."

"Will you let me rub my bare bubbies against yours?"

"Miss Pamela, are you drunk?"

"Perhaps. But I am more stirred than drunk. In school, the girls would sometimes touch each other. I haven't had anyone here I could ask. But maybe we can."

Lucy watched as Pamela undid her dress and lowered it to her waist. Her titties hung heavily in her camisole. Lucy stared at them as though in a trance. Slowly she reached up and untied the string holding up the bib of her pinafore apron. She unbuttoned her dress and then stopped. "Miss, there is nothin' under my dress."

Pamela understood. "That's all right, Lucy." With no hesitation, Pamela pulled off her camisole, allowing her bare breasts to tumble free. "Now, you."

Lucy pulled her arms out of the sleeves and lowered the top of her dress, exposing her bare bosom. "Miss Pamela, I've never felt like this before, except with Jack." She shyly looked away. "It feels good."

"It feels good to me, too." Picking up Lucy's hand, she put it on her bare breast. "Lucy, touch my bubbies, the way Jack touches yours."

"Miss, Jack touches them and he suckles."

The itch between Pamela's legs became a pulse-beat. "Would you like to suckle me, Lucy?"

Lucy squeezed Pamela's breast, her fingertips sinking deep into the soft flesh.

"Oh, my, miss, could I?"

"It would excite me terribly, Lucy, to feel your mouth on me."

Lucy leaned over and kissed the top of Pamela's breast. With feather-soft kisses, she slowly moved down the curve of her bubbie. Pamela cupped Lucy's breast in her palm, and then pinched her nipple. Lucy moaned, her warm breath heating Pamela's skin. Sucking Pamela's hard bud into her mouth, she made a sound like a kitten mewing at a mum cat's teat. Pamela closed her eyes, losing herself in the carnal sensation.

Jack walks into the parlour, continue reading
Peter walks into the parlour, turn to page 262

A male voice cut through their sapphic intimacy. "Well, now, isn't this a fine kettle of fish?"

Lucy jumped so forcefully she nearly fell off of the sofa. Unsuccessfully pulling her apron bib over herself, she gasped out, "Jack Sims, what the bloody hell are you doing here?"

Jack stood in the doorway, holding his open flask of gin, and grinning at the two women. "Master Rennard told me to get the tub and bring it back straightaway. He wanted me to put up the tree, so Miss Pamela could do some decorating today." He paused to belt back some gin before adding, "I'm to stop at the storage house on my way to fetch him home."

Pamela made no attempt to cover herself, rather enjoying the way Jack looked at her. Jack put the cap back on his gin. She pointed to his flask. "Aren't you going to offer us some of that?"

Jack pointed to the open bottle of rum. "Seems you should be offering me some of that!"

"Jack!" Lucy could hardly contain her anger. "You'll be getting us both sacked, you will!"

Pamela patted Lucy's hand. "It's all right, Lucy. No one is getting sacked. Jack is quite right. I should be offering him some of our tea."

Still making no attempt to cover herself, Pamela held her teacup out to Jack. "Here, have a sip."

Jack closed the parlour door. Coming over to the sofa, he took the cup. Smelling it, he said, "There ain't much tea in this!" He drank it in one gulp.

Lucy watched Pamela closely. Seeing her lack of modesty, Lucy dropped her apron, fully exposing her breasts. "Miss Pamela, could I have some more?"

"Certainly, Lucy." Lucy held up her teacup and Pamela poured more rum into it. "Lucy, perhaps Jack would care to sit between us." Pamela slid over to the side. Lucy, following Pamela's lead, slid to the other side. Patting the cushion between them, Pamela invited Jack to sit.

Setting his flask beside the open bottle, he helped himself to more rum. After filling the cup, he sat down between the two ladies. Raising his cup, he said, "Happy Christmas, Miss Pamela. Happy Christmas, Lucy." He downed the contents of the cup and set it back on the tray.

Lucy sat on the edge of the sofa, glaring at Jack. "What the fecking devil do you think you're doing?"

"Miss Pamela invited me to sit. So I sat." He reached out and groped her bare breast. "Seems to me I should be asking you the same question. I didn't know you fancied Miss Pamela."

"You bleeding sod!" Lucy put down her cup and stood, trying to put her arms back into her dress.

Pamela quickly rose and went to her. "Lucy, wait!" Without regard to Jack sitting there watching, Pamela embraced Lucy. Their bare breasts touched and fire moved through Pamela's chest. Holding her close, Pamela whispered, "Don't leave."

"He ruined it, miss. I can't with him here."

Pamela soothed her. "Yes, you can." Responding to the compulsion that bubbled up inside of her, Pamela kissed Lucy full on the mouth. Obviously surprised by the contact, Lucy jerked to the side and fell back onto the sofa.

Lucy scrambled to stand and Jack held her down. "Lucy, mind yourself! If Miss Pamela wants to kiss you, it seems to me you should let her do it."

Pamela, being too stirred and too drunk to think about the impropriety of her actions, knelt on the floor in front of Lucy.

Bending forward, she tenderly kissed Lucy's breasts. Imploring her to stay, she said, "Lucy, please, don't leave. I adore how this feels, being with you like this."

Pamela felt Jack's hand on her arse, pulling at her skirt. She could hardly believe it when he said, "Lucy, wouldn't you fancy watching Miss Pamela spend?"

Lucy took a deep breath. "Miss, he means it. If you don't want him to touch you, you best be telling him to sod off!"

Pamela did not respond. Instead, she leaned against Lucy, their breasts pressing together. Wrapping her arms around Lucy's neck, she kissed her again. This time, Lucy did not resist. She returned the kiss. Pamela lost herself in the kissing, and pushed her tongue into Lucy's mouth.

Jack lifted Pamela's skirt and petticoat. Pamela opened her legs wider, so Jack could wedge his hand between her legs. "Play with her bubbies, Lucy. I'll tickle her clit."

Lucy grabbed one of Pamela's dangling titties and pinched her nipple. Pamela moaned. She felt Jack looking for the opening in her knickers. Immediately upon finding it, he pushed his hand inside and tickled her vulva with his fingertips. Pamela pressed down on his hand. "Lucy, Miss Pamela wants it bad."

Lucy pinched her nipple again. She breathed her question into Pamela's mouth. "Do you, miss? Do you want Jack to rub you?"

"Merciful heaven, yes, Lucy, I do."

"Do you want him to paddle your bottom first?"

"Oh, Lucy, yes!"

"Jack, Miss Pamela likes to be walloped. She wants you to slap her bum."

"Well, now, is that a fact?" Jack gestured to Lucy to have Pamela bend over the back of the sofa.

"Miss, Jack is willing, if you kneel over the back of the sofa."

Pamela crawled onto the sofa. Kneeling on the cushion,

she leaned over the back, with her arse up in the air. Her titties dangled heavily from her chest.

Jack tucked her skirt into the waist of her dress. "Lucy, take her drawers off."

Before pulling them down, Lucy asked, "Miss, is it all right if you are bare?"

Pamela's clitoris throbbed between her legs. "It is quite all right, Lucy. It excites me."

Lucy peeled Pamela's knickers down her legs and pulled them off. Pamela opened her legs wide, in anticipation of the spanking. Jack opened his trousers, exposing his rock-hard cock. Pulling off his belt, he instructed Lucy, "Go around and kiss her. She'll like that."

"You ain't going to fuck her, Jack!"

"The guvner will take care of that bit of business. I'm going to fuck you, my fuckable bit of stuff. Miss Pamela can watch, if she has a taste for it."

"You feckin' bugger! You're as ornery as a tomcat!"

"With what I walked in on, I have a right to be!" Jack folded his belt in half and brought it down across Pamela's arse. Pamela groaned.

Lucy, now in a state herself, chastised him as she went around in front of Pamela. "Don't you be leavin' no marks that the mister will see!"

"I'll be easy on her." He smacked her again.

Lucy retrieved a chair and sat down in front of Pamela. "Are you all right, miss?" Pamela nodded. "Would you like me to kiss ya and pinch your bubbies?"

Pamela whispered, "Yes . . ." just as Jack whacked her again. The sting shot through her and she lurched forward.

"Jack!" Lucy snapped at him. "You said you'd be easy on her."

"I am. Ain't it obvious she's wantin' this?"

Pamela managed to say, "He's right, Lucy. I'm on fire. Kiss me."

Lucy did kiss her, sweeping the inside of Pamela's mouth with her tongue. Each time Jack brought the belt down on her bum, the scorching heat between her legs grew hotter. Lucy twisted her nipples between her thumbs and forefingers, drawing the heat into her chest.

Gasping for air, Pamela pulled her mouth away from Lucy's. "Lucy, I want to watch Jack fuck you. Are you willing?"

"Oh, yes, miss. I would fancy a good poke right now."

"Let's switch places."

Lucy scurried around the sofa. Jack brought the belt down on Pamela's arse one more time before helping her stand. Pamela wobbled. "Miss, can you manage?" Jack held her arm as Lucy took off her drawers and knelt on the sofa where Pamela had been. She pulled up her skirt and opened her legs wide, as Pamela had done.

"I'm quite all right, Jack. But I do need to spend."

Jack grinned. "I'd be happy to oblige, miss."

"I'm sure you would. I can manage myself while you take care of Lucy."

"Certainly, miss."

Pamela went round to the back of the sofa and sat in the chair. Knowing that both Lucy and Jack could see her plainly, she pulled her skirt up and slipped her fingers into her slick pussy.

Unexpectedly, Jack cracked the belt against Lucy's arse. "Loosen it up, my sweet biscuit." Jack slapped her again. "Open your arse up for me, like you have before. I'm going to have me a bit of bum."

"Good Lord, Jack, you're not!"

Jack cracked her again. "Oh, yes, Lucy, I am. Your tight arsehole is begging for some cock."

Pamela saw him watching her frig herself. She pressed her stinging bum against the seat of the chair and propped her feet on the back of the sofa. With her legs spread wide for both Lucy and Jack to see, she pushed two fingers into her cunt.

"You see, Lucy, Miss Pamela wants to see me give it to you up the arse." He tossed his belt onto the sofa. He cupped her vulva in his hand. "Your pussy is so frigging wet, you got plenty to grease up your arse." With his fingers coated with Lucy's moisture, he shoved three fingers into her arse. "Relax, Lucy. You know it hurts if you tighten up."

Pamela diddled her clit, anticipating the sodomy. Lucy's titties jiggled as Jack finger-fucked her arsehole. Lucy closed her eyes and moaned. Withdrawing his fingers, Jack slapped Lucy's arse several more times, kneading her bum between each slap. Cupping his hand under her cunt again, he took her wet to slick up his cock.

Positioning himself behind Lucy's arse, he positioned the tip of his prick against her anus. When the tip of his cock entered her arse, Lucy groaned loudly. Pamela finger-fucked herself watching Jack slide his prick into Lucy's bum.

When he had his cock buried deeply into her rectum, he reached around and grabbed her titty. "I'm going to fuck you until Miss Pamela spends. You best be watching her frig herself real close, now. Maybe you'll have yours when she does."

Lucy focused her eyes on Pamela's cunt while Jack rammed his prick into her arse.

The scalding heat in Pamela's belly could barely be contained as she watched Lucy being fucked. Jack showed no mercy, as he forcefully buggered her. Lucy pushed her bum back each time Jack rammed his prick into her. Delirious with arousal, Lucy climaxed. She squealed and dug her fingers into the back of the sofa, her body trembling uncontrollably.

Seeing Lucy in the throes of her ecstasy triggered Pamela's release. She jabbed her fingers deep into her cunt and lifted her arse off of the chair. Pamela moaned softly, her pelvis thrust upward as waves of pleasure washed through her body. She opened her legs wide for Jack to see.

Lucy had gone limp over the back of the sofa. Jack continued to pound himself into her arse while staring at Pamela's cunt. When he emptied himself into Lucy, he shouted, "Cunting hell! Yes!" and banged his prick into her arsehole half a dozen times.

Pamela drifted back to reality and lowered her legs. Jack still had Lucy pinned over the back of the sofa, his cock buried in her arse. Lucy had her eyes closed. "Lucy?" Pamela stroked her breast. "Are you still in there?"

Lucy sighed. "Oh, yes, Miss Pamela, I'm here."

Pamela smiled. "Good." Leaning forward, she kissed Lucy on the lips, a gentle kiss meant for a lover. "Thank you, Lucy, for sharing this with me."

"Miss Pamela, I have never been so satisfied." Lucy winced as Jack pulled himself out of her. "Now you know one of the ways we use to not conceive."

"I'll have to suggest it to Peter."

Jack cleaned himself with his handkerchief. "If you hope to keep us in your employ, I wouldn't be telling him where you got the idea."

Pamela laughed. "Not to worry. This is our secret."

Go to page 270

Within the misty haze of rum and arousal, Pamela thought she heard the parlour door's hinge squeak. Not wanting to break the spell of Lucy suckling her, she dismissed it as being her imagination. When she heard the door click shut a few moments later, she bolted upright, nearly knocking Lucy onto the floor.

"Peter!"

Peter stood just inside the closed parlour door, his arms crossed over his chest. "Hello, Pamela." Nodding at Lucy, he simply said, "Lucy."

Lucy tried to put her arms back into the sleeves of her dress, only to find they were turned inside out. While she struggled to untangle them, Pamela continued to stare at him in disbelief.

"You are supposed to be in court all day. What are you doing here?"

"Even though I do not owe you an explanation for entering my own house, I will explain. My scheduled session in court was cancelled due to the illness of a key member of the hearing. Rather than going back to chambers, I came home to help you with the Christmas tree."

"Where is Jack?"

"I expect off doing the list of errands you gave to him. I flagged a hansom cab to bring me back."

Lucy, being too flustered to fix her dress, held the bib of her apron to her chest, only partially covering her bare breasts. Her voice quivering with fright, she asked Pamela, "Miss, may I please be excused?"

Before Pamela could answer, Peter replied, "No, Lucy, you may not be excused!"

Not making any attempt to cover herself, Pamela snapped at him. "Peter, don't you dare frighten the poor girl. This is all my doing."

Peter strode across the room, his bearing even more intimidating than usual. His voice had an edge when he spoke. "Pamela, I have no doubt whatsoever that is the case." Turning to Lucy, he softened his tone. "Lucy, I am not angry with you. As long as you cooperate, you are in no danger of being sacked."

Blinking back tears, Lucy muttered, "Sir?"

"Peter, let her go. Do what you would with me. The responsibility is mine. Lucy is not at fault."

"Hush, Pamela. Mind yourself and be quiet. I'm speaking to Lucy."

"How dare you take that tone with me!" Pamela stood to leave, furious with his cavalier dismissal. Pulling her dress up to cover herself, she took several steps toward the door.

"Pamela!" The sharpness in Peter's voice caused her to stop in mid-step. "If you wish for Lucy to stay in our employ, you will come back here and sit down!"

Lucy whimpered, "Miss Pamela, please."

Pamela came back to the sofa, glaring at Peter. "I've never known you to be so cruel. Let her go."

"I am not of a mind to be cruel. But I do believe the two of you have some penance to do in order for this to be forgotten."

Pamela lowered herself to the sofa beside Lucy. Allowing her dress to once again fall to her waist, she put her arm around Lucy's shoulders. "What are you talking about?"

Peter hunkered down in front of Lucy. Taking her chin between his thumb and forefinger, he lifted her head. "Lucy, look at me."

Brushing the tears from her cheeks, she looked at Peter. "Yes, sir?"

"Lucy, when I came in, you seemed to be enjoying Miss Pamela. Is that correct?"

Lucy whispered, "Yes, sir."

Peter let his hand fall from her chin to her apron. He tugged it away from her hands and it fell to her waist. Her bare breasts hung deliciously close to his face. "Would you like to enjoy her some more?"

Pamela hugged Lucy closer. "Peter, what are you doing?"

Peter answered with cool control. "Only what you seem to

want." He turned back to Lucy. "It would be exceptionally satisfying for me to watch you and Pamela together. Would you do that for me, Lucy?"

Lucy glanced at Pamela, not knowing how to respond. Peter also looked at Pamela, their eyes meeting in vaporous heat. An unspoken understanding passed between them.

"Lucy . . ." Pamela spoke softly, her voice seductive. "If we do as he asks, I promise this whole embarrassment will be forgotten. Peter, tell her."

Peter smiled, knowing he had Pamela's acquiescence. "Lucy, Miss Pamela speaks the truth. All you need do is what I ask of you and what has happened will not leave this room."

"You won't tell Jack?"

"I promise not to tell him. Will you do it?"

"What do you want me to do?"

"Nothing more than what you were already doing. It was quite tantalising."

Pamela took Lucy's hand and placed it on her breast. "Lucy, Master Rennard wants to see us together. Entertaining him would be quite exciting, don't you think?"

Lucy moved her head closer to Pamela's. In barely a whisper, she said, "Yes, miss, it stirs me, it does."

Pamela's lips brushed Lucy's. She whispered back, "As it does me, Lucy. Let's give Master Rennard an early Christmas present."

"Yes, miss." Lucy breathed the words into Pamela's mouth as their lips met.

As Lucy and Pamela kissed, Peter sat in an overstuffed armchair facing the sofa. He settled in, knowing his afternoon's entertainment would be much more pleasant than he could have imagined.

Lucy caressed Pamela's breast. Pleasure rippled through his groin hearing Pamela moan. It seemed Pamela's carnal hunger grew more voracious with each passing day, her appetites rivaling his. Her seduction of Lucy, albeit unexpected, did not surprise him.

He sat quietly for several minutes, letting their passion build. As Lucy leaned over to suckle, he stopped her.

"Lucy, help Miss Pamela remove her dress, and then she will help you remove yours."

"Yes, sir." Lucy's face flamed red, but she immediately set to the task. She unbuttoned the last few buttons and tugged the dress from the bottom. Pamela lifted her bum, so Lucy could pull off the dress and the petticoat, leaving her in only her stockings and drawers.

With no hesitation, Pamela turned Lucy around to undo her apron strings. Lucy stood and faced Peter, practically touching his knees. Pamela stood behind her. Peter stroked himself, watching Lucy's breasts rise and fall with her breath as Pamela took off her dress.

"Pamela, put your hand inside Lucy's knickers and stroke her."

Pamela caressed Lucy's belly. "Is that all right, Lucy? May I touch your private parts?"

Lucy didn't answer. Instead she put her hand over Pamela's and guided it to the waistband of her drawers. Together, their hands disappeared inside. Lucy leaned back against Pamela and sighed. Peter, watching the rhythmic caresses inside Lucy's knickers, felt his cock twitch inside his trousers.

He noticed Pamela staring at his crotch. While she watched, he exposed his prick. Lucy's eyes remained closed, her pelvis undulating against Pamela in a most provocative rhythm. Pamela moved with Lucy, beguiling him with a salacious dance. Silently, Peter gestured to Pamela to pull down Lucy's knickers.

With her free hand, Pamela tugged the already loosened drawstring. Lucy started. Pamela kissed her shoulder. "Master Rennard wants to see you, Lucy. You are quite lovely."

Lucy blushed so furiously even her chest turned pink. She

saw Peter stroking himself, watching her. With wanton abandon, she undid the string herself, allowing her drawers to fall to the floor. She kicked them off.

"Now yours, Pamela. I want you both bare." Peter's usually smooth voice sounded throaty and low-pitched, his arousal evident. He could smell their female musk. He reached out and traced a vertical line the length of Lucy's vulva. "Pamela, spread her open."

Cradling her pelvis against Lucy's bare bum, Pamela reached around and pressed her fingertips into Lucy's swollen lips. She opened her labia, revealing Lucy's rosebud to Peter. He gently diddled her clitoris with his finger, carefully examining the pink flesh. Lucy moaned and pressed backward into Pamela.

"Lucy, I want your help now." She didn't respond to him. She continued to lean against Pamela, her legs splayed indecently. "Lucy!" His sharp tone sobered her.

"Yes, Master Rennard?" She closed her legs and attempted to stand straight. "I beg your pardon, sir. I didn't hear what you said."

"I need your help now."

"Sir?"

He reached around Lucy and took Pamela's hand. "It is time for Miss Pamela to receive her comeuppance. Would you help me?"

Again, Lucy looked to Pamela for permission.

"Lucy, we are here to please Master Rennard. If he requires your assistance, then he shall have it." Pamela stepped around Lucy and knelt in front of Peter. "Lucy, behind the picture frame on the piano, you will find something I put there. Please get it for me and give it to the mister."

Completely forgetting that she had nothing on, Lucy quietly went to the piano. She found the hairbrush and the sheath behind the picture. She brought them back and gave them to Peter. Then, she stepped off to the side and waited.

"Now why on earth would you have these in the parlour?"

"I hoped to have them here for Christmas Eve. But perhaps they would be useful now."

"Pamela, you are a constant source of amazement. It is quite extraordinary having my charge, my fiancée and my courtesan bundled up in one beautiful package." He handed the hairbrush back to Lucy. "Lucy, you are in charge of the paddling."

Lucy took the brush. "Pardon me, sir, I don't understand what you are askin' of me."

As Peter took off his jacket and waistcoat, he explained. "You see, Lucy, Miss Pamela has been quite wicked, taking advantage of you as she has." He opened his shirt. "She must now suffer the consequences of her actions. It seems only fitting that it be at your hand."

"Pamela, I want you to kiss my prick while Lucy spanks you. You will show me how sorry you are for seducing Lucy and compromising her position in our household."

Pamela scratched her fingernails down his chest to his groin. Peter stifled a groan, his prick throbbing at her touch. She whispered softly, "Your organ is quite thick and terribly purple. I will do more than kiss it, if you wish."

Peter ignored her flirtatious invitation. "Lucy, please give Pamela ten strokes with the brush, and then frig her with the brush handle."

"Merciful heaven!" Lucy could not contain her astonishment.

Peter fondled Pamela's breast while he spoke. "Lucy, Miss Pamela welcomes the punishment for her outrageous behavior, don't you, Pamela?"

Pamela answered by bending down and kissing his erection.

Peter relaxed into the chair, Pamela's breast filling his hand. "Lucy, I'm waiting. Do it."

With some hesitation, Lucy lightly brought the brush down on Pamela's arse. Peter barked, "For God's sake, Lucy, you are a strong girl. Put some force into it!"

Lucy took a deep breath and brought the brush down again. This time, the sting made Pamela yelp.

"That's better. Now, give Miss Pamela time to kiss my prick before the next stroke."

By the sixth stroke, Pamela's moans filled the room. By the ninth stroke, her legs had opened and her arse jutted upward, wanting his prick inside of her. The tenth stroke landed. Her now pink bum undulated against his knees.

In a hoarse whisper, Peter said, "Now frig her."

Lucy turned the brush, the round handle warm and slick from her sweaty hand. Positioning the end at the entrance to Pamela's cunt, Lucy slid the handle inside. Pamela pushed backward and groaned. Again kissing Peter's cock, she pleaded with him. "Please, I want you inside me. Fuck me, Peter. Put your cock in me, not the brush."

"Not yet, dear Pams." Lucy continued to slowly push the handle in and out of Pamela's cunt. Pamela pressed her face against Peter's cock and again begged him, "Peter, fuck me before I go mad!"

"Is she ready, Lucy?"

"Oh, my soul, yes, Master Rennard. Her wet is all over the brush and my hand."

Peter slid out from under Pamela. Without regard to Lucy's presence, he took off the rest of his clothes. Pamela remained bent over the chair. While putting on the sheath, he instructed Lucy, "I want you to touch my balls while I fuck Miss Pamela. Understood?"

"Yes, sir."

"Oh, and Lucy . . ."

"Yes, sir?"

"Touch up yourself at the same time. Perhaps you will spend with Miss Pamela."

"I would fancy that, sir."

"As would I, Lucy."

Peter knelt behind Pamela. The moment the tip of his prick touched her, she pushed back on him, shoving his full length inside her. The sensation caused them both to make guttural sounds, which resonated though the parlour. Lucy chose that moment to cup his balls in her hand, sending more flames through his groin.

As Lucy massaged his scrotum, he pounded his prick deep into Pamela's cunt. She twisted and writhed against him, her own passion on the verge of climax. Determined to hold on until Pamela finished, Peter hissed at Lucy, "Touch up Pamela, Lucy. Rub her hard."

Lucy reached between Pamela's legs and rubbed her clitoris, as Peter rammed himself deeply into her. Pamela squealed, "My God, Peter!" Peter held her, his weight preventing her from rising up. She thrashed underneath him, her climax upon her.

Lucy moved to the side of the chair. Peter saw her hand working furiously between her legs. Suddenly, she gasped and thrust her pelvis forward. She struggled for breath, trembling with her orgasm. With both women in the throes of spending, Peter allowed his own fire to move. Slamming against Pamela's soft arse, he filled the sheath.

As the heat of the ménàge à trois subsided, he heard Pamela say quietly to him, "Happy Christmas, my darling Peter."

Chapter Seventeen

During the winter months, Pamela's days were full. Peter gave her carte blanche to decorate as she saw fit. More than anything, she wanted cheerful wallpaper. The choices Peter made years before reflected a dreary, masculine sensibility.

For the dining room, she selected tea rose wallpaper, with brown, green and copper on ivory. She did her bedroom in satin wallpaper with small flowers in burgundy, plum and gold. With some searching, she found a carpenter willing to build a canopy for her bed. She covered it with deep rose material and had curtains made to match.

After reminding Peter that she would soon be sharing the master bedroom, he reluctantly agreed to let her redo his room in a lovely cream damask stripe. Room by room, she went through the house. She replaced or added furniture where needed. In the end, Peter's house became a happier and brighter home because of her presence and her hand.

She also spent time with May, learning how to properly run the household. May insisted that as lady of the house, she had to know everything, including how to cook. Pamela had never been fond of cooking. But with May's patience and humor, she actually enjoyed learning.

When Peter heard Pamela would be cooking the Easter

meal, he offered to have food brought in, thinking May had taken ill. Pamela assured him May was fit as a fiddle. With some trepidation and considerable teasing about the possibility of food poisoning, Peter sat at the Easter table. After his third helping of candied ham and scalloped potatoes, he admitted that Pamela had learned to cook a decent meal.

Now, as they approached the end of Eastertide, Peter's birthday on the twenty-eighth of May would be upon her in a few days. She wanted to surprise him with something. What, she didn't know. A party would be out of the question. Because of their unorthodox living situation, they avoided entertaining and selectively received only a few individuals who wished to call. Once they were married, that would change. But for now, Peter preferred their privacy be maintained.

Pamela sighed. A surprise party for Peter would be delightful. Perhaps she could manage it next year, when surely they would be married. The Parliament had taken the Married Woman's Property Act under advisement. Peter had championed the cause, courting votes whenever possible.

He cautioned Pamela that the final vote might not take place for some months, as the debates were ongoing. Already, revisions had been made to the original bill proposed by Richard Pankhurst.

That left her with the problem: what to do for Peter's birthday? She had never been home for it, her school year ending later in June. This being the first year to celebrate with him, she wanted it to be memorable.

Pamela found Lucy changing the bed linens in Peter's room. "Oh, there you are."

"Yes, Miss Pamela, here I am. Where would you expect me to be?"

"One never knows with you, Miss Lucy." Since Christmas, Pamela and Lucy tended toward considerably less formality when alone.

Lucy giggled. "What do you want of me, miss?"

"I want to know what Peter does on his birthday. Do you have any idea?"

Lucy continued making up the bed. "He's never home on his birthday, miss. Jack takes him someplace every year. They always get home late."

"Do you know where they go?"

"No, miss. Jack has never said. When Jack comes back from taking the mister to chambers, you might do well to ask him."

"Thank you, Lucy."

"Certainly, miss."

Pamela went back to her room and considered the possibilities. It seemed unlikely Peter would have celebrated with Constance. It also seemed equally unlikely he would have gone to his club. Then it hit her. Of course. He most probably went to Nellie's.

When Jack returned, Pamela cornered him in the dining room. "Jack, I have a problem I hope you can help me solve."

"Anything, Miss Pamela. What do you need?"

"Master Rennard's birthday is on Saturday. I asked Lucy what he usually does on his birthday. She didn't know. I thought perhaps you might know." Pamela watched him closely, waiting to see his reaction.

Jack hedged, already confirming her suspicion. "Miss, I really can't say."

"You take him to Nellie's, don't you?"

Jack shifted uncomfortably. "Miss, I'm sure the guvner will be spending his birthday with you this year."

"Oh, but Jack, you miss my point in asking. I want to surprise Peter with a present. What better surprise than to take him to Nellie's again."

"Miss Pamela, you have that devil look in your eyes. Don't you be getting any ideas about going there!"

"Too late, Jack. I've already got them. Bring the carriage around to the gate. I'll be calling on Nellie today."

"Miss Pamela, the guvner told you not to go there. I agree with him. That ain't no place for a lady."

"Jack, we've been through this before. I'm going. Either you will take me or I'll call a hansom cab. But I am going."

Jack ran his fingers through his hair, a sure sign she had bested him. "Miss Pamela, don't do this."

"Jack, I swear you to secrecy. I want to plan a surprise for Peter's birthday. If you tell him where I went today, it will all be ruined."

"He'll be surprised all right! Then he will be mad as hell." Jack shook his head and went to fetch the carriage.

Pamela had not seen Nellie since they first met, nearly a year ago. During that time, she had reread Nellie's letters at least a dozen times. Peter still refused to read them, saying they were a private communication that he had no right to see.

Pamela suspected the reason went deeper than that. Nellie's personal correspondence with Sir George spoke of love and a relationship that lasted for years. They showed Nellie to be a woman capable of profound feeling. Peter deliberately distanced himself from such things.

As far as Pamela knew, Peter had not been back to Nellie's tavern since the day he met her at the train last June. Considering he now had Pamela, the need to seek release at Nellie's had all but disappeared. However, Nellie had been Peter's concubine for many years. She had also offered him friendship and solace when he had no one else. Whether Peter accepted it or not, Nellie was an important part of his past. Pamela wanted to understand that past.

When Jack stopped the carriage in front of Nellie's, he didn't bother opening the door for Pamela. He immediately ran around to the back door to find Henry. It still being morning, Nellie's tavern showed no signs of life.

Pamela let herself out, lifting her skirt to avoid dragging it in the muddy street. She quietly waited at the front door. Jack came round to where she stood a few minutes later.

"Miss Pamela, I expected you to wait in the carriage! You shouldn't be standing in the doorway!"

"Good Lord, Jack. We are alone on this street. What the devil do you think will happen to me?"

Just then, Nellie opened the door. "Bonjour, Mademoiselle Kingston."

"Bonjour, Madame. How very good to see you again. You are looking well."

"*Et vous*. Please, won't you come in?"

Pamela turned to Jack. "Could you please wait at the carriage, Jack? I shouldn't be long."

"Certainly, miss."

Pamela followed Nellie inside. "And to what do I owe the pleasure of this early morning visit, Pamela?"

"I have a favour to ask, Nellie."

"*Sacré bleu*! What could I possibly do for you, Pamela?"

"More than you might think, Nellie." Once again, Pamela found herself entranced by this handsome woman. It seemed inconceivable that she had intimate relations with both her father and with Peter. The undeniable truth of their history together still rocked Pamela to her core. She desperately wanted to experience some of what her father and Peter had shared with Nellie.

"*S'il vous plaît*, tell me, *ma chérie*, what do you need?"

"Saturday is Peter's birthday."

"Ah, yes, so it is. If my memory serves me, it will mark his thirty-sixth year."

"You remember well, Nellie." Pamela gathered herself, preparing to make what now seemed an outrageous request. She hedged. "First, let me tell you, Peter and I are engaged to be married."

"*C'est magnifique!*" Nellie kissed Pamela on both cheeks and then hugged her. "For many years I have waited to hear this news."

The genuine warmth and affection she felt flowing from Nellie filled Pamela. She returned the embrace. "Thank you,

Nellie." Tears slid down her face as she said, "It feels as though Papa is pleased, knowing we have your blessing."

"*Ma petite*, my blessing counts for little. It is your happiness Sir George would see." Nellie's eyes also shone with tears. She quickly wiped them away. "Might I offer you a cup of tea? I recall you find it calming."

"Thank you, yes. A cup of tea would be quite fine."

Nellie called for Henry, who appeared from the supply room behind the bar. "Henry, could you prepare a pot of tea for my guest? You remember Mademoiselle Kingston?"

"I surely do. Good morning, miss."

"Good morning, Henry."

"I won't be but a minute. The kettle is already hot." He disappeared through the side door.

Nellie and Pamela sat at a table off to the side. "Tell me, Pamela, why have you come here?"

Pamela felt awkward, faced with explaining to Nellie exactly what she wanted to do. She blurted out, "Peter and I have been intimate for nearly a year."

Nellie's eyes sparkled. "I suspected as much. I have not seen Monsieur Rennard for quite some time."

Pamela smiled, grateful for the opening. "Exactly right, Nellie. That's why I want to give him a special present for his birthday."

"And what would that be?"

"I want to be one of your girls for a night and receive him here, as a birthday surprise."

"Pamela, that is out of the question!"

"Why should it be out of the question?"

Nellie stood, as though in dismissal. "The daughter of Sir George does not belong in a whorehouse!"

Pamela stood, blocking Nellie's exit. "If you will not do this as a personal favour, then let us make it a business transaction. I will pay you well for the use of one of your rooms for the night, with the understanding I only wish to receive Peter."

Nellie's eyes flashed fire. "Do not insult me, Pamela."

"And I would ask the same courtesy from you. Papa found love in a whorehouse. Peter found friendship and comfort, when he had nowhere else to go. The roots of the family tree run deep. In this circumstance, the sins of my father have been laid at my feet."

"Peter will be livid if I agree to this."

"Yes, I am quite sure he will. That should make our night here lusciously memorable, don't you think?"

Smiling, Nellie visibly softened. Sitting back down, she said, "You are a vixen, Mademoiselle Kingston. I know many gentlemen who would pay handsomely for an hour with a coquette such as you are."

Pamela also sat down. "I am only interested in one gentleman. Perhaps it would be appropriate to request payment from him for the evening's entertainment. I am sure he has paid you well on his birthday for many years."

Nellie laughed aloud. "You know he comes here every year? That is what gave you this idea?"

"My presence in his life is hardly reason to break tradition, now is it?"

"Pamela, he has always needed a special woman in his life. God is good. He arranged a perfect match for my Monsieur Rennard."

"Peter is happier than he has ever been. His whistling in the house has become a source of great amusement to our staff."

Nellie put her hand to her heart. "Pardon? Monsieur Rennard whistles?"

Pamela winked and coyly replied, "He does now."

Again, Nellie laughed. "You are a delight! I see why he is enchanted. Your sorcery has made his head spin."

Henry brought the tea. Setting the tray down on the bar, he poured a cup for each of them. He handed Pamela hers with a bow. When he gave Nellie her cup, he asked, "Do you need anything else, *mon petit chou?*"

"No, Henry. *Merci.*" Henry left them alone, going back to his work in the supply room.

Pamela smiled. "Henry calls you 'his little cabbage'?"

"We have been together for many years. We have, shall we say, an understanding."

"What did Papa call you, Nellie?"

"*Mon amour.*"

"And Peter?"

"Only Nellie. Nothing more. You need not concern yourself about that."

"I want you to know over the last months, I have thought of you often. Your letters have helped me to understand Papa more than I ever did while he lived. I also have come to understand how you helped Peter through many dark nights. Thank you for that."

"You are a gracious woman, Pamela, saying these kind words to an old whore."

"I see beauty in you, Nellie, that I have seen little of elsewhere. I know Papa saw it, too. That is why he loved you."

"Sir George respected me. That is what I hold in my heart. When we see each other again one day, I will tell him what a fine daughter he has."

"God willing, you will also tell him what fine grandchildren he has."

"Now that is a vision! Monsieur Rennard fathering Sir George Kingston's heirs! I do not know if *mon cher* would laugh or cry at the thought."

"Nor do I. Perhaps a bit of both."

Nellie studied her for a moment. "Tell, me, Pamela, what do you hope to accomplish by doing this?"

Pamela spoke her mind to the experienced woman sitting beside her. "With the years of intimate acquaintance you have together, you know Peter in a way I do not. I want to be to him what you are."

"My dear girl, he loves you and will soon marry you. It is not your place to be to him what I am."

Pamela flared. "By God, yes, it is! Once we are wed, I will not be relegated to mistress of the house and mother to his children! He has been coming to you for his pleasure for many years. If I am to be the one he comes to in the years ahead, I must learn the secrets you shared. Otherwise, he will come back to you, or go to someone else."

"You want him to be faithful? Men take mistresses as a matter of course."

Pamela stood and paced, obviously agitated. "Nellie, you are aware I never knew my mum. Growing up alone with Papa, I always had a governess, supposedly to care for me. They never did. I spent my time in the kitchen with our cook while they earned their salary in Papa's bed."

"Sir George had a robust constitution before he became ill. His masculine needs had to be managed, which is why he came to me."

"Yes, I imagine that is true, which is why I intend to satisfy Peter's needs in his own bed! If he is to share the bed of our children's governess, I bloody well better be there with him!"

"Would you do that for him, share a bed with another woman?"

Pamela answered without hesitation. "Of course I would! We have already done so in a fashion. Our maid is quite a handsome young woman."

Nellie picked up the squirrel nutcracker sitting on the table and played with its tail. "*Ma chérie*, would you consider allowing me the pleasure?"

Pamela slowly sat down. "You would do that?"

"Mademoiselle, I am a whore. Certainly I would do that. The question is, would you?"

Pamela sat quietly for several seconds. This unexpected enticement both excited and frightened her. "What would you do?"

"Whatever you ask of me. It is my business to satisfy my clients."

A smile tickled the corners of Pamela's mouth. "Peter would go mad, having both of us there."

Nellie patted Pamela's hand. "*Ma petite*, madness would be the least of it."

"Then, you are agreeing to what I have asked?"

"It seems I am. Are you agreeing to what I have asked?"

Pamela felt her face grow warm as she answered, "If you will be patient with my inexperience, I would welcome the liaison."

"You do yourself a disservice, Pamela. If you have shared Peter Rennard's bed for nearly a year, your experience is no doubt enviable."

"Papa mentored Peter professionally and as I now know, personally. I would ask that you do the same for me in this unusual ménage à trois."

"Have you ever told Peter what to do, or is he usually in charge?"

"I sometimes make requests, but he usually decides what we do. Why do you ask?"

"I discovered some time ago that Monsieur Rennard enjoys a strong female hand. If he has never experienced that with you, I think the time may have come to open the door."

"You will help me?"

"Of course, *ma chérie*! And Monsieur Rennard will no doubt compensate us generously."

Pamela giggled. "Us?"

"Your charms are not free if he receives them in my house."

Pamela beamed. "Oh, Nellie, thank you."

"Might I ask how you will get him here? I can't imagine he will come willingly."

"He'll come if Jack tells him I am already here."

"You are as headstrong and impetuous as your father. It is fortunate I have experience with your bloodline."

Pamela rose to leave. "What time should I arrive on Saturday?"

"Can you be here early, before the evening clients arrive, perhaps around three o'clock?"

"I can. Peter has already told me he has a meeting Saturday afternoon. I will tell him I have picked a place to meet him for his birthday and Jack will fetch him there."

"*Très bien*! That will give us time together to prepare." Nellie hugged her. "If you should decide you do not want to do this, Pamela, send word with your man Jack."

"Nellie, I wouldn't miss this night with Peter for all the tea in China!"

"Then, I look forward to our meeting on Saturday. *À bientôt.*"

"*Au revoir*, Nellie. Until Saturday."

Pamela met Jack at the carriage. "Miss Pamela, are you all right?"

"Of course I am. I am ready to go back to Piccadilly now." Pamela waited for him to help her into the carriage. He did not move. "Is something wrong, Jack?"

"Miss, you've been in a bawdyhouse for the better part of an hour. I'm thinkin' I have a right to have a bad temper."

"Nellie and I had a lovely visit. She has agreed to help me on Saturday. I need your promise that you will help me, too, Jack. You will have to bring Peter here after his meeting on Saturday."

"Miss Pamela, this goes against my better sense, it does! The mister will pop some blood vessels when he finds out what you've done."

"Jack, before the night is over, he will no doubt pop several."

Peter stood in the usual spot waiting for Jack to bring round the carriage. For several days, Pamela had been acting oddly. Her chattering on incessantly about drivel had actually become tedious. Every time he mentioned his birthday or what they might do on Saturday evening, she changed the subject.

Jack also seemed on edge. Contrary to Pamela, Jack barely spoke to him. This morning, Pamela announced she had a special birthday surprise planned. She said Jack would know where to meet her. Peter couldn't help but wonder what on earth she could be scheming.

When Jack opened the door for him, Peter noticed his serious expression. Before he got in, he inquired as to the reason. "Jack, is there something wrong? You seem distressed."

"Sir, I can't really say. Miss Pamela swore me to secrecy."

Jack's reluctance to speak to him finally fell into place. "What is she doing, Jack? Something has you in a twist."

"Sir, Miss Pamela instructed me to take you to her. That's what I'm on about."

Trying to control his temper, both Peter's hands rolled into fists. "Where, Jack?" He already knew the answer in his belly.

"Miss Nellie's, sir."

"Cunting hell! Has she lost her bloody mind?" Peter jumped into the cab. "Take me there, Jack, as fast as that blasted horse can manage."

Jack slammed the door shut. "Yes, sir. Right away, sir." He hopped into the driver's seat, muttering, "Happy birthday, sir."

When Jack stopped in front of Nellie's, Peter leapt out of the cab. Jack stayed in the driver's seat, fully expecting Peter to drag Pamela out of the front door straightaway.

It took every bit of self-control Peter possessed to keep from kicking the front door open. Putting his hand on the latch, he took a deep breath and reminded himself of his stature. He would not make a scene, as long as Pamela agreed to leave quietly.

Opening the door, he quickly surveyed the tavern. He did not see her among the few seamen sitting at the tables drinking ale. He also did not see Nellie. Trying not to draw attention to himself, he went up to the bar. "Henry, where is she?"

"Who, sir?"

Peter ground his teeth together, his impatience nearly besting him. "Miss Pamela Kingston. I understand from my man Jack she asked to meet me here."

Henry chuckled good-naturedly, further infuriating Peter. "Oh, yes, of course. She is with Miss Nellie."

"Where?"

"I believe in Miss Nellie's quarters, sir."

With no other formality, Peter went through the side curtain and up the staircase. The door to Nellie's sitting room stood open. Nellie sat at the table, sipping tea. He did not see Pamela.

"*Bonsoir*, Monsieur Rennard. I've been expecting you." Peter had no inclination to be polite.

"Where the bleeding devil is she, Nellie? I want her out of here, now!"

"That is up to Pamela. She is a grown woman. She can do as she pleases."

Peter had never struck a woman in his life. But he found himself gripping the edge of the table to keep from backhanding her. "Nellie, I will rip this place apart with my bare hands if you don't bring her to me this instant!"

"Peter Rennard, you will do no such thing!"

Pamela's voice cut through him like a razor. There she stood in the doorway to Nellie's boudoir, wearing one of Nellie's red floral dressing gowns. "Pamela, put on your clothes. We are leaving."

"No, Peter, we are not leaving."

"Either you put on your clothes now, or I will carry you through the tavern dressed as you are." The blood pounded in his temples as he walked over to her. "How will you have it, Pamela?"

"I am not leaving, Peter." He took hold of Pamela's arm and pulled her toward the door. She struggled, but could not free herself.

Nellie approached them, attempting to place herself between Pamela and Peter. Peter pushed her away, causing her to stumble backward. Nellie grabbed the back of a chair to keep from falling. Gathering herself, she addressed Peter directly, the sharp edge in her voice slicing through the air. "Peter! Let her go!"

Peter stopped just inside the door. Glaring at Nellie, he said with icy resolve, "I'm taking her home. She does not belong in this place."

Pamela wrenched her arm free of Peter's grip. Before he could grab her again, she went back inside the room and stood beside Nellie. Peter came after her. Again, Nellie shouted, "Peter! Do not force her to leave!"

Pamela calmly put her hand on Nellie's arm. "It's all right, Nellie. I will handle this."

With poise and sinuous beauty, Pamela turned her back on Peter's fury and quietly walked over to the settee. Sitting down, she patted the spot beside her. "Come, Peter, sit. We must talk."

Peter stared at her in disbelief. To see her sitting there in Nellie's dressing gown, so calm and confident, he would never guess they were on the verge of an ugly public display. "Pamela, what in the name of God almighty are you doing? Get dressed and we will leave."

Pamela did not move, save for once again patting the settee cushion. "We are not leaving until you sit here and we talk." Turning to Nellie, she added, "Nellie, I do believe Monsieur Rennard could use a brandy."

"Certainly, *ma chérie*." Nellie went to the cupboard and poured a healthy dollop of brandy into a glass. Handing it to Peter, she simply said, "Monsieur . . ."

Peter took the glass without thinking and sipped. Nellie smiled and nodded to Pamela. Once again, Pamela asked him to sit. This time, he did.

"Pamela, your recklessness in doing this is beyond anything you have ever done. I swear to God, you have lost whatever good sense you had. Please, let me take you home."

Pamela put her hand on his leg. "Peter, if you will calm

yourself and listen, perhaps you will understand why I am giving you this gift on your birthday."

"You call this a gift? You truly have lost your wits!" He sipped his brandy as Pamela lightly stroked his leg. In spite of himself, he felt his organ start to thicken.

"Peter, you have been coming here for so many years. I want to know of your experience here, so I may bring it into our bed at Piccadilly, once we are married."

"What I have done here, Pamela, is unsuitable for you."

"Why do you say that, my darling Peter? We have done many things in the last year that most would think improper. I fancy what we do together."

Peter glanced at Nellie, who stood off to the side. "This is a bawdyhouse, Pams. What goes on here can be crude and offensive, more distasteful than anything we have ever done. I do not want you exposed to those things."

"Have you found pleasure in any of the things you do not want me to know?"

Again, Peter glanced at Nellie. "I do not know how to answer that, Pamela. The experiences men have in a bawdyhouse are not fit for the ears of genteel women."

"Well, bugger me! Here I'm thinkin' all the times you've fancied puttin' your fingers in me cunt, you wouldn't be callin' me a lady no more!" Pamela took his glass of brandy and sipped it.

Trying not to smile at her insolence, Peter said sternly, "I did not offer you that glass."

Throwing her leg over his, she added, "Then, guvner, won't you be buyin' a poor girl some gin?"

The dressing gown Pamela wore separated. Peter saw she had on a pair of cotton stockings held in place with black lacy garters. Most girls at Nellie's wore these. He also saw the top of what looked to be a black corset with gold embroidery. He knew Pamela never wore a corset; she didn't like them. He remembered Nellie had one of this design in her special collection. Putting his hand at the top of the stocking, he asked her, "What are you wearing underneath that gown?"

"Captain!" Pamela feigned indignation and wrapped the dressing gown tightly around herself. "That's no question to be asking a lay-dee!"

As she had done so many times before, she did it again. Pamela made Peter laugh. He took his glass back and drank his brandy. "Nellie, could you give this 'lay-dee' some gin? She seems to be thirsty."

Nellie poured some gin in a glass and brought it to Pamela. "*Mon cher*, do you like my new girl? She is special for you tonight."

As Pamela tasted her gin, Peter slid his hand further up her leg. "It is difficult to know what I think of her. She won't let me see."

Nellie stepped into her role as madam easily, saying the words Peter had heard her say so many times before. "*Ma chérie*, monsieur wishes to see. Show him how lovely you are."

Obediently, Pamela stood in front of Peter. "Yes, madame. As you wish." Handing Peter her glass, Pamela slowly untied the dressing gown and opened it. What she revealed to Peter took his breath and made his already hard cock throb.

Pamela did indeed have Nellie's corset on, and nothing else save for the stockings. The bottom of the corset curved into a peak just above her womanhood, the chestnut curls appearing to be an extension of the garment. Her breasts spilled over the top, the lace barely covering her nipples. The delicate gold embroidery traced the line of her bosom, drawing the eye to her voluptuousness.

Nellie took Pamela's dressing gown off and tossed it over a chair. "Turn around, Pamela. Allow monsieur to see your backside, so full and soft." As it did in the front, the corset curved to a peak just above Pamela's bum cheeks. The laces, no doubt pulled tight by Nellie, strained across Pamela's back.

Nellie caressed Pamela's bottom. "She is quite beautiful, no?" Nellie startled Peter by giving Pamela's arse a hard slap as she said, "Go now. Wait in the boudoir for Monsieur Rennard." Pamela quickly disappeared into Nellie's bedroom.

Nellie stood directly in front of Peter. Lifting the side of her skirt, she tucked the hem into the belt of her dress, as whores do when they are working. "Do you still want her to leave, Peter? She is doing this for you, so you will come to her for your needs and not to someone like me."

Peter bolted back the rest of Pamela's gin. "Nellie, never have I been as satisfied here as I am with her. This whole escapade is unnecessary and unconscionable. You were wrong to agree to it."

"That, *mon cher*, is incorrect. You are wrong to refuse her gift. She is giving you a treasure and you are spitting on it."

Pointing to the bedroom door, he asked, "If I go in there and fuck her in your bed, will that satisfy both of you?"

Nellie laughed, a sound that brought to mind the tinkling of a crystal chandelier. "Oh, monsieur, there is much more than a simple fuck waiting for you in there. Come, receive your birthday gift from your amour."

The emotions swirling in Peter's belly reminded him of how he felt after eating tainted fish. Nonetheless, he followed Nellie into her boudoir. At first, he did not see Pamela. Then, he heard her voice from inside the curtains of Nellie's French canopy bed. "Monsieur, won't you join me?"

He walked over and looked inside. It took him a moment to drink in the sight. There lay Pamela, surrounded by the implements of a *maîtresse*—a paddle, a cane, and an exotic French martinet he knew Nellie only brought out for special clients. There were also several sizes of ivory phalluses, a blindfold, and pieces of rope.

As he took it all in, he murmured, "My God."

"Monsieur, I would ask that you take off your clothes now." Turning to Nellie, he endured another shock. She had taken off her dress, and stood behind him. Like Pamela, she wore only a corset and stockings. She held a brown leather strap which he recognised. Over the years, he had paid her well to take that very strap to his backside.

"Peter, it's time." Pamela stood, and took off his coat. Offering no resistance, he allowed her to unbutton his waistcoat and shirt. Nellie finished the job of removing them. Looking to Nellie, Pamela asked, "Madame, should I remove his trousers or should you?"

"You shall, *ma chérie*. Remember, do not touch. Monsieur Rennard knows the rules. There will be no touching until I allow it."

"Yes, madame." Pamela knelt at Peter's feet and took off his shoes and stockings. When she undid his trousers, he groaned. Pamela stopped.

"*Ma petite*, continue, *s'il vous plait*. It is only the beginning of his bittersweet pleasure."

Pamela removed Peter's trousers and pants, leaving him stark naked. His erect cock protruded painfully from his body. He knew Nellie would not allow him relief from his torment until she knew he could endure no more. He braced himself for exquisite torture, which he suspected would surpass anything he had ever known.

"Pamela, tie monsieur's hands behind his back."

"Yes, madame." Pamela picked up a short length of rope from the bed. She wrapped the rope around his wrists and knotted it.

"Tightly, *ma petite*." Nellie walked around in front of Peter and looked him in the eye. "But not so tight that his hands turn blue."

When Pamela finished, she crawled back on the bed. "I am ready, madame."

"*Très bien*. It is wise to tie his hands so he cannot touch. When he sees you in your pleasure, he will ache for his release."

Nellie unexpectedly swung the strap. It cracked against Peter's arse. He flinched and muttered, "You cunting bitch."

"Pardon, monsieur. I did not hear you. Say it louder." The

leather again connected with his backside. He groaned. Glaring at her he hissed through clenched teeth, "You cunting bitch!"

"*Merci beaucoup.* Now, turn and face Pamela." He could hardly fathom doing so. To be humiliated by a whore in full view of Pamela nearly drove him mad. Yet, something inside him yearned for more. With his arse still stinging, he turned to see Pamela on the bed, her legs spread wide.

As he watched, she picked up an ivory phallus of medium size, slightly smaller than his erect prick. Pamela asked permission to touch. "Madame, Monsieur Rennard likes to watch. May I please frig myself for his pleasure?"

"Of course you may, *ma chérie*, but only if you watch his cock while you do so. If you close your eyes, you will be punished."

Pamela focused on Peter's cock. After sliding the phallus over her clitoris to coat it with her moisture, she inserted it into her cunt. Peter watched, mesmerised by the sight of Pamela frigging herself. She sustained her focus well through the first few minutes, staring at his prick, which bobbed from his groin. He watched her face and noticed her eyelids start to flutter. "Pams, keep your eyes open!"

As soon as he said the words, Nellie strapped him. "You are not to help her! She will learn discipline here. These lessons will serve you both well in your marriage bed."

With the phallus fully imbedded in her cunt, Pamela rasped out the question, "Madame, should I continue?"

"*Oui!*" Nellie barked the command and Pamela continued, keeping her eyes wide open. Her arousal increasing with every stroke, Peter could see Pamela struggling to sustain the momentum with her eyes open. Always, with her climax, she closed her eyes. He wanted to give her relief, but knew any attempts would only sustain the agony they must both endure.

Suddenly, Nellie barked, "Enough!" Pamela pulled the phallus out of her cunt with an audible pop. Her scent filled his nostrils as she laid the sticky tool on the bed. "You have done well, *ma petite*. Now, Monsieur Rennard, kneel beside your amour on the bed."

Trying to keep his balance so as not to fall flat on the bed, Peter knelt beside Pamela. "Monsieur has seen all he shall see this night. Put on the blindfold, Pamela." Pamela did as Nellie instructed. "Mademoiselle Kingston, you are now in charge. I give you Monsieur Rennard with my blessing and my heart."

"Thank you, madame." A few moments later, Peter heard the bedroom door close.

Peter felt Pamela move across the bed. He sensed a change in her demeanor, but could not see anything. He assumed Nellie had left them alone, and that he could now behave normally. "Pamela, what are you doing?"

"Hush, Peter. You do not have permission to speak."

"Pamela . . ."

Before he could finish his question, the sharp stroke of a cane creased his flesh. "Peter, I said hush!" His cock threatened to explode with the realisation Pamela had delivered the stroke. "Lie on your belly."

Peter hesitated. The only way he could lie on his belly was to fall face forward on the bed. The cane once again slashed his arse. In a voice he had never before heard Pamela use, she growled, "I said lie down! Do it!"

With the sensation of falling off a cliff, Peter fell forward and hit the bed with his chest, nearly knocking the wind out of himself. His cock bent painfully to the side. He shifted his weight to ease the pressure on his prick. Before he could gather his wits, he heard Pamela say, "I will give you a choice. What would you like, the paddle or the martinet?"

He knew what he wanted. Nellie only used the martinet on him for his birthday, saying the thrill of it should be savoured only once a year. He knew with certainty that was why she gave it to Pamela, allowing him the choice of receiving it at her hand. Turning his face in the direction of her voice, he answered Pamela as he would have Nellie. "*Merci*, mademoiselle, for allowing me to choose. The martinet, *s'il vous plait.*"

With the first stroke, he knew Nellie had taught Pamela well. The leather lashes bit into his rump just as they had in Nellie's hand. Pamela brought the tails down again with equal force, not the least bit squeamish about flogging him. Her zeal for his punishment increased with each stroke. He heard her grunt softly with effort every time she lashed him. On the tenth stroke, she stopped.

Peter's sensual delirium had fogged his mind. He thought he felt Pamela untying him. He knew it wasn't his imagination when she said, "Monsieur Rennard, I am untying you, but you must not touch. Madame is very strict. If you touch, the game we are playing ends."

Then, he felt Pamela pushing at his shoulder, trying to roll him over. He shifted his weight as she pushed and rolled onto his back. He clenched the bedcovers in his fists to keep from touching. He knew Nellie had instructed Pamela to obey the rules. If he touched himself or he touched her, she would leave.

When he felt Pamela straddle him, he begged her, "Sweet Jesus, allow me to spend."

He gritted his teeth as she covered his organ with a sheath. Her hands on him made him ache beyond endurance. The exquisite sensation of feeling her wet cunt swallow his cock brought him close to tears. He could not contain the joy at finally receiving his reward. "Merciful God in heaven, yes. *Merci*, mademoiselle."

Pamela pulled his blindfold off. She lowered the corset, fully exposing her breasts. Her nipples hung ripe and hard close to his face as she bounced on his prick. Her face contorted as her climax grew in her belly. With utter abandon, she rode his cock, crying out, "*Je t'aime,*" as she pressed down hard on his organ. Her body shook, the power of it moving into his groin.

As the scalding heat of his climax moved into her, he echoed her cry. "*Je t'aime, mon amour. Je t'adore.*"

Chapter Eighteen

Pamela studied the volumes of paper on Peter's desk as she worked to close the ledgers for the year. She had been poring over the books for a month now, since the day after Epiphany. Peter usually did it, working on her accounts along with his own during the evenings. This year, he agreed to let her give it a go.

Not only did she want to learn how to manage her holdings, but she also wanted time with Peter at night. She volunteered to review the ledgers and balance them during the day. Much to her surprise, he turned the project over to her. He would answer her questions, but did not interfere with her labours.

His attitude toward her had changed since his birthday. The bond between them had deepened. Not only had their intimacies intensified, but their conversations and their closeness had as well. Over dinner, he would discuss points of law. If something were troubling him from his day, he would ask her advice. Having discovered her reading his legal journals one day, he inquired about her interest. When he realised she harboured a secret desire to study law, he tutored her.

The February wind rattled the library window. Feeling a draught, she wrapped a shawl around her shoulders. The fire had burned low and the library had chilled. It would be the dinner hour soon, but she still got up to throw another log on the fire. Jack had left some time ago to fetch Peter. They should be home soon.

Pamela turned up the gas in the lamp, her eyes not wanting to focus on the small figures in the ledger. As she studied the transactions for November, she heard Peter calling to her.

"Pamela, where the devil are you? Pamela!"

Knowing Peter never shouted in the house, she ran out of the library to find him standing at the bottom of the staircase. "What on earth are you on about? Is something wrong?"

"There you are! Bloody hell, I thought you were dressing for dinner." Jack stood just inside the door, not able to contain his smile.

"You're both grinning like Cheshire cats."

May and Lucy appeared in the dining room door. "What is all the commotion? Did someone die?"

"Dear May, no one has died!" Having said that, Peter laughed so hard he nearly snorted. Regaining his composure, he corrected himself. "Actually, that is not true. Someone did die."

Totally mystified by Peter's uncharacteristic behavior, Pamela asked, "Have you been drinking, Peter Rennard? You appear as drunk as a sailor!"

Peter came to her and blew his breath right in her face. Pamela blinked as the rush of warm air hit her already burning eyes. "You see, I have not had a drop, my beautiful Pamela Kingston. Or perhaps I should call you what you will soon be known as, Countess Stanford."

"You aren't making any sense. Have you gone barmy?"

"Oh, no, my sweet. I have just had the shock of my life. I am an earl!"

"You are a what?"

"An earl! I received the Letters Patent and the Writ of Summons this afternoon."

"Peter, how is this possible? You are not of the peerage."

"Oh, yes, I am! According to the Letters Patent informing

me of my title, my great-great-grandfather was the second Duke of Dorset. The current Duke of Dorset died several months ago, leaving no heirs. Before they considered the title extinct, the solicitors researched the lineage to find any remaining male heirs. And they found me! They delivered the documents this afternoon. I am the heir to the duke's lesser title of Earl of Stanford."

"Peter, this is astonishing!"

"Jack, hand me that envelope." Jack picked up a large envelope Peter had left on the vestibule table. "Take a look at this."

Pamela opened the envelope and took out a piece of parchment with the royal seal. "What is this?"

"It is a Writ of Summons. Read it."

What Pamela read made her weak in the knees.

Her Majesty Queen Victoria by the Grace of God of the United Kingdom of Great Britain and Northern Ireland and of Our other Realms and Territories, Queen Head of the Commonwealth, Defender of the Faith

To Our right trusty and well beloved Earl of Stanford Chevalier Greeting.

Whereas Our Parliament for arduous and urgent affairs concerning Us the state and defence of Our United Kingdom and the Church is now met at Our City of Westminster,

We strictly enjoining Command you upon the faith and allegiance by which you are bound to Us that the weightness of the said affairs and imminent perils considered (waiving all excuses) you be at the said day and place personally present with Us and with the said Prelates, Great Men, and Peers to treat and give your counsel upon the affairs aforesaid,

And this as you regard Us and Our honour and the safety and defence of the said Kingdom and Church and dispatch of the said affairs in nowise do you omit Witness Ourself at Westminster the Fifteenth day of February in the Forty-Fifth year of Our Reign.

Peter asked her, "Do you understand what it says?"

Pamela read it again to make sure she understood. "It is a summons to appear in the House of Lords, isn't it?"

"Indeed it is. The seat of the Duke of Dorset has been inherited by his successor, the Earl of Stanford, namely me! The Queen has called me to service with that writ. I will be introduced and take my oath of allegiance to the Queen on Tuesday next."

"By all that's holy, this is manna from heaven! Peter, it is enormous!"

"Oh, yes, Pamela, it certainly is." Peter took the writ from her hands and handed it to Lucy. Taking Pamela in his arms, he held her tightly against him. "Sir George is winking at you right now, do you know that?"

Pamela smiled. "Is that a fact, my lord?"

"Oh, yes, my lady, it is. His daughter will marry into a peerage."

Pamela's eyes grew wide. "Oh, my word!" She pushed Peter away.

"What? You look as though you've seen Sir George's ghost over my shoulder!"

"Perhaps I have. Peter, you will be able to vote on the Married Woman's Property Act next month. You will be able to support it as a member of Parliament!"

Peter looked up at the ceiling and said, "Sir George, you certainly are determined to get her married, I'll say that."

No one said anything for a moment, the indefinite postponement of the wedding rarely being mentioned. May broke the silence with a well-timed pronouncement. "Here we all are standing around like a flock of chickens! Earl or not, you still have to eat. If I don't get back to it, you'll be celebrating with a burned roast!" She went back to the kitchen. Lucy handed Peter the parchment he had given her to hold and followed May.

"Master Rennard, the carriage needs tending. I best be getting to it."

"Of course, Jack." With that, Jack went out the front door, leaving Peter and Pamela alone in the vestibule.

Peter again took her in his arms. "It occurred to me in the carriage why I am so happy about this."

Pamela touched his nose with her fingertip. "It did? Please, tell me."

"I had you at Piccadilly waiting to share the news with me. If that weren't the case, I doubt the manna would be nearly as sweet."

"Peter, it truly is wonderful news. You are already an influential man. With a seat in the House of Lords, your prominence will only grow."

"There is something I wish to discuss with you, Pams. Come, my lady. Let us sit in the library until Lucy calls us for dinner."

He took her arm and led her through the library door. Together they sat by the fire. The log Pamela had thrown on the fire blazed brightly. "The room certainly is warmer now. I took a chill sitting here today." Pointing to the window, she added, "Jack may need to replace that window. It is terribly draughty when I work in here."

"I will have him look at it tomorrow." Peter's mood had shifted. "Pamela, I want to discuss our wedding."

"Peter, we have been through this so many times . . ."

"I know we have. But you have to realise, we are approaching the end of waiting, one way or another."

"Meaning?"

"Meaning the vote for the Property Act is next month. You know I will continue to work for its passage, now more than ever. But we have to be realistic about this. It may not become law."

Pamela stood and went over to Peter's desk. "I have nearly finished the ledgers. I am up to November and should be able to close the books for the year by week's end."

"You are quite capable. I knew you could manage it."

"Peter, this is so unfair!" Pamela's already watery eyes filled with tears. "I understand my holdings and should be able to legally manage them. It is my right." She ran her hand over the ledger pages. "I shouldn't have to choose between you and my inheritance."

Peter came behind her and wrapped his arms around her shoulders. "And if you do have to choose?"

Lifting his hand to her lips, she kissed his palm. "We cannot continue living as we have been for nearly two years." Pamela turned to face him. "I want to have children with you and a normal life. I want to share your bed every night, not keep separate rooms as we are now. If the law does not pass, I will still marry you."

"My darling Pams, you know you will still manage your inheritance, no matter what the law dictates. I will honour your decisions on matters that concern your inheritance."

"You are an honourable man, Peter Rennard. I know you mean what you say. But what of our daughters and their right to what we give to them? Not all men are as honourable as you." Pamela laid her head on Peter's chest. "It is all so very wrong. It has to change."

"And it will, Pamela. If not now, soon."

"You don't think the law will pass, do you?"

"It is impossible to know. The debates have gone on

longer than anyone thought. The convictions are strong on both sides. It helps that the Prime Minister supports the passage, but many conservatives are opposed."

"Will your voice make a difference?"

"It might, if they give me the floor in my first weeks as a member."

"You have a reason for speaking up. I think you'll get their attention."

"I expect I will at that. I'll have one month to the day. The vote is scheduled for the Ides of March."

During the intervening weeks, Peter's schedule changed. In order to accommodate his new responsibilities in the House of Lords, he left Piccadilly earlier and returned later. He assured Pamela that the longer hours were only temporary, until he established a daily routine and balanced his responsibilities. Pamela missed him terribly the days she had to dine alone, preferring the kitchen and May's company to the empty dining room.

They had more visitors calling. Pamela forfeited more than one weekend tea with Peter to colleagues and well-wishers. There were also more invitations to social events, all of which were addressed singularly to Peter. As far as the world knew, he remained unmarried and uncommitted.

Many of the invitations came from well-placed families with unwed daughters. Peter declined all but a few, but had to attend some for the sake of appearances. It became apparent to her that they would have to announce their engagement soon. If Peter continued to avoid socializing, curiosity about their living arrangement would surely fuel more rumors. Not to mention the thought of Peter escorting one of those husband-hunting prigs during a dinner party made her jealous as a barbary pigeon.

The morning of March fourteenth, Pamela saw Peter just before he left Piccadilly. She came up behind him as he put on his coat to leave. Adjusting the collar of his coat, she reminded him to stay warm. "It's terribly cold today, Peter, and windy. Wrap your scarf around your neck so you don't catch your death."

"You worry too much." He turned around and hugged her tightly. "You realise, of course, it is indecent for you to be downstairs in your dressing gown."

"Had I stopped to dress, I would have missed you. Good heavens, Peter, it is only half past six!"

"I have work to do before today's session. If I am to take the floor today to speak in favour of the vote tomorrow, I must be clear as to what I will say."

"Do you think they will permit your speech?"

"Fortunately, Pamela, I have many years of court experience that most of these chaps do not. I am able to hold an audience when there is reason to do so."

"Thank you, my darling, for being my champion. Now I understand how ladies of years past felt seeing their knights joust for their hands."

"Is that what I'm doing? I thought I'm simply arguing for passage of a law."

"A law that will give me my freedom. Dear God, it has to pass!"

"There are signs the tide may be turning. I must leave now, Pams. I will see you this evening."

"Late, I suppose."

"Most probably. By the looks of it, the weather will be unforgiving today. I suggest you also stay warm and close to the fire."

"Yes, my lord." Pamela kissed him and then backed away. With an elegant curtsy, she said, "I bid you adieu until eventide."

Peter smiled. "My lady, you give me ample reason to make my way home as soon as I am able." Wrapping his scarf tightly around his neck, he left for the day.

Pamela spent her day distracting herself. She made sure the new ledgers were current, she knitted, she played the piano.

When the dinner hour approached and there was still no sign of Peter, she wandered into the kitchen.

"May, it looks as though I will be eating alone again."

"I figured as much, missy. He told me this morning not to expect him."

"He did?"

"Said he would be courting votes this evening, whatever that means."

Pamela smiled. "I know what it means." Walking over to the stove, she asked, "What are you cooking? It smells delicious."

"I made you some chicken and dumplings, figuring one of your favorites would get you to eat. I don't want you fainting on me."

"May, I haven't fainted for a very long time."

"Once was all I needed." She shook a spoon at Pamela. "You shortened my life by five years that day. I can't afford another five if I'm going to live to see you married."

Pamela hugged her. "Do you know I love you?"

"Then, you won't mind my asking when the blue blazes you and the mister are planning your wedding!" She glanced at Pamela's belly. "I don't want no little ones coming until you have a ring on your finger."

"We haven't set a date yet, but I promise it will be soon." She tugged at May's dress the way she did as a small girl when she wanted a favour.

"What you be wanting now?"

"If I want a June wedding, will you help me plan it?"

"Lord have mercy, child!" May wiped her hands on her apron and then practically smothered Pamela in her arms. "I've been waitin' for almost two years to hear that."

Pamela pulled her head back just enough to say, "May, I can't breathe!"

Loosening her arms, but still holding Pamela, May laughed. "The mister wouldn't be too happy with me if I choked ya, now would he?"

Getting her breath back, Pamela concurred. "I think he might be a bit cross with you, to be sure."

"Now, why on earth do you want me to help you plan your wedding? You should be doing it with someone who knows more about such things than I do."

"You're the only mum I've ever known. I don't give a flying fig what you know or don't know about it. I want to do it with you."

"You watch your language, dearie. A countess better not be heard cussin'."

"'Flying fig' is not cussing. 'Flying frig' is."

Pamela saw her smile just before May spun her around and swatted her bum. "You're going to have to start acting like a lady. The mister will expect you to conduct yourself properly when entertainin' ROY-alty."

"I will be entertaining, won't I?" The thought surprised Pamela. She hadn't considered the social implications of her marriage to Peter.

"You surely will! And I'll be cooking for your parties." May went back to the stove to make Pamela a plate. Pamela heard her mutter, "Maybe I should be asking for more wages."

After dinner, Pamela went to her room. The wind still howled outside, rattling the windows. Shivering in the draught, Pamela quickly changed into her dressing gown and crawled under the quilt. She decided to read while waiting for Peter to come home, so she picked up a book from her night table. She snuggled under the downy warmth. After only a few minutes of reading, the book slipped from her hands as she fell asleep.

Pamela woke with a start. Rubbing her eyes to make them focus, she tried to see the clock. She sat straight up in bed when she realised it read half past twelve. As the sleepy fog lifted, she saw the gaslight had been dimmed and her book lay closed on the night table. She had a vague recollection of having a dream about Peter. In the dream, he kissed her. Only then did she grasp he had been in her room and kissed her good night.

Throwing off the quilt, she climbed out of bed. When her bare feet touched the cold wooden floor, goose flesh rippled up her legs. She lifted the chimney on the oil lamp, lit it and adjusted the wick. Carrying the small lamp, she quietly made her way into the hall and went to the toilet. On her way back to her room, she stopped for a moment outside Peter's door, wanting so much to go inside.

Peter goes to Pamela's room, continue reading
Pamela goes to Peter's room, turn to page 305

Not wanting to disturb him, she went back to her own room. With the vote due in only a few hours, Peter would no doubt leave at dawn as he had today. He needed to rest.

The door creaked when she came back to her room. She made no other sound. Cupping her hand over the chimney, she blew out the lamp. The gaslight still flickered softly. She decided to keep it on. If she hoped to see Peter before he left, she would have to get up before dawn.

She slipped back into bed, shivering. Staring at the shadows the gaslight made on the ceiling, she thought of Peter. She couldn't imagine being without him. No matter what the vote tomorrow, she would marry him.

Her life would be good no matter what happened tomorrow. Squeezing her eyes shut to keep the tears in, she pushed away the terrible sinking feeling in her stomach at the thought of forfeiting her inheritance. She whispered a quiet prayer just as her door opened.

"Pams?" Peter's hushed voice startled her.

"Peter?" She sat up. "Is something wrong?"

He closed the door. "Nothing is wrong. I heard you were awake. I wanted to see you."

"I'm sorry. I didn't mean to wake you."

"You didn't. It is not an easy night to sleep, what with the wind shaking the house and the vote tomorrow."

Pamela lifted her quilt. "You'll catch your death. Come, get warm with me."

Peter came across the room to her bedside. "If I get under that quilt with you, I would expect to get quite warm."

"What do you mean, 'if I get under that quilt'? What are you going to do, stand there looking at me and freeze?"

"You have a point, my beautiful one." Peter lay beside her. Pamela threw the quilt over him and cuddled close.

"I don't want to sleep alone anymore. I want to do this every night."

"As do I, Pamela." Putting his arm around her, he nuzzled her hair. "Dear God in heaven, I never knew I could love a woman as I love you." Then, he kissed her, clenching her hair in his hand.

Breathing the words into his mouth, Pamela pleaded with him, "Peter, please, let me move into your room now. I can't stand this any longer. I want to be in your bed every night."

"You will be, Pamela, once we are married. We agreed we would wait until we marry to share a bed. Otherwise, May will surely leave our employ."

Pamela took a deep breath and exhaled. "The fifteenth of June."

"What did you say?"

"I said the fifteenth of June. That will be our wedding day."

"Even if the bill does not pass tomorrow?"

"Even then. I can't live as we are anymore. I want to be your wife."

"As I want to be your husband. We will start planning the wedding tomorrow. Tonight, there are better things to do."

"Peter Rennard, you need to sleep!"

"Pamela Kingston, soon to be Lady Stanford, having you under me will be far more rejuvenating than a full night's sleep."

He tried to pull up her skirt. "What the devil are you doing in bed with your dressing gown on?"

"It has been terribly chilly in here with the wind hitting this side of the house. I'm trying to stay warm."

"I will wager you a honeymoon in Paris that I can warm you without your wearing a stitch of clothing." As he spoke, Peter untied the sash of her dressing gown.

"And if I catch my death letting you undress me?"

"You may book passage to anywhere else you might want to honeymoon."

Pamela laughed as she slipped her arms out of her dressing gown. "You dodger! You know very well that Paris is where I would want to go."

"Then, we both stand to win the wager, now don't we?" Peter massaged Pamela's breasts through her nightdress. "Take everything off. You will be warm under the quilt."

Pamela reached down and caressed his hardened cock. "I see you are already quite warm."

"If you aren't going to take off your clothes, then I have to resort to extreme measures." Peter lifted the quilt and disappeared underneath.

Pamela felt him sliding down the length of the bed. "What the bloody hell are you doing! You'll suffocate under there!"

Even with his voice muffled by the bedding, Pamela heard him say, "I couldn't ask for a better end." She felt him push her nightdress up to her waist as he crawled between her legs. Spreading her legs wide, he found the opening in her drawers.

When his mouth touched her, she gasped. With an intensity that rivaled the wind blowing outside, he sucked her. Not knowing how he could possibly breathe under the quilt, she threw it off. Peter immediately slid both hands under her bum and held her even tighter against his mouth.

She raked her nails through his hair, wanting to somehow touch him while he licked her. The burning in her groin moved through her belly into her chest. She thought surely her heart would burst with the feeling she had for this man. Just as he devoured her womanhood, he consumed her soul. Her girlhood crush on Peter had grown into a deep and abiding love for the man she would soon marry.

Not being able to stand another moment of this torture, she filled her fists with his hair and yanked. When he lifted his head to stop her, she slipped out from under him. With brazen immodesty, she knelt in front of him and pulled her nightdress over her head. He also rose to his knees and took off his pyjama top. As if in a sacred ritual, they knelt facing each other on the bed. As Pamela lowered her drawers, so did Peter lower his pyjama bottoms.

"Pams, get me a sheath from your drawer." She opened the drawer of her night table and took out the tin of shields Peter had given her to keep there. She took one and came to him. Before putting the cover on his stiff prick, Pamela leaned over and kissed the tip, licking off the drop of dew that had formed on the end.

With delicate tenderness, she wrapped his cock in the sack and tied the string. Before lying down, she embraced him. "Peter, no matter what happens tomorrow, I want to spend my life with you. I love you."

Peter gently lowered her to the bed. "My darling Pams, I also want to spend my life with you." Opening her legs, Pamela accepted Peter into her body and into her soul.

Go to page 309

Pamela motioned for Peter to follow her into the alleyway beside Nellie's. Out of sight of the busy street, she took his genitals into her hand and fondled him. He tried to open her dress so he could touch her breasts, but he couldn't seem to manage the buttons. Instead, his trousers opened of their own accord. She knelt in the dark passageway and took his prick in her mouth.

He murmured, "Why are we here? Shouldn't we be home?"

"Peter, darling, we are home. You're dreaming." He opened his eyes. Pamela lay beside him, caressing his genitals as she had in the dream. He had his hand on her breast. Still in a sleepy haze, Peter muttered, "What are you doing in here, Pams?"

She leaned over and whispered, "Enjoying you." Then she licked his ear.

Now more awake than asleep, he still feigned sleepiness. "Hmmmmm? Enjoying me?"

"Enjoying every bit of you." She kissed his neck. Making a trail of kisses to his throat, she kissed the dent between his Adam's apple and the top of his collarbone. Then she unbuttoned his pyjama top and rubbed her face in his chest hair.

Peter tucked the blankets around her, so she wouldn't get chilled. The wind gusting the entire day had chilled the whole house. The warmth of her body and the feel of her next to him made him long for the day when they would share this room. "Pams?"

She looked up at him and asked, "Are you awake now?"

He wrapped her in his arms. "I thought you were a lovely dream. Now that I'm awake, I see you really are a lovely dream."

"Had you not become a barrister, you could have been a poet."

"Pamela Kingston, you are the poetry in my soul. No one else in my life inspires me the way you do. You are certainly the love of my life."

"Peter Rennard, do you realise I will soon be Pamela Rennard?"

"Actually, you will also soon be Lady Stanford."

Pamela reached down and continued to fondle him. The sensation of her hand on him made him ache with wanting her in his bed always. "Pams, shall we set a date right now?"

"Peter, the vote isn't until tomorrow."

"Even if it doesn't go our way, you said you would still marry me!"

Peter felt her inhale deeply. "Yes, I did. You are quite right. We should set a date."

"The fifteenth of June then. If the bill passes tomorrow, the royal assent should be given by the end of May. The law would begin the first day of June."

"I told May just today that we might marry in June. Perhaps we will honeymoon in Paris?"

"If you care to, yes, indeed, we can honeymoon in Paris."

Pamela snuggled in close to his ear and whispered, "Might I share the master bed before then?"

As tempting as the suggestion might have been to him, Peter held firm. "No, Pamela. May made it quite clear she would leave if we shared a marriage bed before we are wed. I know you do not want that."

"No, I do not want her to leave. You are quite correct. I will simply have to visit more often until then."

"Indeed! And what will you do on these midnight liaisons?"

"Shall I show you?"

"Should I leave a few shillings on your pillow when you finish?"

"If you wish. Although, I would think I am worth more than a few shillings!"

Peter could attest to the fact that she certainly would be a wealthy courtesan. But when she became randy, as she appeared to be tonight, he fancied treating her as one of Nellie's girls. "I'll pay you an extra shilling or two if you treat me well."

"Is that a fact, guvner! I'm worth more than that, I am! A wealthy gentleman such as yourself should be paying a girl what she's worth, he should! If he don't, he ain't no gentleman at all!"

Peter's already stiff prick twitched against his belly as Pamela assumed her trollop persona. She had developed quite a talent for mimicking street whores. Every time she played this game with him, he knew she would immerse herself in it. He responded in kind. He relished this freedom to be coarse with her.

"Talk is cheap, m'dear. If you wish to be paid well, you have to earn it."

"And that I will, captain. You'll see you picked yourself a ripe one, you did!"

"I don't believe you are as ripe as you say. Tell me something ripe, so that I will believe you."

"Oh, go on with ya! I know your wantin' me to pull at ya so you can cream in me hand." Pamela loosened the tie on his pyjama bottoms and pushed her hand inside. When her fingertips touched his stiff cock, a guttural sound gurgled in his throat.

"If you want to be paid well, you best be showing me your bubbies. A trollop not allowing me to see her bubbies will never get more than a shilling from me!"

"Well, captain, why didn't you tell me you fancy my bubs?" Pamela untied her dressing gown and undid the buttons on her nightdress. Pulling her night clothes open, she fully displayed her bare titties. "Nice ones, aren't they, captain?"

Peter filled his hand with one of her soft mounds. "Oh, yes, my dear, they are fine ones, indeed."

"Might you fancy sucking my titties, guvner?" Peter moved to take a hard nipple in his mouth. Pamela put her hand on his head and held him back. "Sucking my titties will cost you

two shillings more. A toff like you can afford to pay a working girl her due."

Peter had to stifle a chuckle. She had never used that line
on him before. Keeping to his role as a gentleman, he retorted, "M'dear, I will decide what payment you are due."

"I don't give it away, guvner. You best not forget that!"

"I assure you, miss, I will not forget it."

With his prick throbbing, he took a scarlet bud into his
mouth. She lay quietly, letting him suckle and knead her bubbies. When he licked the underside of her breast, her salty
perfume filled his nose. He adored her scent, a mix of her ambrosial skin and rose water.

She interrupted him. "Now, don't you be thinking I'll stay
here lettin' you lick me bubbies all night! What's your pleasure, guvner? Will you be spendin' in me hand?"

Pamela nodded toward the clock on his night table. He
had only a few hours to sleep before having to leave to prepare for the vote. She knew his habits well. He could spend
hours playing this game, hours better spent on this night
sleeping.

"I'll spend in your hand while I feel your cunt."

"You are a filthy one, you are! Wantin' to touch up me
cunt." Pamela snuggled in close beside him and pulled up her
nightdress. He pulled the quilt up, so they were covered to
their necks. They lay side by side, frigging each other until
they fell asleep.

Chapter Nineteen

Pamela woke before dawn on her wedding day. Thankfully, the house remained quiet. She had a bit of time before the others stirred. After lighting her oil lamp, she quietly opened her bedroom door. Total silence.

Breathing a sigh of relief that even May and Lucy still slept, she crept down the stairs. Given their situation, Pamela and Peter deemed a small wedding at Piccadilly appropriate. The parlour would be suitable for the ceremony and the dining room for the wedding breakfast.

Feeling like a child sneaking a peek on Christmas morning, she opened the parlour door. The scent of roses washed over her. Late yesterday afternoon, the floral arrangements arrived. The flower shop delivered more roses than she had ever seen in one place, even more than the carts held at Covent Garden. Unbeknownst to her, Peter had contacted the shop and doubled her order. He said he could never have enough roses to represent his love for her.

After some argument, Peter put his foot down and told May he would not permit her to cook for the wedding. The food would be prepared and served by a caterer. He told May that being Pamela's substitute mum supplanted her job as cook. Pamela needed her as a family member on her wedding day, not in the kitchen cooking. May finally forfeited her right to cook the wedding breakfast with Peter's concession that she could plan the menu as well as bake the cake herself the day before.

The guests were to arrive at about half past ten, with the ceremony to begin at eleven. Lucy and Jack could hardly believe it when Peter asked them to greet the guests and seat them. Pamela took them both shopping for proper wedding clothes. During the trip, they inquired as to the possibility of Jack becoming a butler and Peter hiring another driver to replace Jack. Pamela suspected another wedding might be in the offing.

Last evening, Jack moved the sofa against the wall and set up rows of rented chairs. Jack and Lucy requested they be permitted to sit together on the sofa, so they could hold hands during the ceremony. May had a reserved seat in the front row.

Pamela walked down the impromptu aisle between the chairs and set her lamp on the small table where the clergyman would stand. The parish clerk had a chair beside the table, so he could witness the ceremony and record their signatures in the parish registry. Their parlour had been transformed into a chapel overnight.

The flower shop built an archway of roses, under which they would take their vows. Pamela stood under the archway in wonderment. In a few hours, they would be married. Peter would finally be her legal husband.

He had fought so hard for the law that meant her keeping her inheritance, using all of his legal skill and influence to garner votes. Pamela smiled remembering the note Peter sent by messenger after the vote on the fifteenth of March. It read simply:

Dearest Pamela:

The Married Women's Property Act has passed. You can be my wife and retain your inheritance. Start planning the wedding.

Yours in love,
Peter

Richard and Emmeline Pankhurst made a trip to London following the passage of the bill. Pamela invited them to stay at Piccadilly. Much to Pamela's delight, they accepted. That visit fostered an unexpected friendship between Peter and Richard. Whereas Pamela and Emmeline corresponded regularly and remained friends, Peter and Richard had never met. During their visit, Peter and Richard had heated conversations regarding certain points of law, which Pamela and Emmeline watched in amused silence.

The night before they left, Peter took Pamela aside and made a surprising suggestion. He asked Pamela if she thought Richard and Emmeline would stand for them at their wedding. Since they had no blood family to ask, Peter thought it fitting that the Pankhursts be included in the ceremony. In an unusual way, the Pankhursts had been an important part of their lives for the last two years. When asked for their participation, they enthusiastically accepted.

She sat for a moment among the roses, taking it all in. She thought of her father. He should be here today, this most important day of her life. The tears came without warning. She sat and wept for her papa.

"Pams, are you all right?" Peter stood behind her. She hadn't heard him come in.

Wiping her eyes on her dressing gown sleeve, she chastised him. "You aren't supposed to see me today until the ceremony." Her voice cracked as she added, "It's our wedding day."

Peter hunkered down beside her and put his arm around her shoulders. "Yes, it is, my darling. Why aren't you asleep? It is still dark outside."

"I wanted some time in here, alone. Then I thought of Papa." She buried her face on Peter's shoulder as the tears streamed down her face.

"He is here, Pams, I know he is. Sir George wouldn't miss your wedding, not even from the other side." He reached into his pocket and took out a small box. "Perhaps you should know about this now."

"What is it?"

"It is something Sir George gave to me to before he died. He told me to see to it on your wedding day." Peter chuckled. "Of course, he never expected me to be the groom. I was on my way to give it to May when I saw the light in the parlour."

Pamela took the box and opened it. "Oh, my!" Pamela took a sixpence out of the box. "It is a lucky sixpence."

"Sir George told me that is the very one your grandfather put in your mother's left slipper on their wedding day. He kept it for you. I am having May do it for Sir George, as she is closest to you."

Pamela brushed the tears from her face. "Oh, Peter, I miss him so."

"I know you do, Pamela. I miss him, too."

"I'm pleased Nellie agreed to come today. It connects me to Papa in a special way on our wedding day."

"Hopefully, Henry will wear the morning coat I gave to him. If he comes in his street clothes and suspenders, more than a few eyebrows will be raised."

"Nellie will see to it. She told me she bought him a new shirt when she shopped for her dress." She ran her finger over Peter's lips. "Thank you for agreeing to invite her. I know you did it for me."

"I just hope none of her clients are among our other guests."

"If some do recognise Nellie, I seriously doubt they will mention it, do you?"

"No, dearest, I don't think they will."

When someone lightly knocked, they both started. Lucy stood in the shadow of the open parlour door. "Pardon me, Miss Pamela, you told me to draw your bath at six o'clock, sayin' not to dare let you be late."

"Quite so, Lucy." Pamela handed Peter the box with the sixpence and kissed his cheek. "I won't see you again until the ceremony. Peter Rennard, I love you."

"And I love you, Pamela Kingston."

As Pamela walked with Lucy to the stairs, Lucy whispered, "Miss, May would be so cross if she knew you saw the mister before the wedding!"

"No doubt. But you aren't going to tell her, are you?"

"Certainly not, Miss Pamela. It is our secret."

Lucy drew Pamela's bath, then went to lay out her wedding dress. She had already packed Pamela's trousseau for the honeymoon. Whatever few things remained, Pamela would manage herself before they left.

Peter handled booking passage to Paris, saying a husband should carry his bride off to a secret place for their honeymoon. They would be staying in Paris for a week, but she didn't know where. He had been so mysterious about it all. Pamela didn't even know where they would spend their wedding night.

Having plenty of time to soak before anyone else needed the toilet, Pamela took her time in the bath. She felt calm sitting in the warm water, but while drying herself, her stomach filled with butterflies.

Keeping with the flower of the day, she splashed rose water on herself before putting on her dressing gown. When she came into her room, Lucy sat at her desk waiting for her. The silver-blue organza wedding gown from the House of Worth lay on the bed. Her veil hung from the bedpost. As she looked at the dress, she started to cry.

Lucy immediately came and hugged her. "Miss Pamela, this ain't a day to cry! You should be laughing your fool head off. You and the mister are getting married!"

"I've waited so long, Lucy. I can't believe the day has finally come." Pamela took a handkerchief from her night table and wiped her eyes. "It is a beautiful gown, isn't it?"

"Miss Pamela, it's the prettiest wedding dress I've ever seen! It's all covered with lace and pearls! And I've never seen such fine embroidery in all my life as is on the bodice and train."

"Do you know Peter hired a man to come here and take our photograph today? He said he wants to always be able to see me in my gown."

"With you in that gown and the mister in his blue frock coat and doeskin trousers, you will be a sight, you will! The mister is right to want a picture of that, he is!"

"He will be so handsome, won't he?" Pamela shook herself as more tears threatened to come. "I have to stop crying, or my eyes will swell shut."

"Come, miss. Let me fix your hair. That will take a bit."

Lucy worked on Pamela's hair and then helped her into her undergarments. As Lucy laced up her corset, she asked, "Miss Pamela, you never wear a corset. Where on earth did you get this one? It is indecent!"

Pamela giggled. "It is supposed to be indecent, Lucy. Someone dear to me allowed me to borrow it for my wedding day." She couldn't tell Lucy that Nellie lent her the same corset she had worn on Peter's birthday.

"Well, miss, the mister is in for quite a surprise on his wedding night."

"Oh, yes, Lucy, he is. Let me show you what else I have." Pamela reached under the bed and pulled out a small traveling bag. "Peter told me to keep my wedding night things separate from the honeymoon boxes. He wouldn't tell me why."

Pamela opened the bag and took out a folded black garment. When she shook it out, Lucy gasped. "Miss Pamela! You're goin' to wear that?"

"I surely am, Lucy. I do believe Master Rennard will fancy it, don't you?"

Lucy took the garment from Pamela. She held a black satin negligee, cut to fit a woman's body like a second skin. Looking a bit bewildered, Lucy turned it over. "Where's the rest of it, miss? There ain't no back or sleeves."

"There's not supposed to be any, Lucy. I had it specially shipped from Paris with my wedding dress. The shop where I ordered my gown had a drawing of it from the designer. I couldn't believe the unabashed immodesty of it! Isn't it scandalous?"

"Miss, if you'll excuse my rudeness, the guvner will cream on himself when he sees you in this."

Pamela's smile lit up the room. "I know! With the front cut so low and the back simply not there, he'll be so hard he'll have to be watchful he doesn't crack it!"

Both women dissolved in hysterical giggles at the absolute wickedness of Pamela's wearing such a close-fitting black gown on her wedding night. It was so risqué! Trying to regain some control, Lucy reminded her of the time. "Miss Pamela, we have to finish dressing you so I can put my new dress on before your guests get here."

"Indeed, Lucy." Pamela hugged her. "Thank you, sweet soul, for getting me through this morning. I don't know what I would do without you."

"Miss Pamela, having you here has made this a place where I want to stay. If you and the mister are willing to keep us, Jack and me want to be the couple overseein' your household staff."

"Lucy, has Jack proposed?"

Lucy's face turned scarlet. "I'm not supposed to say yet, miss. He wants to be sure you and the mister will keep us on as a couple first."

Pamela hugged her again. "I want you and Jack to stay with us. With all the entertaining we will have to do and children in our future, our staff will surely grow. I'm sure I can convince Master Rennard that he should find a new driver so Jack can be our butler."

Lucy squeezed her tightly. "Thank you, Miss Pamela. You have a good heart, you do."

"All right then! Get me into this dress."

Lucy helped Pamela with all of her wedding clothes except her veil, leaving that for May to put on. Leaving Pamela alone, Lucy hurried to dress herself for the wedding.

Once again, Pamela checked off her list, something old—

she had a bracelet that had been passed from her grand-mother to her mother and then to her; something new—her wedding dress; something borrowed—Nellie's corset; and something blue—both her dress and her garters.

Someone knocked on the door. "Who is it?"

"May, dearie. Can I come in?"

Pamela went to open the door. When May saw her, she whispered, "My heavens, Pamela. You are so beautiful. I al-ways knew you would be a lovely bride!"

Pamela fought the urge to cry again. "Come in, May. You have to help me with my veil."

When Pamela sat down at her dressing table, May pro-duced the box with the sixpence. "This is from your father, Pamela. Master Rennard asked me to see to it and put it in your shoe." Pamela lifted her left foot. May slipped the six-pence in her shoe and recited, "With this sixpence, I speak for your Papa and Mum in wishin' you a lifetime of good health, happiness, wealth and happy wedded bliss."

Even with her resolve to keep the tears in, they came any-way. "May, thank you for being my mum all these years. I know it hasn't been easy for you waiting for this wedding." Pamela stood and hugged her tightly. "I'm so glad you didn't leave us. I love you."

May also could not contain her emotion. Crying softly, she whispered to Pamela, "You know I could never leave you, missy. Someone has to have some sense in this house."

Trying to compose herself, Pamela dabbed at her eyes with a handkerchief. "Help me with my veil, so I can go down-stairs and wait in the dining room. I want to see when the guests arrive."

As May pinned on her veil, she asked, "Is Miss Constance coming today?"

"I invited her, as well as her cousins Charles and Sarah. I told Charles early on that I would invite them and didn't want to go back on my promise."

"Do you think she'll show herself here?"

"I expect so. She'll need something to gossip about tomorrow. Peter's marriage to me is certainly grist for the mill, don't you think?"

"Dearie, you are the fruit of Sir George's loins and with you, the fruit surely doesn't fall far from the tree."

"Papa always did what he wanted and never let what other people thought stop him. That's how he raised me. And that's how I choose to live my life."

"You're a strong woman, Pamela Kingston. I'm proud to be here today with you and the mister. You are both fine people. I wish you both all the happiness in the world." May finished adjusting Pamela's veil. "Now I best be gettin' back to the kitchen and checkin' on those caterers. I might not be cookin', but I can bloody well make certain they're doin' things right!"

"I'll go down with you and hide in the dining room."

They left the room together. May held Pamela's train up as she carefully made her way down the back stairs. Cracking the dining room door just enough to peep out, Pamela watched Lucy greet their guests. She looked beautiful in the peach gown Pamela had helped her choose. Jack also appeared quite dashing in his black morning coat. He fussed a bit with the waistcoat, but seemed to forget it once he had to be about ushering the guests.

Pamela stifled a belly laugh when Constance arrived on Charles's arm. She wore a black day dress, with a black bonnet. No doubt her perception of it being a funeral rather than a wedding would be noted by everyone in attendance. Sarah followed on the arm of a handsome young man. His attentiveness told Pamela they were most probably engaged.

Nellie and Henry came in. Pamela opened the dining room door a bit more and blew them a kiss. Henry wore the morning coat Peter gave to him, along with his new shirt. The trousers didn't quite match, but nonetheless, he was dressed suitably. Nellie wore a purple day dress. She looked positively regal. The purple plume on her hat gave her just a hint of flamboyance. Her father's courtesan held her head high as Jack escorted her into the parlour.

Some people arrived that Pamela only knew by acquaintance, all friends and colleagues of Peter. A few of her classmates came. When the minister and parish clerk arrived, Pamela's palms became clammy. They were the last to go in with Jack and Lucy. The pianist began playing. She saw May going into the parlour, followed by Richard and Emmeline. Then she saw Peter. He stood outside the parlour door, waiting for the minister to signal his entrance. Then, he disappeared inside the room.

She picked up her bouquet of rosebuds. Slowly, she walked toward the open parlour door and waited. The bride's processional music began and she stepped into the room. Peter stood halfway down the aisle waiting for her. Having no one to give her away, she asked Peter to wait and walk with her from the midpoint. Standing there among the roses, so handsome and masculine in his frock coat and breeches, he appeared to have just stepped out of a Manet painting.

When she reached the place where he stood, he held out his arm for hers. She threaded her arm through his and leaned against him, grateful for the support he offered. Then, they walked toward the rose archway together. As they reached their proper position under the roses, he whispered to her, "You are a walking dream, my darling Pamela."

The minister nodded at them, and then began the ceremony. "Dearly beloved friends, we are gathered together here in the sight of God, to join together this man and this woman in holy matrimony, which is an honorable estate, instituted of God in paradise. It is a mystical union, not to be taken in hand unadvisedly, lightly, or wantonly, but reverently, discreetly, and soberly, duly considering the causes for which matrimony was ordained. Therefore, if anyone can show any just cause why they may not lawfully be joined together, let them now speak, or else hereafter forever hold their peace."

Pamela held her breath and waited. The room remained

silent, except for May sniffling as she wept. Pamela couldn't be sure the high-strung Constance wouldn't make a scene. Thankfully, she remained quiet.

After that bit of business passed, Pamela relaxed. She focused on listening to the minister. After delivering some preliminary prayers, the minister recited their vows. Without being told, Peter took both her hands in his as the minister spoke.

"Peter Rennard, The Right Honourable Earl of Stanford, wilt thou have this woman to thy wedded wife, to live together after God's ordinance in the holy estate of matrimony? Wilt thou love her, comfort her, honour, and keep her in sickness and in health; and, forsaking all others, keep thee only unto her, so long as ye both shall live?"

"I will."

"Pamela Frances Kingston, wilt thou have this man to thy wedded husband, to live together after God's ordinance in the holy estate of Matrimony? Wilt thou obey him, and serve him, love, honour, and keep him in sickness and in health; and, forsaking all others, keep thee only unto him, so long as ye both shall live?"

"I will."

"Who giveth this woman to be married to this man?"

There followed an infinite moment of silence. Peter glanced at May, having instructed her to speak for Sir George and charge Pamela to him. With tears streaming down her face, May shook her head no. Unable to speak, she pointed to Peter.

Drawing himself up to his full height and with dignity fitting his position, Peter replied, "In the name of Sir George Kingston, whose presence in spirit is felt by us all, and as Pamela's guardian, I do."

The joy in Pamela's heart knew no bounds. For Peter to acknowledge her as his ward during their marriage ceremony, in front of his friends and colleagues, made this ceremony a rite of passage for both of them. Their secret would no longer be considered a sin. They could now love one another openly and proudly.

After exchanging their vows, the clergyman asked for the ring. Peter took the ring he had engraved with their initials and the date of their wedding, and placed it on the Bible. Once blessed, the minister gave it back to Peter. He placed it on Pamela's finger saying, "With this ring I thee wed, with my body I thee worship, and with all my worldly goods I thee endow."

Pamela smiled, noting the emphasis he put on "with my body I thee worship."

They knelt together under the rose archway as the minister instructed them. "Ye husband, dwell with your wife according to knowledge; giving honour unto her, and as being heirs together of the grace of life, that your prayers be not hindered. Ye wife, be in subjection to your own husband, giving reverence unto him, and as being heirs together of the grace of life, that your prayers be not hindered.

"O eternal God, send thy blessing upon these thy servants. May Peter and Pamela ever remain in perfect love and peace together, and live according to thy laws. Those whom God hath joined together let no man put asunder. Amen."

Peter lifted Pamela's veil. Following his instinct and without regard to deportment, he pulled her to him. As he would if they were alone, he kissed her. In front of everyone present, his passion proclaimed they need no longer hide their love.

After Peter and Pamela received their guests at the dining room door, the caterers served the wedding breakfast. When Pamela saw the elaborate trays of food, it seemed a wedding feast would have been a more appropriate description. One tray had cold salmon, pigeons in jelly, cherries, strawberries and cream. Another tray had lobster salad, blancmange, veal galantine, apricots, peaches and grapes. A third had ham, tongue, duck and lamb. The chicken pie and veal pie sat beside a variety of breads, rolls and jellies. And of course, May's wedding cake sat in the middle of the table.

Constance and Charles were the first to leave. Constance murmured congratulations with a limp handshake before she hurried out the door. Pamela noted, almost with pity, that the hard lines creasing her face had become more severe. Charles kissed her cheek and offered his good wishes, saying to Peter he now understood why Sir George would approve of the groom.

As morning moved into afternoon, the guests gradually thinned. Nellie and Henry were among the last to leave. Nellie embraced Pamela with heartfelt warmth, her wishes for a future filled with happiness and love coming on a wave of tears. She also hugged Peter, and whispered something. Pamela could not hear what she said. Peter smiled and nodded, saying nothing in return.

Richard and Emmeline also said their goodbyes. They had to return to Manchester, having left their daughters Christabel and Sylvia in the care of Emmeline's parents. The nine-and-a-half hour train trip would have them arrive home late Saturday night. When Emmeline asked Pamela if she had chosen any names for their children, Pamela whispered, "yes"; the first boy would be George and the first girl, Nellie.

After everyone had left, Peter and Pamela put on their traveling clothes and prepared to leave. Again, Peter emphasised that she should have an overnight bag apart from her boxes for the honeymoon trip. Pamela questioned why they had not left before their guests, as was the custom. Peter would only say the plans for the night did not include an early departure.

Lucy and May saw Peter and Pamela to the carriage. With tearful hugs, Pamela said goodbye, charging them with keeping the house on Piccadilly secure in their absence. Jack already sat in the driver's seat, prepared to take them to the mystery destination. Pamela had meant to corner him earlier and ask for some hint as to what Peter had planned. But the day's events had not allowed for such an interrogation.

Peter helped her into the carriage before climbing in behind her. Jack had piled all of their boxes in the cab, forcing them to squeeze into the corner of the seat. Immediately, Pamela noticed something odd.

"Peter, why are the windows covered with towels?"

"Because I told Jack to cover them."

"What on earth for?"

"So you could not see out of them, of course."

"For Lord's sake, why?"

"I told you, our destination is a surprise. You will not know where we are going until we arrive."

"Aren't we going to the steamer ship that will take us across the Channel to France?"

"Eventually. But the passage I booked doesn't sail until early tomorrow morning."

"Then, where are we going?"

"Ah, yes, that is the question, now isn't it?"

Pamela pinched his arm. "You devil!"

"Now, now, didn't you just swear to obey me and give reverence unto me?"

"When I am inclined to it, I will!"

"I do not recall there being a condition placed upon subjection!"

Pamela cuddled in close as she whispered, "I never swore to subjection. I heard it as an instruction, not a vow." She licked his earlobe and added, "When have you ever known me to obey an instruction?"

Peter caught her breast in his hand and sunk his fingertips into the soft flesh. "Oh, I think you will tonight, my bride. I certainly think you will tonight."

The carriage rumbled along. Pamela had thoughts of beginning the wedding night early, while still in the carriage. Peter caught her hand as she attempted to caress his crotch. Kissing her fingertips, Peter chastised her. "Lady Stanford, you will wait to consummate our marriage at the appropriate time!"

Lying her head on his shoulder, she deferred to his senti- ment. "Indeed, my lord. And might I add I much prefer being Pamela Rennard to Lady Stanford."

The motion of the carriage made Pamela drowsy. Leaning against Peter, she dozed a bit. When the carriage stopped, she started awake. "Have we arrived?"

"We have." Peter picked up his bag. "Hand me your case."

"Where are we?"

"You will see. Wait here for a moment." Peter opened the door and handed Jack the two cases. "Take these inside, Jack. Then, take our boxes on to the dock where we will board the steamer to France."

"Yes, sir." Jack hesitated for a moment. "Master Rennard?"

"Yes, Jack?"

"Might I tell you how happy I am for you and Miss Pamela?" He set the bags down and caught Peter unaware when he enthusiastically shook his hand. "I'm mighty proud to be in your employ, I am! Congratulations, sir!"

Peter smiled warmly. "Thank you, Jack. You are a good man, to be sure. When we return, we will discuss your posi- tion in the house."

"Yes, sir!" The bright-eyed Jack grabbed the bags and dis- appeared around the carriage.

"May I get out now?"

"Quite so! Come, my bride. Our wedding night awaits us."

Pamela took Peter's hand as she carefully stepped from the carriage. When she turned to look behind her, her laughter rang through the street. "You bleeding devil, you can't be se- rious!"

"Oh yes, Pamela, I am quite serious. Welcome to your wedding night." Pamela stared at the sign over the door, the sign Sir George had made nearly ten years before. It still clearly read NELLIE'S.

When she turned back to Peter, she saw him studying her

reaction. "I asked Nellie to hire a room, but she has generously offered us her quarters for our wedding night. It is her gift to us."

"Will we be alone?"

"Quite assuredly! It is our wedding night!"

"Well, then, shall we go in the front door or the back door?"

With obvious relief that Pamela had accepted his unusual wedding gift, Peter smiled and took her arm. "We will use the back door. Jack should have already alerted Nellie we have arrived."

They met Jack at the back door. "Miss Nellie says to go on up to the room. You know the way. She also says to help yourselves to the food and liquor. It is there for you. Oh, yeah, and don't worry. You won't be disturbed."

"Thank you, Jack. We will meet you back here at seven o'clock tomorrow morning, to go to the steamer."

"Yes, sir. I'll know the proper streets to take tomorrow, since I'm taking your boxes to the dock straightaway."

"Good man."

"Thank you, sir." Smiling broadly, he tipped his hat and winked. "Have a good one, now." Pamela heard him whistling the tune Peter often whistled as he left them for the carriage.

"Shall we?"

Pamela went in first, with Peter right behind her. Once her eyes adjusted to the dim light of the back hall, she saw the familiar staircase ahead. Peter came up behind her and whispered into her ear. "Do you smell it?"

Pamela sniffed. "Smell what? I don't smell anything."

Peter salaciously rubbed her breast. "Oh, yes, Pamela, there is a scent to this place. It is the delicious musk of a heated woman. No matter how often I've been here, it always affects me." Peter pressed his groin into Pamela's bum. His hardened prick poked her.

"My scent will soon add to the bouquet, don't you think?"

Peter sniffed her neck. "I think it already has."

When they entered Nellie's sitting room, Pamela found herself surrounded by even more roses. "I don't suppose you had anything to do with this, Peter Rennard?"

"I arranged this with Nellie. I told her what I wanted and she did the rest."

Pamela turned and embraced Peter. "What else did you arrange with Nellie? Is that what she whispered to you before she left Piccadilly today?"

Peter kissed the tip of Pamela's nose. "She told me our wedding bed had been prepared."

Pamela glanced at the closed bedroom door. "I must change into my nightdress. Shall I change here?"

"By all means."

"Since Lucy isn't here, you will have to help me with my dress."

As Peter undid the buttons on the back of Pamela's dress, he chided her. "You know, of course, that it is proper for a young bride to bring a female companion along on the honeymoon. Perhaps I should have also booked passage for Lucy!"

"Oh, no, Master Rennard. I expect you to see to all my needs during our holiday."

"Is that a fact, Mistress Rennard!" He lowered her dress and kissed her shoulder. "And what are the needs you expect to have?"

Pamela stepped away. Turning to face him, she slowly lowered her dress to her waist. Pushing it below her hips, she took it off. "The first thing you can do is unlace this corset."

Just as Pamela's laughter had bubbled into the street, Peter's filled the room. "Well, well! It seems Nellie Flambeau has had her hand in my wife's trousseau!"

Wearing nothing more than the corset, her knickers and stockings, Pamela sashayed up to Peter and put her arms around his neck. Pressing her pelvis into his, she felt his thickened prick. "You like, Monsieur Rennard?"

"Oh, yes, Madame Rennard, *beaucoup*!"

Pamela turned around. "Unlace, *s'il vous plait*."

Peter untied the bow just above Pamela's bum, the one Lucy had so carefully tied that morning. He pulled the crosses loose and the tight garment slackened. Pamela caught it as it slid, and held it to her chest. Turning again to face Peter, she smiled seductively. "Now, my husband, you must allow me a few moments alone to put on my wedding night gown." She pointed to their bags sitting on the floor beside the settee.

Saying nothing, Peter went to Nellie's liquor cupboard and poured himself a brandy. Pamela stood in the middle of the room, holding the corset so it wouldn't fall off. She allowed it to slide a bit more, exposing most of her breasts. Only her nipples remained covered. Peter turned around, his own glass in hand. "Would you care for something, Pamela?"

He sipped his brandy, his eyes moving over her body like an extension of his hands. "I would fancy some of Nellie's gin." As she spoke, Pamela deliberately glanced at the bulge in Peter's trousers and licked her lips.

Peter chuckled as he poured her gin. "Pamela, today I married my inamorata. You are the only consort I will ever want or need." He handed her the glass. "A toast before I bid you adieu." He raised his glass and recited from *The Pearl*. "'The first four letters of the alphabet—A Big Cunt Daily.'"

Without a moment's hesitation, Pamela replied, "'In with it, and out with it, and God work His will with it!'" They both drank. Peter took his bag and set about putting on his own dressing gown in Nellie's boudoir.

Pamela quickly removed every stitch of clothing. She took her salacious gown from her bag and slipped it on. The material clung to her as did the coat of a sleek black cat she had seen outside the house at Piccadilly.

She took her hair down. It fell around her shoulders onto her bare skin, reminding her that the gown had no back. Glancing in the mirror hanging on the wall, she made sure she had properly framed the deep line between her breasts before joining Peter in their wedding boudoir.

When she came into the room, Peter turned around. He froze, as though rooted to the floor. Pamela watched his eyes as they explored her body. His lips barely moved as he breathed the words, "My God!"

Her heart thumped in her chest as Peter circled around and stood behind her. She knew he would be looking at her bare back framed in the gown. Giving him time to take in the sight of her, she did not move.

When she felt his finger tracing a line down the middle of her back to where the gown curved at her bum, she shivered. Lowering a strap down her arm, he kissed her shoulder. Leaning in close to her ear, he whispered, "Pamela, how did you come by this? I have never in my life seen anything like it."

"It is from Paris. For our wedding night, I wanted something wicked."

"Oh, my dear, it is surely that! You must know what it is doing to me."

"Monsieur Rennard, that is exactly the point!"

"I also ordered something from France. It is a special wedding gift for you." He went to his bag, took out a small box and gave it to Pamela. "We will keep it by our bed, as I am sure we will be using it often."

Inside the box, Pamela found an exquisite martinet. The polished wooden handle had been carved in the shape of a phallus. The heavily oiled black leather lashes hung ominously from the other end. Pamela caressed it, her excitement building in anticipation. "Who will be first, Peter? What is your choice?"

Peter took the martinet from her hand. "My dear wife, I told you on this night, you will surely follow my instruction. My choice is to show you what happens to wicked wives who tempt their husbands with wanton actions."

Pamela's entire body throbbed. The heat in her belly threatened to melt her from the inside out. "My lord, what would you have me do?"

"Take off my dressing gown, *s'il vous plait.*"

Pamela untied the sash on his robe and opened it. She had seen Peter's cock innumerable times since they had become lovers, but never had she seen him so thick. She reached down to touch him.

Peter growled, "You will not touch! This time, Pamela, I am the master. You will do as I say, nothing more, nothing less. Do you understand?"

Pamela knew the rules. "Yes, monsieur, I understand."

"Lower the top of your gown."

Pamela slipped her arms out of the straps and lowered the gown to her waist. Peter lightly brushed the leather lashes across her chest. "Pamela, do you think you deserve to be punished for wearing such a sinful gown on our wedding night?"

With her eyes downcast, Pamela glanced at Peter's cock. It twitched as she replied, "Yes, my lord. I should be punished."

"And what do you think your punishment should be?" Again he trailed the lashes over her bare breasts.

"My lord, you are the one to decide, not I."

"Remove that lewd piece of clothing, Pamela." As Pamela slipped the gown down her hips and off, Peter moved an armchair directly in front of a full-length looking glass beside Nellie's canopy bed. "Bend over this chair, Pamela."

Pamela did as he told her. "You are aware of the rules, are you not?"

"Yes, my lord, I am."

"You will keep your eyes open and watch yourself in the looking glass. If I see you have closed your eyes, our marriage will not be consummated on this night. Do you understand?"

In this place, this brothel, the rules never varied. A single moment of disobedience or of weakness ended the liaison. It did not matter it was their wedding night. The rules would not be broken. If Pamela hoped to feel Peter's glorious prick in her cunt on their wedding night, she must be strong. "My lord, I understand."

Pamela fixed her eyes on the looking glass. She saw her reflection, her chest flushed scarlet, her voluptuous breasts swaying with each breath. The image of herself in the throes of passion inflamed her even more. When the first swing of the martinet connected with her flesh, she dug her fingers into the chair. More than anything, she wanted to close her eyes. Peter knew it to be her reflexive reaction. Her eyes teared with the effort to stare at herself.

Peter's voice jarred her concentration. "Pamela, are you prepared to share my bed every night and open your legs to me as my wife?" Again the lashes bit into her bum.

With her eyes open wide, she shifted her focus and looked at Peter's reflection in the looking glass. "Yes, my lord. My body is yours for the asking."

He lashed her again. "That is as it should be." Pamela saw the lust burning in him as it did in her. She knew it would be soon.

"Are you prepared to consummate our marriage and allow my seed inside your belly?"

This time, the sting hit lower, as the leather creased her thighs. Still watching Peter in the looking glass, she answered, "I want your seed inside my belly. I want to conceive our first child!"

His voice hoarse with need, Peter growled, "Spread your legs wide."

Pamela leaned further over the chair and opened her legs. No sooner had she done so than the lashes curled between her legs. She moaned loudly, but did not close her eyes. Again, heat seared the tender flesh between her legs as the lashes cut into her. She pushed her hips backward and pleaded, "My lord, I will die without your cock inside. Please!"

Pamela saw herself bent over the chair, her body consumed with lust and need. Peter stood behind her, also looking at her reflection. In the looking glass, she saw him turn the martinet around. Even as she screamed, "My God, Peter! I want you, not that!" he rammed the handle of the martinet into her.

Her body clenched the intruding object tightly, as everything in her wanted to be fucked. As though possessed by a demon, Peter frigged her with the wooden handle, all the while watching her in the looking glass. Pamela saw a frenzy come over him as he pushed her closer to the edge.

With a ferocity she had never before witnessed in him, he pulled the handle out of her and threw the martinet across the room. When his scalding cock filled her cunt, she knew the game had ended, and she had won.

Don't miss this scorching scene from NIGHT SPELL by Lucinda Betts, available now from Aphrodisia . . .

Closing my eyes, I took a deep breath.

A deep melodic voice interrupted my meditation. "Good," he said, the tone slow, rich, seductive. Otherworldly. "You indicate some ability to control yourself. You show promise."

I tried to scream, but the sound refused to budge from my lungs. I fought the paralysis. And lost. I just . . . couldn't scream. Panic pounded through my veins.

"The Sultan will be extremely pleased with your control," he said.

I tried again. My lungs worked! This time I did scream. So much for control. I screamed for help. I screamed for mercy. I screamed obscenities that weren't nearly as creative as I might have hoped given the situation. Finally, I screamed to a God I wasn't sure existed.

The result of my screaming didn't make me any more religious. No golden chariots appeared at my rescue. No sword-bearing angels came to avenge me. Instead, the implacable voice of the man standing in the doorway responded in an almost gentle fashion.

"Now is the time for screaming—and lack of control," he said. "Scream all you like—today. No one can hear you except for me. Mariah is deaf, and if she could hear, she would not help you." His sensual voice had a husky, mocking quality that sent a shiver down my spine.

Unearthly. Elegant. Did Pierce Brosnan have a younger brother with a habit of kidnapping women? My captor seemed vaguely familiar, like I'd met him in a dream. A feathered memory tickled the back of my mind. There was something . . .

My captor approached me, almost floating in his gracefulness, and he moved to touch my head. Panic swelled, filling me with an overpowering desire to escape this tent. Now. Regardless of the guy's looks, I hadn't signed up for this, and nothing about the situation in which I found myself was consensual.

I pulled away from him wanting all of my strength, but as if in a dream, I was as weak as a child. In slow motion, I tugged my wrists, feeling like I struggled through a sea of molasses. I was so slow, so weak. What was wrong with me?

The drugs . . . it must be the drugs, whatever he'd use steal me from the Morgan Hotel. Telazol? Ketamine? I could barely move, despite my will to run. My bonds held.

I shouted again, but it didn't sound like my voice. Kathleen Battle's voice fell from my lips, singing a passionate scene of anger and rage. Birds took wing from the branches above my tent.

"I would recommend that you cease shouting by nightfall. Why let the lions and hyenas know where you are?" His calm tone ridiculed me.

He touched my head again, despite my noisy writhings. His hand unnerved me, burning into my skin even through my hair.

He paused at the tent's flap and said, looking me in the eyes, "Mariah will be here shortly to see to your needs. When you calm yourself enough to think of escape, be aware that you are several hundred kilometers from the nearest town, and the people of that town do not speak English."

I'd been screaming and struggling through his brief soliloquy, and I was nearly frozen in panic. My mind absorbed only a few words: "lions," "several hundred kilometers," "no

English." I'd also heard the word, "escape." Until then, I hadn't accepted that my situation warranted escape.

Terror rose through my throat.

All parts of my brain agreed upon the next course of action—I cried. I cried until I fell asleep.

But even as sobs ripped themselves from my chest and slept crept up on me, I realized that a man as good-looking as my captor would not need to kidnap anyone, not for himself anyway.

With a few kind words, he'd have the attention of most women I knew. Maybe even me. Images of his dark hair coupled with fair skin, aqua-blue eyes and sharp features danced across my imagination. His easy competence was the sort that generated trust in people.

When he wasn't kidnapping women.

I slid into consciousness again. My mind fought to find the Morgan, but the old woman made it impossible. She silently sponged warm, fragrant water over me. Was the fragrance lavender?

I struggled violently to sit, yanking on my ties. My wrists and ankles burned under the cords, and my feet longed to run.

But the old woman held up a hand. Like magic, I stopped. Panic drained away, leaving dreamy lethargy in its place.

I stared at her a minute, wondering at the power in her hand. She looked like drawings of Baba Yaga from the fairy tales I'd read as a child, wizened and brown. Wrinkled raisin eyes peered from her sunken face.

I still felt fuzzy headed, like if I tried hard enough I could detach myself from my body and view myself from above. I thought I'd woken in a bed, but now I found myself tied to a chair, hard and unyielding.

Heat permeated the air and the mat-covered ground beneath my feet. The intense heat didn't feel like New York, and the dust didn't smell like Manhattan. My captor mentioned lions. Hadn't he?

Lions. I rolled the word around my consciousness. *Lions.*

Like leaves across a late summer pond, the word floated through my mind.

Where did lions live? My mind's eye played pictures of big cats roiling over some dusty land.

But a country's name wasn't coming with the picture of the landscape. Someplace in Africa. They were gone in India, weren't they?

I'd watched enough nature shows to know the answer to this question. Rest would bring the answer.

Closing my eyes, I let the old woman do her job. Cool, fragrant water trickled over my brow. Her strong hands massaged warm oil into my calves, into my arms.

When she finished, she held a drink for me. Cool lemony water. So refreshing.

She untied my hands slowly, letting my wrists memorize the texture of the silky binds. After the tie slithered off, she held it up for me to see. *Do not try to escape,* her expression said. *I am trusting you.*

An aromatic stew appeared on the table near the door flap. It must have been there all along. The scent of fresh tomatoes and Indian herbs filled the tent. Naan bread appeared at its side. I ate it, and I enjoyed it.

The old woman was a witch. The lethargy she'd cast on me was something I couldn't swim past. My feet were bound, true, but escape no longer beckoned me.

Where would I go? Was I really in some exotic land miles—no, kilometers—from nowhere?

I finished the stew, using the bread to suck up every last morsel. The old woman—Mariah, I reminded myself—nodded in approval.

She knelt at my feet with a grace surprising in an old woman. With deliberate movements, with slow and exaggerated hands, she untied the silky cords binding my feet. She stood, and with the elegance of movie star, she held the tent flap opened, and gestured for me to leave my green nest.

I did.

Looking at the landscape, I felt like I'd been sucked into the television and delivered to Discovery Channel land. Dry savannah lay all around me. Thick baobab trees peppered the hills. A river trickled below us.

The air smelled amazing. Had I ever before smelled air free of exhaust? And the heat, it defied description. I'd never been to the Southwest. Could anywhere in the United States be this hot?

Mariah gently nudged me towards a small building. I realized it was a bathroom, an outhouse. I then realized that my clothing were not my own.

Someone had dressed me in a sunflower-colored dress. Finely woven cotton fit tightly across my breasts and stomach, loose and flowing around my legs. Ignoring the achingly blue sky and the strange scent of the dust, I quickly undid the buttons over my breasts and looked down.

My no-nonsense underwear were gone. Now, a leopard-print bra pushed my breasts high, made them look full and tempting. My pink nipples peeked out the top. A tiny triangle covered my pubis, also leopard-print. Tiny black strings ran over my hips, up the back of my ass.

I stumbled into the outhouse in a cloud of yellow cotton. As I closed the door behind me, name of countries that had lions and that looked like this on the television started to filter to the top of my brain—Tanzania, Kenya, South Africa.

Toto, I said to myself, *we're not in Kansas anymore.* But I guess Oz did have lions. If I found myself talking to a tin man, I'd have to question my sanity. The world felt strange—monkeys might fly across the cloudless blue sky.

When I came out of the outhouse, the panoramic view shocked me, took my breath away. I scanned the horizon seeing nothing unnatural, nothing made by human hand. A wide trickling river. Scrubby trees clinging to the shoreline. Huge boulders scattered over the landscape.

Not a house. Not a road. Not an electric pole in sight.

And Mariah was gone. But her witchy magic wasn't. I felt compelled to sit on the boulder. To sit and watch.

In bare feet, I climbed to the top of the big rock. A bright blue lizard with a peach-colored throat scampered away. A bottle-green snake gave me an apologetic look and slithered into the shade. Overhead, a bird of prey cried, sounding like my heart.

And then the old witch returned. With a crook of her gnarled index finger, Mariah indicated I should return to my tent. She wasn't a servant—she was Baba Yaga. Her chicken-legged home lurked just on the other side of one of these boulders. I knew it.

So when Baba Yaga called, I went willingly, filled with the strange lassitude.

I knew I couldn't escape on foot. Where were my shoes? I'd need a car—or a camel. Did they have camels in East Africa?

My knees felt weak. From travel? From fear? I couldn't say. From the witch's spell.

My vision felt strange, wave-like and uncertain. Almost like if I blinked I might see a purple sky, blue and yellow striped zebras, a river running in flamboyant orange.

Jet lag, I told myself. *Drugs.*

I went to my bed in my emerald nest, and I did not object when Mariah fastened the silky cords around my wrists and ankles.

I would have objected to the blindfold, but in my complacency and confusion, she tied it over my eyes before I knew what she was doing.

Mariah was a witch. Black magic was her paintbrush. I was her canvas.

Then she brushed my hair while I lay tied, and I relaxed,

despite my captivity. The mattress beneath me felt like a cloud, like a slow-rolling wave crossing the Caribbean on a sultry day.

The blindfold brought a strange comfort. In the purple blackness, silvery stars danced before my eyes. Gold ones shot past my view.

Maybe the blindfold meant they were going to transport me someplace, and perhaps that someplace would be more amenable to escape. Maybe they realized that they had the wrong girl and they were bringing me home. If they were going to kill me, I thought, they would have done it before now.

Maybe I'd just wake up in my own pillowy bed, in my sea of blue blankets with sun streaming through my white eyelet curtains. Set on a timer, my coffee would just start dripping into the pot, filling my apartment with its delicious scent. I know I must have been smiling as I drifted to sleep.

I thought fates worse than death were literary exaggerations.

"You no doubt have many questions, and I will answer none of them."

His voice seemed to come from a distant place, and it rung with a fantastic vibration—like he was both behind me and miles away. And his words did not reassure me, although I didn't say as much. If I appeared implacable maybe he'd leave me alone.

"I'm going to give you some rules. They are simple and basic. You will obey them." With my captor in the room, the blindfold was no longer comforting. Where was he? What was he doing? Panic threatened to overwhelm me. I couldn't imagine feeling more vulnerable.

"Who are you?" I demanded, doing my best to sound imperious. "My father will pay you, if it's ransom you're after."

"I like your attitude," he responded in a voice as rich as dark chocolate. If a magician could special order a voice, he'd want this one. "But I will not answer any of your questions." I wondered just how much Dad could afford. This guy seemed like he had expensive tastes.

I heard him pause as he approached me, and then he said, "Here are the rules."

I waited, hoping for something like, "Say 'please,' and you can go home."

"I will not penetrate you until you beg for it."

At this, I started fighting my bonds in earnest. My dreamlike weakness of the pervious day was gone. My wrists jerked and flailed, yanking the ties until they were as taut as my muscles.

"Penetrate" could have several meanings, none of which sounded good. "Are you crazy?" I screamed. "Get away from me!" I tried to rub my blindfold off with my shoulder. Was he getting closer? The blindfold stubbornly held. Damn Mariah and her knot-tying skills.

"Don't be afraid. I will not enter you until you ask—until you beg. And you will. Even then I will not harm you."

In my experience, people say, "I'm not going to hurt you," just before they hurt you. What doctor tells a patient that the injection will hurt like a son of a bitch?

I screamed wildly.

When he caressed the arch of my foot I screamed again, kicking my tied feet maniacally. Unperturbed, he waited until I stopped. My throat was beginning to ache. While continuing his caress up my ankle, he said, "I will touch you everywhere, in every imaginable way, but I will not penetrate you until you want it. And you will want it." His voice sounded huskier than I remembered.

I knew then that he used "penetrate" as in "to insert the penis into the vagina or anus of." I'd been—unrealistically—hoping that he'd meant "penetrate" as in "to gain insight."

As his warm palm approached the inside of my thigh, I found myself hoping for a version of "penetrate" that involved knives and hearts, preferably my knife and his heart.

"One day," he said, "just hearing my voice will make you wet." His thumb just brushed through the thin silk of my panties, just above my clit. I jumped, arching my back to get away from him.

"The leopard spots suit you, my little fighter." He chuckled, "and so do the black strings. How does that feel across your clit?" He shifted the string, and I bucked away, screaming.

Then he said, "My goal is to have you wanting me at the sound of my voice. You've had too much control for too long. It's time for a change." His thumb danced gently across my labia, so accessible in this thong, despite my efforts.

I made some small sound in the back of my throat, realizing the hopelessness of my situation. "Today—now—you can fight me without repercussions. But listen to my rules, for I will not change them." I squirmed away again, but no matter where I moved, his clever hands found a light way to tease. His fingertips found my nipple through the cotton fabric of my dress and bra. The gentle pinch sent a shock through my body. What had I done to deserve this?

"Why are you doing this to me?" I sobbed. "Get away!"

"I demand that you will not fight me. That is my rule." Again, I bucked to no avail, and again he laughed. His thumb insistently pushed against my nipple, and the corresponding thrill that ran through me sparked more than fear. "Don't worry. I know that today you can't help but fight. You won't be punished for any recalcitrance today. But tomorrow and thereafter . . ."

The threat hung in the air, and I thought that he was going to leave it unfinished. His breath warmed my cheek as he whispered in my ear, "Tomorrow and thereafter, you will be punished if you fight me."

I froze with the intensity of his whispered voice, and he left before I could respond.